CUCKOO

CUCKOO

Julia Crouch

WINDSOR

PARAGON

First published 2011
by Headline Publishing Group
This Large Print edition published 2011
by AudioGO Ltd
by arrangement with
Headline Publishing Group

Hardcover ISBN: 978 1 445 85808 1
Softcover   ISBN: 978 1 445 85809 8

British Library Cataloguing in Publication Data available

Printed and bound in Great Britain by
MPG Books Group Limited

To Tim, Nel, Owen and Joe.

Thanks to:

Jacqui Lofthouse who helped me decide what to do and to stick to it; Hannah Vincent who spurred me on until I had finally killed the fox; Tara Gould at Short Fuse Brighton for letting me read my stories to real people, out loud; Carmela Marner for being the first to read and feed back; Boo Hewerdine for advice on matters musical; Janee Sa for social work expertise; Chloe Ronaldson for her midwifery advice; Hannah Norden for her ambulance/paramedic insights; Laura Marshall-Andrews for her medical help; John O'Donoghue for saying he thought I had done some writing before; Chris Baty and Nanowrimo; Queens Park Lowbrow Bookgroup for listening to me going on and on; Jane and Roy Collins and Pam and Colin Crouch; Rosemary Pryse for the writing space and a hundred-thousand stories; Simon Trewin, Ariella Feiner, Jessica Craig, Zoe Ross, Giles Smart and everyone at United Agents; my wonderful editor Leah Woodburn, and Imogen Taylor at Headline; Joan Deitch; Amanda Smith and Gary Parker; and my family for putting up with it all.

Aftermath

It could be the scene of a crime, but the real crime happened somewhere else. Nothing is what it had been: everything is cut, or torn, or ripped. Great globs of flesh-coloured paint blight the surfaces; shards of paper curl over edges.

Propped up against the walls are painted repetitions of the same, naked, skeletal form. She is arched, ecstatic, beautiful. And her eyes have been gouged out, stabbed with scissors, sliced with a blade.

It is, in short, a total mess.

One

When Rose heard that Christos had been killed, she didn't think twice: Polly and the boys must come and stay. She and Gareth had the space now, and Polly had been her best friend since primary school. There was no doubt about it: they must come, stay, and let Rose look after them.

The phone call came on the last day of February. Anna and baby Flossie were asleep, and Rose and Gareth had just lit a candle and opened a bottle of wine at the kitchen table. The image of such a nightly routine had been held in their minds throughout the two and a half years they had spent renovating this house in the Wiltshire hills. Now, just one month after they had finally moved in, the vision had been established as firm fact.

The phone echoed across the flagstone floor, breaking into the rural silence they still found a little unnerving. Gareth had wanted a proper, resounding phone bell just like the one he had grown up with in Upstate New York. One you could hear wherever you were. He said it signified, for him, a conscious intent, a state of being here by design, rather than by accident. Rose couldn't see how he took it to that conclusion, but a loud bell was practical because they couldn't get any sort of mobile phone reception out where they were, out in the sticks.

Taking her glass of wine with her, Rose went to answer the phone.

'Christos is dead,' was the first thing Polly said.

Rose had to sit down at the window seat, the

cold stone freezing into her legs.

'What?' She didn't believe it, of course.

'He's been killed. In a car crash. He was drunk.'

'What's the matter?' Gareth drew his chair over and sat by Rose, holding her hand as she took it all in and fought for air.

Rose thought of Christos, the big bear. Christos was, of everyone she knew—except Gareth and the girls—the last person she could ever imagine not living. He was all about life. Once, knowing she craved scallops when she was pregnant with Anna, he had cooked her a full twelve. 'You must follow your body, because it knows you better than you do,' he had said with his infallible Greek logic. She and Gareth had his paintings all over their house. Bursts of colour, life, sex and food, they lit up the cool interior they had made, clashing beautifully with the restraint and symmetry of Gareth's own, more cerebral, work. They even had one of the most erotic paintings Christos had ever made—of Polly, as it happened—hanging in their dressing room.

'When?' Rose asked. She needed facts to help her take it in.

'Two weeks ago.'

Rose thought she could hear the sound of the sea at the end of the line, crashing onto the stone of the shore. She imagined Polly sitting on the terrace of the house in Karpathos, the one that led straight onto the beach. She would probably have a large glass of Metaxa in her hand. But then it was February, so she probably wasn't outside. Was it cold in Greece in February? Rose didn't know—she had only visited in the summer, and the last time she had done that had been two and a half

4

years ago. She and Polly hadn't spoken at all for six months, she realised.

But, however long they spent apart, they always seemed to be able to pick up where they left off. Rose and Polly were entwined. They had grown up together; they lived together in their late teens and twenties. They had both married artists, and had surprised each other by both rather unfashionably moulding themselves around their men and their children.

'He always drives too fast on the roads round here,' Polly was going on. 'Thinks he knows them because he was born here. But he doesn't. It's all bollocks.'

'Poor you.' Rose didn't know what else to say.

There was silence. Just the sound of the sea: crash, pull; crash, pull.

Rose put her hand over the mouthpiece and told Gareth the news. Gareth gasped, closed his eyes and collapsed his face into his palms, pressing his fingertips into his brow. He and Christos had been friends once, before Polly. In fact, it was through Christos that Rose and Gareth had met.

Rose went back to Polly. 'How are you?' She tried to hold her own shock and upset back for the sake of her friend. She wasn't as entitled to grieve for Christos as much as Polly.

'We've buried him and I've been wished an abundant life a thousand times by all the aunts and cousins and his bloody mother. We're waiting for the memorial service, then I'm out of here.'

'And the boys? How are they?' Rose had difficulty finding a voice for this. Nico and Yannis were Polly and Christos's two sons. Rose and Anna had spent a fortnight snorkelling and sunbathing

5

with them, that summer they'd visited, just before the house project had kicked off. Rose remembered Nico, aged seven, surfacing in front of her with a perfect sea urchin shell, his smile as wide as the sandy sweep of bay behind him. Christos's whooping for his son's find reached them across the sparkling sea. Rose thought with a shudder that she should have visited more often. Now there would be no chance of return.

'All I want to do is to touch him,' Polly said. 'And that shocks me. I didn't want to so much before, when I could—but now it's all I can think of. It's like a fire has burned everything.'

'And the boys?' Rose asked again.

'They're too young really to know what it means. They'll realise soon enough, but for now they have no idea of the permanence of it. Fuck.' There was the sound of a glass crashing onto stone.

'I'll come out tomorrow,' Rose offered, catching the warning look Gareth darted at her through tear-rimmed eyes. She knew the minute she said it that the whole idea of dropping everything and taking the baby out to the eastern lip of Europe was ridiculous. Gareth was supposed to be getting back to his work; she was needed to run everything else.

'No,' Gareth mouthed. Despite the painting in the dressing room—which he put up with partly for Rose's sake, and partly because it was an example of Christos's best work—he had never liked Polly. He once said that she gave him the creeps, which was pretty strong for Gareth.

'No. You stay put. Me and the boys are coming back. We're out of here,' Polly said.

6

'Well then, you must come and stay here,' Rose said, looking directly at Gareth. 'Stay as long as you like.'

Gareth went over to pour himself another glass of wine, his back to Rose.

But what can he say? Rose thought. He'll just have to like it.

Two

It was a long phone call. After she put the receiver down, Rose realised that Gareth wasn't in the kitchen any more. She searched the house, but she couldn't find him. Pulling on her Barbour, and slipping her feet into boots, she took a torch and the baby alarm and, still reeling from the news about Christos, still unable to absorb it, she headed off into the moonlight to where she knew he would be.

A slow, deep river ran at the bottom of the field, and beside it stood a big old willow with a flat, smooth stone at its base. Rose had first discovered the spot fifteen months ago, after she had told Gareth she was pregnant.

It had been an accident, the pregnancy—the result of a rather messy topping-out night, when they had farmed Anna out to a friend's house and invited the neighbours round to help them consume a lot of awful local cider. They had hauled a Christmas tree up onto the rooftop, there was a lot of whooping and dancing, and then everyone staggered home. Andy—Gareth's brother, who had come over from France and was

7

helping out and camping in the Annexe with them—collapsed in a drunken heap on the floor of the main house. Rose and Gareth covered him with blankets and tiptoed on their own up to the Annexe, where, after a nearly chaste eighteen months of sharing their bedroom with their small daughter, they let all caution fly to the wind.

So it was that, a few weeks later, when Rose did the test and it came out positive, it came as something of a blow. The plan had been that when the house was finished, Rose would find teaching work for the hours Anna was at school. This would take the financial pressure off Gareth, allowing him to pursue the more creative possibilities of his work. While he had enjoyed the practical satisfactions of putting doors up and knocking walls through, he had begun to feel stunted. In order to reboot his work, he needed uninterrupted, unpressured days in his studio—once he had built it.

Rose had known that this new baby would put paid to all that. She also knew that, for many reasons, Gareth had only wanted one child. So, with a chill in her heart, she had gone out to tell him. He was out in the rain, repointing an old stone wall that had been consumed by ivy. When she gave him the news, he jolted as if she had hit him with a stun gun. Then he dropped his trowel, stood up and just walked off.

She had spent ages trying to find him that time. She ran through the fields for a whole wet afternoon, calling out like a madwoman, growing increasingly desperate at how easily their happiness could be punctured. Eventually she found him sheltering under the willow, smoking

8

and staring at the brown swirl of the water.

'I suppose an abortion's out of the question, then?' he had asked, looking up at her.

It was, absolutely. Rose wanted that baby, and despite Gareth taking to his bed for three days, her pregnancy began to take shape.

'We can make this work,' she coaxed, offering him tea on the first day of his retreat, as the perpetual rain battered through the windowless ground floor of their unfinished home. 'We've still got a bit of money, and I'll give you all the practical support you need.'

Rose knew, from the almost weekly contact that Gareth was getting from the gallery, that there was a demand for his work that his absence had only made stronger.

'And if you have the right conditions you can really work prolifically,' she said on the second day, after she and Andy had worked side by side weatherproofing the house by battening blue plastic sheeting from lintel to sill on every gaping window hole.

By 'right conditions' Rose meant the light, airy studio that they were making from one of the outhouses. By 'work prolifically' she meant churn out more of the same old same old. Gareth didn't have a leg to stand on with the financial argument. But he had planned a return to his more conceptual roots, and there he was being forced back to the commercial concerns he had tried to escape.

'It could be perfect, Gareth. Just think, a baby,' was her offer on the third day, when the first hard frost of what had been up till then a mild, wet winter finally set in.

9

Gareth eventually managed to get up and back to work on the house, but he wasn't himself. His reaction had heralded a long and difficult period for them, from which they had now only recently emerged.

Rose had a nagging worry that this news about Christos—and, more specifically, the bit about Polly coming to stay—might kick everything off again. She knew that quick action was needed, so, drawing her Barbour around her, she hurried across the silvery-blue field towards the river. The picture of a laughing, sun-shot Christos hung in her mind so vividly that she reached out for him in the night air. And that's when it jolted into her that she would never again hear his voice, never touch his skin again. She stopped and held her breath, as the awful fact of his death struck her fully for the first time. For a moment she felt lost, marooned in the middle of the field. If she didn't hold on to herself, she thought she might disappear altogether.

Then she looked up and saw Gareth's willow. Outlined by the moonlight, it looked like a drooping troll in the night. Rose could smell Drum tobacco, and she knew her husband was there. Her bearings recovered, she moved on towards the tree and crept into the tented circle made by what remained of the leaves.

She sat down next to him, joining him in silence.

'Christos. I can't believe it,' he said, his eyes shut.

'No,' she said. 'It's too horrible.'

'He was so . . .' Gareth looked up at the river with red eyes, searching for words.

'He was your friend.'

10

'She's had the funeral, I take it?'

'Yes. I'm afraid she has.'

'I would have liked to have been there to bury him.'

'Me too.'

'That woman stole him and kept him to herself.'

'I know, but—'

'She should have told us sooner.'

'Yes.' She put her arm around him. The river flowed on at their feet, filling their silence with the sound of its journey from hill to ocean.

'It's the wrong time for this to happen,' he said finally, digging his boot into some mud at the water's edge.

'I know,' she said, taking his hand.

'We've had the most difficult two years of our lives, and now, just as we're beginning to settle in and start really living this life we have worked so hard for, we've got to open our doors to that friend of yours and her kids.'

'It's bad timing,' she said.

'Why should we risk it all for her?' he asked, looking straight at her.

'Risk?' she said. 'That's a bit strong, isn't it?'

'It's an invasion.' He threw his dog end in the river.

'Don't be like that.'

'How do you want me to be?'

A breeze ruffled the willow, and they both listened to the rustle and scratch that encircled them.

'But look,' she said. 'We've got the space. We've got the whole big house to ourselves, and Polly and the boys can stay in the Annexe. They'll be entirely separate. They can even cook their own meals.

We'll hardly notice they're there.'

The Annexe stood at the front of the property, just off the lane. It had been a glorified chicken coop for decades, and the first job had been to convert it into a comfortable, if basic, bed-sitting room for Rose, Gareth and Anna, with a tiny antechamber for Andy when he came. There was a fairly well-equipped kitchen area—Rose had to be able to provide good fuel for the workers—and a shower room. She had missed soaking in a bath, though.

'And besides, who else do we know with this amount of space to offer?' Rose went on.

It was true. All their other friends lived in London in tiny flats. Or, if they had children, they were in small terraced houses that were bursting at the seams. No one else they or Polly knew had the money for this sort of property. Even from Polly's music business days nobody was left who ticked all three boxes of unwasted, wealthy enough and still living in the UK.

If it hadn't been for the death of Rose's parents, Rose and Gareth wouldn't have been able to afford a big house either. Her father and mother had gone, one after the other, from, respectively, liver cancer and bowel cancer. Their legacy—the proceeds of the sale of their house in Scotland and a hoard of savings amassed through a result of clever house-buying in the days when that sort of thing had been possible—had been enough to allow Rose, their only child and their great disappointment, to dream a bit. The fact that they had thought to acknowledge her in this way had surprised her. She had expected the money to go to their church, or to a dogs' home, or to distressed gentlefolk. Anywhere other than her.

This old house, The Lodge, which Rose and Gareth had first seen as a ruin with buddleia growing where the roof should have been, had seemed to be just the stuff of a good dream. They decided to do almost all of the work on the house themselves, partly to stretch the money, and partly for the experience. Gareth had declared that he wanted to do it so that they could truly connect with their home. His enthusiasm was infectious. Once Gareth got something—good or bad—into his mind, there was no holding him back. He liked to see things through. And that was why Rose was determined to nip his objections to Polly coming to stay before they even came into bud.

The moonlight wove into the wind-rippled river and Gareth tugged at a strand of willow.

'It's not possible not to notice Polly,' he said. 'She doesn't exactly blend in.'

'That's why I love her,' Rose said. She looked at Gareth as he stared at the water. A nerve was flickering in his cheek, and his jaw was tense.

'Are you OK?' she asked.

'I'm just tired,' he said.

She sighed. This was his way of telling her to leave him alone. But she wasn't going to do that this time. If she left it, there would be a disaster.

Back in London, when he was like this, he would throw himself into his work. He'd disappear to his studio, only to emerge a couple of days later with two or three pieces which went straight to the gallery.

This approach worked for him, but for Rose, stuck at home alone with Anna, it was less satisfactory. She wished sometimes that they could

13

work things out together, that they could sit and talk about things until dawn, like she imagined other people did. Perhaps if they had done that, the whole pregnancy thing wouldn't have made their lives so difficult. She also wished she didn't have to be the gatekeeper, fending off Gareth's behaviour around Anna, who wondered why she didn't see her daddy.

'But he's at work, love,' Rose would say, and they would go off and bake a cake.

This had been easy in Hackney, where the studio was far away, on the other side of Victoria Park. But in this new house, especially during the build, the work was all tied up with the life. There was nowhere for him to go, and he could infect them all with his downturn. It had happened once already, and she didn't want it to happen again.

'Look, Gareth. Christos, your friend, your old, old friend, is dead. For Christos, can't you see a way?'

'I'm not going to get a say in this, am I?' he said, ripping a Rizla out of the packet and rolling another cigarette.

'We're talking about it now, aren't we?'

'But you're decided. I can see that.'

'If you like, I can phone Polly right back up and tell her not to come,' Rose said. Part of her wanted to do that. She knew that Gareth had a point, that it was indeed the wrong time. But she couldn't fully admit it, not now.

'I just wish we could have discussed it before you said she could stay,' he said.

'But what else could I do? Polly and I practically grew up together. She's like a sister to me,' Rose said, counting the points off on her fingers. 'We

14

shared everything until we met you and Christos. And now Christos is gone, she's widowed with two kids, she wants to come back and there's no one else for them to stay with. I don't even know if she's got any money.'

They sat in silence. It was a cold night if you were still. Despite her sensible waxed coat, and the protection of the willow, Rose shivered.

'Man,' Gareth said. 'Christos dead. I can't believe it. Shit.'

'I'll miss him so much,' Rose murmured.

'Me too.'

Rose leaned her head on his shoulder.

'Look. I want us to be together on this,' she said, after a while.

She didn't want it to be like her pregnancy, when she had felt as if she were carrying both Anna and the baby on her own. It had been frightening, feeling so alone. The endless work on the house, and the blustery, wet, psychotic English weather seemed to grind Gareth down. He was tall, with big hands, thick hair, and solid legs. But, over that period, he seemed to get smaller and smaller. Rose's belly had swelled in counterpoint to Gareth's decline, but she had been determined to pull her not inconsiderable weight on the building work. She remembered aching everywhere. Her tenacious optimism, which usually saw her through anything, had started to desert her.

Everything had begun to seem hopeless, when, unannounced and two weeks early, the baby arrived.

The labour was an unseemly two hours, far too short to get to the hospital. So Andy and Gareth—

who had been wrenched from his slough by the pressing nature of the event—delivered her with telephone support from the emergency services.

The minute the baby slipped into his hands, Gareth was smitten. He declared her to be Flossie—not the prearranged Olivia that Rose had whittled out from all the possibilities. Rose was so relieved at Gareth's instant transformation that she would have agreed to Weasel or Troutface if that was what he had wanted.

This new joy had taken them through the last stages of the build—the final fixings, the colour schemes and the flooring decisions—into the completed house, where life was ready to begin as an ordered, organised existence. There was a cupboard for everything; shelves displayed only books or the useful and beautiful. They had space, at last. It was so different from cramming their lives into a one-bedroom flat with no garage and no attic as they had done back in Hackney. And this space was special: they had punched and pulled and sweated to create it. Spring was on the way, and the sun would soon begin to warm their bones again. The forecast was for a great summer.

Rose knew that her instinctive reaction to Polly's situation had posed a threat to all this balance, but she also knew that neither she, nor Gareth, had any real choice now. And she was pretty sure he saw it like that, too.

'Look,' she said to him. 'They're not staying for ever, and if it doesn't feel right, we can always ask them to move. It's only till they get their feet on the ground here, really it is.'

The air shifted slightly in their willow shelter. Very, very slowly, he began to smile, and she knew

16

in that moment that it was going to be all right.

'Oh yeah, I can really see you asking her to move on,' Gareth said. 'You're too softhearted, Rose. You're a pushover, always looking out for something to look after.'

'That's why I chose you,' she said, and he drew her in close.

'But I'm serious, Rose. If it goes tits up, then I'm going to be the one to send her on her way, and I won't take any sort of opposition from you, OK?'

'OK,' she said, curving into him. 'Besides, we're rock solid now, aren't we?'

'Too right,' he said, and he threw a stone into the river, skimming it so that it bounced four times.

Three

'Tell me a story about when you were younger.'

Two weeks had passed. Anna was curled up next to Rose. Manky, the old cat, was sprawled over the two of them, purring like a motorised, heated blanket.

'Did I ever tell you about when I met Polly?' Rose said.

'No.'

'Would you like to hear it?'

'Yes!'

They were on the bed in Rose and Gareth's room. Already it had become the favoured place for bedtime stories. It sat up in the eaves of the house, tucked under the roof whose topping-out

17

was responsible for Flossie's existence. The sloping, oak-beamed ceilings—high enough to stand under except in the very far reaches of the room—made the place feel enclosed, like an embrace. And the low, warm lighting made you feel protected and held, even on a night as stormy as this.

'Well now. When I was six—the same age as you—I lived in a big house by the sea. It was in the middle of a town too, though.'

'That's Brighton.'

'Yes. The house I lived in was a guesthouse.'

'I know that!'

'OK.'

'But what's a guesthouse? A house with guests—like we're going to be when they get here?'

'Not really, it's more a sort of hotel. My mum and dad—your grandparents—let rooms out to people who came to Brighton on holidays, or for business. They gave them breakfast in a room in the basement in the mornings. The people paid. It was hard work for your grandparents. The guests were always coming or going, only staying for a couple of nights at most.'

'Did you like living there?'

'Do you know what? Not really. There were always these strangers shuffling up and down the stairs, waiting for the lavatory, wanting this or that. Complaining.'

'I wouldn't like that.'

'No. But it was all I knew. Your grandparents were kept really busy by it all, so I was pretty much left to get on with things myself.'

'Sounds boring.'

18

'It was. And a bit lonely. I wasn't lucky like you. I didn't have a sister to play with. There were never any children apart from me. Your grandparents didn't allow children.'

'Why not?'

'Oh, you know. Noise. Mess. They hated all that.'

'They sound horrible.'

'I liked living by the sea, though. I used to go down to the beach every day. It was my route to school.'

'You used to walk on your own, right?'

'Yes. Out the house, take a left. Cross the road at the zebra then down onto the beach. I used to cut under the pier, although I wasn't really allowed to.'

'I wish I could walk to school on my own.'

'You're too young. It's dangerous these days.'

'Why weren't you allowed to go under the pier?'

'That's another story. But the thing was, you see, that the sea was extraordinary. Every time it was different. One day it might be flat, like a sheet of silk. The very next morning there would have been a storm, like the one we've got tonight, and it would boil, reaching up and trying to grab you off the pebbles to drag you out to sea. I loved it like that. I'd poke my tongue out at it, following the waves back onto the wet gravel as they pulled outwards, then I'd pelt back up the beach as they threw themselves in again.

'One day, the sea got me and I turned up at school soaking wet, my homework book ruined. The teacher told me off and the other children all laughed. I was freezing cold.

'Then the teacher said there was a new child,

19

and brought in this tiny, skinny girl with a bush of black, matted hair. Everyone giggled again, but she looked back at them like a tiger and that shut them all up.'

Rose made the face for Anna. She remembered it clearly.

'The teacher got us all to sit down. "This is Polly, everyone, and I want you to make her feel welcome," she said. "Polly, would you take a seat, please?" Well, the only seat available was the one next to me. So she came and sat there, right by my side.

'She looked at me, all soaking wet. "I've got some spare clothes in my rucksack, Miss," she said to the teacher. "Can this girl put them on? She's freezing, look."

'And amazingly, the teacher said yes. And me and Polly went out to the cloakroom. Her clothes didn't fit me all that well: she was so skinny, and I was quite chubby back then. But at least they were dry.

'And ever since that moment, we've been best friends. We sat together every day at school and it turned out that her mum lived in the flats in the next street from ours. So at last I had someone to be with at school and at home. We'd spend days rummaging round the guesthouse, hiding from my parents in empty rooms, pretending it was our hotel, or pretending we were newlyweds on honeymoon. We'd dress up in Polly's mother's clothes—she was very poorly and stuck in bed all the time, but she had loads of beautiful things from the days before she got sick—and parade along the seafront in long, floppy velvet coats, too-big platform T-bars and feather boas.

'Polly and I called ourselves twin sisters. And, thanks to her, I wasn't lonely any more. Or bored. She always had ideas about what to do next. So, in the end, I was lucky like you. You've got Flossie and I've got Polly. We lived together in Brighton from when we were sixteen, and then later, when she was a singer and I was a teacher, we shared a lovely flat in London. We had loads of adventures, and sometimes we were quite naughty.'

'What sort of naughty?'

'Ah, now, that'd be telling. Another story for another day. Look at the time. It's bedtime, Mrs.'

'Oh. Pleeease.'

'No! Come on. We've got a long day tomorrow. We're going straight after school to the airport to pick up Polly and the boys. So you've got to be full of beans. Just think, not only have you got your little sister, but you're going to have Nico and Yannis to play with all the time.'

Excited by this thought, Anna picked up her teddy and padded downstairs to her bedroom, where Rose tucked her in and kissed her goodnight. She smoothed her daughter's thick brown hair and felt the warmth of her breath on her cheek. Manky jumped up and took his place at the end of Anna's bed.

Rose turned out Anna's light and went to find Flossie for her bedtime feed. On the way downstairs, she tried to remember what it was really like in her parents' house, on that dark, winding staircase that seemed to go on for ever from the little basement flat that they lived in to the very top attic bedrooms. She remembered landing after landing of closed doors that seemed to draw her to them, tempting her to eavesdrop on

21

the transient lives that played out behind them. But most of all, she remembered that sick, fearful feeling she always had in that house, and she was glad that her daughters would never have to go through all that.

Did she have some of the hotelier in her blood? She hoped not—she would rather not have anything to do with all that—but she had enjoyed preparing the Annexe for the visitors. It had been a bit of a rush: once Polly had the invitation from Rose, she lost no time in organising her departure. But Rose was nearly there. She ticked off in her mind the final things she needed to do to prepare for them: make up the beds in the Annexe, put milk in the fridge, fresh towels and loo roll in the shower room and a bunch of daffs in a vase on the table.

And then, everything would be ready.

Four

'How much longer?'

Anna tugged at Rose's coat. It was getting late, and they were both a little irritable. They had been waiting in Heathrow for over an hour. Polly's flight had been delayed at take-off because of a storm in Crete, and there was no definite landing time on any of the screens, just an annoying message that told them to wait for further information.

They had finished the rice cakes and apples they had brought along as snacks and Anna was getting tetchy and impatient. Rose began to wish that she had left her back at home. Flossie was fast asleep in her sling, thank goodness, so at least she only had one child to contend with.

'All right, let's go to Starbucks,' Rose said. They wandered over and, after a lot of deliberation, Anna settled for a Grande hot chocolate, with cream and marshmallow. Rose had a cup of tea. They took a seat where they could see both the screens and the people coming through the arrivals gate from airside.

Rose loved watching the arrivals. Whenever she had to meet someone she'd always get to the airport early. She'd tell Gareth it was in case there were any problems parking, but what she really wanted to do was to watch the moments of exposure and connection, the bare meeting points between people. It was like theatre: the travellers appear on the stage a little dazed, blinking, dragging their luggage behind them. There's a moment of confusion, then they spot their loved ones and the scene becomes pure and focused as they wave, run, embrace.

'Look at that,' Rose pointed out for Anna, her voice catching slightly. A young blonde woman had pushed a trolley full of red suitcases through the gates and was now standing still, searching. On top of the suitcases, against all safety regulations, she had perched a small, ginger-haired boy. The child's face lit up as a tall, lanky man flew towards him, scooping him up. From the colour of his hair, the man had to be the boy's father. Perhaps they had only been apart for a couple of days, but Rose thought it must have been longer. Were the woman and child coming home? Or were they arriving to join the father away from where they lived? Why did the father only embrace the child

23

and not the woman? They exited stage left, the woman still pushing the trolley and the man holding the child. Their story would live on, and Rose would never know about it.

It contrasted so sadly with the last time she had flown, when she and Anna had got back from visiting Polly in Karpathos. Rose had been excited about claiming their own little scene for themselves, a reunion after being away from Gareth, who had rather too readily volunteered to spend the fortnight in England, making the Annexe habitable for their return.

But he had been late to meet them, and they had stood at the arrivals rendezvous point not quite knowing what to do. As usual, Gareth wasn't answering his mobile; even in range, he had a selective deafness no matter how loud he made the ringtone. Rose could feel the holiday and her suntan draining away with every moment they had to stand there. By the time he eventually turned up, nearly an hour late, she was crabby and resentful. All she wanted to do was get back home. She barely noticed the big bunch of daisies he had brought her from their new garden.

Rose and Anna finished their drinks and went back to the barrier. Anna turned somersaults on the shiny metal rail until a miserable security guard came along and told her off. Rose, not seeing his point, nearly started an argument. But Anna's embarrassed pleading—'please don't, Mum'—stopped her. Finally, the plane they were waiting for was announced as having arrived.

And then, there was Polly.

Dragging a large dusty pink suitcase, a guitar strapped to her back, she looked even thinner than she had two years ago. Bones ridged the deep vee of her black T-shirt. Her stiff, long skirt stood out from her like a gothic lampshade. She looked more like an orphan than a widow. Her two little boys, who were now five and nine years old, wavered, blinking behind her. The three of them, pulling their suitcases behind them, could have been survivors of some kind of apocalypse, facing sunlight for the first time.

Polly was, as usual, commanding attention. People's eyes were on her.

Tucking Flossie closely into her front, Rose ducked under the barrier and ran towards Polly. Anna followed behind them. Taking care to move the baby to one side, Rose took her best friend into her arms and pressed her against her chest, breathing in her unchanging scent, a mingling of Amber and sweat, with a dark Jasmine wound underneath it. Polly just let Rose take her. She stayed very still, held and tense. She felt like a frightened bird in Rose's arms: stilled, only just humming with life. Rose was scared that she might break her, but she knew Polly was tougher than that.

The big suitcase toppled over. Nico, the elder of the two boys, tried to set it to rights, but it was almost as big as him, and probably weighed more. Yannis, his brother, tried to help him, but only managed to get in the way, setting off a skirmish between the two boys.

Other travellers had to skirt around this splayed-out scene—the two women held still, with a baby sandwiched between them; the two skinny boys wrestling with a battered pink suitcase and Anna, the neat little girl, standing to one side, like

25

a lemon. Rose was aware that they were making a scene, a picture for an audience, but she sort of liked it.

*   *   *

It was dark and raining hard as they swung up onto the M4, heading west. Rose turned the heating up full blast in the Galaxy. The green light of the dashboard, the noise of the fan and the swooping of the windscreen wipers seemed to cast a spell over the children. After a couple of minutes of silently looking out of the windows at the rain, the boys were asleep, their brown faces tilted back, their mouths slightly open. Flossie and Anna soon followed.

It didn't seem necessary, even appropriate, for Rose and Polly to talk. Polly sat tapping her knee, sipping at the strong black coffee Rose had bought for her, drumming her bitten fingertips as if she were waiting for something. It was more like sitting next to an electric field than a person. Rose indicated and swung out to overtake a large lorry that was funnelling dirty water straight back at them.

'Was it hideous?' she asked after a while.

'Worse,' Polly said, looking at the muzzled lights of Reading in the rain. 'God, this country's grim. You forget after a few years just what it's like.' She shivered.

'You warm enough?' Rose asked.

'Someone just stepped over my grave,' Polly said, and wrapped her denim jacket tightly around her. 'Look, Rose, I know we've only started, but any chance of a fag break? Is there anywhere in

26

this country you're allowed to smoke?'

It seemed like a good idea. Rose pulled over at Reading West Services and parked up in the rest stop car park. The children didn't stir. Polly got out and climbed a steep grass bank in front of them to sit on a picnic bench. She was trembling in the rain. Rose got an umbrella from the boot, locked the doors and joined her. She had a good view of the car in case the children woke up.

'Want one?' Polly offered Rose her bag of tobacco. She had black smudges under her eyes that could have been mascara, but were more likely down to nights of sleeplessness.

Rose looked back at the car with the sleeping children in it. She knew she shouldn't take a cigarette, but this was a special occasion, and smoking had been one of the things that Rose and Polly had done really well back in their twenties. She could resist in front of Gareth, but Polly was a different matter. For old times' sake she took a Rizla and started rolling. The two of them sat huddled under the umbrella, smoking.

'That's nice,' said Rose, exhaling. 'Haven't had a fag in ages.'

'They all smoke in Greece,' Polly said. 'It hasn't quite got there yet, the Northern European sanctimoniousness.'

'Perhaps the Mediterranean diet benefits outweigh the smoking drawbacks.'

'Possibly,' Polly said. 'It's an old shithole, anyway, Karpathos.'

'Oh come on, it's one of the most beautiful places I've ever seen,' said Rose.

'You don't know anything,' Polly said. 'It's a shithole full of arseholes. Or an arsehole full of

27

shit. In any case, I wish they were all dead.'

'But—'

'Oh Rose. Don't listen to me. I've got issues.' Polly snorted a sort of laugh and stubbed out her cigarette. 'I need a pee.' She buttoned up her denim jacket and darted down the slope and across the car park to the services.

Rose sat there watching the slight figure flit across the shiny black tarmac. She knew Polly had her problems with Christos's family, who would have preferred a Greek girl for their golden boy, or at the very least someone who wasn't an ex-junkie ex-rock star. And his death had clearly not brought any sort of reconciliation. Rose reckoned that was why Polly had come back to England. She had a history of being quick to take offence, flaring up and off at the slightest touch. And after that, she could hold onto a grudge for days, weeks— even permanently.

There was one woman, for instance, who Polly referred to as 'the dead one', who had had some sort of thing with an ex of hers. Polly swore that if she saw this woman while driving, 'even though she's only a walking ghost', she would mount the pavement and knock her right down, reversing back over her head to hear it pop. She had even turned it into a song, 'Piss Redress', which became the title track of her second album.

For the most part, Rose found these florid revenge strategies amusing. Polly outlined them well and was entertaining with the detail. But there was always the suggestion that what she was saying might actually be true, and it was just a matter of luck that the situation hadn't yet arisen where she might act out her plans.

28

Once or twice, Rose had been at the receiving end of Polly's anger, and she hated it. In fact, Rose couldn't cope with anyone being angry at her and often went to great pains to avoid it. When she was younger, she would compare herself to Polly, finding herself a little wet around the edges, a little unformed, a little too eager to pour herself into the mould that her best friend carved out for her. But since marrying Gareth and having her children, she had found more focus and definition. It had probably helped, too, that Polly had moved over two thousand miles away. In the sum of things, though, Rose believed that her own approach, her desire to please, had led to a life less troubled than Polly's.

But the mess Polly was in right now was nothing to do with her anger; it was not of her own making—Rose had to remember that. Polly had just lost her husband: the man who had helped her out of big, big trouble, the man who had given her a whole foundation on which to rebuild her life.

Polly appeared in the brightly lit service station doorway, incongruous against the McDonald's backdrop. She came out and was blown across the car park by the filthy weather. She, and her clothes, were far too flimsy for this English March. She looked as if she might take off, be swooped up across the dark night sky. For a moment, she seemed to have lost her bearings. She stopped to push her mop of black hair out of her eyes, scanning the cars, looking for Rose. A man in a good raincoat, hurrying across the car park, stopped for a second to take her in. You could almost hear him thinking that what he saw was interesting, familiar even; Polly had been a well-

29

known figure fifteen years ago. You could see his calculation, then the decision that, weighing things up, he would just quietly return to his solid Audi and its sleek leather seats.

Then Polly looked up and smiled the first real smile that Rose had seen from her. She flitted past the car and up the bank to sit down again.

'We'd better get going,' Rose said.

'Just one more cig,' Polly said, and she rolled up and lit another. She narrowed her eyes and exhaled a stream of smoke into the night. Then she turned to Rose. 'I want to thank you,' she said. 'You and Gareth are being so generous.'

'It's nothing,' Rose said. 'Besides, we've got loads of space.'

'I know. But I also know that Gareth and I have never really seen eye to eye,' Polly said. 'He hated me because I took Christos away from him.'

'Do you think that was it?' Rose said. It had always troubled her that Gareth could never put his finger on what it was that he found so off-putting about Polly. Her own theory was that it had more to do with his jealousy about their friendship—that he somehow felt threatened by it. In any case, the two couples made up of two sets of best friends didn't hang out together as much as an outsider might have expected. Rose practically moved into Gareth's flat a week after first sleeping with him. It was, she knew now, an avoidance strategy: simply put, Rose found it difficult to be near Christos while she was with Gareth. She was happy to play second fiddle to Polly's lead—indeed, she carried on seeing her almost every day until they moved to Karpathos—but she couldn't bear the idea that she would ever consider Gareth

30

to be second best, when in so many ways he was so perfect for her.

Shortly after they got together he had taken her to the private view for his and Christos's MA Group degree show at Goldsmiths. Gareth's piece, entitled *BloodLine*, was just that: a white box of a room with a thick red horizontal line around it which he had drawn at the level of his heart, using his own blood. At his eye-level, he had gaffa-taped letters and documents connected with his search for his birth mother. In the middle of one of the walls, near the door that swung shut as you entered the room, closing you in, was an original photograph of his mother—the only one in his possession, Gareth said—with holes where the eyes were.

Rose had stood in the middle of the room in a flowered chiffon mini-dress, clutching her wine and weeping, as Gareth told her how Pam and John, the people he had grown up believing to be his parents, had kept the fact of his adoption from him until he was eighteen. When they told him, he raged for a month. He wanted to kill them. He wanted to kill his birth mother, the woman who had abandoned him.

'But weren't you grateful for the life you had? It was a good life, wasn't it?' Rose searched his eyes, desperate for some sort of release from the tension she felt in that enclosed, blinding space.

'No,' Gareth said, resting his finger on the red line. 'My anger obliterated all those years. Why hadn't they told me? Why had she abandoned me? No one could give me answers that satisfied me. And then, by the time I found out who my real mother was, she was dead. Killed herself in

31

Buffalo, New York. And I thought: *Good.*'

Rose gasped and looked away.

'So I came over to England, away from the lot of them. And now my bloodline starts and ends here,' he said, his voice cracking. 'In this room.'

'And how are you with them now, Pam and John?' she asked gently.

'They're deceased. They were too old. It's too late.'

Rose took him by the hand and led him through the swinging white door, back into the bar area, where Christos and Polly were holding court with a group of earnest-looking undergraduates. She knew that, in Gareth, she had found her man. She was going to take his bloodline forward, out of that clinical, angry space, and out into the world. And in doing so, she was going to make her own reparation as well as taking on the son of that poor, eyeless woman in the photograph.

Christos ran out of red dots for his own exhibition that night, but *BloodLine* didn't sell, and no one expressed any interest in Gareth, beyond a general muttering about health and safety and imitations of Marc Quinn. But for Gareth, and, to some extent for Rose too, the work represented a catharsis that allowed both of them to move on together, united on the surface, at least.

'Don't look so worried.' Polly reached across in the rain and took Rose's hand, waking her up out of her dream. 'I want you to know that I am going to be so good, that you are only going to be thankful that I am there. I promise that.'

'I don't doubt it.' Rose smiled.

Polly sat back and smoked for a while, her eyes darting around the car park as if she were searching for something.

'What do you remember of Christos?' she asked.

'I don't know if—'

'No, go on, I want to know.'

'OK, well, let me see. He was always going on. He was always talking, drawing, smoking, drinking, eating. Touching you; making food; clearing up. I never, ever saw him sitting still. Not even when he slept. You always felt you could do, say, eat and drink whatever you wanted when you were with him. He was—I don't know—he was like a dark-haired lion, great in the doorway of your white house, grapevines over his head, raki in his hand. He was a sort of Dionysus.'

'Godlike.'

'Yes, if you like. Godlike.'

And the two women sat there in the rain, under the umbrella, remembering that all this was dead, gone, no longer.

'I've missed you, Poll,' Rose said.

'Me too you.' Polly leaned forward and stubbed her cigarette out on the picnic table.

'You really must stay as long as you like,' Rose said. 'Stay for ever!'

'Well, until we get on our feet again . . .'

'Of course.'

'Oh, by the way,' Polly said. 'The baby was crying when I went past the car.'

'Why didn't you say?' Rose said, scrambling to her feet and running down the slope to get Flossie.

'I did. Just now,' Polly said to Rose's back as she slowly got up and made her way down behind her.

33

Five

It took Rose a while to settle Flossie back into the car seat; she had managed to wake up all the others with her wailing. Anna had been trying to calm her sister, which somehow made Rose feel worse, as if she had committed a double dereliction of duty. Polly just got in the car and sat and waited for Rose to finish, barely acknowledging Yannis and Nico, who were wriggling with discomfort in the back.

Rose eventually climbed into the driver's seat. It was nearly seven o'clock and she wanted to get home to the stew she had cooking in the Aga, to feed the travellers then settle them into their new digs. She was a little angry at Polly for not having told her earlier about Flossie, but she made allowances for tiredness and for grief. By the time they were back on the motorway, she was able to speak again.

'What are your plans then, so far?' she asked Polly, but there was no answer. She glanced over and saw that Polly had curled around her seatbelt and fallen asleep. She looked so calm and so innocent like that—at least ten years younger than she actually was. Rose turned her attention back to the road and quickly had to brake. The car in front was stationary and it looked like there was a long queue up ahead.

As she sat in the traffic jam, Rose felt a growing sense of responsibility for her visitors. Her own and Polly's histories were so bound up together, it was hard to know where one of them began and the other ended. It was Rose who had introduced Christos to Polly, back in the Notting Hill flat days, and it was because of Polly and Christos that Rose had got together with Gareth.

Polly had been very successful in the early nineties. She had ridden high in the indie charts with her raw yet poetic music, and had been the pin-up for a certain type of kohl-eyed boy. When she came up to London to do her teacher training, Rose had rented a room in Polly's velvet-lined Notting Hill flat. Those had been heady days. Polly was Rose's ticket to the glamorous and exciting London that she, a maths graduate and trainee primary school teacher, shouldn't really by rights have had access to. She remembered only too well the feeling of facing a raucous class of seven-year-olds with the dregs of cocaine in her system—and, on one very memorable occasion, her nostrils—from the night before. She was well known as Polly's sidekick, and her photo often appeared in magazines, in the background or in the back of some taxi, behind the main story that was Polly.

And then it all went wrong. Polly's fourth album, a pared-back piano-based series of the darkest songs she had ever written, was universally loathed. 'Music to cut your wrists to,' was one critical opinion, 'and not in a good way'. Polly, who lacked the thick skin to deal with such blows, sank low, and the recreational use of cocaine and heroin that they had both enjoyed soon became, for her, a daily necessity. Sepulchral at the best of times, Polly started to look like a corpse. Her skin greyed, her legs looked like she had rickets, her hair began to fall out. But even like this, she exuded a childlike sexuality that seemed to draw men to her.

Rose, bored by the people that Polly had begun to hang out with—junkies breed junkies—had, for the first time in her life, started going out on her own and making her own friends. She and a couple of her PGCE contemporaries had edged their way into a group of older boy MA Fine Art students at Goldsmiths, where they were all studying. She enjoyed hanging out with them, spending half-term afternoons in lock-ins in smoky New Cross pubs, arguing about minimalism, structuralism and postmodernism over pints of Red Stripe. She was drawn to the conceptual, left-brain stuff they went on about, but was at a loss to understand how they then translated that into creative work. It was something that still both perplexed her and provoked her admiration.

The MA boys were romantic figures, all work-worn fingers, splattered DMs and intense cigarette rolling. Christos had caught her eye from early on, and it wasn't very long before he asked her to go with him to 'this little Greek place my Uncle Stavros runs'.

It was the middle of a heatwave and everything about London was a little heightened. The night they went to the restaurant, darkness had brought no relief from the humidity of the day. It turned out to be one of the most extraordinary nights of Rose's life.

After a dinner of chargrilled souvlaki, thick garlicky tsatsiki and tooth-achingly sweet baklava, Rose and Stavros stayed drinking raki and Greek coffee until the restaurant closed. Opening bottles of cold beer and chilled retsina and handing them out to all the restaurant staff after hours, Uncle

Stavros turned the music up loud, cleared the floor and turned the place into a party venue. This was quite normal, Christos had explained, for a weekend evening.

The night was long and sweaty. Rose found herself dancing next to a dripping, squat Mexican dish-wash boy and a waitress she had decided early on was a great beauty. Then Christos stepped in, put his arm around her waist and in a gesture that was grand and romantic, like something from an old-fashioned movie, he swept her away so that he had her all to himself.

They danced for hours, glued together at the groin—skin on skin with her arms under his T-shirt, twined around his back. He smelled, she remembered, of Eau Sauvage, garlic and fresh sweat. She could recall it so clearly even now, over a decade later, with him in his grave, and it still made her make a small involuntary sound at the back of her throat when she thought about it.

Then at four-thirty, just before sunrise, his uncle called a load of cabs. Everyone poured out of the restaurant into the clammy night and piled in.

'Now for the best part of the evening!' Christos grinned as he handed her into the taxi.

They went up to Hampstead Heath, where, like a pack of giggling children, they climbed over fences to break into one of the bathing ponds. This was how they always ended a hot Saturday night, Christos said. It was a hangover from the days when his uncle had run a restaurant in the Plaka in Athens, and they had all gone down to Rafina to see the dawn in from the Aegean, before a trip to the fish market to buy the next day's menu.

'Hampstead Heath Pond isn't quite the same,

and the fish is delivered in a dirty white van, but what can you do?' Uncle Stavros shrugged, and, tugging off his clothes to reveal a darkly haired body that had seen perhaps too many souvlaki and kleftiko, he belly-flopped into the cold, dark water.

The others followed him. They were all so hot, the water practically sizzled when they jumped in.

Christos swam across the pond, leading Rose off to a dark corner, away from the others. As the shouts and laughter died down, and everyone began to drift off, Rose and Christos made love, naked on the grass, in the early-morning light. He came at her like a hungry animal, licking and eating. She was quick to respond.

Looking back on that night, she reckoned that Christos had lit something up in her that she had never known about before, and she was grateful to him for it.

As they walked back across the Heath in the warm morning sun, Rose thought that she had very high hopes for this one. They kept stopping for deep, devouring kisses, adding more ache to their already tired mouths and faces.

'Would you like to come in for coffee?' she asked with a smile when they arrived on the doorstep of the flat she shared with Polly.

'I'd like to come in and fuck you some more,' he whispered. 'Then I'd like to sleep with you.'

So he did. As usual, Polly had been partying all night and had gone to bed leaving the place looking as if a bomb had hit it, but for once Rose couldn't care less.

They woke in the late afternoon and lay in bed, listening to the Sunday silence. Rose got up to make a cup of tea for them both, and was annoyed to see that Polly still hadn't cleared up from the night before. She also noticed that there, amongst all the beer cans and vodka bottles, was a dirty set of works and spillages of white powder on the coffee-table. Not for the first time, Rose thought that if Polly didn't sort herself out soon, she was going to have to start thinking about taking the almost unbearable step of leaving this flat and living a life apart from her friend. As she crossed the floor towards Polly's room, she indulged in a little fantasy, where she moved into a cottage on a cliff by the sea with Christos and was finally able to stand on her own two feet.

She was working out how many children they would have when she knocked on Polly's door.

'Poll? You awake? Want a cup of tea?'

There was no reply. Rose knocked again. Surely she couldn't have gone out and left all that crap out there?

Carefully, she opened the door and there was Polly, completely naked, sprawled on her back across her bed, strings of drying vomit in her black hair and blood smeared around her face and pillow. She was the same colour that Rose and Gareth would later choose to paint their living-room walls: duck egg blue.

Rose ran to her and took her pulse. She thought she could feel something, but it was hard to tell because her own heart was pounding so strongly. She grabbed a mirror from Polly's bedside table and held it to her face, sprinkling tiny grains of white powder over her as she did so. It steamed up, so she was breathing, slightly.

Rose began shaking her, trying to wake her, but Polly just flopped back like a bluebell a day after picking.

Then Christos was by her side. He was completely naked.

'Is that—?' he asked.

'Yes, it's her.'

'Polly Novak?' he gasped. Rose had kept the fact of her famous flatmate a secret from her Goldsmiths friends.

'Yes. Look, she's not well. You've got to call an ambulance.' Rose held Polly to her breast, shaking now only inside herself. Christos gently put his arms around Rose and kissed her hair.

'You go, Rosa. I know what to do—this happened to a friend of mine. I'll lift her up, get her walking around. You go: I'm stronger, you know the address and everything.'

So Rose went to call the ambulance and the emergency operator asked a whole string of questions like what Polly had been taking, when and how much. There wasn't much Rose could say definitely, but she answered as truthfully as she could. Who cared if it caused a scandal? Polly needed to stop what she was doing or the next time Rose found her, she might not be breathing. Despite the messed-up living rooms and the chaotic lifestyle, when it came down to it, Rose couldn't bear to think of what her life would be without her.

The operator finally let Rose go, saying the ambulance would be there as soon as possible. Talking had calmed Rose down. She went through to tell Christos the news, but stopped in the doorway. He was standing in the middle of the room, naked, holding the equally naked, floppy body of Polly in his big arms. She had come round

40

slightly and had a worn-out ecstatic smile on her face, like the clip-framed print of Munch's *Death and the Maiden* she had on her bedroom wall. She looked beautiful. Christos was singing one of her songs to her, stroking her hair.

Seeing them there like that, fitting together like two worn but beautifully jewelled belt clasps, Rose knew that there would never be a house on a cliff for her and Christos.

And she was right: through Polly's stay in hospital and the media hoo-ha and the rehab, Christos hardly left her side. Rose was forgotten, and all she had of him was that one night. But, in his absence, his best friend and fellow MA student Gareth Cunningham just sort of stepped in. And shortly after that, it was the degree show, and then there was no time for looking back.

Rose could have felt resentful about Christos going off with Polly, but she saw that, once introduced, they had no choice. It was hardly that Polly had stolen him from her—she had, after all, been unconscious when he fell in love with her.

It was just one of those things that Polly did to men.

'Why have we stopped?' Anna had woken up and was leaning forward in the car, tapping Rose on the shoulder.

'Who knows. Some sort of roadworks perhaps, or an accident,' Rose said. 'Try and get back to sleep.'

'I'll just look out as we go along. I like the lights in the rain.' Anna leaned back and pressed her face on the cold condensation of the window.

Soon they were off again, crawling along the shining road, the exhaust from the cars around

41

them like a swirling fog.

Rose saw the ambulance lights up ahead, and the swooping blue light of the police cars.

'It's an accident. Look the other way, Anna.'

They crawled past the scene. It looked as if a lorry had ploughed into a people-carrier that had been parked on the hard shoulder, half crushing it, sending it out into the path of the traffic coming behind the lorry.

'Look away, Anna!' Rose yelled as they went past the people-carrier. It was on their side of the road and, despite her better instincts, she couldn't look away herself. She saw the emergency workers trying to get at the occupants, who looked like a family of puppets with their strings all cut. One small body—it looked like the first to be freed— was being stretchered away under a blanket. Rose looked sharply up the floodlit grass verge and saw a little girl sprawled near the top, one leg bent right under her body, her head at an unnatural angle, her eyes open. A couple of paramedics stood over her. One looked like he was crying.

Six

Gareth was in his studio when they finally arrived, two hours later than planned. He didn't come out to the car to greet them, which Rose chose to see as a good thing. If he was so involved in his work, this was progress, and she wasn't going to spend a moment supposing that his not showing might have more to do with the fact that he wasn't keen on seeing Polly.

'You go in, it's unlocked,' Rose said to Polly and the boys. 'Anna will show you the way.' And her little girl led them off down through the herb garden to the front door.

'Mind the steps,' Anna said, looking back, feeling the responsibility. 'There's lots.'

Rose unbuckled Flossie's car seat and lodged the handle in the crook of her arm. She scooped up the bottles of milk she had picked up at the late-night garage on the main road out-side the village and followed the others down to the house.

'Very nice,' Polly said, standing dwarfed by the vaulted kitchen ceiling. 'Must've cost a bob or two.'

'The house was a wreck, so it was actually quite cheap for round here,' Rose said, as she busied herself setting the table. It was a little annoying that Gareth hadn't done a thing towards getting the kitchen ready. 'But we made up for that with our blood, sweat and tears.'

'It looks very smart now.' Polly curled up in the large old arm-chair in the corner of the kitchen, watching Rose work. 'Very finished.'

Rose wondered why this sounded like a criticism.

'We can't do finished,' Polly went on. 'Christos always gets distracted into other things. He can never settle on the one task. So we live in the middle of ongoing projects—paintbrushes in the kitchen sink, wires hanging down from ceilings. It never ends. Oh, God.'

Polly leaned back in the chair and covered her eyes with her hands. Rose went over to her and put her arms around her.

'Beep beep!'

43

A crowd of children barged past them. Anna and the boys were racing round the circuit you could make around the ground-floor rooms—from hall to living room to study to kitchen to hall and so on. Already, this part of the design of the house had become a major attraction for visiting children.

'Well. They're settling in just fine,' Polly said, wiping her eyes.

'Oy, calm down, you lot!' Rose got up to get a glass of wine for Polly and herself. A panting Yannis bowled up in front of her.

'Rose, can we stay for ever?' He leaned his sweaty little face right into hers. 'I love it here!'

'You can stay as long as you like,' Rose said, giving him a big hug.

'Come on, Yannis, I'll show you my dolls. I've got some Action Men, too.' Anna grabbed the little boy's hand and took him away. Nico, at nine years old too cool to show enthusiasm for dolls, nevertheless followed along up the stairs behind them.

'Oh, happy boys,' Polly said, cupping her wine glass in her dry, cold hands. 'She works well, your girl. But we're not going to stay too long—just until I can get us on our feet again.'

Rose started to slice a loaf of bread. 'What are you going to do about money, Polly? I mean,' she added, detecting a flicker in Polly's eyes, 'not that we're going to ask you for anything. You're our guests and we love you and you must stay as long as you like.' She laughed. 'I keep saying that! But that's because I mean it.'

Polly drew her knees up to her chest, making herself look tiny in the armchair. 'What surprised

44

me most of all about—about what happened to Christos—apart from the actual fact of him dying, of course—was that the month before he died he had actually got it together to sort out some insurance. Against his life, you know?'

'Wow,' Rose said. It was the last thing she would have expected from someone who had lived so very much in the moment.

'I know. He made sure that if anything happened—to either of us, actually—the survivor and the children would be OK. At least financially. At least for a couple of years. It isn't a fortune, but it gives me a buffer. Well, it will, when it's all settled. Greek bureaucracy is a nightmare. Oh, stop me. I hate talking about money.' She drained her wine glass just like that, in one, and Rose topped her up. 'And I've got the money from the house, of course, when it comes through.'

'You've sold it already?'

'His sister wanted it. She was sick of Athens and wanted to get back to the island. There was some sort of expectation that I'd just let her have it for nothing, but that was just mad, suffocating, Greek family stuff. That island seems to pull them all back like Persephone to the fucking underworld. I'm wondering if my boys will be the same, when they grow up.'

'You've left for good, then?'

'Oh yes. I'm done with all that.'

'But what about Christos's mother? Won't she miss the boys?'

Polly sighed. 'She did mention that once or twice. It's like living in a vice grip, being in that family. We're better off out. Anyway, she can come and visit us here when we're settled. It's not the

45

end of the earth. And she's got Elena's lot now. Five boys, God save them. No, I'm not going back there. Not even for a visit.'

Polly got up and wandered across the kitchen. She stopped and stroked the chrome bar in front of the stove. 'Oh, an Aga. How very nice.'

*   *   *

Gareth came through when Rose rang the supper bell. It had been a camp joke to have a handbell to summon the family to dinner—'to call the swains from the far corners of the estate,' Gareth had said. But under Polly's gaze, Rose felt the thing to be something of an affectation.

As she carried the stew over to the table, she looked at Polly, who was already seated, waiting to be served. She was casting her eyes around the objects in the room, as if she were making some sort of mental calculation.

Polly never could keep her mind still and, as with Rose, the years had seen her childhood character crystallise. She had always been a wild, restless little elf, whereas Rose saw herself as slightly bovine, more easily contented. She was home, and Polly was away. She wondered which sat better on a woman in her mid-to-late thirties.

She went back to the workbench to dress the salad, and Gareth bent down and hugged Polly.

'It's great to see you, Polly,' he said, holding her tight. 'I can't say how sorry I am about Christos. He was the guy.'

'He was that.' She looked up at him.

'I only wish I'd managed to have gotten out to see him,' Gareth went on, helping himself to wine

46

and sitting down. 'It's hard to think the last time I ever saw him was five years ago.'

'When he came to England on his own,' Polly said, looking into her glass.

'Yeah.'

'Things weren't too good between us back then,' Polly said.

'Yeah, he said.'

'But they got better again,' she said, looking up, tears in her eyes. 'They did, Gareth.'

Gareth reached across and took her hand. 'They did, Polly. I know that.'

Rose, who had worked hard to stop herself from intervening during this exchange, was impressed at the warmth Gareth had summoned for Polly. She reckoned that he had probably realised how mean-spirited his initial reaction had been to her coming to stay. And, of course, he did realise how important she was to her.

To be fair to Gareth, he had tried to make an effort back in the early days. Perhaps Polly had been right and it *was* due to his jealousy at her taking his best friend. Rose's theory was more simple: she thought it was because Polly rubbed him up the wrong way. She was, after all, an acquired taste.

Once, as an attempt to smooth things out between them, Rose had set up a get-together for Gareth and Polly in a pub in Hammersmith. It was a chance, she said to them both separately, to work out what it was that stood between them.

After all, these were the two people she loved most in the world (three, if she counted Christos, although she tried not to), and she couldn't bear it if they hated each other.

Rose stayed home in Gareth's flat in Elephant and Castle, watched a video of *Pulp Fiction* and drank a bottle of wine. At eleven o'clock, he came back, a little more pissed than she was, and smelling of beer and outdoors.

'How did it go?' she asked.

'Jeez. I'm glad to be home,' he said.

And that was it. After that, he seemed to dislike Polly even more intensely. Rose's plan had failed, and the two of them hadn't spoken to each other again. And now, here he was, in their kitchen, holding her hand, offering her comfort.

He was really trying.

'Where are those boys, then?' Gareth broke away and tapped the table, breaking the moment.

'Gareth has been ever so excited about meeting Nico and Yannis,' Rose said as she carried the salad over. 'He's surrounded by females in this house. He's going to love having someone to kick a ball around and do a bit of rough stuff with.'

'Yeah, Anna's a real girly girl.' Gareth smiled.

'Despite my best efforts at countering gender stereotypes,' Rose chipped in. 'I've bought her cars and balls and books with tomboy main characters. I scoured car-boot sales for those damn Action Men. But it didn't work. She's still seduced by pink.'

'I think Rose had to reconfigure some of those feminist nurture/nature beliefs,' Gareth told Polly, then he stood up and went to the bottom of the stairs. 'Kids!' he yelled. 'Get on down here!'

At the sound of his voice, the children thundered downstairs.

'We were making too much noise to hear the bell,' Anna panted. 'Nico and Yannis, this is my

48

dad, Gareth.'

The two boys stood either side of Anna, suddenly a little shy in front of this towering man.

Gareth squatted in front of them. 'Hi guys,' he said gently.

'He's great fun,' Anna said. 'When he's not working.' She rolled her eyes.

'Hey, madam, less of that,' Gareth said and scooped Anna up, swinging her up, over his shoulder and round again—a complicated manoeuvre that never failed to make her squeal with laughter.

'Me! Me! I want a go!' Yannis said.

'All right, little guy, here's yours,' Gareth said, repeating the trick on him.

Soon all three children—even Nico had begged for a swing—were collapsed on the floor in a giggling heap. The whole kitchen seemed to be filled with a new kind of energy.

'Hey, come and have supper, you lot.' Rose had to strain to be heard.

'I guess we'd better do what the lady says,' Gareth said, helping Nico and Yannis up.

In his big pullover, sheepskin slippers and baggy cords, Gareth looked like a gentle giant set against the two boys. Nico and Yannis were so tiny Rose thought they would probably have had a social worker assigned to them, had they been born in England. She looked at her man and smiled. He was welcoming them all to the cave.

Tucking Anna and the boys into their seats, Gareth kissed Rose and sat down.

'You're going to have your work cut out feeding this lot up, Rose,' he said. And Polly—anorexic, hypersensitive about her size and eating, with a twisted relationship to food—Polly laughed. Such was Gareth's gift at putting people at their ease.

He had once told Rose that his charm was learned as a baby, when he was placed into strangers' hands.

'But Pam and John must have loved you instantly. They wanted you so badly,' she had replied.

'Then why did they lie to me?' he said. And that was that. Rose could say nothing to that.

They sat around the long oak table and Rose served up the beef stew that had been simmering away since dawn.

For a while there was little sound except that of the boys' noisy munching. It was as if they hadn't eaten for weeks.

Rose counted just two forkfuls that found their way into Polly's mouth. She was performing her old trick of pushing food round the plate: a facade of eating that was pretty convincing.

'What're those?' Yannis had bolted his food down and was cruising round the room, taking it all in. Normally, Rose would have told a child to wait until everyone else had finished before getting up. But she decided to make an exception for this one night.

'My eggs,' said Anna, after finishing her mouthful. 'You can get them down if you like.'

'Hey, let me give you a hand,' Gareth said, getting up to lift the basket down from the dresser. 'It's pretty heavy these days.'

Yannis took the basket of polished stone eggs over to Anna, who laid them out one by one on a space he had hurriedly cleared next to her by pushing his plate and cutlery back.

'Careful, Yannis,' Rose said, catching her wine glass as it toppled, knocked over by the displaced crockery. She watched, amused, as her carefully laid table was sent to chaos.

'This one,' Anna said, taking a life-sized, shiny green egg from the basket and handing it to Yannis, 'Daddy brought me back from China.'

'Let me see!' Nico was on his feet, snatching the egg from his little brother.

'Oy!' Yannis cried.

'Never mind, Yannis,' Anna said, lifting a bigger, turquoise-coloured egg from the basket and giving it to the little boy. 'You can hold this one—look. It's my favourite. Daddy brought it back from Japan when I was four.'

'What about this one?' Nico lifted a polished lump the size of an ostrich egg from the basket.

'That's the biggest. It's made of onyx, which is a semi-precious stone. Daddy got it in Singapore.'

'Does your papa bring you eggs from everywhere he goes?' Yannis asked.

'Yes. I've got sixteen. Though he hasn't been anywhere for ages and I want another egg.' Anna looked at Gareth.

'So you want me to go away?' Gareth laughed.

'No! No, Daddy, I didn't mean that. I just want another egg and for you to stay.'

'Oh, OK, that's all right. I thought you wanted me out,' he said. Feigning great relief, he got back to his food.

'Does anyone want any more stew?' Rose asked, trying to change the subject, surprised that Gareth couldn't show more tact towards two boys who had just lost their father. But Nico and Yannis didn't seem to have noticed. They both appeared to be

51

strangely resilient. Perhaps Polly was right—perhaps it hadn't yet sunk in for them. A month can seem like a lifetime when you are young.

'What was your school like in Karpathos?' Anna asked Nico, carefully arranging her eggs back into the basket.

'Small,' said Nico. 'There were twenty-three children in the whole school and we all had lessons in one room.'

'Was your teacher nice?'

'He was OK,' said Nico.

'He was great!' Yannis said.

'And you learned your lessons in Greek?'

'Yep.'

'It's not like that at mine,' Anna said. She went to the village primary, which was a short walk across the fields at the back of the house. 'Each class is bigger than your whole school.'

'Are we going to go there, Mama?' Yannis asked, going over and sitting next to Polly.

'What?' said Polly. She had zoned out during the children's conversation.

'Are we going to Anna's school?'

'I suppose so,' Polly said. 'I hadn't really thought about it.'

'I've spoken to the Head,' Rose said, clearing the table. 'They've got a couple of spaces in years one and four, so you should be OK. But you'll need to go up there tomorrow because I think you've got to fill in some forms or something for the council.'

'There's no hurry, though,' Polly said, pouring herself another glass of wine.

'No, not at all,' Rose said. 'Gareth, could you finish the table while I get the pudding out?'

52

Gareth got up and put the basket of eggs back on the dresser shelf.

'You're coming to my school!' Anna clanged her cutlery together. 'Wicked! It'll be like you're my brothers. Or like Mum and Polly when they were at school.'

'Like we were.' Polly caught Rose's eye across the room, and smiled.

Holding herself slightly back from that dense gaze, Rose thought she detected something a little more complicated than pure nostalgia. Confused, she broke away, and busied herself with the custard.

*   *   *

'So,' Gareth said, as the children raced up the stairs, their bellies full of apple crumble. 'How long are you with us, Polly?' He put another bottle of red on the table and sat back down opposite her.

'I'll get me coat.' She smiled lopsidedly.

'You know that's not what he means,' Rose said, pouring everyone another glass of wine. 'Is it?' She turned to Gareth.

'Of course not,' Gareth said, looking at Polly. 'I was just wondering if you have any plans.'

'Not really.' Polly leaned back in her chair and folded her arms.

'It's early days . . .' Rose said.

'Yeah, all that,' Polly said. 'But I'm sure a plan will emerge, and as soon as it does I'll let you know.'

Rose reached across and took Polly's hand. She wanted to calm her down a bit. They had all drunk a fair bit of wine, and she didn't want anything to upset this first night, not after it had been going so well.

In Rose's own warm fingers, Polly's felt like dry sticks. Rose saw what Polly was doing. This shell, this apparent insouciance, was all a load of armour. This was a woman in shock. Not just anyone, either, but Polly. Her Polly. And she determined there and then that she was going to do everything in her power to bring her back to life.

Polly needed her help.

Unaccustomed as she was to playing the leading role in the drama of herself and Polly, Rose couldn't help but feel excited, even a little relieved. In the years they had spent apart, she had become used to being in charge of her own world. She didn't think she could ever slip back into how things used to be between the two of them.

Flossie had slept so solidly since the car journey that Rose had nearly forgotten that she had left her in the living room in her car seat. But she quickly reasserted her presence by setting up a wail that was in danger of bringing down all the new ceilings and smashing the triple-glazed windows.

Rose gave Polly's hand a squeeze, knocked back her wine, then went to find her book so that she could give her poor baby a good, long feed. This one, the last of the night, was the stocking up that Flossie needed to see her through her six-hour sleep. Rose knew she should really start to think about moving her on to solids, but something in her was resistant to the idea. She was a little guilty about the amount of wine she had drunk, but she knew it had the benefit of making babies sleep that little bit deeper.

'We'll go upstairs,' she called to Gareth and Polly. 'We don't want to get Floss all over-excited.' She also thought that it might be a good move to leave the two of them downstairs alone together, to give them a chance to relax a bit into each other's company without her getting in the way. She knew she was only trying to smooth things out, but it was the grown-up thing to step away, to trust Gareth and Polly to their own devices.

As she carried Flossie up the stairs, she smiled to herself. At least she didn't have to worry about Gareth being drawn to Polly in the way that most men seemed to be. Apart from the fact that she trusted him completely, his former loathing for Polly was so far away from attraction that she knew that wild horses wouldn't pull him in that direction.

Up in Rose and Gareth's bedroom, Flossie fed and sucked and murmured like a hungry little beast. Rose tried to read, but her eyes kept blurring over the same paragraph, and she couldn't take in a single word. Her mind kept going back to that look Polly had given her at supper, to the weight it contained.

Rose edited her past meticulously for public consumption. She had to. Only Polly, sworn to secrecy, knew it all. Had there been danger in that look?

She closed her eyes and tried not to think back, tried not to remember running for her life. As a teenager, she had possessed a talent for provoking extremes in her father. Mostly, she managed to get away and lock herself in a bathroom until whatever it was he was feeling subsided. But sometimes he got to her before she could escape, and he would rain his fists down on her until she screamed so loudly that he had to stop, for fear that the paying guests might hear.

The last time this had happened, when she was sixteen, Polly had been there, thank God. The news Rose gave her father was so terrible to him that he would probably have killed her, had she been alone.

'Slut,' he hissed, holding Rose by the hair, raising his clenched fist, ready to bring it down hard into her stomach.

Tiny as she was, Polly launched herself across the room at him and physically stopped his arm.

'NO,' she yelled, so forcibly that he was shocked into silence.

She stood right in front of him and spat up into his face. Rose, still cowering by the sofa, her arm over her head, looked on in a stunned silence.

Her father turned and fled the front parlour of the family flat at the bottom of the tall dark Regency guesthouse, straight into the arms of his selectively blind wife.

Muttering about how they would never again be able to hold up their heads in Brighton, her parents put the guest-house on the market. They moved up to Scotland, to her mother's home town, a small place north of Edinburgh. They did not invite their daughter to go with them, nor would she have gone had they done so.

If it hadn't been for Polly, Rose wouldn't have known what to do. Polly's mother had been put into hospital, so Rose moved into their flat. Polly took care of everything for Rose, sorted everything out. Yes, if it hadn't been for Polly, she wouldn't be where she was today.

Rose finished feeding Flossie, carried her to her little bedroom and lay her down in her cot. On her back, her eyes closed, her arms flopped out to either side, the baby looked dead to the world.

There was something in that position that triggered an unwelcome reverberation of the car crash Rose had witnessed earlier. She had forgotten about it until then. She closed her eyes and thought about that whole family, wiped out in one wrong move. It was all so fragile.

She touched Flossie on the cheek. After a couple of moments, she murmured and smacked her lips, telling Rose she was still alive, and freeing her to leave.

She went back down to the kitchen. Polly was once more in the armchair, staring into the fire, a glass of whisky in her hand. The washing-up still needed to be done, and Gareth was nowhere to be seen.

Seven

By the time Rose managed to prise Anna and the boys apart, it was gone eleven. While Anna got ready for bed, Rose showed Polly and the boys to the Annexe. She had tried to make the space as homely as possible, scrubbing it clean and putting a load of Anna's old toys and books in the boys' room. Before she left for the airport she had lit a fire in the woodburner they had installed when they first moved in. She was pleased to see that it was still giving off some warmth, hours later.

'Where's my room?' Nico asked.

Rose showed him the little bedroom off the main room. 'In there. You two will have to share.'

'So tell me something new.' He shrugged.

'Wicked, a bunk bed. Can I go on top?' Yannis looked up at Rose.

'Get to bed now, you two,' Polly said from the main room. 'Don't worry about teeth or pyjamas for tonight.'

After a little tussle, they worked out that Nico should sleep on top as he was bigger, so if he fell off it wouldn't seem so far. Finally, Rose managed to get them both settled down. She leaned over and kissed each of them.

'And we can stay as long as we like, you say?' Yannis whispered from deep within his duvet.

'Longer.' Rose smiled.

She came out of the bedroom to find Polly pacing around the main room.

'I know it's rather small up here,' Rose said, 'but the boys are welcome to come down to the house to join us when they wake up, if you want to sleep on. I'm up at six with Floss, anyway.'

'No, it's lovely. It really is. I don't know how to thank you,' Polly said.

'And look!' Rose said, opening the fridge with a flourish. 'Bonne Maman crème caramels. Remember?'

'I used to live on them,' Polly said, holding the little pot that Rose had passed to her. 'Them and Solpadeine.'

She put the crème caramel back in the fridge and went to the window.

'Quite a view of the big house I'll have here in

the morning,' she said.

Rose showed her how to draw the curtains, using the rope rather than just pulling them across.

'Leave them open, though, Rose. I want to look at the sky for a bit.'

Rose took hold of Polly's hand. 'Are you going to be OK?'

'Of course,' Polly said. 'I'm a tough old bird.'

'Don't I just know it,' Rose said, and drawing her close, she gave her a big hug. 'Right. Time to leave you to your own devices. And you've got everything you need?'

'The bed is there,' Polly said.

'And remember, just turf the boys out in the morning. Send them down to the house.'

'I will. Never fear about that.'

*   *   *

On her way back to the house, Rose smelled woodsmoke. She wandered round to the back and found Gareth stoking the woodfired pizza oven that he had built on the terrace. It had been one of his pet projects. Rose hadn't seen the point, but he had just gone ahead with it anyway. She was quietly boycotting it—she had her work cut out enough getting to grips with the Aga. And, as she did most of the food preparation, her inactivity had led to the pizza oven sitting there unchristened by food. But they had spent a couple of family evenings out there enjoying the heat it created when it was fired up with the doors open.

'That's nice,' she whispered, slipping her arm into his. They stood, letting the flames warm their faces, watching the sparks rise and flicker towards the gaping mouth of the chimney.

'Where did you get to back then?' she asked, after a while.

'There was something I needed to finish off in the studio. It wouldn't keep. Polly said she was fine about me going.'

'It just seemed a bit abrupt, you going off like that.'

'She really didn't mind. I behaved really well tonight.'

'You did.'

'I'm trying my best.'

They sat close together on the wooden bench, the light from the applewood flames flickering on their faces. The rain from earlier had stopped and the night was clear and cold. They could see every star up there, and the crescent of the moon was as sharp as a sickle.

'Sometimes the work just screams out for me,' Gareth said. 'I can't believe I was away from it for so long.'

'I know.'

'I didn't draw anything for over a year.'

'You did some lovely diagrams.'

'Yeah, and I painted walls and woodwork.'

'You did it beautifully, though.' She smiled up at him. 'And you did say you wanted to get your hands dirty. And you enjoyed it in a way . . .'

'Yep.'

'It was awful for you sometimes, Gareth. I know that.'

'I lost the plot.'

'Don't say that.'

'I did.'

'We all had our low moments. Remember,

60

"Fuck it, let's go and buy a nice Barratt Home"? If it hadn't been for Andy . . .'

Gareth stared into the flames.

'Without him, I don't know what we would have done,' Rose said, searching for her husband's eyes. 'You have a great brother.'

'He's OK,' Gareth said.

Rose had to be careful about discussing Andy with Gareth. There were issues there. Of course, they had grown up believing they were real brothers. In fact, out of the two of them, Andy was the only birth son of Pam and John, who for political reasons had only had one child of their own—and they had waited until they were into their forties to do that. Their choice had been to adopt a second baby, in order to share their good fortune in life with someone who might otherwise not have been so lucky.

Rose had asked Andy about this on one of the many evenings they spent alone together, while Gareth was hiding under the duvet, battling his demons.

'Why didn't they tell you?' she asked, as they went for one of their evening walks down to the river.

'They didn't want Gareth to feel the odd one out,' Andy said. 'I guess they thought it was for the best.'

'Didn't it come as a shock to you?'

'Totally. I mean, we're so physically alike, people always asked us if we were twins. But it wasn't such a big deal for me as it was for Gareth. He's never gotten over it. He never got beyond formalities with them again, and now Pam and John have passed away and it's too late. They loved him so much, though, Rose.'

Rose looked at Andy. It was true; he and Gareth were very similar. Both tall and strong-looking, both with the same beautiful hands. But it was as if Gareth were made up of two halves—the light and the dark, whereas Andy was just light.

It was because of this lightness that Andy seemed to be able to cope with the residual anger that Gareth sometimes, for want of a better target, directed at him. It was because of this lightness that, from time to time, Rose found herself asking if she had picked the right brother.

'Andy's more than OK,' Rose said to Gareth.

'I guess.' He shrugged.

The fire crackled around the knotty wood, sending a spray of sparks out onto the brick surround of the pizza oven. Rose looked at her husband and wondered how on earth she could ever have doubted that he was the one for her. They sat still, listening. The silence of the night was broken only by a blackbird that Rose had fed throughout the winter. He sat on their chimney, giving perspective to the evening.

'I hope they don't stay too long,' Gareth said at last.

'Oh, she doesn't stop still,' Rose said. 'If I know Polly she'll be up and off—probably with a new husband, band and recording contract—before I get a chance to change their bedlinen.'

'I don't want you running around after her. She's a grown-up, you know. She needs to take care of her own stuff.'

'OK, Dad,' Rose said, leaning into him.

'I'm sorry.' Gareth put his arm around her shoulder. 'I just don't want us to be distracted from the important stuff.'

'No worries about that.' She reached up and kissed him. 'You know, there's something rather wonderful about this fire,' she murmured, as she slipped to her knees and unbuttoned his Levis.

*   *   *

Later, in their bedroom, as she lay next to Gareth—who had gone out like a light—Rose thought about what he had said, about the dark days, about how he had lost the plot. There was a point back then when his silence had been deafening. He had effectively signed out, only showing up for meals.

This evening had been the first time they had ever really talked about it. She didn't know if that was a good or a bad thing. Sometimes it was better just to forget about the unhappy stuff.

Remembering that not so distant time, she again questioned her wisdom in welcoming Polly. But it was unthinkable that she could have turned her away. In any case, she and Gareth had sworn to be generous with their good fortune. After all, just ten years ago, they wouldn't in their wildest dreams have imagined themselves in this comfortable position.

Back then, before Hackney even, they lived in Gareth's rented flat in Elephant and Castle. It actually had two bedrooms, but the landlord wasn't allowed to charge rent for the second since it was too damp for human habitation. This 'condemned' room became Gareth's studio, and it was there, out of necessity, that he had turned his back on the large-scale conceptual installations of his MA days. Instead, he started to work in what later became his trademark style of painting on found wood in oils. The dampness of the room meant that the oils stayed wet for longer than they normally would, and he would move his pictures into the living room to mingle their fumes with those of the paraffin stove that heated the place.

The smallness of the room also limited the size of his work, which further defined his style. The luck of it was that what he had hit upon out of necessity turned out to be very marketable and this had hauled them out of the grim rental market and on to the Hackney flat-owning step of the artist's progress in London.

It had helped that Rose had been earning a regular salary. Without that, the mortgage for Hackney would have been impossible. Her teaching job had also qualified them for a key-worker's loan for the deposit. These days, however, her role in their rise tended to be overlooked: both she and Gareth had a tendency to see their progress as being solely connected to his efforts. Over the years she had changed role from that of principal breadwinner to wife of the successful artist, and mother of his lovely children. While she knew she should probably feel bitter, or at least a little wistful about this, she was in fact genuinely happy with her lot.

Gareth snored softly. Rose sighed and turned over, aware that she had just a couple of hours before Flossie woke up for her feed, and that she must sleep.

After half an hour of lying there trying to empty her mind, she gave up. She knew it just wasn't going to happen. Taking care not to wake Gareth, she got up and slipped on her dressing gown—a dusky pink antique kimono that Gareth had brought back from an opening in Japan—and padded down the stairs in her sheepskin slippers.

She stopped on the half-landing and looked out of the arched window towards the Annexe. The boy's room was all darkness, but Polly's light was still burning, and the curtains were still open. Rose stood still, to one side, and saw Polly pacing back and forth in front of the window, smoking, her hair following her like a dirty fox tail. Rose wondered whether she should go up there and see if she was all right.

But then Flossie started whimpering and rustling in her cot, two hours earlier than usual. Rose cursed under her breath. Floss had slept too long on the airport journey and that, along with the alcoholic milk and missing her usual bedtime routine, had messed her up.

Rose bounded back up the stairs to catch Flossie before Gareth woke up. She was rewarded by the vision of her daughter gurgling in her cot, holding out her arms, delighted to see her mother arrive so quickly. Rose scooped her up and took her downstairs to sit in their favourite feeding chair. She drew a blanket around them both and settling in, she slowly drifted off to the rhythmic sucking of the baby, the tingling of the letting down of her milk.

When she woke, she and Flossie were enclosed in the bubble of their own body heat. Flossie was fast asleep, a trickle of milk drying on her cool, soft cheek. Rose carried her back up the stairs, being careful not to wake her. On the way up to the second floor, she stood at the arched window

65

again, looking at the Annexe. The main lights had been turned off, but there was still a glow in the room. Probably Polly had put the bedside light on. She was reading, perhaps. Or writing—Rose knew she liked to work in bed. Or was she just lying there, thinking of a beach, a house, a man, a life that had been taken from her and her boys?

Poor Polly.

Rose continued up the stairs and laid Flossie down in her cot, tucking her under the little duvet. She tiptoed across the landing to her bedroom, took off her kimono and slippers and put them in their proper places. She pulled back her crisp, clean, lavender-scented bedding and climbed in beside her handsome, capable, alive husband. Her sturdy baby slept solidly just yards from her, and her healthy and bright older daughter was dreaming good things on the floor below in her freshly painted, beautifully large bedroom.

How lucky was she?

Rose lay back and, like a rosary, she counted her blessings until she fell into a deep and generous sleep.

Eight

At seven o'clock, Nico and Yannis ran down to the house. Rose, up again with Flossie, set about making them porridge with maple syrup. They both sat at the big table, tousle-haired, sleep still in their eyes, their voices croaky. Flossie lay on her lambskin on the floor, gurgling and kicking, her eyes fixed on the coathanger hung with shiny toys

66

that Rose had suspended from the ceiling to dangle down low in front of her.

'Mama's still sleeping,' Nico said.

'She's always asleep,' Yannis added.

'It's been a difficult time for her—for you all,' Rose said, placing the porridge in front of the boys. 'Sometimes people get so exhausted by stuff like that, they just have to go to bed and sleep it off.'

She showed them how to drizzle the maple syrup on the porridge to make a spiral shape.

'She's just drunk all the time,' Nico said.

'She is, Rose,' said Yannis, looking up at her.

'I'm sure she's not drunk *all* the time,' Rose said. 'Things'll work out. You just see. Now, eat up.'

They looked at their bowls.

'Go on,' she said.

'What is it?' said Nico.

'Looks like sick,' Yannis giggled. 'Or mushed-up brain.'

'But it doesn't taste like it. Go on, try a bit. Make sure you get a bit of the syrup on your spoon.'

Yannis watched Nico as he put the edge of his spoon into his bowl and, shuddering, slowly lifted the porridge to his mouth.

'Bleurgh!' He spat it out, grabbed his throat and fell to the floor, writhing in agony.

'Nico!' Rose said.

'It's quite nice, actually,' he said, getting up and shrugging. His timing was spot on.

Yannis laughed, and the two boys tucked in. They were both so skinny, Rose wondered where they put it. Humming-bird metabolisms, she

67

thought. Yannis ate messily, spreading it all about the table. A porridge battlefield.

He stopped suddenly. 'Where's Gareth gone?' he said, a slight panic in his voice.

'He's working. He likes to get going really early, before everyone else is up. He just disappears down there and gets on with it.'

'Dad used to paint, too,' Nico said.

'I know,' Rose said. 'Do you know, I knew your father before your mum met him?'

'Oh,' Nico said, busy with his porridge.

'Anyway, you'll see Gareth at lunchtime. He comes out to be fed. Sometimes he comes out earlier, for more coffee.'

'Aren't we going to school today, though?' Nico asked, trying to clear up his little brother's mess with his spoon.

'Leave it, Nico, I'll do it,' Rose said, fetching a cloth from the sink. 'I don't know. It depends on your mum.'

'Please . . .' Yannis pleaded.

'Please, Rose. We're going to be so bored stuck here all day,' Nico said.

'Thanks!' Rose said.

'I didn't mean it like that,' Nico said. 'It's just that Mama will sleep all day and we'll have to tiptoe round like mice, as usual.'

Yannis jumped up and stuck his teeth out. 'Eeek eeek,' he said. He started scurrying around the room on tiptoe.

'And look,' Nico added, pointing at his brother. 'I'm fed up spending all my time with that spastic.'

'Oy!' Yannis said, jumping at his brother, pulling him back off the bench by the hair. 'Oy!'

'Spastic.' Nico got up and turned to face Yannis,

holding him at arm's length, his hand on his head.

Yannis punched at his brother but, being a lot smaller, he couldn't reach. His face exploded with fury and frustration. 'Wanker!' he yelled.

Nico laughed at his brother's anger, but then Yannis dodged under his hold and caught him in the belly.

'Right, shit face. You asked for it!' Nico cried, wrestling Yannis to the floor.

'Hey, you two!' Rose said, stepping in. She was a little stunned. Where in Karpathos did the boys learn all this language?

The boys scuffled their way across the room, towards the corner where Flossie lay on her lambskin, gurgling at the shiny, pretty toys that dangled from the coathanger.

'Cunt!' Yannis screamed and lashed out at his brother with a kick. His foot narrowly missed Flossie's head.

'RIGHT YOU TWO, CUT IT OUT NOW,' Rose cried, leaping over to separate the boys. This was worse than the worst class she had taught back in Hackney. And in her own kitchen, too.

Getting the two boys apart was quite a job. Although they looked as if they were made of thin wire and paper, they had an angular strength that rendered them solid to the touch. The energy beneath their skin made them stick together like glue.

'Right. You sit there,' Rose motioned Nico to one end of the table. 'And you go there, Yannis.' The child-control techniques she had honed at work were being called on in a way that they never had been with Anna. Rose scooped Flossie up, feeling like an idiot to have exposed her to such danger.

'Time out. Five minutes' silence to calm down.' The boys sat there glaring at each other. Rose sat in the armchair by the window and fed Flossie, studying them and thinking.

She had planned that the boys would stay at home with her for a week or two while the school stuff got sorted out and they got used to being in England. She had thought about taking them for long walks around the hills that surrounded the village, showing them the British spring and the new animals at the farm down the road.

But this fight made her think that this might not work out as she had planned. For all his crudeness of expression, Nico had been right: the boys needed to spend time away from each other, to be with other children. And school was the best place to start all that. There was also Anna to think of and, after what Rose had just witnessed, diluting the Yannis and Nico effect with some other children might be best for all concerned.

'OK, look, guys,' she said at length, buttoning up her pyjama top. 'I'm glad you've both calmed down. Let's take you up to the school this morning and I'll have a word with the Headmistress.'

The boys cheered and punched the air, all animosity forgotten.

'I'm not sure what she'll say, but she owes me a few favours.'

'Shall I go and wake up Mama?' Nico said.

'No, let her sleep. I'll deal with it today.'

'Hi.' A sleepy Anna wandered into the kitchen. 'What was all that noise?'

'It was Nico's fault,' Yannis muttered, looking at his brother.

'You started it, runt!' And Nico launched himself across the table, knocking the milk jug over.

'*Enough*,' Rose said. Once more, she pulled them apart. It was only after she had sat them down again that she noticed that Anna, her little doppelgänger, had got the cloth from the sink and was, very quietly, cleaning up the spilled milk.

*   *   *

When everyone was ready, they set off for school. It was quite a cold morning after the clear night, so Rose found a fleece of hers that swamped Nico, but would at least keep him warm. Yannis wore the only warm top of Anna's that wasn't pink or covered in flowers. Rose made a mental note to get the boys wellies.

The way to school was down to the end of the garden, then across the field at the back, skirting round the bottom of the hill that rose up like a lone breast from its middle, to the main part of the village about half a mile away. The earlier skirmishes had been forgotten and Anna, Nico and Yannis ran on ahead, jumping up to catch dew-laden branches, shaking them and running away from the resulting shower.

Rose walked along behind them, Flossie strapped to her front and carefully wrapped up underneath her Barbour. She looked at the boys with their sun-fed skins, their angles and lankiness under their too-big outer clothes. She compared them to Anna, who looked as if she fitted everything completely, from her skin outwards to her pink Puffa jacket. Her hair looked impossibly

71

thick and shiny next to their long rat's-tails, which Rose had earlier tried to comb out. She had met with such screams and resistance that she had given up. Looking at Yannis and Nico, the word that came to her was 'waifs'. Poor waifs and strays.

'Got some new children, then?' Her neighbour Simon bounded up with his usual contingent of Labrador and two elfin children. Rose often bumped into him on the way to school, and he usually went back with her for coffee after. He was a writer and took the domestic role in his marriage to Miranda, who was a high-flying barrister well on the way to becoming a judge. Rose liked Simon very much.

'These are Polly's kids.' She called them over. 'Nico and Yannis, come and meet Liam and Effie and their dad, Simon.'

'Come and pull the trees!' Anna said to Simon's children. Only Nico lingered as the others pelted back across the muddy field.

'Who's the dog?' he asked, standing with his arms folded to show that he knew he was too old for the little kid stuff.

'Trooper,' Simon said. 'Here, throw this for him,' and he handed him a beslobbered ball. Nico took it and charged off with the dog.

'Great lad,' Simon said.

'They're a bit wild,' Rose whispered.

'So she turned up, then?'

'Last night.'

'When do I get the honour? I'm terrifically excited,' Simon said. He had been a great fan of Polly's back in her heyday, and ever since Rose mentioned she was coming, he had been on tenterhooks waiting for her arrival. He dressed up his anticipation with manly irony, but Rose could see through it.

'She's pretty blasted, I'm afraid. It'll be a day or two before she emerges. I was quite shocked when I saw her.'

'She's lucky to have a friend like you, keeping the fans away.' Simon grinned.

The children had run on ahead and were playing a game of catch that seemed to involve the dog in a central role.

'We go back a long way, me and Polly—since we were seven. See this? Blood sisters.' Rose showed him the scar on her index finger.

'I did that, too, when I was about six,' Simon said. 'Can't even remember the kid's name now.'

'We did ours when we were sixteen. After my parents moved away,' Rose said. 'Poll made up this elaborate ritual. We had to put on long dresses and be very solemn. And she wrote this special music for it.'

'How did it go?'

'Don't ask me that.'

'Very gothic, teenage and intense.'

'I know. But back then it seemed so important. We'd been together so much and, with her mother being so ill, her dad off the scene, and my lot disappearing, it really was just us on our own. It seemed like we needed something to underline all that.'

Simon took Rose's finger and bent to look at the scar. 'Quite impressive. Must've been a deep cut.'

'Yeah, it bled for ages. Her scar is much smaller.' She glanced over at the children. 'Yannis, no!' she yelled as she saw him push Anna over into a ditch.

She ran across to help her, but when she got there, she saw that Anna was laughing like a drain.

'Get up, Anna! Look, you're all muddy.'

'So?' Anna said. She skipped off to catch Yannis and get her own back.

'Little madam,' joked Simon, who had crossed the field behind Rose. 'So she's in a bad way then, Polly?'

'Yes. It's almost as if the grief has stilled her. She needs a lot of looking after. I'm sure we'll get the old Polly back eventually. I'm working on it.'

'I've no doubt you are,' Simon said, touching her arm.

'And those poor boys,' Rose said, looking over at Yannis and Nico. 'They must be waiting for their mother to return, too. She can't really see them at the moment—she's too wound up in losing Christos. Life never touches Polly lightly.'

'I know the type. Trooper—come here!' Simon turned to call the dog, who was getting over-excited and making Yannis scream. Rose was almost dazzled by the shine of the sun caught in Simon's white-blond hair. She would introduce him to Polly really soon. He was a good listener. He would cheer her up.

They got to school and Rose kissed her soggy, muddy daughter goodbye. Then, when all the children had gone inside, she took the boys to see Janet Jones, the Headmistress.

The boys sat outside Janet's office with a pile of books. Rose could see them through the glass door and was pleased to note that, instead of beating each other up, they seemed to have got themselves lost in Dorling Kindersley.

As she had anticipated, her record with the school—parent governor, magazine editor, running the maths club and even doing the odd day's sneaky unpaid supply teaching when someone was ill—meant that Janet was fine with letting the boys stay as visitors for the remaining two weeks, while the formal application for a place went through with the council.

'I've got a couple of spaces in Reception and Year Four. How's their English?'

'Perfect. Polly—their mother—had only very basic Greek, so the family language was English.' Rose resisted the temptation to add that the boys' idiom tended towards the Anglo-Saxon.

'Well, it'll be good for the school. We're pretty mono-cultural here and their experience of growing up in Greece will help broaden the other children's outlook,' Janet said. Rose hoped that the broadening effect wouldn't be too wide, given the boys' behaviour that morning, but she kept her mouth shut about that, too.

'Of course, I'd like to meet their mother as soon as is possible,' Janet said, handing Rose the forms. 'How's she doing?'

'I'll bring her down this afternoon,' Rose said. 'She's OK, considering.'

Rose and Janet looked at the boys through the office window. Their faces were hidden in the straggled bushes of their hair as they bent their heads low into their books.

'Poor little fellows,' Janet said. 'We'll make them very welcome here.'

Rose was pleased. That was the boys sorted, then.

Nine

She dawdled on her way back home. Polly wouldn't be up yet, Gareth was working, and Flossie was fast asleep strapped to her front, so there was no hurry. The sky was an extravagant blue with small puffs of white clouds.

She loved this walk home from the school. Knowing that Anna—and now the boys—were safe and happy in the classroom, that Flossie slept securely scooped into her sling, and that the finished house was over there in front of her—it all gave her a great feeling of completeness.

She remembered the trudge through litter and dog shit that she used to take home from playgroup with Anna in Hackney. She shuddered as she remembered the underpass she used to run through each time—her heart in her mouth, the buggy crashing and splashing through the pissy puddles. Once, earlier, when she was seven months pregnant with Anna, she had been coming home from work late on a dark winter's evening when a kid with a knife and a desiccated face jumped out in front of her. Rose thought she knew him—hadn't he been in Year Six a couple of years ago? But if he recognised her as his ex-teacher, he didn't show it. He demanded her purse, and she just gave it to him. There was no point arguing and getting herself stabbed for a tenner and an easily replaced Visa card. But her heart was pounding, and Anna was leaping around inside her, suffering electric shots of adrenaline.

The mugging changed forever the way Rose

viewed the streets around her home. That moment was probably the one that sowed the seed of escape and now, here she was, standing at the foot of a ridiculously rounded green hill that grew out of the field at the bottom of her large, burgeoning garden.

She found the bench with the view; the one that she considered to be hers, even though it was actually dedicated to a seventeen-year-old girl called Martha who had died of cancer in 1985. She sat and took in the village and the far-reaching hills that rose behind the valley. There was still a little mist rising where the river wound its way through the houses and down towards the hidden city of Bath, fifteen or so miles away.

Looking back, part of her felt sorry for that kid with the dry features. Unlike her, he would probably never escape those streets. More importantly, he would never get away from whatever it was that made him feel that he had the right to take other people's things from them. But mostly she had to admit that she just thought he was a little bastard and hoped that he was locked up now. How could he have drawn a knife on her? She was pregnant, for God's sake! And the money he had stolen she had earned working her arse off trying to save shits like him. She still shivered a little with the anger.

Then she breathed and felt her shoulders settle back to their country level. She could sit here on this bench, a woman on her own, with her bag, and she didn't once have to look back over her shoulder. She had brought her family to a place of refuge.

And they were going to stay. They still felt the

dirt of the city on their shoulders, but this was where they were going to dig in their roots. She knew that she and Gareth would grow old here, keeping the family home for their daughters, even after they left to start their own lives. Having not had this for herself, Rose felt strongly about it. Later, there would be grandchildren, who would long for their holidays with Rose and Gareth in the big house in the countryside. Rose had an image of herself, grey-haired, at the head of the table, serving *Boeuf en Daube* like a Boden-clad Mrs Ramsay.

She thought that once the dust had settled from the renovation work, they might dig a swimming pool in the back garden, though she wasn't going to mention it to Gareth just yet. And Andy could come over again from France and help, even perhaps move into the Annexe for good in the end.

In the end. If Polly ever left, of course.

Rose got up, brushed herself down and set off towards the house. She wanted to check on the Annexe, to see if Polly was up.

She stood very still at the bottom of the steps to the flat, and heard nothing. She pushed open the door to the cobwebbed ground-floor storeroom that sat right underneath the bed-sitting room, tiptoed in and stood in the middle of the room, listening with her ear angled up to the floorboards above. Nothing. Not a sound. Polly must still be asleep.

Rose wandered down the flight of stone steps towards The Lodge and let herself in. That was another joy of living here—you didn't have to lock anything. In Hackney, she had felt as if they lived under a constant, low-level siege, with bars on the basement windows, double locks and a couple of bolts each on the front and back doors, and a motion-sensor burglar alarm. They had to be careful not to leave anything valuable lying in view of the street. They had even put the stereo in a cupboard so it couldn't be seen by passers-by.

Despite all of these precautions, they had been burgled twice—the first, shockingly, when Rose and Anna had been taking an afternoon nap upstairs. That time the intruders stood on a dustbin and lifted a first-floor sash window that Rose had left slightly ajar, the way you do when you're in a house on a hot day. The other lot put a brick through the glazed back door and turned the locks and bolts by reaching through.

Both burglaries had been opportunistic and both times the intruders took cash from Rose's purse. The first lot also took an SLR camera that Gareth had left in full view on the table in the front room. The second time they stole a few more things, including a laptop Rose had on loan from the school. That had been a complete pain in the arse. The police said these sorts of robberies were very common in the area—most likely the thieves were junkies looking for stuff they could shift to raise a bit of quick cash. Rose and Gareth were insured, anyway.

But it was the invasion that was the upsetting thing. The idea of some sweating, shaking, dirty stranger roving through her stuff made Rose feel ill. Worse, during the second burglary, which took place while they were up in Scotland trying to make some kind of peace with Rose's mum in the hospice, one of the burglars took a shit right in the middle of their kitchen floor. The police said this,

79

too, was pretty common—due to adrenaline, apparently. But Rose thought it was more that this semi-animal intruder was marking out their territory as his own, scenting it, leaving his mark. It was as if he were saying that all this couldn't ever be just theirs again. If the mugging had been the seed for them leaving the city, this had been the final straw.

After they moved, it took a while to get used to leaving the doors unlocked. It was easier for Gareth, growing up as he had done in the sort of remoteness that only a country the size of the USA could offer. Pam and John's house hadn't even had any locks to do up. It was harder for Rose. While she was OK about it during the day, at first she couldn't sleep unless she had the Annexe doors locked and chained. She was making progress, though. Now they had moved down to the main house, she felt comfortable with only the Yale locks on at night. But that may have been because she was up with Flossie so regularly that she was able to keep a weather eye out for intruders.

She hung her Barbour on the peg by the door and went into the kitchen. It looked like the Hackney flat after the second burglary, minus the shit. But instead of the mess of marauders, it was the leavings of small boys and their messy fights that confronted her. To buy time before she cleared it all up, she made a pot of tea and sat down at the table in a streak of sunlight to feed Flossie, who had just woken up.

They were just settling down when Gareth came in, all afire from a productive morning in his studio. Energy seemed to spill out of his fingertips when he was like that.

80

'Christ, what's been going on here?' He came over and kissed Rose and stroked Flossie's cheek, then set about the ritual of making his habitual pot of dark, strong coffee, grinding the beans in an ancient chrome and mahogany hand-grinder that he had bought in a roadside antiques stall in Maine. It was the only way, according to him, to prepare coffee.

'The boys had a fight.'

'No blood spilled, I hope?'

'No,' Rose said. 'Just porridge.'

'They've grown up pretty wild,' Gareth said. He hadn't seen Nico since he was two, when Christos and Polly moved to Greece. Last night had been the first time he had met Yannis.

'You should know about that!' Rose said. Gareth and Andy had been home-schooled, which Pam and John had interpreted as letting them roam the woods around their land, generally doing what they wanted. They had spent days away in camps they had built themselves. They hardly ever opened a formal textbook. Yet they both came out of it having read more books, and with a better understanding of the world around them, than most regular high-school students.

'No, I didn't mean my sort of wild. That was a gift of freedom. They may have got a lot wrong, but Pam and John knew exactly what they were doing with that. These little guys, they seem to have been, I don't know, neglected. Perhaps not that. Perhaps I mean disregarded.'

'I don't want this to descend into a Polly bashing,' Rose said.

'I ain't sayin' nothin',' Gareth said, holding up his hands and smiling lopsidedly.

'You've got a point, though. Yannis and Nico don't seem to have had much in the way of guidance,' Rose said, changing Flossie over to feed on the other side. 'Certainly not recently.'

Gareth switched on the coffee-maker and went over to stand behind Rose, looking down at his baby daughter's fist as she beat her mother's breast to get more milk. He reached down and let Flossie close her hand around his finger. Milk dribbled out of the side of her mouth.

'I love that,' he said. Rose felt his erection press into her back. He had always been aroused by the sight of her feeding. Rose felt strangely grateful for this. It was extraordinary: connected and intimate, a slightly shameful, shared secret between the two of them.

'Mmm. Do I smell coffee?'

Rose jumped and turned round to see Polly standing in the middle of the kitchen. Gareth slid back and Flossie fell off the nipple and started to cry. Polly was barefoot and wearing nothing but a thin, antique cotton nightdress. She might as well have been naked, the way her goosebumped nipples and dark pubic hair were visible. At least Gareth's used to it from Christos's painting, Rose thought. He's seen it all before.

'Come on in,' she said, latching Flossie back on.

'I'll fix you a coffee. Strong, black, no sugar, isn't it?' Gareth moved over to the stove.

'Well remembered.' Polly smiled. She sat at the table. It was then that Rose realised that she was shaking.

'You OK?'

'I'm a bit cold,' Polly said. 'I forgot it wasn't Greece.'

'Gareth, could you fetch my kimono for Polly?'

'Sure,' Gareth said, placing down a coffee for Polly. Then he turned and bounded up the stairs.

Polly fumbled in the embroidered bag she had slung over her shoulder and brought out a couple of brown pill bottles. They rattled in her shaking hands. 'These bring on the shivers, too,' she said.

'What are they?'

'Greek doctors prescribe willy nilly, thank God,' she said, washing down one pill from each bottle with a mouthful of coffee. 'I'm needing a few pharmaceuticals to help me get over the worst.' She caught Rose's look and smiled. 'No cause for alarm, Mother.'

'I didn't mean—' But Rose knew that Polly and substances were a potent combination. She wondered how much that Greek doctor had known about Polly's past. Even before things got out of hand back in London, she had been a heavy necker of pills. Despite her frail exterior, Polly could party with the best of them, and always managed to last the night through to sunrise, long after Rose had passed out in a corner. Rose hated anything trippy that made her lose her sense of self, but Polly loved all that. She had once said that she didn't think she could have written any songs without her little helpers.

'These are sort of antidepressants. They get me going in the morning, after these'—Polly took another bottle from her bag and waved it in the air—'have helped me sleep through the night. It's all very balanced, Yin and Yang. Really. It's a great help. I'll be back on me feet in no time.'

Gareth came in and handed her the kimono.

'Thanks,' she said, shrugging it around her bony

83

shoulders. Although it was much too large for her, Rose thought that Polly gave the kimono a glamour, a back story. On Rose, it was just a beautiful kimono. On Polly, Billie Holiday loitered in its folds.

A silence fell on them, as Rose finished feeding Flossie and Gareth sat staring into his mug, thinking. Polly shook and twitched, looking out of the window, then sharply down to the floor.

'I have to get back to work,' Gareth said eventually, getting up.

'I wish Christos had your discipline,' Polly said, looking up at him with heavy-lidded eyes.

'But he did loads of work,' Rose said. 'He was incredibly prolific.'

'He was a lazy Greek,' Polly said, picking at her fingernails with the tine of a fork that someone had left on the table.

Gareth exhaled and looked at Rose, one eyebrow raised. Then he stroked her cheek with the knuckle of his index finger and left, shutting the back door a little too firmly.

Rose got up and laid Flossie back down on her lambskin. She fetched the fruit bowl and put it in front of Polly.

Polly took an orange from the bowl and turned it in her hands like a cricket ball.

'So, the boys are at school,' Rose said.

'I thought they might be,' Polly said, clawing at the orange to get the skin off. 'That's good. Thanks.'

'The Head would like to see you at some point today. There's some paperwork that needs to be taken care of.'

'Jesus. That's all I seem to have done since

Christos died.'

'Sorry,' Rose said, 'but you do need to do it. Janet's been incredibly flexible letting them stay today. I'll take you up there at about twelve so we can catch her at lunchtime.'

'If you want.' Polly was picking the pith off the orange now, removing every tiny bit.

'Come on, Polly, you've got to think of Nico and Yannis.'

'Do you think I don't know that?' Polly whacked the orange down onto the table. 'Do you think I'm not trying? It's all right for you, Rose, with all this—your nice house, your nice husband, your nice fucking children . . .'

'Polly . . .'

'It all turned out all right for you, didn't it?'

'That's not fair.'

'Too right it's not fair.'

Rose couldn't say anything to this.

'It's all so perfect here. Perfect Rose and her perfect house,' Polly went on. 'Look, Alessi kettle, herbs dangling from the ceiling, cream fucking Aga.'

'Stop this,' Rose said quietly. Polly had got up and was pacing around the kitchen. Remembering the earlier incident with the boys, Rose moved across the room to stand in front of Flossie.

'It was shit with Christos. *Shit*. You know?' Polly said. 'Nothing ever worked. I never had anything like this, and now—now I've got nothing.' She came to a halt in the middle of the kitchen and looked up at the vaulted ceiling. 'After everything . . .' She screwed her eyes shut tight and hunched her arms around herself, as if she were trying to force the world back into focus.

'He didn't love me, you know. Not really. Not like—like that.' She almost spat as she pointed to the door through which Gareth had disappeared. 'He only wanted my magic. And when he'd had that, when he'd drunk it all up, he'd had enough.'

She turned to Rose and looked her straight in the eye.

'You're lucky, Rose. You never had any magic to be stolen. You'll never know what it's like. It was shit with Christos in Karpathos. Shit. And then he died.'

I'm not going to take this personally, Rose thought, fighting to stay on the side of compassion.

Then Polly jolted, as if reality had bitten her sharply in the skull.

'He died, Rose. He actually died.' She drew a breath and twitched again. 'I don't think I can go on like this.'

Then her face crumbled, and her eyes filled with tears.

That was what Rose needed. She went to Polly and wrapped her arms around her. She held her tight and felt her crumple beneath her, great walls of sobbing shuddering through her tiny body.

'Let me in, Poll,' she said. She felt a small tingle of satisfaction that she hadn't risen to Polly's criticisms. She had, after all, to make great allowances for grief.

'It's going to be all right,' she said. 'You're going to be fine. You're a survivor, Polly, remember? You get through everything.'

She pulled Polly to her again, smelling the travel in her hair, the perfume and the unwashed scent of her. She rubbed her back, feeling the ribs and the outline of her pelvis at the base of her spine. She was brittle, almost crackling under Rose's touch.

'Remember?' Rose urged.

'I'm a survivor.'

'You're a survivor. You helped me through all that when we were younger. Now I'm going to help you, Poll. I'm here for you.'

They stood there for a while, until the air around Polly had settled, until she was still.

'Are you, Rose?'

As she looked up, Rose thought she saw the green flecks in Polly's irises flicker with gold. She pressed her scarred index finger to Polly's, finding the ridged line that matched her own.

'You helped me, and now I'm going to help you. However I can.'

'However you can?'

As the scars touched, Rose felt the familiar lurch in her belly, something between fear, pleasure and excitement, the feeling that only Polly could arouse in her.

'However. And I'm sorry if you felt I was putting you under pressure,' she said, stroking Polly's hair and holding her face in her hands. 'I'll tell Janet you can't make it today.'

'No,' Polly said. 'You were right. I'll go. I've got to hold it together for the boys.' She looked up at Rose. 'You know that was just me going on, back then? I loved Christos—you know that, don't you? I loved him so much.'

'I know. You were made for each other. Anyone could see that.'

'And I miss him. And I'm angry at him for driving so stupidly and getting himself killed.'

'I know.'

'And leaving us all alone.'

87

'Yes.'

They moved apart a little. Rose took a tissue from under her sleeve and dabbed at Polly's eyes. 'You go and have a bath, Poll,' she said. 'Use my bathroom, and put a slug of bath oil in. Wash it all away. Take your time. Then we'll go to the school. OK?'

'All right. Thanks, Rose,' Polly said. 'Thank you. I don't know what I'd do without you.' She moved back towards Rose and reached up, taking her face between her cool, dry hands. She pulled her down towards her and kissed her on the lips.

Again, Rose felt that surge inside, and her eyes pricked with tears.

Polly clutched the kimono around her, and climbed the stairs slowly, as if each step hurt her.

Rose sighed, and looked over to her baby, who was lying on the floor, gazing at a shaft of sunlight as it hit the stone floor.

'Blimey. What are we going to do with her, eh Floss?'

And, at last, she set to clearing up the mess of the kitchen, putting it all to rights. But before she did that, she ate the whole, perfect, pithless orange that Polly had left on the table, letting the juice run down her chin.

Ten

Polly pulled out all the stops for the meeting with Janet the Headmistress. After her bath, she washed and brushed her hair, and managed to assemble an outfit that wasn't ripped, dirty or transparent. Apart from her spectral thinness, she could have passed for a normal mother. Rose went up to the school with her partly to give moral support, but mostly to be on hand to ease out any wrinkles that might spring up.

As it turned out, the meeting went smoothly. Polly was on her best behaviour: articulate, charming, and only as sad as was appropriate to her position of new widow. She filled in the forms for the local authority and handed them over to Janet with a smile.

'From first impressions, they're going to fit in marvellously,' Janet said. 'The other children seem to be very taken with them.'

'They're quite a pair,' Polly said, getting up and reaching her hand out to shake Janet's.

'Thanks, Janet,' Rose said.

'Don't mention it. Baby's looking gorgeous.' Janet took Flossie's hand, which she had flung out from the sling like a little drama queen. 'I'm so glad you're preparing another little Anna for me.'

They took their leave and walked off down the clattery school corridor with its tang of school dinners and plimsolls.

Outside in the playground, the home lunch children were just being brought back to school by their parents. Rose could feel the ripple Polly caused as they crossed the playground. Even before she was famous, she had managed to turn heads, with her ingrained glamour and angular swagger. Now, more than a decade after her most recent album, people would still do a double-take. Even with her hair so neatly combed, and her clothing tuned down, Polly still had a distinctive look that was hard to obscure.

In an attempt to defuse the spell that she knew Polly could cast—and the trouble that generally resulted—Rose introduced her to a couple of people as 'my old friend Polly, whose kids are starting at the school'. But it was pretty pointless. As Polly held out her hand for shaking, Rose couldn't help feeling as if she was introducing the Queen.

'I thought I was going to have to start signing autographs,' Polly said as they walked back across the field.

When they got back, Polly went up to the Annexe to lie down.

'Can you get the boys, please, Rose? I'm wiped out,' Polly said, as she set off.

'Of course,' Rose said. Nico was nine, and she reckoned that pretty soon, with their strength in numbers, Anna could have her dream and the children could make their own way home. There were no roads to cross, and most of the journey was across the fields.

She hadn't let Anna know during her stories of when she was a girl, but the reason Rose's parents had forbidden her to take the short-cut under the pier on her way to school back in Brighton was that it was a notorious gathering-place for all sorts of undesirables. Rose had disobeyed her parents and, on one occasion, a man grabbed her. He had something purple and hard sticking out of his trousers, which he put her hand over, moving it up and down. She had squeezed it really hard, and dug her nails in, which had made him swear and loosen his grip, allowing her to beat him off with her satchel and run away. But she couldn't get the stink off her hand, no matter how hard she washed it. For weeks afterwards, she suffered nightmares where he followed her home, climbing in through her window and sticking that stinking thing at her with his smelly hand over her face.

After that, at least for a while, she tried her best to be a Good Girl, to obey her parents. But her efforts always seemed to backfire, and she invariably found herself thundering up the stairs of the guesthouse in an effort to lock herself inside the bathroom before her father caught her. In the end, she had just stopped trying—the outcome always seemed to be the same, whether she was good or bad.

In any case, this was why she wouldn't let Anna wander on her own. But now that Anna had two wild and unruly guardsmen, she supposed she would be safe. Another advantage, Rose thought, of Polly, Nico and Yannis staying for a while.

Thinking about this, Rose went up to the school a little later to pick up the children. She brought them back, listening to Nico and Yannis's excited chatter about their first day at Anna's school.

'It's your school now,' Anna said to them, swinging her schoolbag round and round over her shoulder.

When they got back, Rose gave each of them a glass of milk and a slice of cake. Then she turfed them all out into the back garden, where they started to build a den in the overgrown patch at the very end. Rose smiled to herself, thinking how much this would please Gareth.

At six-thirty, Rose sent Nico up to the Annexe to fetch Polly for supper. A while later, he came back, alone.

'She's in bed and sort of sleeping. She says go on

without her.'

'I'll put a plate out for you to take up for her,' Rose said.

'Nah, don't waste it,' Nico said. 'She said she's not hungry.'

As far as Rose knew, Polly hadn't eaten a thing all day. She was really going to have to keep an eye on her.

At seven, Gareth came in from the studio and they all sat down to supper without Polly. The boys tucked into their lasagne like hungry animals, taking second helpings and licking their plates clean.

They had spent their first day at school as rather glamorous exotica: their accented English and olive skins were a novelty at the village school.

'Me and Yannis decided we wanted to run round the playground, so we did, and soon everyone in the school was charging round after us,' Nico said.

'The whole school!' Anna hammered it home for Gareth.

'Like a crocodile,' Yannis said, and Anna and the boys beamed at one another. Anna had spent the day basking in the reflected glory of being associated with the boys, and Rose saw that she liked it. A lot.

'Like a bunch of idiots,' Nico added. Then the laughter died down and he yawned and shivered. 'I'm cold,' he said.

'Ah, you're not used to our nights yet. It can get pretty chilly,' said Rose. 'Now, finish up, and we'll get you to bed. It's really late.'

'At home, we stay up as long as we like,' Nico said.

'Well, we do things differently here,' said Gareth. 'And while you're with us, you'll do them like we do.'

'And you must be exhausted anyway, after your journey and going straight to school and all that,' Rose said.

'Come on Anna banana,' Gareth said, taking her and Flossie up for their bath.

Rose found blankets and wrapped them round the boys. She walked them up the garden towards the Annexe. The sky was clear now, and the air still. A touch of frost was biting into the air and the stars were like tiny stabs in backlit silk.

'Look,' she said, pointing up. 'The Plough, see?'

'We've got that back home,' Nico said. 'We see it from our terrace every night. But it's over there.' And, with an astronomical rationale all of his own, he pointed further south.

She bundled them both up the Annexe stairs to the darkened room above, and they tiptoed past Polly, who lay huddled asleep on the big bed. Rose took them into the bathroom, and switched on the light. Polly had taken a shower, Rose noticed. The floor was covered in water, there were damp towels bundled in a corner, and talcum powder covered the surfaces.

'Where are your toothbrushes?' Rose asked the boys.

They both shrugged.

'Well, your toilet bags then?'

'Toilet bag? *Ewww*,' Yannis giggled.

'Your washbags, I mean.'

Both boys looked blank. So Rose made them use their fingers with the toothpaste she had put out before they had arrived. Tomorrow she would

93

buy them warmer clothes and toothbrushes. And pyjamas, because it turned out that they didn't have any of them, either.

She tucked them into the bunk beds in the little bedroom—which, she noted, was very small indeed once there were two boys in it. There was also a faint whiff of damp, which she had never noticed before.

She went to turn the light out, looking back to smile at the two brown faces peering out from identical striped duvets.

'Rose?' Yannis said from his nest, in a small voice.

'Yes, Yannis?'

'Do you know any stories?' he said. 'Not scary ones, though.'

'Let me see now,' said Rose, curling up on the end of his bed. She could hear Nico sigh and turn noisily to face the wall. 'It won't be long, Nico, just to get Yannis settled.'

'Whatever,' Nico said.

'Do you want to hear how me and your mum met?'

'All right,' Yannis said.

'Well, it was a very rainy day by the seaside where we lived, and we were at school—our primary school, which was just near the beach.'

'Ours is too, back home,' Yannis said.

'Yours opened right onto the beach, didn't it? So at lunchtime you played out there. Well, ours was in the middle of a big town and there were a few roads between the school and the beach, so it was quite different, and the weather was very chilly and rainy that day, so everyone felt a little mean and cold. Not like in Karpathos, where the sun

94

shines almost every day.

'Anyway, we were all sitting down at our desks, when the teacher said there was a new girl, and in walked your mum. She was thin as a stick, and tiny, and her hair was like a frightened black cat sitting on her head.'

Nico let out a snort of laughter from the bed above.

'She was soaking wet, and looked like a little ferret, staring out with her beady eyes. And she was wearing what looked like a purple tutu, stripy pink and black tights and big silver boots that made her feet look like a hooligan's. Everyone in the class laughed.'

'No one laughed at me today,' Yannis said.

'No. They're nice at your new school. Back then, every—one laughed at your mum, except me. I stood up and said, "Can she come and sit by me, Miss?" And I looked after her. I took her hand and said, "We're going to be best friends". And we were.'

Nico had turned round now, and he hung his head down from the top bunk, listening.

'That afternoon, I took her back to my house after school. We stopped off at her little flat on the way to let her mum know, but her mum was sleeping on the sofa, so we left her a note. Did you ever meet your granny?'

'I did, when I was a baby,' Nico said. 'But I don't remember her.'

'Well, she was very beautiful. She was a model and her photo was in a lot of magazines when she was younger. But by the time she had your mum she wasn't all that well, and she wasn't able to look after her properly. So we went back to my house

95

and we had tea, and Polly told me all about her life. She and her mum had just moved down to Brighton from London, and they had spent some time in Italy before that, and Morocco. But they stayed in Brighton when they got there, because her mum was too tired to move anywhere else. Which was lucky for me and Polly.

'So if we weren't at school together, we were round each other's houses. My house was a sort of hotel, and we'd play in the empty bedrooms.'

'Can we go there, to that house?' Yannis asked.

'Oh, it was sold a long time ago,' Rose said. 'Still, we've got *this* house now. And I hope you two and Anna will grow up to be as great friends as me and Polly.

'Now then, it's time to call it a day,' she said, tucking them both in again and smoothing their duvets down. 'There'll be plenty more evenings for stories.'

'I can't sleep, Rose,' Yannis said, his lip trembling.

'Oh dear, Yannis, come here.' Rose lay down on the bed next to him. She knew that Flossie would be wanting a feed soon, but she couldn't let this poor little boy lie here in the dark on his own. She held him close and hummed and stroked his head, sure she could still smell wild oregano in his hair. In a matter of minutes, he was asleep, a tiny smile traced across his lips.

Rose got up. 'Is it OK if I go, Nico?' she whispered.

'He's asleep?'

'Yes.'

'Then go, Rose. I'll be fine.' He reached over, and rubbed her shoulder.

Like a little old man, she thought as she made her way back through the main room, past Polly's bed.

'Liar,' Polly muttered from her bed.

'What?' Rose said, startled.

'It wasn't like that,' Polly mumbled, half under her breath as she turned and huddled back down under the duvet. Then she sighed and softly started to snore.

Eleven

The next morning there was a deep frost. Pale gold sunlight was just beginning to soften the crunch underfoot as Rose, Flossie, Simon and Trooper crossed the field towards The Lodge on the way back from the school run.

'So, I hear she caused quite a stir yesterday,' Simon said, swinging the lunchbox he had forgotten to leave with Liam.

'What?' Rose said, watching a swift as it swept across the sky. Surely it was too early for swifts?

'Ms Novak. She was all the gossip at the school gate.'

'Oh, yes. Well, it makes a change from you, I suppose,' she said, arching an eyebrow.

More often than not, Simon was the only father on the school run. What with that, and his being tall, blond and not in bad nick for a dad, most of the other mothers had their eye on him for one reason or another. He had a reputation for being a bit of a flirt, but Rose put it down to him being an open and friendly sort whose good nature was

97

misinterpreted by the claustrophobic school community of mothers who had very little else to turn their minds—or eyes—to.

For example, the fact that Simon and Rose often left the school gates together had not gone unnoticed, nor that he had regularly been seen going into her house. Rose thought the whole thing with the gossip was ridiculous. The Lodge was on the way home for him, and he had often admitted that he was all about procrastination in his morning writing schedule. It quite annoyed her sometimes, the meaningful looks directed at her outside the school. Some of those people had very small lives.

Trooper bounded up with a drool-soaked stick and Simon threw it again for him. It arced up through the air, landing at the far side of the field.

'I haven't seen her since yesterday, when we met up with Janet,' Rose said.

'So you had the boys all evening?'

'Oh, I don't mind that. They're rather charming in their way. I'm getting quite fond of them. In fact, I'm thinking that it might be more practical at the moment if I move them down to the main house—at least until Polly's well enough to pull her weight.'

'From what I heard, she looked quite well enough,' Simon laughed.

'It's all a front. She knows how to pull off a performance,' Rose said.

They reached the entrance to Rose's garden.

'Got time for a spot of coffee?' Simon asked.

'Oh, go on, then,' she said, holding the gate open for him.

Rose was glad Simon was coming in. He

brought something of the outside world to the house—he was always going up to London for meetings with agents, editors and journalists— people who wanted his work and his wisdom. She enjoyed his talk of Soho House and the Groucho. It made her nostalgic for a life she supposed she had left behind when she moved out of London. In reality, she had rarely ventured further west than London Bridge when she lived in Hackney. But the fact that Simon managed all that urban, cultural life while still living out in the sticks reminded her of the possibilities of this place she and Gareth had chosen as their home. When Flossie got to school age, who knew what Rose might manage for herself?

Rose was surprised to see Polly in the kitchen, sitting in the armchair, with Manky the cat in her lap and a mug of coffee in her hand. She was wearing a different nightdress from the day before, but this one was just as revealing—an ankle-length skin-tight red tee with a low, curved neckline that barely contained the skinny little nipples that jutted from her chest. Her eyes were ringed and smudged with a mixture of sleep and yesterday's make-up.

Rose looked at Simon, who reddened. He was one of those fair-skinned people who are quick to blush. 'Polly, Simon. Simon, Polly.' While she was glad to see Polly up, she was a little irritated that her morning coffee with Simon was being gatecrashed.

Polly lifted her free hand from the cat and held it out. Simon, rather surprisingly, bent and kissed it. Once again, Polly was having regality bestowed upon her. Rose moved over to the other side of the room, unwound Flossie from the sling and lay her in her morning sun spot on her lambskin.

'I see you've reacquainted yourself with Manky,' she said to Polly.

'What?' Polly said.

'Manky. Surely you remember Manky? He was yours first of all.'

'The cat? My God, I never even thought—how old is he?'

'About thirteen now. Getting on a bit. Christos got him for you, remember? When you came out of hospital. Poor old Manky. I've got to take him to the vet later on—he's got something wrong with his teeth.'

Polly looked down at the cat who, having just spied Trooper, leaped off her lap, digging his claws into her legs.

'Oh my God,' Polly said in a small voice.

'And I took him on when you went to Greece, remember?'

'Yes.' Polly buried her face in her hands. They all stood there for a couple of beats, Simon turning redder by the second.

'I'm sorry,' Polly said suddenly, putting her hands down onto her thighs, shrugging her shoulders and smiling up at them both. Then she got up. 'Look at the state of me,' she said, holding her hands up like Shirley Bassey. 'I wasn't expecting company. Anyone want coffee?' And she moved to the coffee machine.

'Yes, please,' Simon said.

'I'll get myself some tea, thanks, Polly. Sit down, Simon,' Rose said, busying herself with the kettle. 'Would you like a brownie?'

'Yes, please, Rose.' Simon made himself

100

comfortable at the kitchen table. 'I'm a great fan, Polly,' he said.

'Thanks,' she said, sliding the coffee-holder into the machine.

'You were the soundtrack of my twenties,' he told her.

'I've got some new stuff I've been writing. Perhaps I'll play it for you, give you the first performance,' she said.

'I'd be honoured,' he said, his eyes on her.

'Simon's kids are in the same class as Yannis,' Rose said, putting a brownie in front of Simon. 'He's a writer. He's married to Miranda, who's a glamorous, big-shot barrister.'

'I don't think she'd describe herself like that,' Simon blustered.

'What do you write, Simon?' Polly asked, putting a cup of coffee down in front of him, then sitting herself opposite.

'Novels, mostly. And the odd bit of journalism from time to time.'

'He's being modest,' Rose said. 'Simon's a top crime writer.'

'Not really, I—' he protested.

'I'd love to read your books,' Polly said, leaning forward so that her breasts squashed together into something approximating a cleavage.

'I'll drop one by,' Simon said.

'You could form a mutual appreciation society,' Rose said, tucking into a brownie that she hadn't meant to eat. 'How is the marvellous Miranda?' she asked Simon, swallowing. 'I haven't seen her for ages. We must have you both round for dinner soon.'

'She's great. On a long case right now, up in

London during the week. It's some complicated corporate fraud case. Frightfully dull, but she seems to find it all fascinating.'

'She's so lucky she's got you,' said Rose. 'To hold the fort, I mean.'

It was just then that Gareth came into the kitchen. He'd been in his studio since dawn—his best time, he always said. Things were beginning to go well. As usual, Rose didn't know the details, but he had said that he was starting on a series of drawings, or diagrams, as he called them, that took the colours and shapes of the fields around them as a starting-point.

The night before, he and Rose had made love— the second night in a row, which was unusual—and afterwards he had said that he thought that, even given the arrival of Polly and the boys, their big life experiment was going better than planned. Rose had held him close.

'Hi, Simon, how's it going?' Gareth went over to Rose and kissed her on the cheek. 'I'm dying for a coffee.'

'You sit down. Let me get it.' She jumped up.

'Now who's the lucky one?' Simon winked at Rose.

'I'd better go back to my Annexe and have a shower,' Polly said, stretching her arms up above her head, more like a cat than Manky had ever managed.

'I'll walk up the path with you,' Simon said, getting up to join her. 'Bye, Rose, Gareth. Ta for the coffee and brownie. Delicious!'

'Oh. OK. Bye, then,' Rose said, Gareth's coffee cup in hand.

'That was a bit brief,' Gareth said after they had

gone out of the front door.

They watched through the kitchen window as Simon and Polly dawdled up through Rose's herb garden. Polly stopped and picked a head off a lavender bush—Rose had left them on for the winter—rubbing it between her palms. She held her hand up to Simon's face and he breathed in the scent.

'The little minx,' Gareth muttered.

Rose sat down next to him, looking out of the window. 'He's a big boy,' she said. 'He can take care of himself.'

'I wonder,' said Gareth. 'Simon's not famous for his discretion.'

'Oh, that's all just bollocks gossip,' Rose said. 'I hate all that.'

'Easy, tiger,' Gareth said, stroking her back.

They sat in silence, sipping their coffee, looking at the sparkle on the garden as, framed by the stone-edged window, it warmed in the sunshine.

'Rose?'

She felt Gareth's hand as he moved it gently to her shoulder, and turned to face him.

'Yes?'

'I love you so much,' he said.

And they kissed, in the sharp sunlight.

Twelve

Gareth finished his coffee and went back to the studio, leaving Rose and Flossie alone in the kitchen, which seemed, for a second, a little too empty. She switched on the radio and set about clearing up the breakfast and coffee things to a discussion on *Woman's Hour* about whether it was possible for modern women to have it all.

The cat came and rubbed himself against her legs.

'Oh Manky,' she said. 'She didn't even recognise you, did she? How shocking for you.'

Later, she took Flossie to Tesco to get toothbrushes, pyjamas, fleeces and wellies for the boys. She also bought a stack of boy-type magazines, a football net and football and some giant water-blaster gun things.

Before unloading the car, Rose knocked on the Annexe door to see if Polly was about. There was no reply. She went down to the house to look for her, but she wasn't there either. Rose was a bit put out, because she had wanted to ask Polly before she moved the boys. But, she thought, it was a favour she was actually doing for them all, so she just went ahead and sorted out the spare bedroom anyway. She made up the beds, cleared out a set of shelves and swapped a couple of Gareth's more cerebral paintings with two of Christos's colour bursts.

When she brought the children home from school, she sent them to the Annexe to pick up the boys' stuff.

'Was your mum in there?' she asked Nico as the three of them returned laden with the toys and books she had carried up there just days before.

'Yeah, but she's resting.'

'Sleeping?'

'Nah, just lying there. She said hello to us, though.'

'Ah.' Rose helped the boys set out their

104

belongings. Very soon, the rather bare guest room had been transformed into a proper boys' bedroom.

'Wicked!' Yannis said.

Rose fetched the new wellies and clothes she had bought from Tesco and gave them to the boys to try on. Everything fitted beautifully, although Nico said he didn't like his new fleece, declaring it to be lame. He took himself off to the corner of the kitchen in a half-hearted attempt at a sulk.

'Do you guys want to come and feed the chickens?' Anna said. It was her job, and she did it every day. She loved the chickens, which she viewed as her own.

'We can see if they've laid,' she went on. 'Though Peck probably won't let us get near. She's very broody right now.'

'OK, then.' Yannis jumped up. Nico tagged along behind them—again, too cool to show interest, but unable to keep away.

While the children got on with feeding the livestock, Rose took her trowel out to her herb garden at the front of the house, thinking that she could keep half an eye on the Annexe to see if Polly stirred.

This part of the garden had presented a lot of challenges for Rose. Before the renovations, it had been a steep slope. Then Rose, Gareth and Andy spent a weekend carving it into terraces that led down, with the help of stone steps, to the front door of the main house. When you arrived by car—which you invariably did, because most trips beyond the school involved a motor—you parked up by the Annexe and took the steps down towards The Lodge.

Gareth hadn't been sure about this at first. Backed up by Andy, he had said that carrying the shopping down all those steps would be a pain. The two of them had spent an evening drinking beer and thrashing out a plan for moving tons of earth to bring a driveway down to the house. They filled up one of Gareth's rough sketchbooks with diagrams and lists.

When the two of them worked together like that, Rose could see the two boys who had grown up in each other's pockets, miles from anywhere. They were so alike, it was surprising. Raised for self-sufficiency, they had been equipped with a deeply practical response to anything life might throw at them. Andy had told her that once he and Gareth had built a party hut: a two-roomed log cabin on the edge of Pam and John's land. They had cleared part of the forest and fashioned the structure from the trees they had cut down. It had taken the entire summer. How different Gareth and Andy's teenage years had been from the boozy, lazy time Rose and Polly had spent in Brighton, taking drugs on the beach, hanging out with boys on sofas.

Despite admiring the way the two of them worked, Rose had argued passionately against their pragmatic drive idea. She said they needed to separate the car from the house. She wanted to stand at the sink and see a garden, not a driveway. The backdrop to the view was the Annexe, and the car could hide behind that. If they had a beautiful old Saab, or a Maserati or something, then that might be a different matter. But seeing their practical, ugly, big old Galaxy sitting there would just be depressing.

106

The men couldn't really argue with that, so Rose was very careful that, the decision having been made in her favour, she would never, ever complain or ask for help when faced with hauling a week's worth of shopping down the steps to the house.

And she loved the herb garden that stood where the drive might have been. The space and scope for growing all sorts of esoteric varieties of thyme and lavender excited her. She was happy, while the children fed the chickens, to take the opportunity to spend a little time out there, picking around the earth, getting rid of the baby weeds that were already pushing themselves up so early in the year. Flossie sat beside her in her car seat, gurgling in the sunshine.

Rose heard the children clatter round from the back garden to the side of the house, towards the stone table and benches that stood by the pizza oven. This was where Anna sat and counted the eggs each day.

'Well, my papa's dead,' Nico was saying.

'Yeah, yeah, I know that,' Anna said. 'Now you've made me lose count.'

'But he might come back, though,' Yannis piped up. Rose's heart contracted.

'No, he won't, *malaka*,' Nico said.

'He might, though.'

'And my mama's famous, though. And she's pretty and thin,' Nico went on.

'Well, my mum's pretty, too,' said Anna, Rose's loyal little girl.

'And, well, my mama's very brave. She sometimes has little cuts here and here, and sometimes they bleed,' Yannis boasted.

'Shut up, Yannis,' Nico hissed.

'And my yaya is a witch because she says Mama killed Papa,' Yannis added.

'She doesn't,' Nico said, his voice rising.

'She does, though. I heard her, and Mama said back to Yaya that *she* was a witch.'

'Yaya doesn't mean Mama actually killed Papa,' Nico said.

'She does. I heard her.'

'You didn't, though—you just shut up, Yannis,' Nico yelled, and there was a crash and a gasp from Anna.

'MUM!' Anna shouted.

Rose arrived just in time to pull Nico off his brother. He was screaming, Yannis was crying and the eggs lay smashed all around the patio. Anna stood there wringing her hands.

'That's enough, you lot,' Rose said, holding them apart, at arm's length, wondering how she was going to sort this one out. Then, out of the corner of her eye, she spied the fox creeping into the space between the apple tree and the pear tree at the far end of the back garden.

'Anna, are the chickens in?'

'Yes, of course,' Anna said, following Rose's gaze. 'Oh, Foxy!'

'Look,' whispered Rose, putting an arm round each boy. 'See?'

'Won't he eat the chickens?' Yannis asked.

'Not if they're in. They've got a fox-proof run. We love our fox,' Rose said. 'In fact, we'll leave these smashed eggs for him to clear up after we've gone.'

'Most people in the country hate foxes, but we think he's strong and proud,' Anna added, using the exact words that Rose had used when they first saw him a couple of weeks after they had moved in.

The children gazed at the grizzled beast. Rose's theory was that he had more or less taken over the garden when The Lodge had stood empty. In spite of the chickens, she was glad of his presence because he kept the rabbits away. Or, more likely, he kept the rabbits down. She didn't like to think about it all that much.

'The poor old fox is hunted and hated by humans,' she said to the boys, 'but he sees our garden as a safe place in a hostile world.'

'And we love him.' Anna beamed.

You've certainly earned your keep this afternoon, Mr Fox, Rose thought. The two boys, their fight forgotten, now stood transfixed as he dawdled across the lawn, completely unconcerned by the presence of the humans.

'Let's make supper,' Rose said at last. 'Will you go and bring Flossie in, please, Nico?' she asked, offering the task like a gift, a proof of her trust in him after having to handle him so roughly to get him off his brother.

They went in and she set the children tasks to help prepare the meal, which she reconfigured from a roast leg of lamb to a pie, because it involved stirring stuff in pots, rolling out pastry and decorating with little leaves and initials. It was far more complicated and took longer to do than a roast, especially with an army of inexperienced sous chefs, but Rose was a great believer in the healing power of the kitchen.

Soon, Nico was cutting the lamb into cubes, and trimming it of fat, Anna was frying onions, and

Yannis was rubbing flour into butter between newly washed fingers.

'Phew—it's hot in here,' Rose said, and flung open the kitchen window. It was true, the early March sun had a strange intensity to it that afternoon.

When the pie was in the oven, she set the younger ones to cutting out biscuits from the leftover pastry, while she and Nico peeled some spuds.

'So, Nico,' she said. 'How was your second day at school?'

'S'OK,' he said. 'Except—'

'Except what?' Rose asked.

'Well, a couple of the kids, they take the piss.'

'Why?'

'They say I speak weird.'

'Who says you speak weird?'

'Oh, just a couple of kids in my class. They're morons, anyway.'

'Names?'

'Nah, it's OK.'

Rose made a mental note to have a word with his teacher in the morning.

'And how are you liking it, staying here with us?' she went on.

'It's OK,' he said.

'Just OK?'

'Yep,' he said, nodding and frowning over the potato he was slowly scraping right away with the peeler.

'You've finished that one, I think.' Rose took it from his hand and put another, unpeeled one in its place.

'And how do you think your mum is?' she asked.

'She's all right.'

'Yes?'

'Yes. Well . . . she's sad. About Papa.'

'Of course she is.' Rose put her peeler down and bent down towards him, trying to catch his eyes. 'It's normal, you know, to be sad when someone you love dies.'

'I know,' he said, his eyes fixed on his work.

'And—are you sad, Nico?' she asked.

'I . . .' He looked up, over her shoulder, and a flicker of something Rose couldn't define—was it fear?—passed over his face.

She turned to see Polly shivering outside at the open kitchen window, looking straight at her. Her black hair flared out around her, making her face appear small and ill-defined. She was wearing the long, semi-transparent white nightdress again. Rose noticed that in the sunlight it looked a little ripped, a little stained with what looked like dried blood. Her eyes were red-rimmed and bloodshot.

Her voice was quiet when she spoke. 'Of course he's sad—aren't you, Nico?'

The boy nodded dumbly.

'We're all sad, Rose. In case you hadn't noticed, our entire world has fallen apart.' Then, in a burst of energy released from somewhere deep inside her, she yelled, 'God!'

The children stopped what they were doing and looked up, stunned. Across the other side of the kitchen, a knife fell from the magnetic block to the stone floor with a metallic clatter. Rose shuddered and blinked. Then, thinking quickly, she pulled herself together and clapped her hands.

'OK, kids. Why don't you go and watch *The Simpsons*? Nico and Anna, will you keep an eye on

111

Flossie for a moment?' She ushered them through into the TV room and thrust the remote control into Yannis's hand, who took it as if it were a piece of treasure entrusted to his safekeeping.

Rose hurried out of the house, round to where Polly was still standing, looking out now, up at the Annexe, her stained nightdress fluttering in the breeze.

'Come on, Polly, let's go up to your room, make a cup of tea, have a sit down.'

'You always think putting things in stomachs will mend things, don't you?' Polly said.

'I know,' Rose said, putting her arm in Polly's. 'But, you know what? I really do need a cuppa. Come on.'

Steering her by her sinewed, downy arm, Rose led Polly up the stone steps towards the Annexe. Her skin felt rough to the touch, dry like paper. But she came readily enough, offering little resistance.

'I'm sorry I've been so busy today,' Rose said. 'I wanted to spend some time with you, but I had shopping to do. I checked on you earlier, but I think you were asleep. It must be a long time since you've had some time to yourself, without the boys to take care of.'

'Yes.' Polly drew her arm out of Rose's and wrapped it round her thin frame. The sun was going down now behind the Annexe, and the shadows were lengthening, revealing the true chill of the breeze. They stopped at the bottom of the wooden stairs that led up to the bed-sitting room.

'Don't come in yet,' she said to Rose. 'Just give me a second, will you?'

'Of course,' Rose said. She stood and waited for

ten minutes, listening to Polly moving around upstairs, shifting things, rubbing and banging. She heard a tap running for a while, then the toilet flushing. Then Polly, breathless, was at the door again. Her mood seemed to have been lightened by the work.

'Sorry about that,' she said. 'The boys—they leave such a mess!'

But they've been out at school all day, Rose thought. As she followed Polly up the stairs, she got an overwhelming, amber-heavy blast of Polly's perfume, which had quite clearly been sprayed around the room. But why? What was she masking?

'I'll put the kettle on,' Polly said, moving over to the kitchen area. Rose sat at the table.

She had no idea what Polly had been clearing up. The bed-sitting room was a mess, the bed unmade, rumpled, the sheets torn away. And there were clothes and underwear strewn around the place, as if the open suitcase in the middle of the room had projectile-vomited its contents in a 360-degree trajectory. Polly's guitar was out of its case and the table was blanketed with sheets of yellow paper, all covered in tiny writing and drawings, crossings out and hieroglyphs. Rose knew what this meant, having seen it many times before.

'You're writing.' She looked up at Polly.

'Oh? Oh yes,' she said, hurrying to gather up the paper, as if she hadn't noticed it before. She dumped the lot on the bed and pulled the duvet over it. 'It's one of my ways of coping, as you know.' She sat down on the bed, on top of the papers.

'And the others are?' Rose asked, getting up to

113

finish the tea-making that Polly had abandoned.

'Oh, you don't want to know, Miss Rose.' Polly started to laugh, and Rose joined her. But Polly went on laughing a little longer than was necessary, or normal, until the noise became a mechanical-sounding tic in her throat.

Rose turned to add milk to the mugs then took one over to Polly, putting it carefully in her hands.

'Polly, are you sure you're all right?'

'To be honest?' Polly said, taking a sip out of her mug and making a face. 'I've been better. But just give me time, OK?'

'Of course,' Rose said. 'There's all the time in the world.'

'I'll be fine,' Polly said, and set about drinking her hot tea as if it were a task she had set herself. When she had finished, she put the mug on the floor and looked up at Rose, who had sat back down at the table.

'Look, Rose,' she said. 'I'm really grateful for what you're doing for me. I really am. Just—just please don't think you can make it all better by talking, by having cosy little chats with me, or with my kids. It's not going to work like that. What we've gone through is not solvable by that. The only way that is going to work is my way. And I do things differently to you. I always have. So please don't think you can put it all right with some words and plates of food, because you can't. The truth is that nothing will bring Christos back. And that is what we—the boys and I—are dealing with. And how could you ever know what that means to us? So please—you know. Back off.'

Rose looked at the floor and exhaled slowly. 'OK then,' she said.

114

'I know you want to be everyone's mummy, Rose. And we both know exactly why that is.'

Rose gasped, shocked at what Polly had just said.

'Don't worry, Rose,' Polly went on. 'Just don't take it out on my kids, eh?'

Rose got up and turned to go. She noticed that her knees were shaking. At the top of the stairs, she turned to face Polly, forcing a smile.

'You'll be coming down for supper?' she said. 'The children have made a pie.'

'I'm sure they have,' Polly said, hugging herself and avoiding Rose's eye.

'Seven-thirty, then. Please don't be late. The pie won't hang around.'

'OK. Cheers then,' Polly said, getting up to close the door behind Rose.

Rose turned to take one last look round the blasted room that she had spent so long sorting out for Polly's arrival. She noticed, for the first time, that on the little table by the bed there was a brand new, hardback copy of Simon's latest novel.

Polly followed her gaze. 'Oh, Simon brought that round at lunchtime. For me to read. It looks rather good,' she said. She turned back to Rose.

'It is,' Rose said, looking straight at her. 'You'll really love it.'

Then she turned and went back down to The Lodge, counting her steps carefully.

Thirteen

Led by Anna, the children had decided to make the meal into a big event. They laid the table with a white linen cloth and the best cutlery. They picked daffodils from the bottom of the garden and put them in a vase as a centrepiece. As a final touch, with help from Rose, they lit two candelabras, setting them at either end of the table.

Gareth, who came in from his studio just as the candles were being lit, saw the spread and declared that it was going to be the most special meal of the year, worthy of a bottle of champagne from the case he had received from Andy for his fortieth birthday.

He popped the cork right across the room, and the children caught the overspill in tiny glasses, which they held up in a toast. Their enthusiasm was infectious. It thawed the tiny part of Rose's heart that still held ice from earlier, so that when Polly finally arrived—late, of course—she was able to look at her.

And she was quite a sight. She had put on a long black, bias-cut dress and pinned her hair up in a distrait bun. Red lipstick made her slightly too-large mouth bloom like a rose, and her pale cheeks were fringed by impossibly long, mascaraed lashes. She looked, Rose couldn't help thinking, extraordinarily beautiful, like a character in a novel, like *La Dame aux Camélias*. Rose drew her own worn and pilled cardigan around herself and wondered how one suitcase could contain so many different outfits, so many different Pollys.

Unlike Rose, Polly seemed to have completely forgotten what had happened up in the Annexe. She made her entrance, then, seeing the splendour of the table, took Rose by the hands and kissed her, once on each cheek. She moved to Gareth and repeated the gesture, then went on to the children and formally shook their hands, one by one.

'This looks gorgeous,' she said, sitting down, her skin glowing in the candlelight. 'You've all been working so hard!'

The children smiled, ripples of pride running through their shoulders. Rose and Anna served up.

'This pie is delicious,' Polly said, as she nibbled at her portion. And it was. Despite enthusiastic over-handling by the children, the pastry was light and flaky, the lamb and vegetable filling melting and tender.

Rose looked at Polly. That outpouring back in the Annexe must have been useful for her, she thought, because she was on incredibly good form. Well, if it made her feel better, then that must be a good thing, she supposed.

Polly asked the boys about their day at school. She even sat with her arm around Yannis while they waited for Rose, Anna and Nico to serve up the dessert of baked apples stuffed with dates. In his mother's arms, leaning back against her breast, the little boy had the relieved look of a survivor pulled from a sinking ship.

Polly looked almost beatific, with her arm round her boy, Rose thought, as she ladled custard into a jug.

'How's your work going, Gareth?' Polly asked, turning the beam of her attention towards him.

'I'm getting there,' he said. 'I'm looking away from the fields now—at the river. Hand-generated prints of some sort, I think. Maybe a book.'

'Our river?' Rose asked. This was news to her, but she was glad of it. Gareth hardly ever talked about his work while he was developing ideas. 'And printmaking? That's interesting,' she added, handing out the apples. Gareth's more recent artwork had mostly been digital, with a little oil paint added along the way, for old times' sake.

'I guess I've been taken up by manual labour,' he said, getting up to fetch a bottle of red from the dresser. 'I'm feeling the need for something solid, something real under my hands.'

'I know the feeling.' Polly smiled.

'I might try to trace the river back to its source, document the journey,' he said, filling up her glass, then his own.

'I'd like to come with you!' Polly said.

'I'm not sure—' Rose started, but Gareth spoke over her.

'If I do the trip, it will have to be alone. It'll take days,' he said. 'I'll take a sleeping bag and just spend the night where I find myself.'

How wonderful it must be, Rose thought, to feel free enough to just do that. But it was part of what made her love Gareth—the way he could make an idea become a fact, a reason for spending days and weeks and months on something. Years, even, in the case of the house. Tenacity was a good quality for a husband. And, more than that, when it came to his artwork, he could turn this ability into a way of making money to put food on their table. That Rose could ever think it possible to take off alone for a couple of days to follow a dream seemed so

118

remote that for a second she wanted to weep. What dream would it be, in any case? She wasn't so sure she had one. But then she was living her dream, wasn't she? She didn't need to go anywhere.

They finished the apples—all plates except Polly's scraped clean. Rose got the children up and organised them into a washing-up team.

'Polly's been doing some writing, Gareth,' she said.

'Really?' He turned to her.

'I'm just digging out some work I've done since Christos . . . Well, I've always written my way through trouble, and the conditions are certainly good right now. It's spilling out of me.'

'Songs?' Gareth asked.

'My *Widow Cycle*,' Polly said in a small voice. Then she ground to a stop, spreading her hands out in front of her and examining her nails. She suddenly looked very fragile.

For a thin woman in her late thirties who had taken a lot of drugs and spent five years living in the sun, Polly had a remarkably smooth face. Rose had a belief that it was your arse or your face for women of a certain age, using it to comfort herself about the extra stone she carried. Polly defied this, as she did with so many of the rules set for the majority. In the candlelight she looked like a girl of twenty.

'I so admire you two for being able to do that, to use your lives and surroundings to create stuff,' Rose said, sitting down next to Gareth.

'You do it too, Rose, but your creation is life itself,' he said, putting his arm around her with a cheesy smile.

119

'Oh per-lease,' Rose said. 'You sound like a fridge magnet.'

'Yeah, I know. But you make all of this come alive,' he said, gesturing around the room. 'Without you, all this would be nothing. Without you, I'd be nothing.'

He was pushing it a bit far. Over by the sink, the children started giggling, then Rose and Gareth joined them and soon the five of them had tears of laughter streaming down their faces. Polly smiled from her different place, across the table. Rose watched her from the corner of her eye. She had that look on her face again, the one where she appeared to be working out some sort of sum in her head.

'Without you, I'd be nothing!' Nico was down on his knees, his eyes closed, holding Yannis's hand to his heart. He had taken Gareth's American accent and exaggerated it perfectly. Yannis looked heavenward, flipping the plate he was drying up to give the moment dramatic flourish. Unfortunately, it parted company with his hand and arced across the room to land in a shattering crash on the stone floor, sending Manky yowling for cover. There was a brief, stunned pause, then everyone turned to Rose who, despite losing one of her best plates, led them all as they collapsed, once again, into snorts of laughter. When they had finally exhausted themselves, Rose got up and cleared up the smithereens of the plate.

'All right yeah,' Gareth said. 'But see what I mean?'

'When can we hear your new songs?' Rose asked Polly as she sat down again.

'When they're ready, you'll be the first to hear

120

them. Well, second. I think I promised first dibs to Simon.'

Rose and Gareth exchanged a look.

'I suppose they're about the essence of what you just said to Rose, Gareth. But it's me saying it to Christos,' Polly went on. 'And then there's the anger at being left.' She stared into her wine glass.

'He didn't choose to leave you, Polly,' Rose said.

'At least I can say that, can't I? Funny how it offers such scant consolation.'

'Mum, we've done,' Anna said, coming up and putting her arms around Rose, hugging her from behind. 'Come and check.'

Rose got up, realising she was a little drunk. She cast an eye over the washing-up. There were a couple of pans that she would re-do later when they had gone to bed, but on the whole it was passable.

'Right, get your pyjamas on, guys.' She clapped her hands and they ran upstairs. 'Clean the teeth, get into bed and I'll be up in a bit.'

'I'm assuming, from all the disruption this afternoon, that you've decided the boys are staying up here,' Polly said.

Gareth looked surprised. 'Is this right, Rose?' he asked.

'It seemed practical. I just thought that you could do with a bit of space, Polly. It'll take the pressure off. And the boys were really keen.'

'It would've been good to have discussed it beforehand,' Gareth said.

'And would you have objected?' She turned to face him.

'Well, no, but that's not the point.' He looked her in the eye.

121

'Oh come on, Gareth,' Rose said, sitting down again. 'They're going to be down here every morning and evening, round here after school, and it's tiny up there. Polly needs to be alone to work. It's all good,' she said.

'Gareth's right, though,' Polly said, looking up at Rose.

'But it's the best thing.' Rose poured herself another glass. 'I mean, it's not exactly as if you've been around to ask. I did go up earlier, but you weren't there.'

'I've been in all day,' Polly said.

'I couldn't hear you moving about.'

'So you came and had a good listen, did you?' Polly said.

'Look, for fuck's sake, I'll go up and tell Nico and Yannis to move back to the Annexe.' Rose stood up, ready to march upstairs. She had just about had enough.

'Oh Rose,' Polly said. 'Come here and sit down. Flouncing really doesn't suit you. Look, I'm fine with it, really I am. It's just that you went ahead and did it without even considering what I might feel.'

'Believe me, what you feel is foremost in my mind at the moment, Polly,' Rose said, still standing.

'Look, Rose, will you come and sit down, drink your wine and shut up,' Gareth said.

Rose stayed standing. She didn't know what to do. Go upstairs or sit down? Which would seem less like a capitulation? Then Polly gave an involuntary shiver. Seizing her opportunity, Rose went over to the sofa and pulled off one of the throws. She took it to Polly and wrapped it round her.

'You really should get some warmer clothes,' she said.

'Look,' Polly said, drawing the blanket around her, 'I'm sorry. I know I'm being a bit spiky. I'm really grateful for all this. You're being really generous. I can't begin to thank you . . .'

'Then don't start,' Rose said, sitting next to her. 'I know you'd do the same for me if—' She looked over at Gareth, and she couldn't go on. 'God, Polly, I can't imagine what it must be like for you.'

'It's like having your arm torn off,' she said. 'Without your consent. How dare he? How dare he go and leave us?'

Gareth got up and fetched what they called the drugs box, which they kept on the top shelf of the dresser, above Anna's nest of eggs. He sat down again and started to roll a joint.

'There was no one to talk to there. His mother was awful,' Polly went on. 'She blamed me. Said I'd driven him to it. She even had the gall to suggest that I'd tampered with the truck.'

'No!' Rose said.

'I mean, do I look like I'd know my way around the mechanics of a pick-up truck? She's always hated me. If you haven't been on the island for ten generations you're an outsider, and there was no room for me. After he died. I had to go.'

'How did it happen exactly?' Gareth asked.

'Christos and I had this argument. It was serious, but not out of the ordinary. I told him to fuck off, so he did the usual and drove off down to the town, to George's taverna—remember that friend of Christos's?' she asked Rose.

'The impossibly handsome one?' Rose said.

'Yep. Anyway, apparently he spent hours in there, drinking beer and raki with his cronies, no doubt telling them all what a witch I was. Then, instead of coming home, he drove right up to the top of the island, up the new road, into the mountains. I don't know why. Sometimes he'd go up there and spend the night—he never told me much about it and I wasn't all that interested. But he was going too fast. And he was drunk, of course. Then he just took a bend badly, one of those hairpins up a mountain, and instead of going up, he went right over the side. The truck was mangled, and so was he.'

'He died instantly?' Gareth asked.

'They think so. But it was a while till he was found. By a shepherd, who, coincidentally, was a distant cousin. Hence the brainless gossip about tampering.

'The night it happened, I'd gone to bed and didn't realise that he hadn't returned till I woke up the next morning. I thought perhaps he'd stayed at George's down in the town. As I said, it wasn't unusual for him to spend a night or two away. Later on in the evening of the next day, when there was still no sign of him, I got a taxi down to the town to find him. I was furious by then, of course. But no one knew where he was. We weren't all that concerned. He had set a precedent for disappearing, after all.'

Rose passed the joint to Polly, who drew deeply on it and exhaled slowly.

'Then, five days later, they found him. What remained of him. The wolves had got there first. We didn't have much to bury,' she said.

'Oh God, Polly,' Rose said, taking her hand.

'The worst part, though, was that during those five days, I got more and more angry at him for staying away. I never imagined . . . You'd think you'd know, wouldn't you? Somewhere in your heart, if . . . Anyway, I was so mad that by the time they found him, my first reaction was that dying served him right.'

Gareth blew out his cheeks, and Polly sat back and looked at Rose. There was something terrible in her eyes, some sort of glimmer of triumph. Rose felt herself shiver.

'He fucked other women,' Polly said, smoke trailing out through her nostrils. Lost in her story, she hadn't passed the joint on.

'I know,' Rose said, her eyes level. Gareth kept very still, very quiet.

'All the time,' Polly went on. 'All through our marriage. But until that last time, he always came back to me in the end.' She fell quiet. Then she smiled and looked up. 'Not that I was an angel, of course. Don't feel sorry for me. I got what I deserved.'

'Don't say that,' Gareth said, leaning over and touching her arm. A sudden draught pushed the candles and the flames guttered, threatening darkness. But as quickly as it appeared it passed.

Rose got up. 'I'd better go and tuck the children in,' she said. 'If I can make it up the stairs. Polly, do you want to come and say goodnight to the boys?'

'I think I'll pass tonight,' she said, taking a final draw on the joint and handing it over to Gareth. 'Nico'll just smell my breath and tell me off. He hates me smoking. Thinks he'll lose me too. Give them a kiss from me, will you?'

125

Rose tiptoed up to see Anna first, who was fast asleep, buried in a mound of teddies, her duvet cocooned around her. Then she went to the boys in the spare room. Nico was reading a comic, and Yannis was lying curled under his bedding.

'I said I'd stay up till he went to sleep,' Nico said.

'He's lucky to have a brother like you,' Rose said, leaning down to give him a kiss on the head. She then went over to Yannis, who pulled her close to him.

'I wish you were my mama,' he whispered in her ear.

'Shhh. You mustn't say that,' she said, putting her finger over his lips. 'Now, go to sleep, you.' And, as she kissed him on the cheek, he closed his eyes and smiled.

She went out onto the landing and put on the night-light. Anna was scared of the dark and, if Rose was honest, so was she.

On the way downstairs, Rose realised that the story of Christos's death had not contained one single reference to the boys. It was all about Polly. She had made it her story. But then it was one thing, Rose thought, to stand on the shore thinking how Polly should be swimming to save herself. It was another thing altogether to be in the water, flailing against the current, trying not to be pulled under.

She paused on the landing to look down at Polly and Gareth, who were deep in conversation, handing another spliff backwards and forwards. This was good.

As she went down the stairs into the kitchen, Gareth held out his hand for her to come and sit

126

next to him.

'We were just sharing memories of Christos,' Gareth said. 'He was quite a guy.'

'He certainly was,' Rose said.

Polly, who was beginning to shake, took a couple of pills from one of the rattling bottles in her bag and knocked them back with the remains of her glass of wine.

'I really must be going,' she said, glancing at the clock.

'But it's only ten,' Rose said.

'I have my pharmaceutical schedule to keep to,' Polly said, getting up and glancing out of the window over the sink, the one that looked up towards the Annexe. Something seemed to have caught her attention up there.

'OK, then,' Rose said, getting up. 'You sure you're all right? I'll come up the path with you, if you want.'

'No, I'm fine and dandy,' Polly said. 'Just tired. Look, thanks for tonight. It was good to talk. I'll see you in the morning.'

'Don't get up early,' Rose said.

'As if.' Polly left quickly, with the throw still wrapped around her.

'That was a bit hasty,' Rose said, puzzled. Then she noticed that Polly had left her bag on the table. 'I'd better take this up for her. It's got her pills in.'

'She can do without them tonight,' Gareth said. He had got up and was looking out of the window. 'Come and see.'

He took Rose's arm, blew out the candles and pointed up through the window to the Annexe. There, in the shadows, waiting for Polly, was a tall, male figure that was unmistakably Simon. He and

Polly exchanged a few words in the doorway. She seemed not to be too pleased to see him, but after a few moments she went in and he followed her. Very shortly after that, the lights went out in the Annexe.

'Bloody hell,' Gareth said. 'I'd forgotten quite what a fast mover our Polly is.'

Fourteen

The rest of the week fell into an easy pattern, with the boys sleeping in the big house, and Polly joining everyone for supper. As far as Rose could tell, Simon hadn't visited Polly again after that night. He certainly hadn't been stopping for morning coffee. He had a deadline, he told Rose, as he hurried home after the school run each day. She missed their chats, and she couldn't help wondering what had gone on between the two of them. But whatever had happened seemed to have had a good effect on Polly. She seemed more relaxed, less barbed. And she was working during her hours up in the Annexe. Sometimes, on the way to the car, Rose would catch a snatch of guitar and Polly's unmistakable voice picking its way around a new tune.

The boys' new Tesco clothes only lasted a couple of days and then they were all caked in mud. Rose couldn't wash and dry them quickly enough. So, on the Friday, she decided to take them into Bath to extend their English wardrobes.

She picked them up from school in the Galaxy. It was the first time the boys had been in the car since that first journey from Heathrow, and it took a good deal of bargaining to organise who was sitting where. They both wanted to be next to Anna, but on the very back row, where there were only two seats. Then there was a long argument about why they should wear seatbelts. Finally they set off, bombing down the narrow, banked country lanes through the drizzling afternoon. In a month or so, the cow parsley would be dwarfing them, but right now they were able to see the fields and the hills beyond.

'All this green—it hurts my eyes,' Yannis said.

'It gets worse, believe me.' Rose smiled over to him. In losing the back-seat argument, he had won the not inconsiderable consolation prize of sitting in the front, next to Rose. Flossie, backwards facing in the middle row, was being watched over by Anna who was whispering and giggling with Nico in the row behind.

'I want to be in the back,' Yannis moaned, looking over at the two of them.

'On the way home you can,' Rose said. Only partly satisfied by this, Yannis turned again to look out of his window.

'Back home it's all brown, blue and grey,' Yannis said. 'We get flowers in the spring, but then the sun comes and kills them all.'

'We get flowers here all through to the end of the summer.'

'Really?' He considered this, twirling his long hair round his index finger.

'And, hey, Yannis. You could start thinking about this all as your home now, too.' Rose put her hand on his knee.

'It's too cold here.' He scowled, looking out of

129

the window at the fields as they streaked past.

Rose parked in the multi-storey and filed them all out into the street. There was a lovely shop called Jabberwocky which sold really good quality, rugged clothes for middle-class country children. It was a little more expensive than Tesco, but Rose thought the cut was better, and the clothes lasted longer.

On the way there, she realised how unaware Yannis and Nico were of the traffic. She had to intervene more than a couple of times to stop them stepping out without looking. In the end, she made them hold on to the buggy, one each side. It was, she thought, better to force passers-by off the pavement than risk these loose cannons careering off into the road. It wasn't that they were just looking the wrong way when they crossed the road. It was more that they had no idea of danger. Nor, it seemed, did they possess the ability to follow her instructions.

They piled into the shop, and the children sat in the play area with Flossie, while Rose went around collecting a pile of possible outfits for the boys to try on. The shop was pretty child-friendly, but even so she had to mediate a couple of times: once to pull Yannis off Nico, then to tell him to tone the language down. She wasn't used to shopping trips being so wearing. Yannis, who was normally the easiest of the boys, was proving to be quite a handful today.

They crammed into the changing room. Yannis immediately stripped down to his underpants, slipped his way past Rose and ran back into the shop.

'I'm a weirdo!' he cried out, turning a couple of

130

cartwheels across the shop floor.

'I'm a weirdo!' He bounced and lunged his face into that of a nice little girl with plaits and the straw-boatered uniform of a private girls' day school. She shied away and buried her face in her mother's heavy floral linen skirt.

Rose darted across the shop to catch Yannis and finally managed to corner him by the shoe department.

'Come on, Yannis,' she said, holding him by the arm. 'You've got to act a bit more grown up. It's like being with a toddler.'

'But I'm a weirdo.' He stood there, panting and glaring at her. 'I'm a weirdo. They all said!' Sniggers racked him until, like a tap running dry, it all stopped and his wiry little body, at first so tense and fizzing, seemed to fold before her eyes. She followed him to the ground, still holding him.

'Who said, Yannis?'

'The kids at school. I hate them.'

'We'll see about that,' she said. 'They can't do that.'

At last, the tears came.

'I hate that school. I want to go home, Rose. I want it all back how it was,' he wailed.

The shop was, thankfully, fairly empty, and the few other customers and sales staff kept a discreet distance from Rose and the melting, wild little boy.

She folded him up in her arms, pressing his hot head into her breast. 'There, there, Yannis. It's OK, shhh, it's OK.'

'I want my papa,' he sobbed.

'I know,' Rose whispered into his hair. 'I know, Yann.'

It was horrible to think, but in a way she was

glad that he was reaching out for her like this. The poor boy had to go through this grief. Even a child had to reach the bottom, before they could move on. She felt privileged that he had chosen her for his witness.

'And Mama's just rubbish.'

'Shh,' Rose said. 'She just misses him too, and it's making her sad, like you. But she'll be better soon. And I'm here, and whatever happens, I promise, promise, promise that I will never, ever let you down.'

He looked up at her, his eyes red.

'Look, Yannis, Gareth and I—well, we love you. As if you were our own sons. And Christos—your papa—he loves you too. He's up there, looking down and giving you all his love.'

'In heaven?'

'Yes.'

'But Mama says that's just bollocks. I heard her tell Yaya that, when they were at the funeral.'

'Do you think it's bollocks?'

'No.'

'Well then, nor do I.'

'I talk to him sometimes.'

'Do you know what? So do I.' She smiled at Yannis. She hadn't noticed before, but he really had the eyes of his father. 'I can see him right there, inside you, right now.'

'How can he be up there and in me at the same time, though?'

'Well, nothing's impossible. Your dad is on an awfully big adventure. One we can't even begin to imagine.'

'And that's a good thing?'

'Yes. Yes, it is.' She gave him another hug.

'Here,' she said, breaking away a little. 'I know what'll make you feel better. There's this place round the corner that serves the most amazing hot chocolate. It's so thick you can stand your spoon up in it.'

'Really?' he said, the cloud passing as quickly as it had descended.

'Yes, but come on, first we've got to get you kitted out,' she said.

'What?'

'Buy you some clothes, I mean. Come on.' And she led him back to the changing room.

Behind the curtain, a scene of calm and order confronted her. Nico was sitting playing with Flossie, who was awake in her buggy.

'Those are the ones Nico wants,' Anna said, pointing to a pile of clothes that were neatly folded on a chair. 'And these,' she said, putting the final pair of trousers back on a hanger, 'don't fit or they look rubbish.'

Nico smiled up at Rose. 'They're really cool clothes. Thanks, Rose.'

'That's nothing, Nico. I'm glad you're happy. Now then, Yannis, let's get you sorted.'

And she set to helping him into the lovely, German-made trousers and Swedish fleeces she had piled up, ready for him to try on.

*   *   *

She ended up spending over £300 in the shop, but she felt Jabberwocky had earned it, having had to bear witness to Yannis's moment. The boys insisted on wearing their new clothes and she paraded her freshly smart crew into the special hot

133

chocolate café. They emerged half an hour later, happy but somewhat less well-groomed, with chocolate moustaches and splatters on their new tops. The children, sugar riding high in their bodies, skipped and chattered all the way back to the car park. Yannis seemed to have entirely forgotten his earlier outburst.

Just before they got to the car, Rose was surprised to spot Simon. He was standing outside a pub on the other side of the road, a pint in his hand, smoking. He was on his own, and he looked awful. She tried to catch his eye, but he wasn't looking outwards. If she hadn't had the children with her, she would have gone over to him. But as it was, they had to get back. She had never seen Simon like that before, though, and it made her wonder just what exactly was going on under her own nose, in her own home.

Fifteen

'I'm gonna get you!' Gareth roared, waving his sword in the air as he charged down the grassy mound.

The children screamed and fled in all directions.

Polly and Rose, basking in the unseasonal sunshine, stretched out and smiled at each other.

'So this is why we have men,' Polly said, lying back on the tartan blanket and tickling Flossie while Rose began to put the picnic things away.

'He certainly loves to play,' Rose said, crinkling her eyes and looking at her husband as he galloped and whooped over the crumbling castle ruins. It

134

had been Gareth's idea to come up here. Now he had the boys to play with, he wanted to reconstruct a game he and Andy had invented in their childhood, called Invaders. The rules were labyrinthine, but the children seemed to grasp them immediately, and, armed with the wooden swords and shields Gareth had made the day before, they were well into the inaugural game.

Gareth had found the castle just after they had moved to the village, on one of his early reconnaissance walks. He had once told Rose that, throughout his adult life, he would subconsciously size up various landscapes for their Invaders suitability. When he first clapped his eyes on this site, he knew it would be perfect, and he had just been biding his time, waiting for the right moment to put it to use. The castle was in fact the remains of a badly built Victorian mock-medieval folly, and it sat on private land. It therefore didn't have the health and safety restrictions and censorious caretakers that were normally assigned to more historic, nationally adopted, remains.

The landowner was an aging, absentee American movie star more famous for his involvement in Tantric practices than his acting work. He happened to own a couple of Gareth's pieces and was only too pleased to think of their creator frolicking on his land with his family. So the Invaders had the place to themselves.

Gareth had recruited Yannis to be on his side, and they were stalking Anna along a precipitous four-foot-high stone wall.

'Be careful!' Rose cried.

'They're fine,' Polly said, looking on.

'Christos was great with the boys, too, though,'

Rose said, after a while.

'He was a good father,' Polly said. 'But he wasn't rough and tumble like that. He didn't have that sort of energy with children. He was more interested in adults, really. Children he enjoyed talking to, but he'd never have had them on his back like that.' She waved her hand at Gareth, who now had Nico down on the ground, tickling him, while Anna was behind him, her hands on his shoulders, trying to pull him off. Yannis was running circles around them, whooping, and all three children were giggling like puppy hyenas.

'That surprises me,' Rose said.

'That's the thing with Christos. Nothing was expected.' Polly lay back and lifted Flossie up to lie on her stomach.

Rose packed everything into the picnic baskets, then she joined Polly on the blanket and lay back too, looking up at the breezy sky. She and Gareth had agreed that it was far bluer here than in the city. Gareth said he was going to test it in paint one day. He was going to paint canvases of blue sky in different parts of the world—just the blue— then put them up on a gallery wall and compare them. Rose had argued that it wouldn't be scientific, because the blue varied from day to day, and he couldn't be all over the world in one day. He had laughed, but she had been serious.

Polly stroked Flossie's chubby arm, softly kneading the flesh. 'When Christos died,' she said, 'all I wanted to do was touch someone. His body was the part of him I no longer had. I could still sort of talk to him, still feel his presence, but the actual physical part of him had been taken away from me.'

136

'When we can't have something, it's what we want most,' Rose agreed.

'Well, you'd know that, more than anyone.' Polly looked over at Rose.

Rose stopped what she was doing and looked down at her hands, picking a little dirt out from beneath her fingernails. For a moment, she lost all sense of where she was. The laughter of Gareth and the children was lost to her ears.

'Sorry,' Polly said.

'We don't talk about that, Poll, remember? Not ever. Pain of death.' Rose held her scarred index finger out in front of her as if it were a magic wand.

'OK, then. Sorry.' Polly looked away.

Rose forced herself back into the now, and smiled a little too brightly, her eyes dazzled from the sky.

'Do you know what, Polly? I can't think of a thing I want that I haven't got!'

The minute she said it, she wished that she hadn't. How horribly smug it must have sounded. Rose wanted to apologise to Polly, to tell her that she had only said it to convince *herself*, and that in no way was she trying to rub her unhappy friend's nose in her own comfortable situation. But if she said that, she would show her own vulnerability, and she wasn't going to start down that road.

'Well, that's marvellous. I'm really glad for you.' Polly frowned and drew her arms closer around Flossie. Rose couldn't help thinking that her baby couldn't be too comfortable there on that rack of bones.

'At the funeral,' Polly said, after a while, 'I wanted to rip off the coffin lid and jump in and

137

screw him there, in front of everyone. I wanted him to be cremated. I wanted his body fully over and done with. I thought that would stop the feeling. But the idea of his body still there somewhere, mouldering away under the ground: it's too horrible.'

'So why didn't you cremate him?' Rose asked, shuddering too at the thought.

'His mother. She said it was illegal in Greece. I didn't know any better. I believed her. But she was lying. The state permits it but the Orthodox Church doesn't. Despite the name old Yaya Maria had lumbered him with, Christos was not a believer.'

'He was anything but Orthodox,' Rose said.

'And I should have gone with what he would have wanted. But there you go. I was weak.'

'Don't say that. His mother sounds like a force of nature.'

'Tell me about it. Anyway, so I let us all down. And there I was, the days after the burial, going to the graveyard, touching the fresh earth that contained him, burying my face in it. And just itching, like an animal on heat. I surprised myself.'

'How do you mean?'

'I mean I hadn't really wanted him all that much when he was alive. Not for a couple of years, really.'

She lifted Flossie off her front, sat up and rummaged in her bag for her pills. Rose, taking Flossie from her, noticed that Polly's hands were shaking again. She watched her as she necked four pills from three different bottles, washing them down with her cava.

'That seems like a lot of pharmaceuticals, Poll,'

Rose said gently.

'It's just what the doctor prescribed.' Polly rattled the bottles. 'And who am I to disagree?'

'So did you get over it?' Rose asked.

'What?'

'The itching feeling?'

'No. It got so bad I had to ask Taverna George for some help.'

'No!' Rose said.

'He didn't seem to mind,' Polly laughed. 'It did us both a lot of good. It wasn't as if it was the first time, me and George, anyway.'

'Jesus.'

'Yes, Jesus.' She put on the air and accent of a scandalised Greek grandmother and waved her arms in the air. '*Chreeestos*!' She laughed and lay back down again. 'Oh Rose, you can be such a prude. Remember, neither of us had been complete angels when he was alive.'

Rose knew this was true of Christos, at least. She had never been entirely honest with Polly about the extent of the feelings she had for him. This had partly been down to her own pride, partly because she knew that telling Polly wouldn't help anyone deal with anything any better. But there was that time, on Karpathos during that visit two years ago, when they were supposed to all be going to see a one-off showing of *La Dolce Vita* at the open-air cinema in Pigadia, but Polly had been feeling ill. She stayed in and Rose and Christos had gone without her. The night had ended with a moonlit motorbike ride to a beach, where a reenactment of the Trevi Fountain scene had turned into a midnight skinny dip. Rose had tried to draw a halt to things before the sense of déjà vu became too precise, but she had only been partly successful.

'It was an exorcism of sorts,' Polly went on. 'Besides,' she shrugged, 'George is, as you yourself noted, impossibly good-looking.'

For a number of reasons, Rose was quite relieved when Anna bounded up towards them.

'Come on, you two! Dad says you've got to join in. He says it's not fair three kids against only one adult.'

Rose got up. 'I'll come, but someone has to stay and look after Flossie. Poll, are you OK with that?'

'Oh no,' Polly said. 'Does that mean I've got to just lie here in the sunshine while you run around up and down hills? I'll do my best to cope.'

Rose joined Anna and ran off, stopping to pick up one of the extra swords Gareth had made.

There was much whooping, charging and over-dramatic rolling down banks. What was surprising was that it took over an hour for someone to hurt themselves. Nico tripped while running away from Anna, and got a nasty gash on his knee. It wasn't serious, but there was enough blood to get him bawling. The other children squatted in front of him, grimacing, at once repelled and fascinated by the gore. Gareth ran back to the car for the first-aid kit.

After she had cuddled the tears out of Nico, Rose walked him back to the picnic blankets to find a medicinal bar of chocolate she had stashed at the bottom of one of the baskets. She stopped short in her tracks as she saw Polly and Flossie. Flossie was wobbling, but, for the first time in her life, she was standing unaided. She had just let go of Polly with one hand. In her other, she was rattling a bottle of pills.

'Look!' Polly said. 'No hands!'

Flossie, who hadn't even begun to crawl yet, stood for a moment, held up at the top of the arc of a wobble, then she tumbled to the ground, rolling down a tiny slope that was right behind her.

'Oops a daisy!' Polly sang.

Rose rushed to scoop up Flossie, who screamed and stuck out her lower lip.

'What's this?' she said, picking a pill off the ground.

'Oh, thanks,' Polly said, taking it from her. 'The lid came off when she was rattling them. I thought we'd got them all.'

'I hurt my knee, Mum, look,' Nico said, tugging at her arm.

'Ow,' Polly said. 'Does it hurt?'

'Course it does,' he said.

'Never mind, here comes Doctor Gareth,' Polly told him, shielding her eyes from the sun and watching Gareth hurdling back across the stone walls, bearing the big blue plastic first-aid kit. 'Big, strong and capable.'

'Are you sure you got all the pills, Poll?' Rose said. 'Floss puts everything in her mouth at the moment.'

'Yeah, yeah. Chill, Rose. Look, she's smiling now.'

Flossie, who had seen her daddy charging towards her, had lit up like a little candle and was leaning away from Rose, holding her hands up towards him.

'Perhaps you can show your dad how you can stand up, Floss,' Polly said, taking her by her waist and putting her on her feet.

141

'I'm not sure it's so good for her legs, Polly,' Rose said.

Flossie wobbled, tried to take a step, then fell down on her bottom, making everyone but Nico laugh and applaud.

'Hey, what about my knee?' he complained, looking up at them all, one by one.

Sixteen

They got back after dusk in the end, with the tingle of a day in the sun on their faces. Rose, who had probably sunk a little more cava than she should have, laid out the remains of the picnic on the coffee-table and the children had the rare treat of a TV dinner while the adults retired to the kitchen to drink another bottle.

They lit the candles and settled back in the golden glow.

'I'm so glad I'm here,' Polly said, hugging herself. 'I can't imagine being anywhere else than here with you, my best friends in the whole world.'

Gareth gazed into his glass, twirling it around in his big hands and smiling. Then he looked up and raised a toast.

'To having a blast!'

They all clinked glasses.

By about ten o'clock the children had all fallen asleep on the sofas, faces smeared with the Eton Mess Rose had made from the leftovers of the picnic meringue, cream and strawberries. Rose, Polly and Gareth lifted them up to their rooms.

'They can clean their teeth in the morning,

Rose,' Gareth said.

'Yeah, yeah,' she said.

Back downstairs, Polly hugged both Rose and Gareth at once.

'Well, goodnight, guys. And, once again, thanks.'

'Look, stop all that thanks now, OK?' Rose said. 'Let's all be equal in this from now on.'

'I agree,' Gareth said.

They saw Polly to the door, and stood on the threshold watching her weave her way up the steps towards the Annexe.

'So long as she stays up there,' Gareth whispered to Rose.

She smiled and leaned into him.

'I've just got to feed Flossie, then I'll be up,' she said.

'I'll be waiting,' he said.

But by the time she got to the bedroom, Gareth was lying on his back, his arms outstretched, snoring.

Poor man, Rose thought. He's not used to running around after boys all day.

*   *   *

Rose woke at four in the morning. Flossie hadn't cried for her two o'clock feed, which was something of a first. Initially, this didn't worry Rose. Anna had kept her up all hours until she was two years old; perhaps Flossie was going to treat them all a little more kindly.

The clear night had made the house very chilly. Rose could see her breath as she tiptoed across the landing to Flossie's bedroom; the grass outside glowed with a peppering of frost.

143

It was when Rose leaned over to look into Flossie's cot that the cold jolted out from the air and plunged deep into her belly. Her baby was still, breathing in shallow rasps, with a sheen of sweat over her face. Rose grabbed her. Flossie's skin was burning, and when Rose picked her up, her body flopped in her arms. She put her back down and pulled open her Babygro. A rash purpled over her chest.

Clutching the baby to her, Rose charged back to her bedroom, yelling for Gareth.

*   *   *

'What's the number?' Rose pressed, as Gareth searched their address book for the village GP's out-of-hours contact.

'I think we should call an ambulance,' he said.

'Kate will get here quicker. And she knows us.'

Kate was the village GP, and the closest to a female friend Rose had managed to find since they had moved.

Rose dialled and waited for an answer. *Come on, come on,* she thought.

'Hello?' Kate sounded sleepy.

Rose told her what had happened.

'You stay there. I'll be with you in a tick,' Kate said.

*   *   *

True to her word, she was at their door in five minutes, a duffel coat thrown over her pyjamas, her feet in Birkenstocks. She took one look at Flossie and ordered Gareth to call for an

144

ambulance.

'We need to get her to hospital as soon as possible,' she said to Rose, pulling up Flossie's eyelids and shining a light into her pin-prick pupils. 'She has a high fever, poor muscle tone— and look,' she said, pulling aside the Babygro pyjamas '—she's starting a rash. It could be meningitis.'

Rose gasped. She knew it.

'It's OK, Rose,' Kate said, putting a firm arm around her shoulders. 'We've got it early. But I'm afraid I'm going to have to put a line in, so that they can get antibiotics into her as soon as possible. It's not nice, but you've got to hold her arm down like this.'

She showed Rose exactly how to extend Flossie's arm as she inserted a large needle into a vein by her wrist. Flossie moaned and wriggled, but Rose held her firmly. Rose saw that Kate kept looking up to check that she was all right. She wasn't. Watching all this happen to her baby, she felt like collapsing onto the floor.

'I'll go and wake Polly,' Gareth said. 'She needs to be here to take care of the others.'

'Rose, you go and get dressed. I'll finish up here,' Kate said, winding bandages round Flossie's hands. 'This is just to stop her pulling her line out,' she added, seeing Rose's concerned look. 'Now, go.'

It seemed like an age before the ambulance arrived. Rose had followed instructions and was dressed. Kate held Flossie in a shawl, ready to carry her straight out; Gareth had come back and was making a pot of tea. Then Polly rushed in, clutching a blanket around her, wavering slightly.

145

'What's happened?' she slurred. 'Is she . . . ?'

'She's stable, but very poorly,' Kate said.

'Oh, when will they come?' Rose wailed.

'When will who come? What's the matter?' Polly said.

'The ambulance,' Kate said. 'It takes twenty minutes. Even with blue lights, that's how long it takes.'

'Kate, this is Polly, our friend from Greece,' Gareth said.

'We've met,' Polly said.

'Yes. Hello again,' Kate said.

'She wouldn't give me what I wanted,' Polly said, smiling at Rose. 'British docs aren't quite as cavalier as their Greek counterparts. Oh—is that tea? I could kill a cuppa.'

Gareth handed her a mug. He sat with a pen and pad and started writing a list for Polly.

'So, you take our bed, Polly. The kids need to be at the school by nine a.m., two pounds each for dinner money—we'll scrap the packed lunches for tomorrow, OK?'

'Yeah . . . I'd better set an alarm,' Polly said.

And then two green-suited paramedics arrived. With them was a young male doctor in a tweed jacket. There were only three of them, but they swarmed into the room, seeming to fill it, making everything look small. Kate handed Flossie to the doctor, and, in an almost balletic movement, he took her in his arms and moved her out of the door, up through the herb garden and into the ambulance. Kate followed him, reciting a list of statistics about Flossie's condition.

Rose, tagging along behind, found this ordering of Flossie's state, this putting of it into so many

146

words and turning the horror of it into a strategy, strangely comforting.

'We've got to get her to hospital as soon as possible,' the female paramedic said, climbing into the ambulance. 'Come on, Mum.' She held an arm out to Rose, to help her in. Gareth made to get in behind them.

'No. You stay, Gareth. Anna will freak out. Please,' Rose said, as the young doctor attached a drip to Flossie's line.

'But I want to come,' Gareth said. He was pale. His teeth worked away at his lips.

'No, no, you stay, Gareth,' Rose said, her hand on his chest, nearly pushing him away. 'I'll call from the hospital. Be here for Anna. Polly: look after him.'

But Polly hadn't come out into the cold air.

Kate jumped into the ambulance. 'Room for one more, then. Look, Gareth, Rose is right. It's better that you stay here for Anna. Your friend there doesn't exactly inspire confidence,' she said, looking down at Polly who was standing at the kitchen window—Rose's window—hugging a mug of tea, looking up at them as if her mind were somewhere else entirely. 'I'll make sure Rose and Flossie here are OK, and I'll drop by on you in the morning before surgery, to keep you posted.'

The paramedics slammed the doors shut, then the ambulance lurched off into the night, its blue lights illuminating the Annexe, the blip of its siren as it turned the blind corner into the lane surely waking the whole village.

Seventeen

They rocketed through the night. the two doctors worked on Flossie while Rose sat at her head, her hand on the small fluff of fine hair that her daughter had managed to grow so far.

Flossie was deeply unconscious now. Even the little moan she had put up in the kitchen had stopped.

'It's the drugs,' Kate said to Rose as the young male doctor—who looked more like a teenage public schoolboy with his blond curly hair and bow tie—prepared a third syringe to go into Flossie's line. 'We're sedating her. Shutting her down so that we can work out what's going on.'

My poor baby, Rose thought. She had taken such enormous care to put nothing but good, honest, organic food into Flossie's body and now all of that was being wiped out by a whole laboratory of drugs.

'It's not responding like a typical meningitis,' the boy doctor was saying.

'No,' Kate said, moving over to sit by Rose and taking her hand. 'Rose, I want you to think: is there any way Flossie might have eaten something unusual? Put something in her mouth? Cleaning fluid? Medicine?'

A piece of ice shot into Rose's heart as she remembered Polly's pills, the ones Flossie spilled on the grass.

'Polly, our friend . . .' she began to say, then Kate, seeing the picture, took over.

'OK, it's a prescription drug overdose, and

148

possibly some sort of allergic reaction. We need to reverse the sedation. Now!' she roared at the young doctor, who started emptying a clear fluid into a syringe. 'And an emetic!'

'Polly. She dropped a bottle on the grass, while Floss was there,' Rose said. 'But she said she'd got them all.'

'In my opinion, your friend wouldn't know her arse from her elbow,' Kate muttered. Rose looked up at her sharply. 'Sorry, but I've seen her in a different light.'

The doctor stuck the edge of his tongue out of the side of his mouth as he injected the new fluid into Flossie. Kate held an oxygen mask over her face. 'I need the names of the pills right now,' she said, thrusting her phone at Rose with her free hand.

Rose was having difficulty staying conscious, but she managed to punch her own number into Kate's phone.

Gareth answered.

'What's happened?' he said, his voice strangled.

'I need to talk to Polly—now,' Rose said.

'Why?'

'I'll tell you later. I just need to talk to her right now, Gareth. It's really important.'

He put the phone down. She heard the front door open, and his footsteps as he ran out of the house. Minutes later, Polly was on the phone.

'Sorry, I'd just got back to bed,' she said.

'Polly, listen, you've got to tell me what those pills were yesterday, the ones that spilled on the ground.'

'My pills? But—'

'No, listen. Just get the bottle and read to me

149

what it says.'

'They're back in the Annexe, though.'

'What is this?' Rose could hear Gareth asking.

'She wants to know what my pills are.'

'Just do it!' he yelled at her. 'Just go and get them. *Now*.'

There was a scuffle on the end of the line and the sound of Polly's footsteps stuttering up the garden steps.

'We think Flossie's had some of Polly's pills,' Rose said to Gareth in a small voice. Kate was now working on Flossie, pressing two fingers onto her chest.

'I'll kill her,' he said quietly.

'We've got her back!' Kate smiled up at the doctor, who cheered as if his cricket team had just scored a century.

'How's Floss?' Gareth asked.

'Not too good, Gareth,' Rose sobbed. Then she heard Polly breathless on the end of the line, the rattling of pill bottles, and Gareth's voice as he made Polly read out the long, complicated names from the Greek writing on the bottles.

Rose repeated the words to the woman paramedic, who wrote them down and repeated them to Kate.

'OK, these are pretty strong drugs. Stronger than we'd normally prescribe here,' she said. 'And Flossie is presenting with classic overdose symptoms. We'll do what we can to get them out of her, but, if she took them yesterday, it's late. We'll concentrate on minimising the effects on her liver and brain.'

Rose felt all of the blood drain from her body.

'But she'll be all right. Rose?' Gareth shouted

150

down the phone. He had heard all of it.

'But she'll be all right?' Rose whispered, repeating his question.

'I hope so,' Kate said. 'Can we get a move on?' she barked at the ambulance driver.

'I love you, Gareth,' Rose said, and hung up as they blasted into the hospital Accident and Emergency Department.

Everything from then on was a bit of a blur. A team of doctors and nurses greeted them and whisked Flossie away with Kate still holding the oxygen mask to her face. The female paramedic took Rose to a row of vinyl easy chairs outside the room where they were working on Flossie.

'Stay there, dear. They're working in her best interests, but to the untrained eye it can look a little brutal.'

Rose had nothing left in her with which to protest. She sat there and shivered. Someone passed her a blanket and a cup of tea. Good old tea. She sat there for what seemed like days. She prayed. She made pacts with God: she would never take anything for granted again; she would be good forever; she would never lie again; she would go to church, wear a cross, give away money, never ever question His existence; she would award Him title case, even in her thoughts. If only Flossie could be saved.

'D'you want a cigarette, lover?' An older woman with an alarming black eye had shuffled along the corridor. She leaned over Rose; her breath smelled of port and tobacco.

'I saw them bring your baby in,' she slurred. 'I hope he's all right, my darling. Here, have a ciggie if you like.' She proffered a pack of Embassy.

151

'She,' Rose said. 'My baby is a girl.'

'My baby was a boy, my baby was,' the woman muttered, and wandered off towards the ambulance bay, lighting a cigarette as she went.

So was mine, Rose thought before she could stop herself.

She pulled the blanket closer around her. It was being here that did it. She hated hospitals. To her they spelled nothing but loss. She remembered sitting in another hospital, in Brighton, over twenty years ago, an empty, leaking shell. And here she was, again facing losing her baby. Again . . .

I mustn't think about it, she told herself. It's bad luck. She had sworn she would never let herself go back there. She folded the partly unravelled thoughts back up and stuffed them away. Why had she been so weak, though, back then?

A little later, still with no news of Flossie, an efficient, kind-looking young woman came up to Rose and took her to a side room. She offered her a low, wooden-armed chair, then she sat down facing her, on the other side of a Formica coffee-table. The woman—Rose didn't catch her name—opened a laptop and asked Rose her name, date of birth and address.

'That's a lovely village.' She smiled across the coffee-table at her.

'Yes.' Rose looked down at her feet.

'Now then. Flossie—that's an unusual name. Is it short for anything?'

'No, she's just Flossie,' Rose said.

'She hasn't been seen a great deal, has she?' the woman asked in a bright voice. Like the doctor on the ambulance, she looked impossibly young to be

152

so authoritative. She even had a rash of what looked like adolescent acne on her cheeks.

'Sorry?' Rose didn't understand.

'By the doctor. You haven't brought her to the doctor a lot. And there's no record of any health visitor involvement?' The woman was scanning something on her screen, frowning and leaning back slightly in her chair.

'One came, but she didn't ever come back,' Rose said. 'She said we'd do fine and just to get in touch if we needed anything.'

'I see.' The woman looked over and smiled again. 'They do that when they think a second-time mother can manage. Cuts, you know.' She went back to her screen and typed something. 'Now, I need to ask a few more questions, Rose, about the household. So we can get a complete picture.'

'Right,' Rose said. Why was this girl needing all this information right now, when all that really mattered was whether Flossie was going to be all right or not?

'Do you have any over-the-counter medicines in your house?'

'Some. Not many, just Paracetamol, aspirin, that sort of thing. Calpol.'

'And where do you keep them?'

'In the medicine box. On a top shelf in the pantry.'

'Out of children's reach?'

'Yes.' Rose was beginning to feel like running away and hiding. She scanned the room for exit points—the door, the windows, any gaps in the skirting boards.

'Is anyone in your house on prescription drugs?'

'Polly.'

'Who?'

'Polly—she's staying with us. Not in the house, though—she's staying up at the end of the garden.'

'I see.'

'In the Annexe.'

'Right. And is there anyone in your household—and let's take "the Annexe" into account here—who might take illegal, non-prescription drugs?'

'Not really.'

'Not really?'

Rose suddenly felt a shot of alarm. 'Oh my God—you're the police, aren't you?'

'No, I'm not police. I'm the hospital social worker. Sorry, I thought I said. Look, these questions are just procedure in these sorts of cases. A child comes in with burns, say—any kind of injury that could just be an accident, but which could also be down to neglect or abuse. Or poisoning, say. It's routine for everyone, Rose. It doesn't mean you're under suspicion, but we have to keep an open mind. Explore each situation without prejudice. I'm sure you understand.'

Rose nodded, and looked down again.

'So,' the woman went on gently. 'Drugs?'

'It's nothing to do with us!' Rose slammed her hand down on the coffee-table, making the spotty woman jump. 'It's her. It's Polly. She let Flossie play with her pills. She didn't pick them all up afterwards. She let my baby poison herself. She's so fucking careless!'

'Rose. You're upset, that's understandable. But behaving like this won't help matters at all.'

'My baby is ill, I don't know what's going on,

154

and you're talking to me like I'm some sort of criminal,' Rose said. 'Like you think I don't know how to take care of my own child.'

The young woman sat back, folded her arms and looked at Rose, who, feeling her scrutiny, drew back inside herself, wrapping her arms around her body.

'Someone will be visiting your friend tomorrow,' the social worker said after a long pause. Then she returned to her computer.

There was a brief knock at the door and Kate came in.

'There's some news,' she said, as she took Rose's hand and sat down next to her.

'Oh God,' Rose began. 'Oh no, no nonono.' She tore her hand away and buried her face in her palms, pressing them deep into her eyes so that all she saw were dark spots. Her milk, long overdue for Flossie's feeding time, leaked through her swollen breasts, crying lactose tears in place of the salt ones Rose was too scared to weep.

'Rose,' Kate said, taking her hands again, trying to make her listen. 'It's all right. She's still with us.'

Rose looked at Kate with red-rimmed eyes.

'She's out of the woods for the time being. We've done everything we can, and she's stable. But she's poorly, Rose. We don't quite know yet what's going to happen.'

Rose didn't move.

'We've put her into a deep sleep. Her organs have a better chance of recovery that way. We won't know till she wakes up what has happened.'

'What do you mean?'

'I've got to tell you, Rose, that there's a risk that there will be some sort of permanent damage. It's

155

less than fifty per cent. But it is still significant.'

'What do you mean, damage?'

'It's too soon to say, but it could be liver, or it could be kidney. Or, Rose, it could be brain damage. But we can't say for sure, and even if we could, we wouldn't know to what extent it might be.'

Rose closed her eyes and pressed her palms to her forehead. Please, she prayed. Turn back the clocks. Make this not have happened.

'Apart from this, Floss is a very healthy little girl. You've done all the right things up to now, and she has the best chance in the world, given her current situation. There's a good chance she'll come out of it completely unscathed.'

'So,' Rose said, her eyes still shut. 'You're saying to me that she will survive?'

'Yes. We're almost entirely certain of that.' Kate nodded, squeezing her hand.

'But you're not sure whether she'll end up a vegetable?'

'That's most unlikely, Rose.'

'But it is possible.'

'Remotely.'

'Thank you,' Rose whispered. An angry heat took hold of her, brutally melting the chill that had set in since she found Flossie in her cot. She wanted to kill Polly. She wanted to force her head back, possibly by pulling her hair, and fill her mouth full of every single one of her bloody pills. Then she wanted to put stones in her pockets and kick her down the field and into the river.

'Come through and see her.' Kate took Rose's hand and led her away from the social worker through to a cubicle at the far end of the A&E

156

ward, where Flossie lay in what looked to Rose like a plastic box, with tubes and wires going in and out of her.

Rose walked slowly up to her, horror rising in her throat.

'What's that?' she asked, pointing at a mask that was taped over Flossie's mouth and nose.

'That's to help her breathe. Just to give her lungs a rest,' Kate said. 'And these, these and these . . .' she pointed out wires that disappeared into dressings that covered unseen holes in Flossie's body '. . . are to make sure she gets enough fluids and nutrition.'

'And this?' Rose pointed to two long, red tubes leading from somewhere on Flossie's body into a big, whirring machine.

'It washes her blood,' Kate said. 'She's on dialysis, just to keep her kidneys happy.'

'Can I feed her?' Rose whispered, pressing the damp patches on her T-shirt.

'I'm afraid not right now,' Kate said, hugging Rose. 'She wouldn't be hungry for it. She's getting the nourishment she needs from the IV.'

Rose looked at her little girl, who seemed more machine than human.

'Did you get all the drugs out of her?' she asked.

'We've done what we can. We've gone a long way to neutralising the overdose, but there's a bit of that work that's down to the liver, I'm afraid. It had gone too far through her. But she's fighting.'

Flossie looked tiny. Stretched out inside the box, wearing nothing but a nappy and bandages, her arms flung upwards and her fists clenched, she looked as if she had aged backwards. As if she had lost her earthly months of life and reverted to a

157

fragile, pre-birth state. Rose needed to touch her, but she couldn't get at her through the plastic box and the wires and the tubes.

'There's a hole in the side of the box, here,' Kate said, as she guided Rose's hand to Flossie's stomach. The bare skin felt like silk, and Rose could sense—thank God—the tiny thrum of life beneath her fingertips. She decided she would stay like this, her hand through the hole in the box, until Flossie got better.

'They haven't got a bed in the Children's Centre ICU right now,' Kate said, 'so she's going to have to stay here, I'm afraid.' She went and found a chair, which she placed behind Rose so she could sit without breaking contact with Flossie. 'It's not ideal, but I've asked them to bring a camp bed up here for you.'

'I'm not sleeping,' Rose said in a low voice.

'I know how you feel,' Kate said. 'But really, Rose, you need to think about getting some rest. The next couple of days are going to take it out of you. Flossie needs you to be strong.'

'Thanks, but I'll just stay here.'

'Look. I've got to go,' Kate touched her shoulder. 'I've got surgery in half an hour. I'll call in to see how she's getting on this afternoon.'

'Yes. Thank you,' Rose said, never taking her eyes off Flossie.

'Take care.' Kate leaned forward and kissed Rose on the head. She stepped outside the cubicle that contained Rose and Flossie, but instead of footsteps, Rose heard her stop and sigh, shuddering in a way that she didn't think Kate was capable of.

Thank God for the good people, Rose thought.

Eighteen

Rose didn't know how long she sat there, stroking Flossie's side through the hole in the plastic box. The regular beep of some machine she knew was playing a part in keeping her baby alive had also, in some way, sustained her. But the dim light that bled through the drawn blinds of their A&E cubicle had grown stronger, and she felt the glow of sunlight on her hunched back.

Then something else joined the warmth and she turned to see it was Gareth, who had placed his hand on the space between her shoulder blades. With a jolt she remembered she should have called him, kept him informed. Despite any reluctance from him during the pregnancy, Flossie was now as much his as she was hers.

She often forgot this.

'Kate called by on her way back this morning,' Gareth said. 'I knew you would be too busy.'

Rose winced. She couldn't have left Flossie's side, and even if she had a mobile phone, she wouldn't have used it, because she was scared that it might interfere with one of the life-saving machines that were ranged around them.

'I'm sorry . . .' she began, but he hushed her and drew up a chair to sit with her, his eyes on Flossie.

'Look. She's calm now, and not so floppy,' Rose whispered, guiding Gareth's hand into the hole in the box. Flossie's fist closed lightly around his large, work-worn finger.

'And she's going to be all right,' she added. 'They think.'

'They don't know, though, do they?' Gareth said. 'Kate said there could be liver damage, or brain damage. They don't know, Rose. And we won't know for sure for years.'

Rose leaned against him and closed her eyes. It was like a bad dream. She kept thinking about the family in the car crash, feeling common ground with them, as if she were now placed right there in amongst them all.

'I took Anna to school,' Gareth said. 'I don't want that woman near my kids any more, Rose. I've told her I want her out by the end of the week.'

Rose nodded. 'Yes.'

Gareth shook his head. 'There's something wrong with her. Those boys, they're moving back to the Annexe tonight and that's it. The lot of them. They're out of our lives.'

Rose felt a lump grow in her throat.

'The boys . . .' She had forgotten that they were attached to Polly.

'I know, but they can't stay if she goes.'

For Rose, the thought of the boys leaving was as if the last string that had been holding her up had been cut. Losing everything when it had nearly been so perfect was too much to bear. She remembered the promise she had made to Yannis in Jabberwocky, that she would never let him down. The fear pressed down on her like a heavy weight, making it hard for her to breathe. She fell against Gareth and cried until snot was hanging from her nose in strings and every ounce of tears had been squeezed from her body. He held her, his arms wrapped around her, until she had nothing left to grieve with.

'I can't bear the thought of losing them,' she whispered into his shoulder. 'I don't want Nico and Yannis to get lost in it all.'

'She nearly killed our daughter,' Gareth said, his voice ice.

Rose looked up at him. 'She's not herself, though, Gareth. It was an accident.'

'Was it?' he asked, looking straight at her. 'Do you know,' he said, walking around to the head of Flossie's box, and gesturing at her prostrate body, 'do you know, I'm not so sure about that. I'm not so sure she didn't put those damn pills right down Flossie's throat.' He leaned forward, grabbing onto either side of the plastic box, and he roared at Rose: 'I'm not so sure that Polly Novak didn't come here on purpose to fuck everything up!'

'Is everything all right?' Two nurses hurried into the cubicle and took positions either side of Rose, protecting her from Gareth.

He put his hands up. 'It's fine,' he said. 'It's fine.'

'I know you're upset, but please can you keep it down, Mr Cunningham?' the nurse said to Gareth. 'We've got some very poorly people here.'

'Like my fucking daughter,' Gareth spat, making the nurse jump back and draw her shoulders up around her ears.

Rose grabbed his arm. 'Gareth, please. It's not their fault. It's not anyone's fault. Why would Polly want to hurt Flossie? Look.' Rose didn't know what she believed, but her overriding concern was to keep the boys safe with her, to give them a chance. 'Look, Gareth, please, for me. For Flossie, for the boys. Please, go and find Polly. Bring her in here. I need to see her.'

161

The nurses shifted on their feet, looking uneasily at each other.

Gareth looked at her. 'You remember what you promised before they came, Rose. You said you wouldn't argue with me.'

'I know, but it's more important than that now. Please. Bring her in.'

Gareth glared, first at Rose, then at the nurses.

'I'll be back.' He turned and left.

'Well!' The nurse who had jumped let go of her breath.

'Sorry,' Rose said, rubbing her eyes. 'We're just a bit upset right now.'

'Just take it easy, Mum, all right?' The other nurse, a round girl with a lilting Somerset accent, came up and put her arm around Rose. 'Baby needs you.'

*   *   *

By lunchtime, Gareth hadn't returned. The round nurse came through and ordered Rose to go and get some food.

'I'll stay and watch Baby,' she added.

Rose went down to the canteen and got herself some beans on toast and a cup of tea. She didn't want to stay downstairs to eat, so she put her food on a tray and carried it back upstairs. Halfway up, she tripped and fell forward, hurting her shin and spilling food and drink all over the floor and herself. Once down on the stone steps, she couldn't find the energy to get up. She just put her head down between her arms and closed her eyes. People had to step around her to get on their way.

'Where do you belong, love?' A kind orderly

162

finally stopped and squatted down to talk to her.

He scooped her up and led her back to Flossie. He used his walkie-talkie to call someone to clear up the mess on the stairs. 'We don't want any more accidents,' he said, smiling at Rose.

The round nurse, who had been as good as her word about looking after Flossie, looked up sternly when Rose came back empty-handed, but the orderly explained what had happened. The nurse sat Rose down next to Flossie, then slipped away. A little while later, she returned with a large Kit Kat and a cup of tea.

'We've got to keep our energy up, Mum,' she said. 'I've seen it so often. You always forget to look after yourselves, but we're no good if we're fainting all over the shop, are we?'

Rose nodded, unable to speak. The nurse pointed to the front of her T-shirt, with its dark stains where her milk had leaked earlier on.

'Oh dear, you're not still feeding, are you? Poor Mum. If you were in the Children's Centre, they'd have sorted you out with a pump. I'll see what I can do.'

After about half an hour, she came back with a breast pump and a hospital issue dressing gown with an open back.

'There we go, Mum. Use this to get the milk out; then you can change into this. Hubby'll be back soon, I'm sure, with some fresh clothes. You can either throw the milk away or donate it,' the nurse chirped as she positioned a table next to Rose, to support her arm while the pump worked. 'I'm afraid they don't have any storage facilities down here. When you get upstairs to Blue Ward they can keep it chilled until Hubby comes in and then he can take it back home to freeze for later. Baby won't be taking any milk for a while.'

'Gareth,' Rose said. 'His name's Gareth.' The pump, clamped over Rose's nipple, whirred and pulsed. Despite the indignity of her situation, Rose felt an enormous sense of relief as her swollen breasts discharged their load into the sterilised bottle.

'So what do we want to do with our milk, then?' The nurse stood back, a hand on her plump hip.

'Let someone else have it. I don't want it to go to waste,' Rose muttered.

The nurse slipped behind the cubicle curtain then returned with a sheaf of forms for Rose to fill in about consent and screening. Rose wished she had chosen for the milk to be thrown away, but to please the nurse, she filled them in.

'Now, let's get our dressing gown on, eh?' the nurse said. 'All that smelly dried milk. It isn't the most hygienic, is it?'

*   *   *

Much later that afternoon, Gareth still hadn't turned up. Rose and Flossie were finally transferred to Blue Ward, which seemed to be full of very sick babies. A large, open-plan area with spacious, curtained-off stations for each tiny inhabitant and his or her retinue of drawn-looking parents and grand-parents, it was more thoughtfully lit and laid out than the corner of the Accident & Emergency Ward they had been in. Flossie had a station with a comfortable chair that could be folded out into a bed for Rose. They also had their own TV—not that Rose could even think

164

about watching it. She couldn't concentrate on anything other than Flossie, who was still deep in her induced sleep. Their new nurse introduced herself. In contrast to the A&E nurse, this one was quick, calm and unobtrusive. She checked Flossie's machines every half-hour and kept telling Rose that Flossie was doing very well.

Whatever that means, Rose thought.

She hated being around all those tiny, half-alive babies.

A while later, the quiet of the ward was broken by a flurry of noise and activity at the main nurses' station. It was Gareth, who came rushing up to Rose and Flossie. In one hand he was carrying a rucksack. The other was firmly wrapped around Polly's wrist, dragging her like a reluctant, naughty child, or a prisoner. He looked demented.

'I couldn't find you,' he panted. 'I thought—why the fuck didn't anyone tell me you'd been moved?'

A palpable shiver rode through the ward as the attendants of every baby looked sharply up at the cause of the disturbance.

'Please, sir, you have to keep the noise down.' The efficient nurse moved towards him.

Ignoring this, he turned to Rose. 'I thought she was— No one said—'

'I'm sorry you had a fright,' the nurse said, holding her ground. 'But look, Flossie's here, and she's doing well.' She turned to Rose, bent down and put her arm round her shoulder. 'Rose, is it OK if he stays?' she asked.

'Thanks, he's fine to stay.' Rose smiled faintly at the nurse.

'Look,' Gareth said to the nurse, forcing a calm note into his voice, 'I just couldn't find them, OK?'

165

He fell to his knees in front of Rose and put his arms around her, burying his face into her shoulder. She realised he was crying.

Polly, abandoned in the middle of the room, stood there, looking nervous and tiny.

'Thank God you're both all right,' he said, looking up at Rose at last.

'You've been ages,' was all she could say.

'It's been a bit of a ride,' said Gareth. 'Long story. How is she?' He turned to Flossie, reaching through the box to touch her belly. 'She looks as if she's got a bit more colour.'

Rose couldn't see it herself, but she nodded anyway.

'We had the police round earlier,' Gareth whispered. 'Asking about drugs. They interviewed her,' he pointed at Polly. 'I showed them her prescription pills. Luckily they didn't search the house or anything. Anyway, I've flushed my weed down the toilet as a precaution. In case they come back with dogs or something.'

'That's wise,' Rose murmured, still looking for the signs of improvement in Flossie that he had seen.

'I brought her in, like you asked,' he said, pointing again at Polly, but not looking at her. 'I'm not changing my mind, though.'

'Let me talk to her,' Rose said.

'Ten minutes. I'm getting a coffee. I'll be back.' And he left, striding across the ward, like a giant in his dirty suede jacket. He didn't even glance at Polly as he passed her.

Polly stood still, twisting her long loose hair around her index finger, a nervous smile nudging at her mouth.

166

'Come here,' Rose said, gesturing to a seat by her side. 'And look.'

'Oh God.' Polly hovered towards the end of Flossie's box and stood there like a tragic angel in a Victorian engraving. She was dressed, Rose couldn't help noticing, immaculately, in a flowing black dress with a transparent black floaty thing over the top. Her make-up was sombre, but beautiful, despite—or because of—the red-rimmed eyes. She was hugging herself and blinking.

'I'm so sorry, Rose. It's all my fault,' she said. 'It's all my fault.'

'It was an accident. Wasn't it?' Rose said, searching Polly's eyes for clues.

Polly rushed and threw herself at Rose's knees, clasping her hands together in her lap, looking up into her eyes. 'Oh yes, it was, such an accident. Please, Rose. Forgive me.'

Rose felt her own hand rest on Polly's praying palms. It sort of floated there, not really connected to her wrist, acting on its own will. She was unable to speak, yet she felt a well of pressure in her ribcage. If she sat there for much longer she would burst and the contents of her heart would spill all over this woman who suddenly seemed so alien to her.

Polly broke down, collapsing her face onto Rose's knees. 'I'm sorry, sorry. I can't believe it,' she sobbed. 'You offer me everything you have and I do this. What kind of monster am I? I don't deserve a friend like you.'

Rose watched as, once again, her hand found its way onto the back of Polly's head, then lifted and patted as it stroked her hair.

'Everything I touch turns bad. I nearly killed myself. I couldn't even keep my husband alive. And now this. I'm cursed, Rose. Cursed.'

'Shhh,' Rose said. She really did want her to shut up. 'Now stop this. Get up. Look.' She stood and turned Polly round to look at Flossie. Polly swayed as Rose took her hand and put it on Flossie's chest. The sight of those thin, fragile fingers with their rounded, bitten nails on Flossie's tiny tube-studded ribs was almost too much to bear. Rose caught her breath at the same time as Polly shuddered.

'So tiny, so innocent,' Polly said, shaking.

They stood there, Rose's hand on Polly's hand on Flossie's body.

'She's going to be all right?' Polly said at length, taking her arm back to place it back around her own body.

'They say her chances are good,' Rose said, repeating the doctor's words.

Polly sank back into Rose's chair. 'I can't believe it. I'm so sorry.'

Rose knelt down beside her and took her hand. 'I know you are,' she found herself saying.

'Gareth is really angry at me,' Polly said. 'He says we have to go, and I don't know what I'm going to do.' Her lower lip shook, then her face broke. 'I don't know what we're going to do, Rose.'

'Shhh, shhh,' Rose said, holding her.

'I'm so sorry. I'm so stupid. Please, please forgive me? You're the one person that I've got left, Rose. I need you more than you could ever imagine. We've known each other forever and there's nothing—*nothing*—we don't know about each other—and I couldn't bear for Gareth to

168

throw all that away, to come between us like that and ruin it all. I don't know what I'd do . . .'

Rose looked into Polly's eyes.

'I don't know what I can do to make him change his mind,' Polly went on. 'Don't know what I'd say . . .'

Behind the pleading and the guilt, Rose saw something glittering, steely. Was it determination, or was it something more?

'What do you mean, Polly?' she asked.

Polly grabbed Rose's hand and rubbed the scar on her index finger against her own. She knew more about Rose than anyone else. She knew things that could threaten everything, everybody's happiness.

Rose shook her head and blinked. She was being stupid—wasn't she? Polly wouldn't tell on her. She had sworn, after all. Bloodsworn. They were best friends. They were like sisters.

'The boys are beside themselves with worry about Flossie, about what's going to happen. Gareth has been shouting at me in front of them. Yannis is frightened, Rose. I don't know what's going to happen,' Polly went on.

Rose had to stand up. She knew she couldn't take any chances. She was feeling dizzy. She saw what could be at stake here.

'Look,' she said, turning away. 'It's a mess. I'm going to talk to Gareth, and we'll have to take it from there. You go now, go and wait in the café. I'll talk to him.' She was so tired, she was nearly hallucinating. Something like a smooth, round pebble had lodged itself in her throat, holding back things best left unsaid.

'Thank you. Oh, thank you. You're doing the

right thing, Rose, believe me.' Polly kissed her on the cheek then skittered away across the ward.

*   *   *

A little while later, Gareth returned, bringing a cup of tea for Rose.

'So,' he said, handing it to her.

'So,' she said, looking up at him.

'Let me guess. You told her you'd have a word with me,' he said.

'Hmm.' Rose stroked Flossie's belly.

'She's a little witch,' he said. 'She's got a hold on you.'

'Look, Gareth, I'm as angry as you are. She was careless and stupid. But despite all that, it was an accident. She hasn't had a baby to look after for a long while. She's forgotten what they can do. And she's strung out; she's ill. Perhaps I was to blame more than her, for leaving her with Flossie. I should have known.'

'Shhh,' Gareth said, putting his finger on her lips.

'I should have known.' She took his hand and held it. 'It's just the boys. Can't we give her another chance for the boys' sake?'

He sighed and put his arm round her shoulders. 'Rose, Rose, Rose,' he said. 'I don't know what to think. It's all gone a little crazy again, hasn't it? I was so mad at her . . .' He sat down and ran his fingers through his hair. 'Look. Just for you, I'll talk to her. And tomorrow I'll let you know how it goes. Tomorrow. But right now, we've got more important things to concentrate on,' and he turned to look at Flossie.

'How's Anna?' Rose asked.

'Why don't you ask her yourself?' A voice came from behind her.

Rose turned and saw Kate standing there, holding hands with Anna.

Anna was making a brave fist of putting on a cheerful face, although she was clearly shocked at the sight of the tiny, wired-up scraps of humanity that were dotted around the room.

Rose jumped up and ran to her girl, hugging her so tightly it almost hurt.

'Thanks, Doc,' said Gareth, getting up and kissing Kate on the cheek.

'No problem. I have to pick my kids up anyway. One more didn't make any difference.'

'I don't know what we'd do without you,' Rose said.

'For you,' Anna said, presenting her mother with a box of Roses chocolates. 'They've even got your name on them!'

It was a well-worn joke, paraded every Christmas, birthday and Mother's Day, and it never failed to make Rose smile.

'Thank you, darling.' Again, Rose pressed Anna to her. But Anna couldn't stay that way for long. She was too concerned about her sister, and she moved away to approach the box.

'Can I touch her?' she asked Rose.

'If your hands are clean and if you're very careful.'

Rose and Gareth watched as Anna laid a finger on Flossie's cheek, then bent over and kissed the box, just above her forehead.

'I love you, Floss. Get better soon, now. I can't wait till you walk and we can have lots of fun

171

together,' she whispered. 'Can she hear me?' she asked Rose.

'I'm sure she can,' Rose said as calmly as she could. But the pebble that had lodged in her throat when she was with Polly was expanding. Very soon, she thought, I will explode.

Kate went off to talk to the nurses, and Gareth and Anna settled in around Flossie. Gareth handed the rucksack he was carrying to Rose.

'Why don't you go take a bath? Take a break. There's enough of us here to hold the fort for Flossie.'

His words brought back a fleeting image of the day before, when everyone had been charging around the grassy ruin, oblivious of what was to come. How she wished she were back there again.

She took a bit of persuading: her instinct was not to leave Flossie. But, in the end, she took herself off to the bathroom.

She glanced at herself in the mirror and splashed cold water on her face. She looked ten years older than she had the day before, when the world had been in the right place.

Her body reeked of the sour milk that seemed to cling to every pore, and her hair had absorbed the stress of the past twelve hours and turned it into dirt. Gareth had packed a bottle of her bath oil, so she filled the parents' bathroom with scented steam, then lay in the bath and tried to clear her head.

She put on some clean clothes, and her favourite socks and slippers. Her newly cleansed body felt an incongruous shiver of pleasure as she thought about how, despite the anger and the worry he was feeling, Gareth had put so much care into putting this bag together.

When she came out, Kate had returned and she, Gareth and Anna were seated around Flossie's box.

'You look a million times better.' Gareth jumped up and let her take her seat again.

'Fabulous!' Kate said. 'And they're really pleased with how young Floss is doing. It's all going well.'

'Look, Rose,' Gareth said, 'we're going to have to get back now. Simon's got the boys and I need to pick them up and feed everyone.'

'There's a stew in the freezer,' Rose said.

'Don't worry. Dad said we could have takeaway pizza tonight,' Anna told her. Despite all of Rose's cooking, Anna's professed favourite food of all time was a Domino's Meateor.

'Are you still here?' a small voice asked. Rose turned to see Polly, who had crept up behind them. For a second, everyone stopped talking and looked round at her, as if a collective breath were being held. Then, with a sigh, the moment was broken.

'Right then, I'd best be off.' Kate stood up and put on her coat. 'Or my family will forget what I look like.'

'Thank you for everything,' Rose said.

'Don't mention it,' Kate said as she breezed away. She had completely ignored Polly.

'I guess you've been waiting for a lift?' Gareth turned to Polly.

'Sorry,' Polly said. 'I don't know about the buses.'

'There aren't any buses, Polly,' Anna said. 'We'll take you back.'

'We're just going. Come on,' Gareth said, and

173

he and Anna stroked Flossie, then kissed Rose, and then they left.

On the way out, Polly turned to Rose. 'Thank you,' she mouthed. But she didn't smile. Not even a bit.

Nineteen

That first night in the hospital was long, overheated and uncomfortable. The armchair bed seemed too small, and the covers too heavy for Rose. She woke herself up every half-hour to check on Flossie, who showed no signs of change one way or another.

Morning came. Or rather, the dim pools of light that glowed around each baby in its station were replaced by a sharp blue over-washing of fluorescent strip-lighting. Rose had a headache and, after checking that a nurse would keep an eye on Flossie, she shuffled off along the corridor to get coffee and a doughnut. She was beginning to feel the fug of the hospital seep into her. Her skin was becoming pasty, her movements slower. It took an effort to imagine another world outside those walls.

She could just about see the children back at home, sitting eating their pizzas in front of the TV, as they would have done last night. But she had difficulty picturing what Polly and Gareth would have been doing while that was going on. The way they were when they both left last night: what sort of evening could that have led to? She had never seen Polly like that. It was as if the wind—the very fabric had been sucked from her sails. And Gareth had been *so* enraged—that, too, was rare.

Perhaps it was because she was having difficulty thinking straight any more, but Rose didn't know what to pray for—that Gareth had stuck fast and sent Polly away, or that he had changed his mind and said that she could stay. And then there were the boys. Perhaps Polly could go, and the boys could stay? Surely that would be the best thing for everyone? Even as she dismissed this thought as ridiculous, part of Rose wished for it.

She went back to the ward, clutching her scalding cardboard coffee cup. The other parents looked up at her as she went past. She tried to smile, but her face wouldn't work. Was there a way you were supposed to behave in these situations? She felt scrutinised by the others, as if there were some rules that she didn't know about; as if there were a race of worried parents of infants that she didn't belong to. To Rose, they all looked the same—greyscale and drawn. How long would it take until she became one of them?

She was glad to get back to Flossie, to be able to focus the beam of her attention on what was most important. Relieving the nurse, she sat and drank her coffee and chewed on her doughnut. She hadn't realised just how hungry she was.

She tried to read her book. Gareth had carefully packed it with a marker where, two nights ago, she had turned it face down on the floor by her side of the bed. But it was useless; her eyes kept running over the same words, and nothing went in. She flicked through a magazine from a pile the nurse fetched for her. But the dog-eared pages with their full-colour clamour and pictures of expensive clothes offended her. How could they be here, in this room, where her daughter lay so ill over there? Instead, she switched on the TV and watched the parade of tragic lives on *The Jeremy Kyle Show. My Best Friend Drugged My Baby and Nearly Killed Her* would make a pretty impressive episode, she thought.

Drop by drop, Rose's will and self-determination sapped from her. Her world shrank to the tiny bubble of air that contained her, Flossie and the TV. She was just beginning to doze off when a commotion set off across the ward. It was the morning round of consultant and hangers-on. The consultant, a tall, sharp-nosed woman Rose had not yet met, made straight for her.

'So this is Baby Cunningham,' the consultant said to the nurse who was at her side.

The nurse handed her the clipboard that lived on the end of Flossie's box. Rose had earlier tried to make out what the notes said, but despite her Biology A-Level, she had been able to make neither head nor tail of the marks and graphs that defined Flossie's progress.

The consultant stood and looked at the chart. Rose wondered if perhaps she might have turned a little invisible over the course of the morning.

'And this is the mother?' the consultant finally said to the nurse.

'Rose Cunningham,' Rose said, getting up and extending her hand. She suddenly remembered she had to be in charge here, for Flossie's sake as well as for her own dignity.

'Hello. Well—ah—Flossie here has had a lucky escape,' the consultant said.

Rose wondered if that was an accusation.

'Mrs Cunningham's house guest left her anti-depressants within reach of the child,' the nurse said.

If the nurse felt compelled to step in and defend like that, then Rose thought she might have been right about the accusation.

'It's all looking good, Mrs Cunningham,' the consultant said. 'We're going to try to get Flossie off the ventilator today, and her bloods are looking fairly clean, so we'll review the dialysis in a day or two.'

A day or two—that sounded such a long time.

'Do you have any questions?' the consultant asked.

'Um, I don't think so,' Rose mumbled. Her mind was blank. She was sure there was something she needed to ask. Possibly it would come to mind later. If so, she would write it down for the next time.

*   *   *

A little while later, Rose was leaning over Flossie, willing her to get better, when she felt a touch on her shoulder. She turned and there was Gareth.

'It's been a long night,' he said.

'Yes.'

'How's my girl?' He reached through the hole in the box and touched Flossie's cheek.

'She's doing well, they say,' Rose said, and repeated what she thought the consultant had said.

'How long are we looking at till we can get her home?' Gareth said.

Rose kicked herself. That was what she should have asked the consultant.

'I don't know.'

'We all want you both back,' he said. He went and found a spare chair and brought it over to sit down beside Rose. He took her hand.

'So?' Rose said. 'How did it go with Polly?'

'I've never seen her like she was last night,' Gareth said. 'I think I finally glimpsed the human being in her.'

'Is that a good sign?'

'I hadn't processed just how much you mean to her,' he said. 'She begged me to forgive her. She's destroyed.'

'What did she say?'

'Look, Rose. Here's how it is. As far as I can see, even without taking Polly into account, it would be terrible for all of us if she went. You'd never forgive me, I'd feel guilty, and it would be the worst thing ever for the boys. I've even had Anna on my case this morning.'

'Do you believe it was an accident?' Rose asked.

'Do you know what? I think I do. She was stupid and careless—those are her words, not mine. She swears it will never happen again. And, you know, I can't get that day at the castle out of my head. How much fun it was, how things were looking so good—before it all happened, I mean.'

Rose was taken aback. Gareth's conversion had been so sudden, so complete, that she couldn't help wondering what Polly had said or done to change him. Rose knew from experience that a few tears worked very well at focusing his attention. She wished that she had seen what had happened between them. But that was beside the point. What was important was that things were going to be all right.

178

'Thank you!' she said, and put her arms round him.

'Now all we've got to think about is our Flossie getting better,' he said, turning back to the baby in the box.

Twenty

The following days seemed to compress into the grey fabric of the curtains around Flossie's little station. Rose wasn't sure in fact if it was days or weeks that passed. The routines of doctors' visits, nurses' checks and cups of tea should have helped mark the time, but they didn't. Rose developed a theory that they put tranquillisers in the urn that the WRVS trundled round. Keep everyone calm, keep the lids on.

She tried to share this idea—half-joke, half-conspiracy theory—with the women on either side of her, but they just stared at her as if she were some sort of lunatic. It came to a point where she began to feel like an alien in that room. The others talked easily among themselves, with their backs turned to Rose. Perhaps it was a class thing. Perhaps it was because they were all neat and well-groomed—Rose couldn't find it within herself to drag a comb through her hair, let alone trowel on the slap like the other women. Or, possibly, wind had got to them of the reason why Flossie was in there, and they disapproved of Rose for being a careless mother. Whatever it was, she felt a bit of a freak. It brought back memories of other times in hospital, times at school—times she thought she had succeeded in forgetting.

There was one moment only when she felt a common bond with the others. On the second day of their stay, a baby in the room died. It wasn't unexpected: sustained only by a battery of machines, the half-formed scrap had never really stood a chance.

Rose heard the consultant gently tell the defeated parents that there was no hope. She got their consent to remove the wires and tubes that had connected their child to this world.

The mother howled. She had barely been into her pregnancy when the baby had fallen out of her. There had never been much hope. Nevertheless, her devastation was equal to that which Rose knew she would feel if the unthinkable happened to Flossie. Loss, as Rose knew only too well, is the worst sort of despair. Particularly—and this is where her heart contracted so badly that she thought she might fall to the ground—when it concerned a child, a baby, that you would never have the chance to truly hold, to love, to know.

The nurses guided the parents away. Bereaved, the sobbing woman and her grey ghost of a husband had gone in an instant from being permanent residents to having no reason to be there. The whole room joined together in a silent prayer of thanks that it was happening to someone else. Every adult pair of eyes watched the deposed parents make their fragile exit.

Gareth visited twice a day. Once in the morning and once in the evening, when he brought Anna, Nico and Yannis with him. Fascinated by the machinery and other accessories of infant medical care, the boys had shown none of Anna's initial reticence. They dove in, asking questions, trying things out and creating their own brand of hubbub around Flossie's station. The nurses had to ask them to be quieter more than once. After their visit, the Sister had a quiet word with Rose: they really only liked one sibling at a time in Blue Ward, so could her sons please come separately in the future.

Polly didn't come while Flossie was in her induced sleep. She couldn't get in by herself because she was one of those people who, incredibly to Rose, had managed to survive well into adult life without ever learning to drive. Or swim, come to that—despite having spent a large proportion of her years living within sight of the sea. She had joked when younger that she had an inner life to maintain: the acquiring of mere practical skills was an annoying distraction.

But Polly didn't visit with the others, either. When Gareth came in the morning, it was too early, way before she woke up, but Rose didn't really understand why she couldn't come in for the evening.

'She's ashamed,' Gareth said. 'And we have to remember that, on top of all this, she is still dealing with Christos dying. She sends her love, though, you know.'

'Yep,' Rose said.

The other visitor was Kate, who came in daily. There were messages from Simon and a couple of the other parents at the school, but no one else was allowed to visit. Only immediate family were allowed in Blue Ward, to keep the risk of infection down.

Gareth brought in tasty food for Rose to eat. He

181

had always been a good cook, but had stood aside for Rose since the children had been born. His current return to the kitchen accentuated her feeling of powerlessness: she was so out of the picture, she couldn't even fill her family's stomachs. Instead, Gareth got stuck in there, making samosas, little pasties, tabbouleh—all sorts of pizzas and tortillas and pies. Loads of pies, like a good American boy. But Rose was thankful for the cleverly designed portable snacks he brought in. It kept her away from the hideous gloop that passed for food in the hospital canteen.

When he turned up on the ward, all the other women turned their heads to look at him. Their faces registered mild amusement, as if he were part of the Joke of Rose. The first time he left some food, Rose had offered it around but had been turned down. One woman even grimaced at the mini-pasty she had been offered, as if it might in some way harm her.

Gareth also brought in a bottle of Laphroaig, which he and Rose sipped as they sat watching Floss. On the second night, he brought a bottle of Rioja for Rose to enjoy after he had gone. Rose wasn't going to offer that around. In fact, she detected an air of disapproval, as she sat there with her wine. But after the second glass, she didn't care. How else was she supposed to get through having a sick baby?

Flossie began to look stronger. On her fourth day on Blue Ward, they unhooked her dialysis and took away her airline.

'She's breathing beautifully,' a young, dimpled Polish nurse said, beaming.

Rose wondered at what a strange, sad thing it

182

was, to celebrate the fact that your child can breathe on her own.

Flossie's colour returned from a rashed-over pallor to a more general, healthy pink tinge. Her grip got stronger by the hour, and her eyelids fluttered from time to time. They seemed less translucent, somehow; more as if they were housing something concrete, durable.

Rose reported these developments to the nurses and doctors, who continued to work from their own, less subjective, charts and measurements. They must have found hope there, though, because gradually the sedative was reduced.

On the sixth day, they woke Floss up and let Rose hold her and put her to her breast. Rose wept and wept as she felt the familiar pulling on her nipple, the gasping and breathing. Flossie couldn't at first settle into a rhythm, but it came back, and with it, the hope of a future; a promise that things would get better and go back to normal.

Flossie was moved from the plastic box into a little cot. This was more, Rose suspected, for psychological rather than practical reasons. It signified that she was out of the woods, that soon they would be able to go back home.

That was the day that Gareth brought Polly in. He guided her across the ward, his hand on her back, as if he were pushing her slightly, as if she were a little reluctant to enter. She moved up to Rose, her head bowed, as an errant child might approach her Headmistress. Rose surveyed her, holding the moment. She thought Polly looked a little better than she had when she had stepped off the plane. Gareth's cooking must be doing her good.

'I'm going to leave you guys alone for a bit,' he said, stepping back. 'I've just got to go to Waitrose, pick up a few things.'

He kissed them both—Rose on the mouth and Polly on the cheek—then he left. Polly watched him go, then turned to Rose.

'I'm so sorry I didn't come before,' she said.

'Gareth told me.'

'I just had real difficulty getting my head round everything.'

'Don't worry about it.'

Polly went over to Flossie's cot. 'She looks so much better. Like she's just sleeping.'

'She is just sleeping,' Rose said.

Polly leaned over and stroked Flossie's cheek. Rose was surprised by the violence of her urge to pull that hand away from her baby and repel its owner from the cot. It took all of her strength to resist it.

'Hello, Flossie,' Polly whispered, and two long dark hairs drifted from her head down to rest on Flossie's face. Rose leaned over and picked them out. Polly looked up at her.

'Rose, I'm really, really sorry, you know. I'm such an idiot.'

'Can we move on from apologising?' Rose said. She didn't think she could bear much more of it.

Polly grasped Rose's hands in hers and held them tightly, squeezing her eyes shut. 'Thank you,' she said after some time. She looked up. There were tears in her eyes.

'Sit there, I'll get us a cup of tea,' Rose said.

When she came back from the parents' kitchen, a mug in each hand, she found that Polly had

184

drifted away from Flossie and was standing chatting to the mother who had rejected the pasty. Rose parked the mugs on the top of Flossie's locker and Polly came back across the room to join her, as bright as a shot of sunshine.

'What were you talking about?' Rose said, handing her the tea.

'Oh, just this and that,' Polly said. 'She had been trying to work out all of our relationships.'

'Oh,' Rose said. 'I thought she hadn't even noticed me.'

'It's quite funny.' Polly smiled. 'She thought I was Gareth's wife!'

'Who did she think I was, then?' Rose asked.

'Do you really want to know?' Polly said.

'Go on.' Rose forced a smile.

'His ex!' Polly sniggered, delivering it as a punchline.

'And how did she explain Flossie, then?' Rose said. 'And how Gareth has come in twice a day to see us, and brought us food and drink?'

'Steady on, Rose,' Polly said. 'It's just what she—mistakenly—thought she saw. It's funny.'

'Stupid cow,' Rose muttered, sitting down in her seat and taking a slug of her tea. She stretched her legs out and rubbed her eyes. 'Shit, I need to get out of this place.'

They sat drinking their tea and talking about the children.

'It's so brilliant the way they get on, Rose. It is like they're all in the same family. Anna loves my boys.'

'And how about you, Poll? How are things with you?'

'I'm doing OK, you know?' she said. 'My widow

185

songs are nearly complete. Gareth's talking about having a word with the landlord at the Lamb about me doing a little preview.'

'Wow,' Rose said. The Lamb was the village pub, and it had a reputation for putting on surprisingly good music nights. The better Bristol and Bath bands lined up to play there, as well as more famous national acts. Once, the story went, Jarvis Cocker had done an unadvertised acoustic set, a couple of years before his renaissance. It would be a perfect venue for Polly to try out her songs.

By the time Gareth returned, Rose had told Polly all about the problems she was having with the other parents.

'Rose needs to get out of here, Gareth,' Polly said. 'It's driving her cuckoo.'

'I'm not surprised,' he said. 'How about you go home tomorrow morning? I'll come in and sit with Floss, and you can drive back, take a bath, spend a bit of time in the garden or whatever you want to do, then come back in after you've picked the guys up from school?'

It was a good idea, and Rose had stockpiled enough breast milk to make it work. They toasted Flossie with a drop of whisky, then Polly and Gareth left. As they crossed the ward, Rose saw how that woman might have got the impression that they were husband and wife. There was a rangy similarity to them both, an alikeness of hair and gait, that made you think they belonged together.

Rose shook herself. I really am going crazy in this place, she thought.

Later that evening, the Ward Sister came round

to check on Flossie. Rose told her the plan for the next day, asking her what she thought. The Sister looked at Rose as if she were some kind of imbecile.

'You don't have to ask our permission, you know,' she said. 'Twenty years ago, the parents wouldn't have been here except for visiting hours and, in my opinion, it allowed us to do our job far more efficiently.'

Rose laughed, as if the woman were joking, but the look on her face made her realise she was serious, so she stopped.

That evening, Rose sat and watched Flossie, who looked right back at her.

Was she imagining things, or was there something different about her baby? Something missing? Before the pills, every day had seen Flossie grow more into focus, a baby on her way to becoming a toddler. But now it seemed as if the process had been reversed. There was a sort of blur about her now.

Now Flossie was awake, the doctors could be more definite about her prognosis. It was clear, for example, that they could rule out severe cognitive or physical impairment. But when it came to the more subtle effects, they couldn't be so sure. The damage, if any, they said, would probably be slight—an occasional stutter, perhaps, or a tiny setback in her reading age. Or there might be no discernible difference. In any case it would be hard to tell what was a result of the poisoning and what would have happened anyway.

It was all most unsatisfactory. Rose wanted the empirical results she loved so much. Not knowing was like a footing was missing from her foundations. From a world that had promised everything, now nothing seemed certain at all.

Twenty-One

The next day, as planned, Rose drove home, leaving Gareth with Flossie. When she arrived, she took one look at the house and wished she had stayed in the hospital. Anna and the boys were all at school, and Polly was probably still in bed. The place was deserted.

The kitchen was in chaos. A cake with one slice cut out of it stood, uncovered, in the middle of the table. Around it was a jumble of packets of flour, dirty mixing bowls, eggshells and used cups. It looked as if the cake had made itself. The floor was covered in a drift of peelings and flour. Jam jars of daffodils, pussy willow and catkins stood on every surface, their water rank and stagnant: the kind of water you knew would smell of death. The clothes basket stood in the middle of the floor, full of screwed-up, damp washing that was beginning to smell musty. Rose took the whole lot through to the pantry and set it going through another wash cycle.

Then she went upstairs. Every bed was unmade, including hers and Gareth's. Defeated, she threw herself onto the rumpled sheets. None of this should matter, but it did. She had been away less than a week and everything looked, smelled, felt different. Surely that couldn't just have happened so quickly of its own accord—without some sort of effort on someone's part?

She batted these thoughts away. She was tired and this was all strange. She closed her eyes and drifted off. Twice she jolted awake, thinking that the beeping of Flossie's machines had stopped. Each time it took her a while to think through where she was, and why she was staring at a white wall instead of a beige curtain.

When she woke for good, her face was jammed up against the pillow, resting in a patch of her own drool. She lay very still, her eyes focusing slowly on the white pillowcase. They came to rest on a foreign object: a single, long, dark hair, right against her cheek. Her brain caught up with her vision and registered just what she was looking at. She sat up and examined the hair, holding it up against her own, which was shorter, mousier. There was no doubt about who this stray belonged to.

Polly's head had been on this pillow.

'Don't be ridiculous, Rose,' she heard herself say out loud into the silence of the room. Polly must have been up in the bed reading to the children. Anna had probably dragged her up here for a bedtime story. Rose had to work very hard to conjure up an image of Polly, with the children gathered around her, sharing a book. And even if she could bring herself to believe it, stomaching it was completely beyond her. It would be as if Polly were being Rose, and Rose found that almost revolting. It put a scent in her nostrils of the time the burglars shat on the Hackney floor.

Rose pulled the duvet right back and closely inspected the rest of the bed. There was one pubic hair on Gareth's side—his, she decided with relief after a close inspection. There was nothing else,

189

except the old black mark from a time when, a little drunk, she had fallen asleep in bed over a shopping list, letting her pen bleed into the sheets. She had never been able to get that mark out.

Then Rose got down onto her knees on the bed and pressed her face to the sheets, running up and down them, sniffing like a curious dog might at the rear end of a bitch. She was certain that there was a tinge of Polly to them. But then she had the physical evidence of the hair, and if she had actually been in the bed—which she had—then of course it would smell of her.

Rose sat on the bed, twisting the hair around her scarred index finger, winding it tight until the tip grew white. Then she glanced across the room at the big mirror to her side of the bed and caught sight of herself, hair awry, eyes open a little too wide.

She smiled at her reflection. 'You're being absurd,' she said out loud to herself.

She pulled the Polly-hair until it snapped. Cooped up in that ward, she had quite clearly lost the art of perspective.

She got up, shook the duvet and plumped the pillows. Then she went to the bathroom, cleaned the bath and ran herself a deep, hot tub. She washed her hair and every part of her body. Then she lay back in the water, counting the puffs of cloud through the skylight above the bath. She was on her way to feeling reborn. The world began to settle. She tingled with the feeling of work to do. Soon she would have order restored, and then they could all move on ahead.

She got out and cleansed, toned and moisturised her face. She rubbed body cream on her body, foot cream on her feet, hand cream on her hands and elbow cream on her elbows. After a moment's hesitation, she decided also to put the elbow cream on her knees.

It was time to get on. She went, naked, to the bedroom to get her kimono from the hook on the back of the door, but it wasn't there. Possibly Gareth had put it away somewhere. She searched through her drawers, but it wasn't there, either. The kimono was special to her, and quite valuable. Perhaps Anna had needed it for comfort? She told herself not to worry. Gareth was sure to know what had happened to it.

Instead, she pulled on some tracksuit bottoms and a long-sleeved tee. She went down to the kitchen, put the radio on, then cleared everything up, scrubbing down the cleared floor, table and work surfaces. She put fresh water in the vases, gagging as she tipped away their old contents—her suspicions about the smell had been well placed. A closer look at the cake showed it to be heart-shaped, studded all over with little sugar flowers, with *Rose* written on it in a wobbly, child's icing hand. Anna's work, Rose thought, smiling. She cut herself a slice and sat down with a cup of tea, looking at the light dappling on her herb garden. The chives were beginning to sprout their purple tufts already. Should she remove them and keep the herb for cooking, or let them grow on as flowers?

Then, guiltily, she remembered Flossie. There were more important things to worry about than flowers on herbs.

A flash of pink drew Rose's eye up to the Annexe door. It was Polly, wandering down the steps towards the house, singing to herself. She looked rumpled, as if she had just risen from sleep. But what Rose particularly noticed was that she was wearing her kimono, drawing it around her, stretching it tight across her hips, belting it up as if it belonged on her.

She came into the kitchen and, without noticing Rose, went straight to the coffee-machine.

'I was looking for that,' Rose said.

Polly jumped. 'Oh, I didn't see you there! Hi, Rose,' and she went over and put her arms round her and kissed her on the cheek. 'Want a coffee?'

'I don't do coffee,' Rose said.

'Oh yes, sorry, of course, I forgot. I'm still half-asleep!' Polly chirped. She turned to the machine and performed the coffee preparation ritual as perfected by Gareth. Grind, scoop, fill, level off, switch, froth, steam.

'I was looking for my kimono,' Rose said.

'What? Oh God, I'm sorry. I meant to put it back, but you beat me to it,' Polly said. 'I had a bath down here and didn't want to put my dirty clothes back on, but I didn't want to go up the garden in a towel and frighten the neighbours, so I just grabbed this off your bedroom door. You don't really mind, do you?'

Rose did mind, but she didn't say anything. 'That level of modesty doesn't sound like you.' She forced a smile.

'Well, you know, it's the countryside. When in Rome,' Polly said, using Gareth's wooden spatula to scoop froth from the milk jug onto her coffee.

And what neighbours? thought Rose. No one overlooked their house and garden. That had, after all, been the point of moving out here.

'Do you like the cake?' Polly said. 'Anna spent hours on it.'

'It's lovely,' Rose said.

'And the pussy willow! We had fun gathering that from the river. Feel,' and she brought a jug over for Rose to touch. They both stroked the velvety buds in silence.

'I'm sorry, Rose,' Polly said. 'About the kimono. About Flossie. About it all.'

'Remember what we said about apologies.' Rose smiled and put her hand on Polly's.

They sat and drank, and a bright shaft of sunlight pierced the morning sky, pouring through the window, illuminating them like a follow-spot on the two main characters of a play.

Twenty-Two

'He was going to die, but he'll be all right now, won't he?' Anna said, looking up at Rose, her large brown eyes circles of concern.

'I think you've saved him,' Rose said, her arm around her daughter. It was later in the afternoon, and Rose had just fetched Anna and the boys from the school.

'He was on the grass at the back, and he was all like this.' Anna crossed her eyes and stuck her tongue out.

'He must've fallen out of his nest.'

'Or perhaps he was pushed by a baddy bird,' Anna added. 'Anyway, I picked him up—I made sure not to touch him with my scent—and I saw he was still alive, so I brought him back in here, and put him in this little box. I'm feeding him five times a day with bits of cut-up worm.'

'Yerk.'

'I do it myself. I don't mind. His name is Jason.'

Rose looked at the fledgling in the box of cotton wool that Anna had lodged in the airing cupboard. She didn't hold out much hope for its survival, but she liked Anna's optimism.

'Jason will think you're a hero, Anna,' she said. 'If he pulls through.'

'Oh, he will,' Anna said.

'Do you fancy a walk down to the river?' Rose asked. 'Before I go?'

It was nearly four and she had to get back to the hospital. After Polly had gone back to the Annexe, Rose had spent a restorative afternoon in the kitchen and now there was a stew in the Aga, a pie in the fridge and a level of peace in her heart. But Gareth would be wondering where she was if she didn't leave soon.

'Come on then!' Anna said, jumping up and taking Rose by the hand.

They wandered across the field towards Gareth's willow. It felt good to be in the open again.

'Come on in,' Rose said, holding the willow branches to one side. Anna followed her and they sat on the smooth stone.

'How have you been with all this Flossie stuff?' Rose asked.

'She'll be better soon and we'll all be back to normal, won't we?' Anna said, picking up handfuls of earth and sprinkling them through her fingers. 'I miss you, though. And Floss.'

'I miss you,' Rose said, and kissed her. 'And

194

you're right. We'll be back really soon.'

'Good,' Anna said, and she clenched her fists.

'What is it?' Rose asked.

'Nothing.'

'No, there's something. Tell me,' she said.

'Well . . .'

'Go on.'

'Well it's the boys. They're fine,' Anna said. 'We have fun. I really like Yannis.'

'And Nico?'

'He's OK.'

'OK?'

Anna went silent and let her eyes rest on the swirl of the river as it rushed past their willow. It must seem so immense to her, thought Rose. Enough to take her away.

'It's just he gets so cross, Mummy. Not only with Yannis. Sometimes with me, too, even when I don't do or say anything. It's like he's got an angry dog or something inside him, trying to burst out.'

'Has he hurt you at all, Anna?'

'No, no. It's just it scares me. Sometimes I think he *could* hurt me if he got a little bit crosser. And . . .' Her voice trailed off and she pulled a strand of hair through her lips.

'What, love?'

'And I want you back, and not Polly.'

Rose felt the blood prick to her face.

'I'll be back as soon as I can, Anna. I promise.'

They walked arm in arm back to the house, and Rose let Anna ride to Bath with her in the car. They got to the hospital to find Gareth sleeping, with Flossie tucked up against his chest.

Anna and Rose smiled at each other. It looked as if he had fallen asleep breastfeeding. It was such

195

a sight, the baby in the arms of the big man, holding his broad finger in her little fist.

As they drew near, he woke and looked up. 'She's perfect, Rose. Perfect,' he said.

Rose sent Anna to get some chocolate from the WRVS stall just outside the ward, then quickly turned to Gareth.

'Anna is being freaked out by Nico,' she said. 'She says he's always angry. She says she's scared.'

'He's definitely not been himself the past couple of days,' Gareth said. 'But I haven't picked that up.'

'It's what she says, Gareth.'

'Of course. She's not going to lie about it.'

'No.'

'Look—I'll keep an eye on it. I'm not going to let him scare Anna. No way.'

'But he already has,' Rose said.

'If it was that bad, she would have come to me,' he said.

'Perhaps she didn't feel able,' Rose said. 'Perhaps—' but she had to cut short because Anna was skipping across the ward with five bars of Galaxy.

'I didn't get one for Polly, because she'd never touch chocolate,' Anna said. 'But there's one for you, one for you, one for me, one for Yannis and one for Nico.'

'I don't think we need to worry too much about our Anna,' Gareth whispered to Rose.

But don't you know how brave she is? Rose thought.

Twenty-Three

By Thursday, the doctors said Flossie could go home. She would have to come in every six months for long-term monitoring, but she was beginning to put weight back on, her temperature had returned to normal and she passed all the tests they ran on her for alertness. She had been moved out of Blue Ward onto a regular ward for young children. Most of their fellow inmates were tonsillectomy and acute asthma attack patients. Their immediate neighbour, aged four, was nursing a broken leg. He lay there strung to a traction contraption like a wriggling fish on a line.

'It's extraordinary,' Kate said when she visited on the final evening, 'how resilient healthy babies like Flossie are. Whatever's thrown at them, they hold on to life for all it's worth. As if they can't wait to see what's coming.'

'If only they knew . . .' Rose, who was lying on the bed, jogged Flossie up and down on her knee. She turned to Kate and looked directly at her.

'Can I ask you something, Kate?'

'Of course.'

'And I want a straight answer. Don't you think Flossie looks a bit . . . lost? Behind the eyes, I mean.'

Kate held Flossie's head and had a deep, long look.

'She's had a rough time, Rose, and she's taken a lot of drugs. It's going to be a humdinger of a hangover for Flossie, and I don't know if you remember those from your youth, but they are enough to take the spirit out of anyone.'

'Hmmm . . .'

'Really. Anyone would take a good long time to get over such a big shock to the system. It's far too early to say if there's been any lasting change.'

'Why does that not sound encouraging to me?'

'Look. What you've got to do is stop looking for signs of damage and start looking for signs of improvement.'

Rose thought about this.

*　　　*　　　*

Gareth picked Flossie and Rose up, and the three of them drove home out of the clogged, rush-hour city and the busy A36, onto the country lanes that were lined with trees just bursting into leaf. It felt so good to be leaving the hospital for good. Like hostages taking their first steps into freedom.

But the past eleven days had drained Rose. She felt like a lamp that someone had slipped a low-wattage bulb into by mistake. She felt like she had been filleted. By way of contrast, Gareth was on top form. His effervescent good humour was almost infectious, but she couldn't take it on.

'You'll be fine. It's just been a really stressful time. Let's get you home and look after you both, get everything back to normal,' he said.

'I'm not the one that's been ill. You don't need to look after me.'

'Yes, I do. You look so tired, my love.'

Rose felt tired, too, at the thought of how much work would be facing her in the house since she cleared up three days ago. She sighed and looked out of the window. The green shoots in the fields calmed her.

They swung into the driveway and Gareth unbuckled Flossie's car seat, clicking the handle into place above it and holding it in the crook of his elbow like a pro. Rose got the bags.

The three of them made their way down the steps to the house. A foul stink hit Rose as she passed the manhole cover that went over the mains.

'What's that smell?' she asked Gareth.

'Oh, there's been something wrong with the drains. I've tried rods, but I think we're going to have to get some of those water-jet guys. It's been throwing it down all week. You probably didn't notice, cooped up in the hospital, but it's been biblical. It's most likely just some silt and stuff left over from building work that's all got flushed out at once. And now all the shit's backing up. They're coming tomorrow.'

'Good.'

'Mum! Floss!'

The front door burst open and Anna rushed up the final two steps to throw her arms around Rose and press her face against her belly. The heat and love of Anna's embrace gave Rose a little more energy. Enough, at any rate, to make the final few yards to the kitchen.

'Put Floss on the kitchen table, Gareth,' Rose said. 'I'll strap her to me.'

'Sure. Hey, guys!' Gareth boomed into the sitting room. 'Look who's back!'

Rose put Flossie in the baby sling then followed him through. She was greeted by the sight of Polly and the boys sprawled on the sofa, in front of *The Simpsons*. Polly had a large glass of red wine, and

199

the boys had a can of Diet Coke each, which Rose never normally had in the house. Polly jumped up and threw her arms around her.

'Welcome back, Rose, welcome back, Flossie. We're so glad you're home.' She leaned in and stroked Flossie's cheek. 'Get up, boys, and give them a kiss.'

Yannis and Nico did as they were told, without removing their eyes from the screen.

'I must apologise for my sons, Rose,' Polly said. 'We didn't get much of this back in Karpathos, so it's a bit of a novelty.'

'Let's leave them to it, then,' Rose said. It was extraordinary how quickly Polly's warm welcome— on top of Anna's embrace—had drawn her in and turned her energy around. She wondered for a moment what it would have been like if Gareth hadn't relented; if he had gone ahead and thrown Polly out, and it had been just the four of them at home tonight.

Rose, Polly and Anna went through to the kitchen, where Gareth was tossing a salad to go with the stew he had made.

'You sit down, Rose. Me and Anna'll set the table,' he said.

'If you insist,' Rose said. Anna poured her a glass of wine and set it in front of her.

'It's good to be back,' she said. And it really was.

'It's such a beautiful evening,' Polly said. 'After all that rain.' She opened the window above the sink to let the sun-warmed evening air stream in.

'This is going to be awesome,' Gareth said, tasting the stew and adjusting the seasoning.

'You can't really go wrong with a kilo of organic beef, two bottles of good red wine and some of

200

Rose's thyme, Gareth,' Polly said, going over to breathe in the steam that rose from the casserole dish. 'Come on, chaps!' she called into the living room. 'Oh, sorry, I forgot,' and she got the handbell and, ever so daintily, rang it.

Rose had never seen Polly with so much positive energy. Not offstage, anyway. She welcomed it. She was happy just to sit, drink her wine and let it all happen about her.

Gareth carried the casserole to the table, where he set it down on a board next to a pile of bowls that Anna had put out.

'I think you're going to be proud of my stew, Rose,' he said as he ladled it out.

'Well, I'm very impressed with the look of the kitchen,' she said. And she was: it looked like he had made a real effort to clean up.

'It's not just housework, though, Rose. It's how I've really managed without you. I even surprised myself. It's gone really well, hasn't it, Anna?'

'Yeah,' Anna said. 'Though we did miss you, Mum.'

'Course we did,' Gareth said, lifting his spoon to his mouth. 'God, this stew is really something.'

'Men can never eat something they've cooked without constant self-congratulation,' Polly said. 'Christos was exactly the same. It was all, "This is the best stifado ever", and, "My mother doesn't make it as good as this".'

'I don't remember Papa doing that,' Nico said, not looking anyone in the eye. These were the first words he had said since Rose got back.

'Well, he did, Nico. It was funny,' Polly said, pushing a bit of meat around her plate. Rose noticed that, despite all the talk about food, she

201

still wasn't eating much.

'God, those drains are really bad, Gareth,' Rose said. 'Can we close the windows?'

'It is a bit high, isn't it?' he said, getting up and pulling the sashes down.

'Mama's got a jig,' Yannis said.

'A what?' Rose said. She realised she was so tired, it sounded like everyone was speaking from another room.

'A gig, spastic,' Nico said to his brother.

'Nico, we don't use that word, remember?' Gareth said.

'Whatever, Gareth,' Nico muttered.

Gareth bristled.

'This is the thing at the Lamb?' Rose said.

Polly nodded.

'Yeah,' Gareth said. 'I went down and had a word with Charlie and he said he'd be only too happy to have Polly do her try-out in there. In fact, he was as excited as a little kid.'

'He was one of my boy fans.' Polly rolled her eyes. 'Still dyes his hair—what's left of it—jet black.'

'Well, that's wonderful,' Rose said. 'When?'

'Next week,' Polly said. 'It's quite bracing. But it'll only be to an invited audience and locals—we're not doing a big load of publicity or anything. I just need to give the new work an airing. Get me feet back again.'

'It's great work, Rose,' Gareth said. 'Very moving. It's your best yet,' he said to Polly, who smiled and lowered her eyes.

'I'm going to do some old numbers too—unplugged—for Charlie and his mates,' she said. 'But mostly it'll be my Christos songs. My *Widow*

Cycle.'

There was a pause, and Nico stared at his mother as she fiddled with her food.

'You've written songs about Papa?' he asked.

'Yes.'

'Why? Why did you do that?'

'Because it's something that has happened to me—to us—and it's important to record it and express it.' She spoke slowly, choosing her words with care.

'You can't use him like that!' Nico jumped up.

'Nico . . .' Gareth warned.

'He's only just died. You can't use him like that!' Nico was waving his finger in the air, stabbing it towards his mother.

'Shut up!' Yannis put his hands over his ears and screwed up his eyes.

'You always do that—you always just use us for yourself, Mama. You never see anything from our point of view,' Nico railed.

'Nico, be quiet. *Now.*' Gareth stood up, pulling his great height against the small, wiry boy.

'Shut up.' Nico turned on him. 'You're not my papa.'

'I am quite aware of that, Nico,' Gareth said. 'Now, come with me into the back garden and we're going to have a little talk.'

'Make me, cunt.'

Anna gasped; Rose looked at her and blanched. Why wasn't Polly doing anything to stop this?

'That's it!' Gareth stormed. He grabbed Nico by the arm and dragged him out of the back door. Everyone stopped eating. Yannis hid his face in his hands and Anna sat looking at her plate, her lip trembling. Rose, who had never seen such

203

forcefulness from Gareth, looked over at Polly and was shocked to see that she had the ghost of a lopsided smile on her face.

'He deserved that,' Polly said. 'He's getting out of order, that boy.'

'He's remarkably articulate about his feelings,' Rose said.

'He doesn't understand a thing,' Polly snapped. 'He's a fine one to talk about not seeing things from anybody else's point of view.'

'He's nine years old, Polly!'

'And how else am I supposed to get us on our feet again? It's all I know, Rose—how to use what's in here.' She punched her breast, just above her heart. 'It's the only way I know of making a living.'

Rose thought Polly was missing the point entirely, turning it all onto herself, but she didn't have the energy to pursue it.

After a while, Gareth brought Nico back in, his arm around his shoulder. The boy looked tinier than ever.

'Nico is sorry, Polly,' Gareth said. 'Aren't you, Nico?'

'Yeah,' said Nico. 'Sorry, "Polly".'

Polly held out her hand and Nico reached over and shook it. He quietly went back to his seat.

'Right,' Polly said brightly. 'Who's for pudding? We've got something rather special made by our little Rose-in-waiting.' She gestured over to Anna, who got up and started clearing the table.

'It's just chocolate ice cream,' she said blushing.

'Home-made, Rose,' Yannis whispered over to her. 'Anna made it all by herself.'

'She's a clever, brilliant girl,' Rose said, smiling

204

at her daughter.

The chocolate ice cream was very good, with sauce swirled around inside it. Afterwards, Polly made coffee.

'Gareth has shown me how to do it,' she said.

'There's only the one way,' Gareth said, holding his index finger up.

'I'll have tea, please,' Rose said. 'And I'm really, really tired, I'm afraid. If you don't mind, chaps,' she turned to Nico and Yannis, 'I'd like to do Anna's bedtime, just me, her and Flossie. Just this once because we've been away so long.'

Yannis nodded, but Nico, still stinging from his outburst, wrapped his arms around himself and shrugged.

'I'll have the boys up at the Annexe tonight,' said Polly. 'Give you lot some space. But we'll clear up first. Come on, guys.'

'Come on, Nico,' Gareth said. 'Let's put it all behind ourselves, eh?'

Nico slowly got up and joined Polly, Gareth and Yannis at the sink. In no time at all, Gareth was leading the boys in a rousing chorus of '99 Bottles of Beer on the Wall', and everything seemed to be forgotten.

Rose looked at the scene of domestic near-bliss and wondered what had happened. When she and Flossie had left, she had felt that she was running the show single-handedly. Now everyone was pitching in and it looked like a well-oiled machine. Did she really get in the way that much?

She bathed Anna and Flossie together. Flossie was on good form, but a little dazed, as if she were getting used to everything again—at least, that's how Rose was trying to see it. How wonderful, in any case, to have her two girls together again in their own bath. Anna was so good with her sister, helping to wash her hair, wiping the water from her eyes with a flannel.

Then, with their pyjamas on, they went up to Rose and Gareth's room, lay on the bed and read *Winnie the Pooh*. It was one of the few things Rose had kept from when she was a child, and her name was scribbled hundreds of times on the flysheet—autograph practice for when she grew up and became famous, she remembered.

Anna loved *Winnie the Pooh*, and was soon tucked into Rose's side, giggling at his misadventures. Flossie curled into Rose, sucking her thumb, not reacting at all when Anna pointed out the pictures to her.

They finished reading. Rose lay Flossie in her cot, which Gareth had moved, at her request, into their bedroom. Then she went down with Anna to her room, where they tucked up together on her pink princess bed. Anna held her face right up by Rose's. For a long time she was silent, as if framing the best way to say something.

'It's funny they've all moved back up there tonight,' she said at last.

'What?' Rose said. She had been starting to drift off.

'To the Annexe.'

'Well, Polly thought it would be better for the boys to be there tonight, while we get back together as a family. I think it was very kind of her. She's absolutely right.'

'You know, I prefer *this* family,' Anna said.

'What do you mean?' Rose asked, stroking her cheek, her eyes half-closed.

'Just you, me, Floss and Dad,' Anna said.

'Yes,' Rose murmured.

'Not me, Nico, Yannis, Polly and Dad,' Anna whispered.

Rose jerked. It was one of those twitches that wake you from half-sleep, shaking you out of yourself.

'But it's not going to be like that again,' Rose said. 'We're back now.'

*   *   *

She called goodnight down the stairs, then went up to her room, checked on Flossie, and climbed into bed. Gareth wasn't long after. He got in next to her, leaned over, kissed her, and fell straight asleep. After nearly two weeks apart, they didn't make love. This was unusual enough to be slightly disturbing for Rose. She could have reached over and drawn him in, but, to be honest, she didn't really feel like it. Flossie being in the room with them didn't help much, either.

They both fell asleep back to back, warmth radiating into the cold bed from where their spines met. At some point in the night they parted company and, when Rose was woken by Flossie wanting a feed, she found herself clinging on to her side, perched on the edge of the bed as if it were some overhanging cliff. Gareth was miles away, over the other side of the sheets. She felt she would need a limb extension, or a loudhailer, to get to him.

Twenty-Four

Rose slept like a piece of lead. After Flossie had woken her up, she had brought her into bed, lying on her side and letting her feed like a piglet on a sow.

She was awoken by the sound of Anna howling. Gareth wasn't next to her. A lump of panic stuck in her throat as she looked at the clock: eight-thirty. She had overslept. She should be taking the children to school. Why was Anna crying?

She jumped up and moved Flossie to the middle of the bed, using pillows to fence her off from the drop on either side. She grabbed her kimono, which was back hanging on its peg, then she flew down the stairs.

'Anna!'

She stopped in her tracks on the landing. Anna stood by the bathroom door, sobbing. Nico and Yannis were further inside, looking down with ghoulish fascination at something in the toilet. And there, standing behind Anna, her hands on her hips, was Polly.

Nico, who had a pencil in his hand, leaned forward and prodded the thing in the pan.

'Get off him!' Anna roared, darting in and pulling him away.

'Anna, what happened?' Rose said.

'She's thrown him down the toilet,' Anna wailed, darting round Polly and throwing herself into Rose's arms.

'Who threw who down the toilet?' Rose asked.

'Jason,' Anna sobbed. 'She's just thrown him

down the toilet. I went in for a pee and I saw him there.'

Rose and Anna both looked up, horrified, as they heard the sound of the toilet being flushed. Polly came out, brushing her hands, followed by Nico and Yannis, their eyes round with a mixture of shock and suspense, their hands over their mouths.

'What? It was dead,' Polly said, looking at Anna and Rose.

Anna wailed. 'I couldn't save him, Mum.'

'She thinks she's failed.' Polly smiled at Rose.

Rose stroked Anna's hair. 'Oh darling, he was very young. It's almost impossible to save a baby bird like that once it's fallen from its nest.'

'I told her that,' Polly said.

'But he was doing so well . . .' Anna collapsed into sobbing again, and Rose held her close.

'It was a bit insensitive, just throwing him away,' Rose said to Polly. 'I think we would have preferred a funeral or something.'

'Oh, good grief,' Polly muttered, and started to go downstairs.

'Where's Daddy?' Rose asked Anna.

Polly turned on the stairs. 'He went down to his studio about an hour ago,' she said. 'He said to say hi.'

*   *   *

Rose said she would take the children to school, and by the time she had got Flossie wrapped up and strapped to her front, it was very late indeed.

'It's not the first time,' Yannis said as Rose hurried them across the field. 'We've sometimes

209

not got there till gone ten.'

'Things are back to normal now,' Rose said. 'This is the last late start.'

The two boys forged across the field, running from tree to tree, but Anna clung to Rose.

'Jason was getting better, though, Mum. Yesterday he ate loads of worms.'

'It's just nature's way.' Rose squeezed her hand. 'It's cruel. But perhaps he just wasn't meant to survive.'

'I don't know how he did that to his neck, though,' Anna murmured.

'What?'

'It was all like this.' Anna put her head over on one side. 'Like it had snapped.'

'Perhaps he tried to get up and stumbled,' Rose said, not wanting to think anything else. She had noticed how fascinated Nico had been with the bird. He had even told Rose when he came into the hospital to visit that he was going to take it into school to show the teacher. Anna had turned on him like a little lion and roared, 'No!'

Rose went into the school with the children to sign the late book. The boys charged off to their classrooms, but Anna hung back.

'I don't want to go to school,' she muttered. 'I want to stay home with you and Flossie, Mum.'

'You know you can't do that,' Rose said, holding her. 'You've got to be strong, and go to school and learn. If you mope at home all day, you'll never get the bird out of your mind.'

'Do I have to?'

'Yes, you do. Now get along, or you'll miss assembly.'

Anna gave Rose one last hug then pulled her

strength around her and walked off along the corridor. She looked back just once.

'Rose. And Flossie! Welcome home.' Janet put her head round her office door. 'Have you got a moment?'

Rose went into the office and sat down in the armchair in the corner. Janet sat next to her.

'How is our baby?' Janet asked, stroking Flossie's head.

'Oh, fine now,' Rose said. 'Though she gave us the runaround.'

'So I hear. It's great to have you both back with us, in any case. I just thought I'd have a quick word. You see, things went a little . . . slack in your absence, Rose. The boys became—well, feral is the only word I have for it. Nico is a particular worry to me. There have been fights. And they've been late almost every day.'

'Have you spoken to Polly about it?'

'Not seen her. I've tried to phone The Lodge, but there's never a reply.'

'But surely you could get her in the morning?'

'She doesn't come in the morning. Or the afternoon.'

'What about Gareth?'

'The children came on their own, Rose.'

'They walked here on their own?'

'Yes. And from what I've managed to glean, when they do eventually turn up, it appears that they haven't had any breakfast.'

Rose felt sick. She looked around. There was a sturdy wastepaper-bin that she could vomit into if she had to.

'Rose? Are you all right?'

'What?' Rose forced her attention back to the

room. She swallowed. 'Look, Janet, I can assure you that things are going to change. Nico can't carry on like that, and I'm back in the driving seat. Don't worry. Things will be back to normal in no time at all.'

'Good. I knew it was only a matter of waiting till you got back. That Ms Novak, though—I know she's had a rough time, but really. It's unprofessional of me to say this, but to be honest, Rose, I view you as more of a colleague than a parent. She has two sons. She needs to put her own interests to one side and start thinking of them instead.'

Rose opened her mouth, starting to defend Polly, but no words came. She found she agreed entirely with Janet. She felt honoured that she had chosen to confide in her. So pleased was she, in fact, that she had to suppress a little shiver.

*   *   *

Thinking about what Janet had said, Rose crossed the field back to The Lodge.

'Little cow,' she said out loud, kicking at a brittle cow parsley skeleton.

She stopped short. There was a man sitting on her bench. Should she turn round and take the road? But then she saw with relief that it was only Simon.

'Hi,' she said, as she closed in on him. He was hunched over, hugging himself tightly, smoking a roll-up.

'Rose!' He unwound his arms and stood up to kiss her on the cheek. 'And Floss. Thank God you're both back. You've been sorely missed.'

'You can't believe how glad I am to be at home again,' Rose said, sitting down next to him.

'I tried to come in, but when I said I wasn't family, they wouldn't let me,' he said, stroking Flossie's head.

'I know. And thanks for the card.'

'How is she now?'

'A bit dazed. But she's getting over it. The docs say she's got every chance of going on as if nothing ever happened.'

'*What* happened, Rose?' Simon said.

'It was an accident.' Rose found that this response came almost too automatically.

'How can a baby take all those pills by mistake?' Simon looked straight at her.

'She puts everything she sees in her mouth.'

'Is that what you think?'

'It's what I want to think. It's all there is to think,' Rose said, closing the subject.

Simon sat back and rolled another cigarette. He offered the tobacco packet to Rose.

'No, thanks,' she said. 'Not with Flossie here.'

He lit his cigarette and blew smoke into the golden morning light. 'Can I tell you something?'

'OK.'

Simon paused. A crow rose from the grass and cracked the silence.

'I think you know some of what was going on,' he said eventually. 'Between me and her.'

'I suppose I do.'

'You won't mention it to anyone, will you? I mean, Miranda and I are, well, relaxed about that sort of thing, but, well, this got a bit tricky.'

Rose wasn't sure if she wanted to hear what he had to say. It was like standing on the edge of a

213

cliff and feeling the urge to jump.

'That night I turned up. You know what I'm talking about, Rose. I saw Gareth switch off the kitchen light and you both were clearly silhouetted in the window. She took me upstairs, and, well . . .'

'Go on.'

'It's extraordinary, Rose, what she does. What she wants me to do. It went beyond what I'm comfortable with. I'm gentle—I don't like hurting people. But I couldn't stop, and I couldn't stop going back.'

'Spare me the details, Si, please.' Rose wasn't sure she wanted to hear any more, especially with Flossie strapped to her chest. It seemed wrong, indecent. He gathered himself.

'She made me do it, Rose. And every hour, every minute of the day I found myself wanting to be back there, doing it to her again and again. She opened something up in me that was—well, very dark. Something I didn't want to know about myself.'

Rose was stunned. Too stunned to walk away.

'Then she just shut the door. Last week. Said she didn't want to see me any more. Said she'd had enough—I don't know why.'

'You're not asking me to be your go-between, are you?' The kernel of anger that Janet had planted with her news about the children was beginning to flare up again, hurting her, deep beneath her solar plexus. Why did everything have to get complicated?

'I'm just trying to say that you may think you know that woman. But there's part of her that is so dark . . .'

'Why are you telling me this?' Rose felt she

needed to go home now.

'Just . . . Just, things aren't always what they seem.'

Rose stood up. 'She won't sleep with you any more, Simon. She's got bored with you. That's all it is. I don't want to talk about it. I didn't need to know all that. I don't want to get tangled up in whatever games you and Miranda play around at. I don't judge people, but I won't be forced to understand what you're getting up to, and I hate having to take sides or lie. So I'm not the best person to start confessing to. And Polly is—' and here she hesitated for a minute, trying to find the right term '—my best friend. And her husband died not more than two months ago, so she's bound to be a little messed up.'

'Rose . . .' Simon said, taking her hand.

'You know what? I don't want to know what you fancy or not about her.'

'Please. I'm sorry.'

'*No*, Simon. I'm going home now.' She set off across the long wet grass, lifting her feet high to trample it down.

'There was blood!' Simon cried. 'Lots of blood.'

*　　*　　*

Rose had stopped shaking by the time she got to The Lodge. Gareth was there. He jumped when Rose opened the kitchen door. She moved into the room and planted herself in the middle.

'Gareth, what do you know about Simon and Polly?'

'And good morning to you too, darling.' Gareth went over and kissed her on the head.

215

'Morning. What do you know about Simon and Polly?'

'Well, nothing more than you, I guess.' Gareth shrugged.

'We saw them go into the Annexe that night.'

'Yeah. So? They're all grown-ups, aren't they?'

'It's just . . .'

'What?'

'Nothing.'

'I've got to get back to work, Rose. You OK?'

'Do you want coffee?' she asked from the middle of the kitchen floor.

'No, thanks. I just had one. See you.' And he went off out the back door, which slammed as he passed through, making the kitchen windows rattle.

Rose realised that she had forgotten to ask him about the children going to school on their own. She went to follow him, but a great feeling of weariness overtook her. Perhaps it would be better just to start anew, now she was back, rather than rake over the old.

With Flossie still strapped to her, she sat at the kitchen table and gazed out of the window, up at the Annexe, where she could see Polly outlined in the bed-sitting-room window, holding her guitar.

It appeared to Rose that she was looking straight down at her.

Twenty-Five

Rose soon discovered that the outward appearance of order the house had presented when she got back from hospital was a piece of fiction. When she opened cupboards and looked under sofas, the chaos was revealed. Everything had just been shoved away, out of sight. She had her work cut out. She spent the day putting saucepans back in their right places, stacking plates correctly and sorting out the cutlery drawer. In between all that, she prepared supper and sat for a long while, feeding Flossie and looking out of the window.

She was far too busy to catch Polly or Gareth and ask them about what had happened while she was away. During the course of the day, she decided to let bygones be bygones. She had been away; all had fallen into chaos. It was a special case. It was to be expected, really.

She didn't see either of them all day. Gareth had tucked himself away in his studio and didn't even come up for lunch, and Polly was busy with her guitar in the Annexe. Occasionally the breeze carried a waft of a chord down and through the open kitchen window. Rose turned on Radio 4, to drown out the sound.

The men came to clear the drains at one. They backed a great, stinking lorry into the driveway. Then they sent a camera down the offending manhole. A tall, scabby-cheeked man—obviously the boss—sucked his teeth and muttered something about critters, then they blasted fearsome jets of water into an outlet behind the house. With a great gasp and a retch, the drain gave up its blockage, the water ran clear and the stink evaporated. The man with the cheeks presented Rose with a bill for over five hundred pounds.

'What on earth did you do for all that money?' she asked.

The man shrugged and gestured to the camera, the hoses, the four expensive men who had been operating them.

'And what was the problem?' she asked.

'You don't want to know, madam,' he winked. 'Payment in seven days, please. The address is on the bill.'

Rose stood in the driveway, her mouth open, as the men jumped on the lorry and disappeared.

*   *   *

Rose was sitting with the children at the kitchen table, attempting to get them to do their homework. She was trying to help Nico with his maths. It wasn't his strong subject, and it failed to hold his attention.

'So what's the answer?' she said.

But Nico was far more interested in goading Anna, who was still tender about what had happened that morning.

'But it was only a bird, Anna,' he said, rolling his eyes.

Anna looked at him over the top of her reading book as if she wanted to kill him. Rose had never seen her like that before. Nico's insouciance worried her. She wasn't entirely sure that he didn't have anything to do with the little bird's death. While she couldn't believe that he had deliberately killed it, she did think that perhaps he might have handled it too roughly, accidentally breaking its neck or something.

'Rose,' Yannis said, looking up from the elaborate drawing he was doing of an Egyptian corpse having its brains drawn down through its nose prior to mummification.

'Yes, Yannis?'

'Please can we come back to live in the big house again, please?'

Anna looked up sharply.

'It's just Mama has taken the whole place over up there, and she plays guitar all night long, and she smokes and smokes, and I want to be back in my proper room down here.'

Rose looked over at Anna, who was entreating her with her eyes. She looked back at the boys, who were doing the same thing. She felt as if she was in the Mexican stand-off scene from *Reservoir Dogs*, where everyone has a gun pulled on them and no one can shoot. Then she remembered that it wasn't like that at all. In fact, she was in control here.

'Of course you can,' she said to the boys.

'No!' Anna whispered.

'Yay!' whooped the boys.

'We'll go and get our stuff. Come on, Yannis.' Nico got up and ran out.

'Thank you, Rose.' Yannis made a little bow then hurtled off after his brother.

'Why, Mum?' Anna looked up at Rose.

'Sometimes you've got to think of someone beside yourself, Anna. The boys need to be

219

properly looked after and that isn't going to happen in the Annexe. They need to be here.' The more Rose discovered about Polly, the more sure she was that this was the case.

'But Nico . . .'

'I know. But I said I was going to make sure you were all right, didn't I? Don't you trust me, Anna?'

Anna looked down. 'I trust you, Mum,' she said.

'Good. I know things got a bit topsy-turvy, but believe me, they're going to be right as rain now.'

*   *   *

Rose made lemon roast chicken with small cut roast potatoes and a green salad for supper. It was a bit of a scratch meal. She had got the chicken out of the freezer—she always liked to keep one in there in case of an emergency. She really should have gone shopping, but she had been too busy sorting things out.

When the food was ready and the table laid, she rang the bell. There was a groan from the living room.

'Can we finish this episode?' Anna asked. She, Nico and Yannis were watching *The Simpsons* in the living room. Anna was clearly trying to put the lesson Rose had taught her earlier into practice. She was a good girl.

'How much longer?'

'Fifteen minutes.'

'All right, but then you've got to come straight through.' A chicken was never harmed for resting another fifteen minutes. And, in any case, neither Gareth nor Polly seemed to be in any sort of hurry to come in from their work.

Finally, Gareth put his head round the kitchen door.

'Hello, stranger,' she said, and went to kiss him.

'Hi.' His head was still in his studio. She recognised the signs; while it was a little frustrating for her, it augured well for the work.

'Good day?' she asked as she poured him a glass of wine.

'It's been hard, getting back into it,' he said, taking the drink and knocking it back in one. 'I didn't get much time when you were away, of course.'

'Sorry.' She bit her lip and turned to stir the gravy.

'I didn't mean it like that.' He sat down at the table, rubbing his eyes. 'It's just hard to find the rhythm of the work when you're only dotting in and out of it.'

'Well, we're back now, and you can spend as much time down there as you like. I'll even bring your food down for you if you want.'

'Oh, I don't think it'll come to that,' he said as he poured himself another glass of wine. 'How's Floss?'

'Sleeping in the buggy. It's all she's done all day. Oh, Gareth,' she said, taking her own glass and sitting down next to him. 'I'm not sure she's all right.'

'Stop worrying, love,' he said, holding her hand. 'Kate said it's going to take time. There's nothing else we can do but sit and wait.'

'That's what's so annoying.'

'Eat my shorts!' Nico led the snickering big children through from the living room with a perfect Bart Simpson impression.

'Nico, would you go up to the Annexe and get your mother?' Rose asked. 'I don't think she heard the bell.'

He groaned, but nevertheless belted off up the front garden.

'Jason died,' Anna said to her father.

'Who?' He ruffled her hair as she sat down, something he always did. From the way the hair was instantly smoothed back to its original state, it was obvious to Rose that Anna would rather he didn't.

'My bird.' Anna looked offended that Gareth didn't know.

'Your bird? Oh honey, I'm sorry.'

Rose realised with a pang that Gareth had been in the studio when the death had been discovered, and had remained there all day. A whole, formative episode from his daughter's life had been lost to him as he buried himself in whatever he was doing now.

'There's blood,' Nico said as he came back.

'What?' Rose turned sharply.

'Mama's fingertips are bleeding from so much playing,' he said. 'She's mental.'

'Is she coming down for supper?'

'She says thanks, but no. She's too busy. She says save her a little and she'll come and get it when she's got a moment.'

It was less than a week to the gig, so this was probably going to be the pattern from now on. Rose plated up a meal for Polly, covered it with another dish, and after the meal, she sent Anna up to the Annexe with it.

Twenty-Six

Flossie lay inert on the activity mat. Before the hospital stay—this was how Rose chose to see it, her shorthand for a nightmare—the plan had been to put the mat away. When she had last been on it, Floss had been able to sit, supported by cushions. She had even been showing signs of wanting to move away, a baby's mental preparation for crawling.

Since they had got back, Rose had tried to sit her up, but Flossie had just keeled over. She had consulted her well-thumbed babycare book. *After an illness, particularly one that necessitates a hospital stay*—ah, the dreaded euphemism again—*be prepared for him to take a step or two backwards on the developmental scale. For example, a baby who was sitting may not be able to do so. But don't worry. In most cases, things will soon be back on track.* This gave Rose a flush, a burst of hope.

Back on track. That's what she wanted for Flossie. *Things will soon be back on track.* It all sounded so scientific, so ordered. So achievable.

But for now, Flossie lay on the mat, her legs not kicking. Her fists not beating. Her eyes were open, though, and they returned Rose's gaze, following her finger as she moved it around her face. She smiled a little bit, too, from time to time. But Rose couldn't help thinking there was something missing. Something *vacant* about her. Not the tabula rasa of a newborn, but more the sense of something lost.

Rose had rung Kate several times since they had

223

got home to discuss this. Kate had been very kind, very accommodating, but by her third call, Rose had been made to feel that she was being a little unnecessary.

'You just have to be patient, Rose. I'm sorry, but despite what most doctors would like you to believe, medicine isn't a precise science. There are too many grey areas, and I'm afraid that Flossie falls into one of those.'

Rose turned to her grey area of a daughter, lying on the mat. She had let her down, and she couldn't make it all better. But she had to force herself to have hope. She just needed to scale down her expectations, take a step or two back.

None of this came easily to her.

Twenty-Seven

The days leading up to Polly's gig were strange and solitary for Rose. She saw Polly three, maybe four times, when she came down to the house to return plates and pick up more coffee or wine. There was never an occasion where a conversation was possible; when they did manage to exchange a few words, they were about the gig, and how the songs were coming on. Gareth seemed to be in a similarly work-oriented mode, only coming in for coffee refills and supper.

On the Monday after the hospital stay, a large parcel arrived from Amazon, addressed to Gareth. Rose went down to the studio, skirting her way around the wet grass and thinking about the stepping stones she would like to lay when time and money allowed. She could see him bent over a sketchbook on his angled wooden table, a daylight lamp illuminating his work. She felt privileged to have this spider-on-the-wall glimpse into his world. It all seemed so mysterious and exotic to her. She knocked on the door and waited at the window—he hated to be burst in on in mid-flow.

He jolted, startled by the sudden intrusion, but then, hand to his chest, he turned, saw Rose and smiled.

'There's a parcel for you,' she said, motioning through the window to show him it was over at the house.

He gave her a thumbs-up.

'I'll be up in a sec,' he said, and she trailed back to the house, to wait for him to appear.

'Aha—here's the beast!' he declared as he came through the kitchen door a good half-hour later.

'What is it?' She had been dying to open it.

'Just look here, Rose,' he said as he ripped open the box to reveal an expensive espresso machine not unlike the one they already had in the kitchen. 'It's state of the art, it has a hard-water filter, and a guaranteed clog-free, self-cleaning milk steamer.' He got the thing out of its box and caressed its black and chrome curves.

His enthusiasm was endearing, and normally Rose would have left it at that, but she had seen the four-figure cost of the thing on the invoice, which fell out of the box as Gareth lifted it out. It seemed so wasteful.

'I don't see why we need another coffee-maker, Gareth. The one we've got's perfectly fine, isn't it?'

'Yeah, it's great, but this one's for my studio.

225

Saves me having to trail up here whenever I need a drink.'

'Sounds very time smart,' she said as he folded the cardboard box ready for putting it in the recycling.

'I'll still have to grind the beans up here, though. There's nothing like my old grinder.'

'I know,' Rose said.

'I'm going to give her her maiden voyage.' With that, Gareth kissed Rose on the cheek, then set off for the studio, grabbing the tin of coffee he had ground for the day when he got up. He tucked the new coffee-maker under his free arm, resting it on his hip like a particularly lumpy and hard child.

Rose would miss him coming up for coffee. Since she and Flossie got back, he had taken to ducking back into the studio after supper, leaving her to put the children to bed on her own. She would then spend the rest of the evening sitting alone with a book and a glass of wine. She had begun to move the older children's bedtime back a bit to postpone the moment of solitude, which always felt to her as if she had failed at something, but she didn't quite know what.

Some nights she wasn't aware of Gareth's presence at all. He would climb into bed when she and Flossie—who was back in the bed with them for the time being—were fast asleep. Then, when they woke in the early morning, he would already be gone. Rose suspected that sometimes he worked through the night, because some mornings she couldn't detect any evidence of his presence in their bed at all: no crumpling of the pillow, no smell of him on the sheets.

The only chance she had for conversation with

him was at dinner, when the clatter and bickering of the boys gave little space for anything other than crowd control. She had to keep reminding herself that this was a stage that Gareth had been through many times before, one that had always previously boded well for his work, and therefore, ultimately, for the family. But she couldn't help feeling that this time there was something different. Perhaps it was just because his studio was so close to the house? She couldn't put her finger on it.

Polly's gig drew closer. Anna, Nico and Yannis had all wanted to go up to the Lamb to hear her play, but children weren't allowed on weekday nights. In any case, Rose felt it might not be appropriate for Nico to hear his mother's songs about his father so soon after his death. She wondered how appropriate the event was for anyone, given the circumstances. But she let it ride. In her view, anything that led Polly towards a path of independence was a good thing.

The boys couldn't believe that they couldn't come. In Greece, they argued, they were able to go anywhere anytime, and children could just do as they pleased.

'It's not like that here, I'm afraid, chaps,' Rose said.

'But it's our mum singing . . .'

'Sorry. The landlord said very firmly, no exceptions. They're expecting a big crowd, and it won't be safe or right to have you there.'

'Fuck what the landlord says,' Nico snarled.

'Nico!' Rose said.

In the end though, Rose felt sorry for them. To make up for them missing the gig, she promised to video it. That way, Nico's first viewing of the songs would be mediated, and any reactions would be in private, where, if necessary, she could quash them.

*   *   *

'I'm off, then—see you later.'

On the day of the gig, Polly put in one of her rare appearances at The Lodge to say goodbye to the children before she went down to the Lamb to do her sound checks. It was an acoustic set, but Polly said she needed to get a feel for the space.

'Wish me luck, then,' she said as she ruffled Nico's hair. He scowled back at her.

'Bye, Mama.' Yannis reached up to her and gave her a big hug. For a second, she closed her eyes, her soot-black eyelashes grazing her white cheeks. Her gash of red lipstick broke into the hint of a smile as she placed her large, bony hand on his small shoulder. Then the moment passed.

'Gotta go,' she said, breaking away. 'My public awaits me.' And she strode out of The Lodge, her guitar slung across her back.

Rose stared into the bolognese sauce she was stirring. Polly had barely registered her presence. But it was good to see her so enlivened. Movement of any sort was a good thing. Once it had started, momentum could build, and perhaps on a high, upward swing, Polly might take it into her head to just keep going and leave. But then Rose started to worry about the boys, and what would happen to them once they were outside her sphere of influence.

She turned to see them standing at the door, looking at the front garden, at the space left by

Polly.

'Can you make sure the video camera's still charging, Nico? It's plugged into the socket by the telly.'

*   *   *

Thirty minutes later, Gareth came in from the studio.

'Isn't it ready yet?' he asked, looking at Rose, who was still standing at the sauce, stirring it. 'We've got to get changed, don't forget.'

She was wearing an old, unwashed T-shirt and her gardening dungarees—an ancient, baggy pair she had lived in during her pregnancy, when she was working on the house. They were paint- and cement-splattered, with a gaping hole through which her muddy knee protruded. She had been wearing them a lot recently. Something in her wanted to keep them on to go down to the pub. She didn't want to appear to have made an effort. But of course, to do so would be out of the question. People would talk.

'Sorry. I got into a bit of a daze.' She blinked and set about putting the spaghetti water on and laying the table, while Gareth scrubbed his inky fingers in the kitchen sink.

'Great day today,' he said. 'A breakthrough on the river project.'

'Oh yes?'

'I've found the language I'm looking for. All that work with the digital manipulation, the etching and the cross-hatching seemed wrong somehow, dishonest. So it's woodcuts, Rose, definitely.'

'Woodcuts!'

'I'm going to take the wood from trees that grow along the banks along the way.'

'Is that sound?' She imagined a riverbank lined with bare stumps, like a photograph in a colour-supplement article on the destruction of the Amazonian rainforest. Acres of decimated land.

'I'm only going to take a branch here, a limb there. Cutting the wood is part of the work. My intervention on the material is going to be minimal, just a suggestion, to make sense of the flow of the water. Let the grain talk. And then . . .' He paused as he dried his partially cleaned hands on a tea-towel, leaving black smudges that meant it would have to go straight into the laundry.

'Then what?' She was having difficulty picturing what he was talking about. She always did when he got onto his work. He took a long time to arrive at his conclusions, but the way he tried to explain them to her made them sound so obvious and simple that they seemed too easy somehow, not worthy of all the effort he had put into arriving at them.

'Then I'm putting the human form into the pieces. Not sure how. But it's about beauty and destruction. About how we put ourselves in our world and then in doing so, we despoil it, grind it to pieces.'

'I'd love to see what you mean.'

'There's nothing to show yet, but when there is, you'll be the first, I promise,' and he leaned over to her as she drained the spaghetti, and kissed her hair.

Rose broke away and rang the bell. 'Dinner!' she called.

'Yep, a good day.' Gareth rubbed his hands together and sat down.

Rose didn't know why, but she felt her heart resting around her navel. Perhaps, she thought, wine would help lift it up again. So she opened a bottle from the bottom shelf of the wine rack—the better shelf—and poured herself a large glass of blood-red Bardolino. She was just turning round with it when she realised she had forgotten to pour one for Gareth. Slapping the side of her head, she went back and got a glass out for him, polishing it carefully with her T-shirt before she filled it.

*   *   *

After supper, Rose organised the older children into a clearing-up party while she bathed and fed Flossie, ready to put her down for the night. Flossie kicked a little in the bath, stirring up a few soapy bubbles. It was the most animated Rose had seen her since the hospital stay. For the first time, she felt perhaps that her daughter wasn't damaged goods. She managed to see a glint of hope, but then again, it could have been the wine.

She was just putting Flossie down when the doorbell rang. That would be Janka, Simon's au pair, who was babysitting for the evening. Simon had chosen not to go to the gig, so it seemed a perfect solution to the problem of both Rose and Gareth going out.

'Can you get it, Gareth? I've still got to get changed. Just give her a cup of tea and I'll be down in a sec.'

Rose felt her belly turn over, as she tucked Flossie into her cot, which had been moved back

231

into the nursery. The plan was to put her in there until they got back, when Rose would take her into their bed, which was the only place she felt safe with her. Putting her in the cot was difficult in itself. But the whole night was going to be a big test. It was the first time she had left her children at night, ever—except for the topping-out ceremony when Anna went to that sleepover. And coming so hard on Flossie's hospital stay, well, Rose didn't quite know how she could do it. Her stomach had been quite upset with the nerves of it over the past few days. She kept on having to rush to the loo. But she had to do it. When she had confided in Gareth about her fears, he had just patiently pointed out that the Lamb was only a few hundred yards down the road, that Janka knew the children, that she had the phone number and that he would tell Charlie the landlord that he had to get Rose immediately if Janka were to call.

He just couldn't see it.

Rose went to her dressing room and leaned against the full-length mirror, eyeball to eyeball with her own reflection. Perhaps if she were to say she were ill? If she were to have a headache, or make herself sick—and here she knew she had form—then she wouldn't have to go. But when she looked over at Christos's painting of Polly, she remembered everything that once was. She bore a loyalty, almost a debt to Polly, and there was no way she couldn't drag herself up the road to the pub for her.

What to wear, though? She picked out the black dress with the sequinned band under the breasts, the one that Gareth really liked. She pulled off her dungarees and T-shirt, leaving them in a pile on

232

the floor, and squeezed the dress over her head. It was quite a bit tighter than it had been the last time she had worn it, back in London for a private view of Gareth's just before they left. But it was empire line, so she could just about get away with it pulling a little across her stomach. She looked in the mirror. The way her breasts squashed up and spilled over the top was all right, she thought. She didn't dwell overlong on how the rest of it looked.

She grabbed her hair, twisted it up and clasped it at the back with a large claw of a hairgrip. She splashed her face with water and put on a smear of lipstick—the first she had worn for months. She stopped for a moment and looked closely at her face in the bathroom mirror. In the brutal blue light that burned from the bulbs over the top of it, she looked shadowed, tired. She rummaged in her side of the bathroom cabinet for the Touche Éclat that was her one bit of cosmetic extravagance, but, to her annoyance, it seemed to have disappeared.

But there were more important things to take care of, so, slipping her feet into her black suede flats, she went downstairs to find Janka and show her around.

She was a little taken aback to find their babysitter at the kitchen table, having a glass of wine with Gareth. Surely it wasn't wise for her to drink before taking charge of four children? The thought of cancelling and sending Janka back flashed through her mind. Surely that would be the most sensible thing? Just one drink can impair the judgement, after all.

But of course, that was for driving, not childcare, and Rose had to admit that she often looked after four or more children after considerably more than just one glass of wine.

'Hello, Rose.' Janka, a handsome Slovakian girl, unfolded herself to her full height and shook hands with Rose.

'Hi, Janka. I'll just show you round. You haven't been here before, have you?'

'Oh yes, Rose. I have being here fivesix times, when you and baby are away,' Janka smiled and nodded.

Rose looked over at Gareth, her eyebrows arching.

'Someone had to look after the kids when I was visiting,' Gareth said.

Rose didn't even bother to wonder why Polly couldn't have done it.

'Well, then, I'll just show you what to do if Flossie wakes up. You've got the pub number, and Gareth has told you to phone it if she shows any sign of being in trouble, and you must check on her every hour, OK?'

Rose really did intend just to show Janka the Flossie part of the operation, but she found herself instead taking Janka round everywhere and introducing her to the children, who looked up and said, 'Hi, Janka,' then carried on watching *Futurama*.

Janka followed Rose around, nodding uh-huh, uh-huh to all Rose's precise and detailed instructions. She did it in such a way that Rose wondered if she were taking anything in at all. Again, Rose felt like calling the evening off, but she couldn't begin to think of a way of extracting herself now without appearing incredibly rude.

*   *   *

She and Gareth kissed the children—all the children, because Rose had persuaded Gareth that they must treat the boys as if they were their own in that respect—and set off along the lane to the pub.

It was a cold, cloudless night, with the type of chill that froze into your sinuses and evaporated in your breath. The air made Rose's eyes water slightly, bringing the moonlit hedgerow into sharp focus. Clarity, she thought, is what's needed tonight. Just keep things clear.

They wandered down the lane, and Rose tucked her arm into Gareth's. He talked about the night sky, about how it made outlines of the trees against the rim of the horizon. She was happy to listen to him.

They stopped and held their breath to hear the nothingness of the country night around them, until it was broken by the screech of an owl and the scream of something tiny. They moved on. As they neared the pub, which was on the outskirts of the village proper, streetlight took over from the moon and stars, and the clamour from within swallowed the silence of the night outside.

It was a full house inside, for sure. For someone with only a telephone and the postal service at her disposal—she claimed not to know even how to turn a computer on—Polly had managed to pull in an audience of two hundred or more, enough certainly to cram the Lamb. Rose looked around as Gareth went to the bar. With a few exceptions, this wasn't a local crowd. The Lamb couldn't have seen so many piercings and leather under one roof in all its five hundred years. There were quite a few raddled, excited thirty-somethings in black, necking what looked like Snakebite. These were obviously fans from the old days. But there were also some better-groomed, more blasé types, drinking white wine and trying to get a reception on their iPhones, which, of course, as Rose knew, was impossible. These must be the industry people, the ones that could shape a future for Polly. An independent future. Rose was very glad to see there were quite so many of these people.

If it took off for Polly and she went back to gigging and recording all over the world, perhaps, Rose thought, she could look after the boys for her on a more formal basis.

Gareth brought her drink over and handed it to her.

'There's Jon.' He waved across the bar. 'Do you mind if I go and see him? He's been on at me about joining the cricket team.'

'How very Archers,' Rose said.

'My final assimilation into English culture.' Gareth put his hand on his heart.

'You go, then, you old Limey. I'm going to find a good spot for filming.'

She perched on a bar stool by the fireplace, quite near the front, where she could see over the heads of the standing crowd, and peered at the video camera, checking that it was on the right setting. She was always the one in charge of the camera. To look at their family photographs, one might think that she didn't exist, because she was always the wrong side of the lens. Gareth took a lot of photographs for his work and said he tended to view any other camera use as a bit of a busman's holiday, so it was left up to her. She didn't mind

236

though. She thought she was rather good at photography, that she had an eye for composition.

The phone rang at the bar. Rose felt a sharp prick of fear as she swung round to see Charlie the landlord pick it up. He laughed down the receiver, a nicotine-stained croak, greeting an old crony. Rose's panic subsided into its usual remnants of a shuddering heart-beat. To calm herself, she looked around and tried to tune into the crowd. There was a definite trend for people to stand facing the stage. Every time there was a movement up front, there was a pause in the conversational buzz. They were waiting.

'I've said I'll go down to the nets next Wednesday. Anything to get him off my back.' Gareth had crossed the bar and was standing at her side. 'I'm just off for a smoke,' he said, and disappeared again.

Rose drained her drink and, leaving her jacket on the stool, went up to the bar to get another. She wished Simon was there, but his absence was understandable. She tried to catch Charlie's eye as he served the throng at the bar, but he wasn't bestowing any favours tonight, and she had to wait what seemed an age to be served. So long was it, in fact, that she decided to buy a whole bottle of wine and tuck it over on the mantelpiece by her stool, to save having to go back.

She had just got herself settled when there was another, more definitive hush in the crowd. She looked up and saw Polly flit across the small raised area that did for a stage, guitar slung across her front. She stopped in front of a microphone and pulled it down closer to her mouth. Her lips were painted blood red, and she wore a long black dress that looked like a spider's web. She appeared a little nervous.

'Hello.' She looked at the audience without a smile. 'It's good to be back.'

With that, the audience erupted into a passionate cheer, which brought a flicker of pleasure to Polly's face. Rose set the video camera going. Polly bent down to her guitar and strummed a few minor chords.

'I'm a widow and this is my story,' she said through half-closed eyes. Then she launched into her first number.

*   *   *

Polly was on great form. Her voice soared from a low growl to a banshee wail in no more than a beat. Her new songs touched on pain, love, blood and death. All her anger and disappointment were unleashed there, in that tiny room. It was obvious, from the quality of their attention that, for many in the audience, the night was a transcendent, even transforming experience.

Rose once looked over to Gareth, who had come in from his cigarette at the first sound of Polly's voice. The crowd had been too thick for him to make his way over to Rose, so he had positioned himself at the other side of the room, leaning against the bar in a slightly proprietorial way. Looking at him watching Polly, Rose felt uncomfortable. There was something in his face that she didn't want to see; something that made her feel very ordinary, as if she wasn't really worthy to stand in this room, listening to this music. She suddenly felt disappointed in herself,

238

ashamed that she hadn't managed to turn out as magnificent as her friend up there on the stage. The advantages that she had thought she had gained over the last ten or so years were obviously just some sort of mythology; she was back where she deserved to be, playing the triangle in Orchestra Polly.

Polly squatted and swung her guitar around as if it were her slave, bound to her hip. The crotch of her knickers was all on display, but in an earthily erotic way that went beyond any sort of sleaze. Rose was, for a moment, in awe.

She remembered very clearly one hot summer's day when she, Polly and a couple of other girls were supposed to be doing shot putt, but instead were just lazing in the sun at the top of the games field. Rose and the others were sitting with their legs curled by their sides, tucking their short games skirts around themselves. Polly, however, sat splayed out, her skirt hitched up and everything fully on display. But there was not a spare pube protruding, nor a wet or grey patch to be seen on her pristine white knickers. Oh, to have that confidence even about that most difficult and wayward part of your body, Rose had thought then. And there it was again: Polly, still as unbridled, so easily on display. Like her thirteen-year-old self.

Rose, stuck there with the video camera, felt like a big lump.

The steady Eddie. That's what she had become. The one who had done the sensible things. Her most outré, risky gesture of late had been to buy an old house and spend two years working hard to do it up. Not all that extraordinary, comparatively.

239

Faced with the electricity on stage and the way it was holding this cool, aloof audience, she felt like the bourgeois, middle-aged housewife she had probably become—and by far and away the least exciting prospect in the room.

The twelve new songs that Polly played that night, together with the famous title track of *Running Scared*, her 1992 album, and a couple of other oldies, put the audience in the palm of her hand. Acoustic pieces, with only her own guitar-playing to accompany them, they nevertheless filled the small space in a way that seemed to transform even the smell of it.

At the end, the audience erupted. They stamped the ground, whooped, yelled for more. People holding glasses tapped their heavy silver rings on them. Polly stood on the stage and, smiling, she put her hands together in a *namaste* then propped her guitar up against the wall and turned and walked through the audience towards the bar. People tried to touch her.

Rose, still filming, attempted to follow her path through the audience, but for the main, tiny Polly, who from the stage had filled the corners of the room with her energy, was swamped now she was down on the floor.

Rose was just putting the camera away when she heard a gasp in the crowd and looked up. A space had cleared around Polly, who was being confronted by a tall blonde woman in skin-tight jeans and an expensively soft-looking leather biker jacket. The woman was blocking Polly's path, standing over her like an evil Disney witch. Rose craned her head to hear what was going on.

'You know,' the blonde woman was saying, 'the

fact that your husband has died is the only interesting thing about you.'

Polly was looking up at her with one hand on her hip, staring her out. The woman swooped forward and slapped her full on the face, catching her by surprise and cutting her cheekbone with a large diamond ring.

Polly went down, and five men, Gareth amongst them, leaped to her aid.

Another man, tall and dark, with a black fringe falling across his tired blue eyes, took hold of the blonde woman who was, it was now obvious, very drunk indeed.

'You said you'd behave if we came here,' he hissed.

'During the gig, I said. DURING THE GIG!' she snarled back.

Rose was quite put out that she had zipped the camera back in its padded bag.

'How many times have I told you? It's all in the past!' the man was yelling.

'I saw your face,' she came back at him. 'Don't tell me you don't still want it, that filthy little piece of stinking fish.'

He took her by the arm and hauled her away, out of the pub. Rose looked down at Polly, who was still on the ground, surrounded by a circle of men. One of them had got a glass of water from the bar and Gareth was using a napkin to wipe the admittedly nasty-looking cut that the woman's ring had left beneath Polly's left eye.

'Are you OK?' Rose leaned forward and asked Polly.

'I'm fine.' Polly smiled up at her, but her mouth was twisted. 'Forget about it, won't you? I know her from a long time back. She's a mentalist.'

Gareth and another man—a great, glossed and suntanned bear of a man—helped her up.

'Now what I need is a drink,' Polly said, looking up at Gareth.

'A bottle of champagne for the star, Charlie!' Gareth yelled as he cleared her way to the bar. Someone slipped off a stool and offered it up to her.

'It's on the house, mate,' Charlie said, and reaching behind the bar, he picked up a bunch of red roses and presented them to Polly with a bow. If she hadn't seen it with her own eyes, Rose would never have believed that such a gesture could have come from this beer-bellied, pock-nosed, coarse-veined bloke. He was far better known for his ability to eject troublemakers by literally pulling them up by the seat of their pants and throwing them out into the road than for his way with chivalry and flowers.

Gareth poured the champagne and handed it out to Polly and Rose.

'That was great, Poll,' Rose said.

'Thanks.'

'Wasn't it awesome?' Gareth put his arm round Polly's shoulders. 'You're not going to have any problems getting back into it, girl, are you?'

'I dunno.' Polly shrugged.

'Excuse me?' A well-spoken white guy with dreadlocks down to his waist came between Polly and Rose and held out his hand. 'I was blown away by that.'

'Thank you.' Something in Polly that had been dimmed after the confrontation with the blonde woman was beginning to come back to life.

242

'Jem Williams, Karma Records,' the guy said.

'Wow,' Gareth said.

'Cool.' Polly smiled.

Rose's attention wandered across the crowded bar, until her eyes came to rest on a figure leaning against the wall near the door, cradling a pint and looking right over in their direction. It was Simon.

'Just going to the loo,' she said to no one in particular, and made her way over to him. She couldn't believe he was here.

'What are you doing here? Who's looking after the kids?'

'They're all asleep. I just slipped in for a quickie. Don't tell Miranda,' he said.

'That's the least of the secrets I've got to keep from her.'

'I trust it went well, then. I didn't get here until the applause.'

'It was—brilliant,' Rose said, searching for the word.

'Great.'

'Yep.'

'Look, Rose,' he said. 'I'm sorry about the other week. I was a bit . . . lost. I just want you to know that, if ever you need to talk, I'm here. I don't want us not to be friends. I miss our chats.'

'I've forgotten about it already.' She reached up and kissed him on the cheek. 'But I'm only going to be your friend if you go back right now and babysit your children.'

'Yes, ma'am,' he said, handing her his drink. 'I'm gone. Remember, though, just grab me—OK? Any time.'

'Right,' Rose said, although she didn't quite know what he meant about her needing to talk.

About what? He was the one in the state. She knocked back the remains of Simon's pint and headed across the bar.

'Where were you?' Gareth put his arm around her.

'Loo,' she said.

He looked like he had been edged out a little. Polly was sitting on a bar stool, holding court. She was surrounded by a group of men who were listening with hungry, yet sympathetic faces to what she had to say. Rose noticed that the dark-fringed man from earlier was among them, standing right by Polly, so close that he must surely be touching her thigh with his own. He must have lost the blonde woman somewhere, Rose supposed.

'Time to get back for Janka,' Rose said. 'You stay if you want.'

'Nah, I'll come back. I've got to be up early in the morning, anyhow,' Gareth said.

They said their goodbyes to Polly, who looked like she was getting stuck in for the night. Outside in the lane, the moon had travelled over the sky, hanging in the night as if it were keeping a big, cautious eye on them. The air, while still chilly, had something of the smell of summer to it. Rose leaned against Gareth on the way home, glad to be out of the crowded pub.

Gareth laughed to himself.

'What?' Rose asked, looking up at him.

'I was just thinking that tonight might find its way into a couple of autobiographies in a decade or two.'

'It was an event, that's for sure.' Rose noticed that over in the far west, clouds were gathering, pastel grey in the moonlit sky. It was going to pour down later.

They went back to a calm household. The evening there had been uneventful. The children had gone to bed when they were told, no one had woken up, and yes, Flossie was fine. Rose and Gareth sent Janka away with twenty pounds, then—after Rose had checked that Flossie was still soundly asleep—they fell, slightly drink-dizzy and exhausted, into bed. For the first time in what seemed like months, she felt that she wanted her husband. She started stroking the small of his back and he turned to her and held her face in his hands. He kissed her then rolled her over onto her back, where he moved his mouth towards her breasts, first kissing, then sucking, then biting so that she yelped in surprise.

Not that she didn't like it, but he had never been that rough before. He moved his hand between her legs and started gently stroking her until she was wet. Then he put one finger deep inside her, then another. He moved his fingers around inside her then pushed in a third and a fourth. It was making her wild, and she moved herself up and down on him. He pushed further, up beyond his knuckles until he finally, gently but firmly, slipped his thumb and whole hand right up inside her so he was wearing her like a glove puppet. This was all new. Their ten years of lovemaking had been, up to now, characterised by a gentle intimacy. She came quickly and explosively, bright lights exploding in her head, as she collapsed on his hand. He rolled over on top of her, took her fingers and closed them around his penis, pumping it furiously up and down until, with a cry, he exploded over her breasts, rubbing his sticky semen in and around her nipples.

'I do love you, Rose,' he said, and, turning his body onto his side of the bed, he fell instantly asleep, tangled in a sweaty heap in and around her legs. She lay there on her back, her vulva burning and still contracting from time to time. She hadn't had an orgasm like that for years.

'We mustn't forget about all this,' she murmured into the silent night of their bedroom.

But, as the rain began to spot onto the dormer window, she couldn't help wondering: *Where did he get the idea for all of that?*

Twenty-Eight

The next morning Rose woke to the sound of Gareth singing one of Polly's old songs in the shower. She lay there in the square of thin morning sun that hit her from the Velux window above the bed, trying to remember what had happened the night before, wondering what it was that made her feel a little stomach-churned. Then she moved and felt the soreness between her legs, and shivered a little.

She felt like she had on her first day at school.

'Hi, my love.' Gareth walked in from the shower, rubbing his hair dry with one of the thick white towels that Rose always left beautifully folded on the slatted oak bathroom shelves. He bent to kiss her on the lips.

'I'm out of studio coffee,' he said. 'We steam through the beans down there, me and my new coffee-maker.'

'I'll put it on my shopping list,' Rose said.

'I do love you, you know.'

'You said that last night,' she told him.

'I said it because it's true.'

He pulled on his work clothes of old 501s and a loden green jumper that Rose had knitted for him when she was pregnant with Anna. Then, running his hands once through his hair, to make sure it dried in his favoured tousled style, he left.

*   *   *

Humming, Rose went to the farmers' market straight after taking the children to school. It was held in the next village, three miles away, so she had to drive there, but it felt so right to be using the market rather than Waitrose. She flung her special wicker basket onto the back seat when she got into the car. She had bought it specifically for these market visits. It was a little difficult to carry tucked under her arm with Flossie in the sling, but she couldn't imagine going there without it. It reminded her that she was a village woman now, and it made her feel complete.

The morning mist was fading away to reveal a blue sky as Rose turned the Galaxy into the car park of the village hall where the weekly market was held. Despite rain at night, the days seemed to have been getting warmer and warmer for the past week or so. She was pleased to see that this morning, despite a little muddiness, someone had decided to move the market to its summer pitch on the playing field at the back of the hall. As usual, it was bustling, full of parents she recognised from the school. She nodded and said hello to a few of the more friendly ones as she waltzed around, humming and packing her basket with artisan French cheeses, local jam and a kilo of bacon that she secretly felt was inferior to (and more expensive than) the supermarket's deli brand, but which she bought because it was produced by a farmer whose fields she could see from the top of her garden.

She closed her eyes and felt the sun on her face and imagined that she was in some sort of French street-market in the Dordogne.

'Coffee, mustn't forget coffee,' she sang to herself as she headed towards the stall that sold the home-roasted whole beans in the particular blend that Gareth liked.

Her spirits were soaring as, babbling on to Flossie back in the kitchen, she tidied the last jar into the correct cupboard. She got the coffee-grinder down from its shelf then processed enough beans to keep Gareth going till suppertime. Gareth. She shivered again, remembering the night before. It was incredible, she thought, how, in amongst all the stuff of day-to-day life, a good bit of sex could make all the difference to how one felt. Looking up from putting the bacon away in the fridge, she saw Polly wandering down the garden path towards the kitchen, clutching around her a black satin dressing gown that Rose had never seen before.

Rose took her basket and put it back in its place in the cool pantry, which smelled of the apples she had wrapped in newspaper and stored there in the autumn.

She walked out to the kitchen and saw Polly

248

sitting at the table, watching her.

'You look happy, Rose,' she said.

Rose smiled.

'Did you and Gareth have a nice time last night?'

'We loved it. How did it go after we left?'

'OK,' Polly said.

'What?'

'I dunno.' Polly stretched. 'I've got a touch of anti-climax about me.'

'You get back late?'

'I think so.'

'Anyone interested?'

'Oh, I dunno. They say they liked it, that they'll get back, but it's all blah blah blah.' She twisted a lock of hair around her finger, inspecting it for split ends. 'Where's Gareth?'

'He's in the studio.'

'It's great he's working again.'

'What do you mean?'

'Well, you know he hardly went into his studio when you were away.'

Rose looked over at Polly, who was still fiddling with her hair. A flush of something bled into the contentment she had felt all morning. What was this all about?

'It was probably the worry. About Flossie,' Rose said curtly.

'He was always around, here in the kitchen.' Polly shrugged. 'Is there any coffee going?'

'I'll put some on in a sec.' Rose remembered she had to get that coffee down to Gareth. He'd be gasping now, with his North American inability to work without caffeine. She pulled on her sawn-down wellington overshoes and padded across the back garden to Gareth's studio. On the way she called out for Manky. He hadn't been home in the night, not that this was unusual. But he hadn't dropped by to eat his breakfast, either. Rose hoped that no one else was feeding him. She knew that this was not what you were supposed to do, but that people often did it out of misplaced kindness.

She knocked softly on the studio door. The blinds were drawn, as they often were, against the morning sun.

'Yes?' he said from within.

She opened the door and gasped. Since she had last seen the studio, less than a week ago, every surface, every spare centimetre of wall space, had been covered with drawing after drawing of the river, of trees, of figures, moving—was it dancing?—in an abandoned, loose-limbed way. There was something about the attitude of the figures that looked familiar to her.

'You've been busy,' she said, looking at the frenzy of work around him.

'Yup,' he said, putting the paper he was working on face down on the floor. He turned to her. 'How can I help you, Rose?' She knew he didn't like anyone to see his work in progress, not even her.

'I brought your coffee,' she said.

'Oh yeah. Of course. Great. Thanks.' He looked at her as if waiting for her to go.

'OK, then, see you at lunchtime.'

'I'm going to work through. Sorry. But don't forget me for supper.'

'OK, then. See you then.' Rose backed out and clicked the door shut behind her.

The sharp sun made the lawn seem to tilt on the

way back to the house, and she felt herself shrinking, Alice-like. The house seemed to get farther away rather than nearer. Suddenly she stopped. Idiot! She had left Flossie in the kitchen, in her car seat, on her own with Polly.

An invisible hand pushing at her back, she tore up the lawn and threw herself into the kitchen, making Polly—who was still sitting at the kitchen table examining the cut beneath her eye in a small turtleshell hand mirror—jump. Flossie was still in her seat, over the other side of the room, fast asleep. Rose ran over to her.

'What's up?' Polly said, putting the mirror down.

Rose was almost weeping with gratitude. Polly hadn't even noticed Flossie. She was asleep, untouched, unscathed.

'How about that coffee, then?' she asked Polly.

Once she had a bit of caffeine inside her, Polly was far less gloomy about the outcome of the night before. It turned out that she had a whole string of meetings lined up in London and Bristol about possible recording contracts and other putative small-scale unplugged gigs.

'Did you see the skinny old guy with short grey hair and a nose ring?' she asked Rose.

'The tight jeans and the leather?'

'Yes. He's Steve Blow.'

'Not?'

'Yep, the bassist. He wants me to guest on a gig he's doing next month in Camden.'

'You going to do it?'

'Why not? The only way is up, really, isn't it, Rose? I thought I'd go up for a couple of days, show the old face around. You'll be cool with looking after the boys, won't you?'

'Of course.' More than cool, she thought. Delighted.

The garden door opened, and there was Gareth, silhouetted, resting his weight on one hip and running his charcoaled fingers through his hair, raking it back out of his face, waiting for his eyes to adjust to the dark in the kitchen.

'I ran out of milk,' he said.

'You need to rig up some sort of pipeline,' Polly laughed. 'Then you need never come up here again.'

'Oh, hi.' Gareth came in and kissed her on the cheek. 'You star, you.'

'Aw, shucks,' Polly deadpanned.

'Use the bottle from the front,' Rose said, as Gareth rummaged through the fridge.

'Oh yeah. Is there any chance anyone's going into Bath today? I've broken a string,' Polly said.

'Sorry,' Rose said, apologising for both of them. Gareth was working, and she couldn't go: there wouldn't be a chance of getting in and out before it was time to pick up the kids.

'Hang on there.' Gareth turned, with the milk bottle in hand. 'I guess I could take you. I need some more paper. I was planning to go tomorrow, but today'll do just as well.'

'If you're sure . . .' Polly said.

'No worries. We'll go after lunch. What's for lunch, Rose?'

Rose was certain he'd said he was going to skip lunch.

Twenty-Nine

Rose made a French onion soup, which they ate at the kitchen table, with bread and goat's cheese from the market. It was strange having everyone around—she had begun to get used to her solitary days. She felt a little as if she was sitting between two bush fires, as both Polly and Gareth talked about their work, about their plans.

Gareth outlined his ideas for his river series, and Polly listened, leaning in and nodding to show she could see what he was talking about. Rose began to drift away. She pressed her right breast to see if it had any of its telltale premenstrual ache. If so, this would be the first period she would have had since Flossie was born, and it would explain the way she was feeling. The morning had started well, she remembered, bright and sun-filled. But now she felt as if she had climbed into a box that was very slowly being closed around her.

Polly went up to the Annexe to get herself ready, and Rose cleared the lunch things as Gareth sat at the table drawing up a list of things to buy in Bath.

'Is there anything I can get you, while I'm there?' he asked.

'I can't find the nit comb,' Rose said. 'And Anna's been scratching again.'

'OK, it's on the list.' He stood up and fetched his car keys from the wooden cabinet by the back door. 'We shouldn't be back too late,' he said, kissing her on the head. Then he went out, bounding up the steps to the Annexe, like a dog let free in a field.

Rose saw Polly turn out of the Annexe door and smile at Gareth. She had on a loose white shift dress that dazzled in the sunlight, making her look a lot younger than her years, like a little virgin bride.

Once she had cleaned the kitchen and checked the garden again for the cat, Rose broke the habit of a lifetime and took an afternoon nap alongside Flossie. Perhaps she would feel better for a sleep, she thought. But she woke up with ten minutes to go before she had to leave to pick up the children, and found that now, not only did she still feel boxed in, but she also had a muzzy feeling in her head, as if someone had crept in while she was sleeping and replaced the sentient part of her brain with cotton wool.

So, when Simon called out to her when she was crossing the field, she didn't hear him at first. But he ran to catch up with her, and the first thing she felt was the friendly brush of Trooper against her leg.

'Hi.' Simon bounded up, more puppylike than his dog. 'Anyone in?'

'Sorry.' Rose turned and made her mouth smile. 'I was in a daze.'

'You're telling me.' He fell into step beside her. 'Do you fancy coming round for a cuppa after school?'

'Why not?' Rose said. There was no reason to go home, in any case, and she could get a lasagne out of the freezer for supper. She didn't feel all that much like cooking.

At the school, the children whooped when they heard the plan, in a way that made Rose wonder what was wrong with going back to their own house.

The field seemed to have filled with black crows in the short time it had taken to gather children, book bags and lunchboxes together and head back. The children ran at the birds, which rose like great black ghosts, filling the air with their caws. Anna, Yannis, Nico, Effie and Liam took the hint from the wheeling birds and flung their arms out, spinning around underneath them until they all fell down in a dizzy heap.

Simon's children were twins. Tiny for their seven years, they had their mother's pale Celtic skin and round dark eyes staring up from underneath Simon's blond thatch of hair. Rose always saw them as little elf children, light of foot and full of a mischief that was much more carefree than that of Polly's boys.

'Where's your weirdy aunty?' Effie jumped up and ran alongside Anna. Both girls were now pretending to fly, too involved in what they were doing to notice that they had got very close to Rose and Simon.

'She's not my aunty,' Anna said, swooping away from her.

'She's weird though, eh?' Liam zoomed in, more plane than bird.

'Fuck off!' Anna said to Liam.

'Anna!' Rose said.

'No, it's OK. He was winding her up. He deserved it.' Simon touched her arm.

Rose looked at Nico, who was smirking. He caught her eye and held it defiantly for a few seconds, then went over to join Yannis, who had taken himself away and was swiping at nettles with a muddy stick. She had no doubt whatsoever where Anna had got the idea from that using that sort of language was acceptable. Since the boys had arrived, Rose had discovered that she hated children swearing. In the past she had thought that explaining context and understanding was more important than banning naughty words, but now she realised she hated filth coming out of the mouth of her daughter, and she had to fight the urge to slap her.

She watched Anna whirling around, and realised that she had become more wiry. It must have been a growing spurt. She had a tendency to fill out, grow up and thin down, but Rose usually was aware of it going on. Now, she saw that her daughter's clothes no longer fitted her—there was a good two inches of wrist showing at her sleeves. But it wasn't just that. Anna had a sort of tension about her that Rose had never seen before. She tried to think back to how she had looked just a month ago, and the way she had contrasted with the harum scarum boys. Now, she realised with a thud, there was little to tell between the three of them. They all looked as if they had come out of the same mould. The discovery shocked Rose. She had always seen her family like a piece of algebra, neatly tucked inside its own brackets.

Then, as she tripped on a tree root, the revelation came to her that she, Anna, Flossie and Gareth simply hadn't had long enough on their own since the finishing of the house to make their family enclosure solid. It had been a ghost wall they had built, and now it seemed to have been breached.

She snatched in her breath and just managed to

stop herself from falling.

'Steady, Rose.' Simon caught her by the arm.

'I'm fine,' she said, looking up at him. 'I just tripped.'

'Let's stop at the shop and get a cake,' he declared, and all the children turned as one and cheered. The village shop sold a secret recipe chocolate cake that was famous throughout the local parishes.

*   *   *

Simon and Miranda's house was about half a mile beyond Rose and Gareth's, which meant that they were next door but one. The house was very different from the pristine newness and clean lines of The Lodge. A ramshackle building, it was full of clutter, with piles of letters and books on every surface. There had been little of the expensive renovation that Rose and Gareth had exerted on their home. The garden was, even at this time of the year, something of a jungle, with stuff that should have been cut back in the autumn throwing weedy sprays of new growth into the air.

Simon cleared a space on the table by swiping what looked like a week's worth of papers down onto a stool. He made tea for everyone, without thinking to ask if that was what they wanted, and served it up in stained mugs. Nico and Yannis, strangers to this English ritual, sipped their drinks and made faces, as if they had been handed moonshine.

They set about the cake with less hesitation. Almost fluid with chocolate, it was made by a woman who lived in the next village, who had baked for Konditor & Cook in her London days. All the children cleared their plates, then, with chocolate faces and fingers, they begged for more, which was forthcoming from Simon before Rose could intervene.

'So Tiger got sent home again,' Anna said.

'Please don't speak with your mouth full, Anna.' Rose touched her on the wrist.

'He punched Sammy in the face,' Yannis said.

'Not hard enough,' Nico muttered.

'It made his nose bleed, though,' Anna reassured Simon, who winced.

'What do you mean, not hard enough, Nico?' Rose asked.

'He was saying stuff about our mum,' Yannis said.

'Shut up, Yan,' Nico said.

'What sort of stuff?' Rose gently put herself between the boys.

'He said—'

'Shut UP!' Nico yelled at his little brother. 'It doesn't matter *what* he said. He shouldn't have *said* anything.'

'Well, whatever he said, he didn't deserve to be hit,' Rose said.

'He fucking did. And Tiger didn't deserve to be sent home. He was being a mate,' Nico grumbled.

'And Sammy *is* a shit, Rose,' Yannis said earnestly.

'Quite possibly so, I suppose.' Rose looked down at her hands. She just didn't have the energy to draw a conclusion from all this. Unusually, the ability to make it into a lesson for the children escaped her.

The room fell into an awkward silence, with just

258

the sound of Flossie breathing heavily as she tried to cram a squashed-up ball of chocolate cake into her mouth.

'Well then—who wants to watch a DVD?' Simon clapped his hands. 'We've got a top quality pirate of *Pirates of the Caribbean Four*. You can even see the people getting up to leave the cinema to pee!'

'Yess!' Liam and Effie stood on their chairs and punched the air. Evidently this dodgy sort of DVD was a top treat in their household. The Tiger business was forgotten as the children bundled through to what Simon called the screening room—in reality just a second living room with a laptop projector trained on a large white wall.

'Now then, me hearties,' Simon said as the children made themselves comfortable on the velvet beanbags that were scattered around the carpet. 'When you see signs of a getting up to pee-er, you've got to go *Harr Harrrrr*, OK? And there'll be Seaworthy Simon's special toffee popcorn for them as stay quiet except for that—all right, me hearties?'

'Aye aye, Cap'n.' The twins saluted. Even Nico couldn't help a smile. The DVD started and soon the children settled down into a concentrated silence.

Rose and Simon went back to the kitchen.

'That's bought us a bit of undisturbed time, thank God,' he said. 'Those boys are something of a handful.'

'Tell me about it,' Rose said. 'Do you mind if I feed Floss?'

'There's no better sight.' Simon got up to make more tea. Rose unbuttoned her shirt and latched

259

Flossie on, then looked around at the drifts of clutter, the half-finished projects by the twins. There was a miniature garden in a shallow dish, with moss pressed down into earth to make grass. There was a papier-mâché and poster-paint fort, with plastic soldiers guarding toilet-roll ramparts. Rose remembered how the Annexe had been full of similar efforts, and she sighed as she tried to remember the last time she and Anna had sat down to get on with something with no one else around, no bickering boys, no clamouring baby.

'Is everything all right, Rose?' Simon sat down facing her and put a mug of tea by her side.

'What do you mean?' She jumped out of her daydream.

'You just seem a little—disconnected today. It's not because of me and her, is it?'

'What? Oh, no. Like I said, that's all forgotten.'

'What's on your mind, then?'

'Oh, nothing. I'm probably just a bit tired out. Still not quite got into the swing again after the hospital stay. And the worry. You know, about Flossie.'

'Of course.' Simon drank his tea and looked closely at Rose. 'Everything's OK at home besides that, then? Between you and Gareth, I mean?'

'Of course,' Rose blurted out. 'We're rock solid.'

'Of course.' Simon looked down.

'Always have been. Nothing wrong there,' she said.

'Good. And how's things with Polly?'

'Fine.'

'Any sign of her moving on?'

'Possibly. After last night—but, it's her shout, you know?'

'Yes.'

'I can't make her do what she's not ready for.'

'Of course.' Simon let his gaze wander out of the window. Then, as if making a decision, he turned back to Rose and, reaching across the table, he grabbed her hand.

'Rose. You have got to get her out of your house. You are being set up for a disaster, Rose. She's dangerous.'

'You're just saying that because you got hurt.'

'Possibly, but I've got eyes in my head and I know what I see. I've had to listen to her talking about you two when you're not around to hear. Get her out, Rose.'

'I don't want to listen to this, Simon.'

He got up and went round to her side of the table. He sat next to her and held her by the shoulders. 'Look, Rose, I'll spare you the details, but I can't say it strongly enough. Get her out of your life. If there's an applecart, she'll upset it. She's already got mine toppled all over the place. I'm not just being selfish—although it'd do me no end of good if she weren't just down the road. This is because of you, my dear friend, and I don't want you upset as well. Regroup, get her out.'

Liam bounced through to the kitchen. 'Oy, Dad, where's our popcorn?'

Simon moved away slightly. 'Coming, Lee. Just doing it.'

'Get on with it, then, Dad,' Liam said, disappearing back into the screening room. 'We've got Greek boys waiting!'

'I don't want to hear any more,' Rose said, straightening her back and stroking Flossie's cheek.

'Just ask yourself, Rose. How does a baby take all those pills, eh?'

'It was an accident, Si.' But even saying it, Rose flushed.

'And Rose,' said Simon, getting up to haul out his heavy-based pan for popcorn. 'Where is Polly now?'

'Gareth took her to Bath,' Rose said. 'To get guitar strings.'

Simon looked at Rose for a moment, then turned to make his special toffee sauce for the popcorn for the children.

Thirty

Simon gave them all supper, a quick tuna pasta bake. Rose tried to call Gareth to tell him to come over and join them, and to bring Polly too, if she felt like it. But his mobile was off, and he wasn't picking up the landline.

It was gone eight when Rose and the children got back to The Lodge—later than she had planned, but it was a Friday, so there was no school the next day. The house was dark and the car wasn't in the driveway. Polly and Gareth were still out.

She went to the place around the side of the Annexe to switch the outside lights on so that they could see their way down to the house, cursing as she stepped in something that she thought might be a pile of animal mess.

When she flipped the switch, she saw the full horror of what she had felt underfoot.

'Look away, Anna!' she gasped.

But it was too late. Anna had seen Manky, or what remained of Manky, in the driveway just outside the Annexe, underneath where the Galaxy usually sat. Something had got hold of him and torn him to bits, so that at first Rose had thought Polly might have dropped a red-lined fur stole on her way to or from the car.

But no, the mangled mat of fur, blood and viscera was her faithful old cat. Whatever had killed him had left his head intact, so she could tell.

Anna screamed, turned away and vomited tuna, pasta, chocolate cake and popcorn into Rose's vegetable patch. Nico and Yannis squatted by the pitiful corpse, wrinkling their noses in disgust, but unable to look away.

'It must be the fox,' Rose said, helping Anna away towards the house, trying to find an explanation. 'Or a badger, perhaps. I've heard they can be quite vicious with cats.'

'Foxy wouldn't hurt Manky, though,' Anna sobbed.

'Come on, boys,' Rose said. She felt very cold, and very tired.

*   *   *

'I want to sleep with you tonight, Mum,' Anna said, as Rose towelled her dry after a troubled bath.

'Of course. You, me and Floss will all sleep together,' she said. She would be glad of it. She didn't want to let anything else precious out of her sight tonight.

263

She tucked Anna and Flossie into her bed, then went to switch off the boys' light. Nico was reading and didn't look up, but Yannis peered, pale and tiny, from the folds of his duvet.

'Rose,' Yannis said, his voice very small. 'Is there a cat heaven for Manky to go to?'

'I'm not sure, Yannis,' she said. She wasn't feeling very generous. 'I'm not so sure about anything,' she went on, and he put his fists to his eyes.

'Goodnight,' she said and turned the light out.

She went down to the kitchen, turned on all the lights and opened a bottle of wine. It was the second of the evening—she and Simon had shared one earlier.

Standing vigil in the middle of the room, she looked up at the Annexe, willing the car to return as she drained her glass and refilled it.

By the time she had reached the end of the bottle, there was still no sign of the Galaxy. She realised her legs were aching from standing still. She was also drunk, cold and weary. She took herself upstairs to her girls and, tucking herself under the duvet, lay down between them.

*   *   *

'Rose, Rose.' Gareth was shaking her awake. 'Hey, Rose.'

She had been dreaming of falling down a sort of Alice in Wonderland hole, where scenes of her life were playing out in layers: here was her mother, being stern about something Rose had done wrong; there was Christos, smiling with the sun in his eyes as he lay beside her; there was Manky,

264

running around after a toy Anna had made; there was the baby being taken away.

She landed with a bump in the bed. 'Where were you?' she whispered.

'I'm so sorry. We bumped into Dave Morgan, and he took me and Polly round to his studio.'

'Who?' Rose was bleary.

'You know, Dave the sound guy—with the studio in Lansdown? He'd heard about the gig. Looks like he and Polly are going to work something out. I tried calling. Did you get my answerphone message?'

Rose couldn't work out why she hadn't thought to check. But then she remembered. 'Manky . . .'

'Manky?'

'You'll have to clear him up, Gareth. I can't do it.'

'What do you mean?'

'He's dead.'

'What?'

'In the driveway. You probably didn't see. You probably parked the car over him.'

'God.'

'He was attacked, he's—' And Rose started shaking, until she couldn't hold back the tears any longer.

Moving Flossie to the other side of her, Gareth sat and held her close, stroking her hair, until she was done.

'He was part of me.'

'I know.'

'I don't know what to do, Gareth.'

'I'll deal with him, love. Don't worry about a thing.' He lifted Flossie and put her into Rose's arms. 'You take your girls and get some sleep now.

Don't worry about me. I'll bed down in the studio. And don't go out in the morning until I've sorted it all out, OK?'

'OK,' Rose said, allowing herself to be tucked in like a child. It took a while to stop shivering, to stop the pictures of her ripped-apart cat playing themselves on her eyelids, but in the end, she fell again into a deep, black sleep. This time there were no dreams. Nothing at all.

Thirty-One

Flossie woke Rose at dawn, grizzling and patting her on the face with tiny open hands. They were mini-slaps, sweaty and sticky. Rose had a panic for a second, unable to find her arms; each had gone completely numb from being tucked around a daughter. She retrieved her limbs and clenched and unclenched her fists until there was enough feeling in them for them to work. Screwing her eyes up against the sore weariness of such a deathly sleep, she picked up Flossie and tiptoed downstairs with her, careful not to disturb Anna, who had turned onto her side and was curled around her pillow, snoring softly.

The house was still and silent downstairs. It felt strangely empty. Then Rose remembered why that was. There was no cat accompanying her downstairs, no one rubbing against her legs wanting food, water and a morning scratch under the chin, or between the ears.

She put Flossie into her high chair and gave her a rusk. Then she scooped up Manky's water and food bowls. She tipped the unfinished portion of Iams into the bin, then thought again and threw both the bowls away as well, as a sort of gesture towards closure. Then she stood at the sink and looked up towards the Annexe, wondering if Gareth had cleared up the remains yet.

'Won't be a sec, Floss.' She slipped on her overshoes and climbed up the steps away from the house, breathing clouds of body warmth into the morning air that still held a little chill. It had rained in the night again: the leaves held more than dew drops, and there were little puddles in the indentations of the York stone treads. It was just that moment before the sun hits the earth, when the air still wears a thick cloak of the night.

Death is as much a beginning as an end, Rose thought, but this gave her little comfort as she searched out the corpse of her cat. Getting down on her knees, wincing as the gravel stuck into her legs, she looked beneath the dusty undercarriage of the Galaxy. Manky was no longer there. The gravel had been scooped away, and all that remained of him was a small dollop of what looked like squashed raspberry. It had probably been too dark for Gareth to have seen that.

She hoped he had saved something to bury, to give her and Anna the chance to give their grief a ritual upon which to hang itself. Two animal deaths in a fortnight. It wasn't looking good for the lesser species at The Lodge. She hoped that Gareth had concealed any remains within some sort of box. Not a bag: the idea of Manky's remains laid in the ground flopping around in a sack made her stomach heave.

Rose sat back up on her haunches and leaned

267

against the blue side of the car, fighting the urge to retch. The air filled suddenly with an alarming sound, like a school guillotine, chopping pile after pile of stacked-up sugar paper. She flinched and cowered, covering her ears. When she brought herself to look up, she saw the noise was coming from a pair of swans crossing the sky, slicing the air with their wings.

Then they were gone, leaving a resounding vacuum in their wake. She stood and brushed the nips of gravel from the indentations in her knees. She looked through the car window. Inside was an empty pizza box and—she counted carefully— eight empty Mexican beer bottles. Someone had been feasting last night.

She fixed her gaze up at the Annexe windows and listened very closely for any hint of life inside. But the silence, now the swans had passed, was impenetrable. All she could hear was a buzzing in her ears as if she had spent the night before with her head in some loudspeakers. It got louder as she climbed back down to the house, and she had to rub her ears with the flats of her hands to try to stop it. She looked in through the kitchen window at Flossie, who was very involved in smearing her half-masticated rusk around the tray of her high chair.

Good, Rose thought.

Taking a deep breath, she decided not to go back inside. Instead, she skirted round the side of the house, past the pizza oven and out across the sodden grass to Gareth's studio. We really must put some stepping stones down, with all this rain, she thought.

She stopped in the middle of the lawn, hearing

now her own blood pushing around her body like the swoosh of a foetal heart monitor. She breathed deeply, the freshness of the air catching her throat and burning her chest. What a smell the morning had. The sweet scent of a too-early honeysuckle just tinged the air. It could all have been so beautiful, if it weren't for the noise in her ears, the sting in her eyes.

'A beginning means a death,' she said out loud.

Gently, she tried the door handle to the studio. It was locked. But Gareth never locked doors. Hadn't he always laughed at her for finding that fact about him difficult? She bent and put her eye to the keyhole. The blinds were drawn—blackout blinds that let light neither in nor out. She held her breath and listened. She was sure she could hear his breathing, deep and slow. Or could she? And if she could, was there a counterpoint there? A lighter sound? Could she hear a duet?

She wished she could stop the noises that kept on coming up from within her so that she could listen more closely. But she seemed incapable of doing anything about it. The morning already felt as if she were trying to swim through a heavy syrup. Perhaps, she thought, I need to see a doctor.

She stood up and stretched her back out, turning to face the house. Just then, the fox streaked halfway across the lawn, his redness almost painful against the lush green of the wet grass. He stopped in the middle and stared right at her, eye to eye. She looked into him. It felt as if she were looking at herself.

It was impossible that he could have harmed Manky. She had read somewhere that foxes steered clear of cats; that they knew that in a fight they would come off a lot worse. And Foxy had other fish to fry. Or rabbits to tear to pieces. Why bother with a skin-and-bone moggy?

Again, she had to fight back the nausea that swooped up to her head from her belly. The fox slunk away into the bushes that stood between the house and the land.

'Don't go on the road,' she warned him.

Then she heard Flossie cry out from the kitchen. She sprinted back to the house, not noticing till it was too late that, as she rushed in, her overshoes covered the kitchen floor with muddy footprints.

She looked over at Flossie and let the relief seep in: her problem was just one of a completely disintegrated rusk. Rose handed her another from the packet. Then she quickly got out a mop and bucket to clean up the floor. If it had been Anna, Gareth or the boys coming in with their feet like that, she would have lost her rag. She let herself off the hook, however. She had been having a bit of a time of it recently.

'But if the kitchen gets in a mess, that's the end of everything,' she said to Flossie, who was watching her with a blank expression.

She squeezed out the mop, then, with a clean dishcloth, she tidied up Flossie's rusk-crusted tray. She reached down Anna's basket of onyx eggs then chose two smallish (but bigger than mouth-sized) specimens for Flossie to hold and roll around her tray. They were clean, smooth and perfect. She sat and watched as Flossie clasped first one, then the other, bringing each up in the air, tightly holding it in her hot little fingers and slamming it down on the tray. If she had laughed or smiled, Rose would have found the whole process a little less disconcerting. But Flossie performed each lift like a grim little automaton, like a bored person in a gym.

Rose turned her back on her baby and went to put the kettle on. She had turned it on twice already this morning, yet had so far failed to get any further towards making a cup of tea. This time, though, she forced herself to pour the water into the waiting mug, fish out the teabag, then top it up with milk. Task completed, she stood in front of the Aga, warming her legs and drinking her tea from her favourite big, clean mug. The reliability of the Aga's heat, the fact it was always there, comforted her. It was like a rock, standing firm in the middle of foaming rapids, and it helped her internal noise to subside, until there was little more than a gentle hum, like the silence at the end of an overture.

She let her eyes move up to the Annexe again. Was this morning going to go round in circles? she wondered. Would she have to go up and check under the car, then skirt round again to the studio to see if she could detect any signs of Gareth? If nothing happened, she felt she might have to.

But the moment was quickly broken. Polly appeared from the back of the Annexe. Rose watched as she carefully made her way down the stone steps to the front door, in her slippers and nightdress. It was very early for Polly to be about. She looked tired.

'Oh Rose, I'm so sorry.' Polly came into the kitchen and put her arms around Rose, holding her to her, taking her warmth and pulling it into herself.

Rose drew away and looked at her friend. She could feel a flush spread up her neck.

'What?' she whispered, afraid of the answer. 'What?'

'Our poor old cat. Our poor old Manky. So awful,' Polly said, taking Rose's face between her hands. 'You must feel so awful, Rose.'

'Yes.'

'Come, sit down. Can I get you anything?'

'I'm fine, thanks.' Rose showed Polly her cup of tea.

Polly started the Gareth-approved coffee-making ritual and Rose sat at the table as directed.

'Gareth was such a hero last night,' Polly was saying. 'He's put him in one of those wooden champagne boxes that Andy got him. We can have a proper burial. Put him to rest properly.'

'Your slippers are muddy,' Rose said.

'God, sorry.' Polly went over to the door where the shoe rack was and slipped them off her feet. 'Is it OK if I wear these?' She prodded Rose's Birkenstocks with her big toe.

'Go ahead,' Rose said. 'They'll probably be too big, though.'

'It's just the floor's a little chilly this morning.'

Rose got up and fetched the mop and bucket again, to wipe away Polly's footprints. How, she wondered, do you get muddy slippers coming down a flight of stone steps? She knew about those steps. She had laid them carefully, on her knees, in the eighth month of her pregnancy.

'Did you have a good time yesterday?' she asked Polly.

'Great!' Polly said. 'We tried to ring, but you weren't in.'

'I was at Simon's,' Rose said, watching Polly for any sign of a reaction. But she was a cool customer. Always had been.

'This friend of Gareth's, with the studio. He's a really interesting guy. He played me some of his stuff. He worked with PJ Harvey, you know.'

'Yes.'

'My Nemesis, of course. If she hadn't been there, I would have been her, they say.' Polly ran her fingers through her hair, tangling them in the knots.

Rose sat down opposite Polly and took the largest egg from Anna's basket. It was a heavy, yellow thing with amber-coloured swirls around it, too big to fit in one hand. She rolled it over and over underneath her palm.

'Same name and everything,' Polly said.

'Where's Gareth?' Rose asked.

'I suppose he's lying in.' Polly shrugged. They both paused and sipped their drinks. The only sounds were a rhythmic clunking from Flossie as she lifted and lowered the marble and onyx eggs onto her tray, and the roll and thud of the egg Rose was palming on the table.

'Do you think we could stop that?' Polly turned and took the eggs from Flossie, who just looked at her hands as if the things had disappeared from them. 'It gets on my nerves,' she said as she took the large egg from Rose, put everything back in the basket, and, stepping on a chair to reach, put it all back on the dresser shelf.

She looked over at Rose and sighed. 'What are we going to do with you, eh, Rose?'

Rose squirmed.

'I've got a great idea,' Polly said. 'Might cheer

273

you up.'

'It'll have to be pretty good,' Rose said.

'Oh, poor Rose,' Polly said. 'You can't think straight, can you? I mean, you're so cut up about Manky—' Rose wished she had used a different expression '—and I'll bet anything Anna's not going to take it well. She's so *sensitive*, isn't she? Well, here's the plan: we'll have the little ceremony later on in the morning. Gareth's cool about digging a hole, and he says he'll make a sort of wooden headstone. Then perhaps we could go to the river bathing-place? Have a picnic? Forget about it all for a bit?'

'That sounds . . .' Rose looked up to see Anna standing at the stairs, scratching her head, looking like a lost little ghost '. . . great. Really.'

'It's going to be a beautiful day, according to the weather forecast. Even hotter than yesterday. One of those freakish April days. Oh, hi, Anna. Porridge?'

Without waiting for an answer, Polly took herself over to the pantry to reach down the oats. Anna came and sat next to Rose, burying her face in her shoulder.

If only it were just us, Rose thought.

Thirty-Two

Later that morning, they held a solemn little service for Manky. Anna wept and threw handfuls of narcissi in the grave that Gareth had dug at the far corner of the orchard. Polly played the guitar and sang a plaintive version of 'Cool for Cats' with

274

customised, Manky-themed verses.

Rose could have done without that. It seemed a little too ironic for what was after all, for her, a small personal tragedy. But it seemed to cheer Anna, who sang, seriously, along to the chorus:

Cool for Cats.
Cool for Cats.

Gareth stood and leaned on his shovel, respectfully grim-faced, like a professional gravedigger. Even the boys were subdued. The sun was high, and as Polly had predicted, it was unseasonably hot. Rose felt a pool of sweat gather in the small of her back. This was crazy weather for April.

Gareth wasn't going to come to the picnic. He wanted to stay behind, he said, to fill in the grave and make the headstone structure. Rose had tried to change his mind, but he was adamant. She hadn't seen him for what felt like years, not properly. She wanted to spend the afternoon with him, even if it was in Polly's company. But clearly he felt differently.

'Can't we leave the river trip for another day?' she said to Polly as they filed back up to the house from the orchard where they had buried the cat.

'What, and miss this beautiful weather?' Polly said, turning her face to the sun. Her pallor almost glowed.

'Well, I—'

'Oh, Mum,' Anna said, slipping her hand into Rose's and looking up to her with damaged eyes. 'Please can we go?'

'How can you say no to that?' Polly said, tossing

her hair back. 'See you in about half an hour. Boys, get yourselves together, and be sure to help Rose.' Swinging her guitar over her shoulders, she broke away from the rest of them and headed up to the Annexe.

Gareth organised the boys and gathered up the rest of the swimming things while Rose attempted to piece a picnic together with what she could find in the kitchen.

'Are you OK, love?' he asked as he put the packed swimming bag on the kitchen table.

'I've been better.'

'It does seem kind of quiet here without him, doesn't it?'

Rose looked in all the biscuit tins. Apart from visiting the farmers' market, which, as far as getting supplies in was more ornamental than practical, she hadn't been shopping for ages, and everything was empty. She was losing her touch.

'It's no good,' she said to Gareth. 'I've got to go to the village shop.'

She went off with her basket tucked under her arm, taking Anna with her to help choose some treats, while Gareth got Flossie ready. On their way back, they were accosted by Polly, who stuck her head out of the Annexe window.

'Aren't you changed yet? Best sundresses, Rose! You and Anna! We're doing this thing in style.'

Rose looked up at her and squinted. 'I don't think—'

'Ten minutes to get them on, starting from now.' Polly slammed the window shut, allowing no argument.

'Come on, Mum, it'll be fun.' Anna dragged Rose towards The Lodge. They put the basket down on the kitchen table and went upstairs.

It was completely ridiculous, of course. Rose sat on her bed and looked at herself in her dressing-table mirror while Anna sped off to her room. In an impossibly short time to have wreaked such a change, Anna reappeared in her favourite—or rather, only—sundress. White and full-skirted, it was covered in a giant cherry print.

'Come on, Mum, you've got to make an effort here,' she said, rummaging in Rose's wardrobe.

She pulled out Rose's old sundress. It was a vintage thing she had picked up at a car-boot sale a couple of years back, before she had had Flossie. It was covered with shouty large rose blooms. She tried to remember what it was like, being the woman who had picked this extravagant thing out thinking that it was 'her'.

'I don't think I'll fit into that any more.'

'Course you will. Just try it on.'

To Rose's amazement she filled the dress as if it had been made after a series of long and painstaking fittings. Anna led her down the stairs to a small round of applause from Gareth. Flossie, who was in his arms, registered nothing.

'You look a million dollars,' Gareth said to Rose and Anna.

'Can you get Flossie in the car seat, Gareth?' Rose said, packing their new purchases into the picnic bag.

'Come on, you boys!' Gareth called.

Laden with picnic and swimming things, they trooped up to the car, just in time to see Polly come down the Annexe stairs holding up two chilled bottles of champagne.

'Oh, my,' Gareth said under his breath.

'Snap!' Polly said.

Polly was wearing a sundress very similar in style to Rose's. The big difference was, Rose noticed, that it was a size six, whereas her own was a generous fourteen. Like hers, Polly's was tight around the bodice and full-skirted. It, too, was covered in roses, but in amongst the blooms were—and this was a typically edgy move on Polly's part—tiny white skulls, with the thorny rose stems curling in and around their eye-sockets.

Polly did a twirl for them all, holding the champagne aloft, and Rose saw, and remembered, the tattoos on her shoulders. On the left she had a rose, on the right, a skull, perfectly matching her sundress. Rose had been there when she had them done in a shady parlour in Streatham, one coke-fuelled evening in their early twenties. The idea was that Rose was going to have the same designs on her own shoulders, that same night. But she had decided against it when she saw what the process entailed. She had very forcibly shown her change of heart, she remembered, by first passing out, then throwing up, right there on the tattoo-parlour floor.

'See how the dress matches the body,' Gareth said, appraising her with what looked like an artist's eye.

'I'll get a coolbag for the bottles,' Rose said. 'Gareth, will you strap Flossie in, please?'

*   *   *

After a final check that everyone had their seatbelts on, Rose started up the car. The children waved goodbye to Gareth, until they turned the

278

corner in the lane and he could no longer be seen.

The river bathing-place was a field with a few huts, on the riverbank, about four miles downstream from The Lodge, beyond the next village. It was a private club and, like most of their neighbours, Rose and Gareth were members. For such a landlocked area, it provided welcome hot-weather relief. Although it was usually closed at this time of year the club had sent notes home with the schoolchildren a couple of days earlier saying that, due to the unseasonably hot weather, they would open for the weekend. Rose had been pleased when she saw the note. She loved swimming in wild water. The sea was the only thing she missed from her childhood in Brighton. She had swum in it almost daily, whatever the weather.

She parked the car in a gravelled patch at the entrance to the field. Anna and the boys flung open the car doors and started off towards the river.

'Oy, you lot, come back here!' Polly yelled. 'Help Rose with the stuff.'

The three of them groaned, but came back and stood impatiently at the rear of the car, getting in Rose's way.

She opened the hatchback and handed out the picnic basket, coolbag, rug, swimming bags and rubber rings. She hooked Flossie's car seat into the crook of her arm, balancing it against her hip, and passed what she called the beach bag to Polly. Fully laden now, they clambered over a wooden stile and padded across the grass towards the river. The swimming spot was perfect here. There was a shallow paddling place for younger children, edged

279

by a weir that was more or less impossible to go over by accident. The weir was a great water slide for the older children and it plunged mossily into a cool, deep pool that provided more challenging swimming for the serious-minded. The river was quite wide on that side—about thirty metres—ideal for catching up on widths.

The ground was still a little soft underfoot from the night's rain. It gave slightly under their feet like not-quite-set fudge. But the sun was now so hot that the field was drying rapidly, filling the air with a steamy, earth smell that, had Rose grown up in the countryside, would have had a tinge of nostalgia to it.

'Ugh,' Polly said, as they stood looking for a space on the grass. 'People.'

The field was packed, it couldn't be denied. Little family groups covered it almost entirely, stretching their pale English legs out in the sun on brightly coloured Mexican blankets, tucking into their picnics. The sound of middle-class chatter filled the air, men talking about how it was like Tuscany today, mothers calling to their children.

'Leo!'

'Anastasia! Come here, darling!'

'Let's go over there.' The children groaned as Polly led them all to a place far away from the crowd, at the top of the sloping field, at least fifty metres from the river. Rose would never have chosen that spot. It was impractical, a choice made by someone who obviously didn't care if her children swam or drowned.

Rose was feeling the heat; her body was damp with it. She was sure her dress was showing her sweat. Her belly was hurting, too, that unmistakable, hot pain of a period about to start. She had once heard it described as a worm slowly eating its way out of you. That's exactly how it felt to her.

Polly put the blanket down, and the children started tugging on their swimming costumes. Yannis threw off his clothes completely to get changed, but Nico and Anna were a little more circumspect, hiding their bodies by twisting and turning with towels and, in Anna's case, shrouding her secrets with a long towelling robe that belonged to Rose.

'Can we go now, Mum?' Anna asked, hauling a rubber ring onto her shoulder.

'Yes, but don't go over the weir,' Rose said. 'And that applies to you two as well,' she said to Nico and Yannis.

'Do you think so?' Polly turned to her. 'They're strong swimmers.'

'There's a current,' Rose said, looking over at the strong flow of the river, which was still a little swollen by the recent rain. She didn't really care what the boys did, but she didn't want Anna to follow them.

'Ohhh . . .' Nico wailed, trying to attract Polly's attention. But she was too busy now, changing into her own little bathing suit, to pay him any notice.

'How about you play in the pool section until after lunch, then when Flossie's asleep, I'll take you over the other side,' Rose offered.

Nico, realising that he didn't have any alternative, shrugged his assent then turned and led the other two down the slope to the river.

'Aren't you going to get changed?' Polly said, sitting down in her perfect fifties bikini. Rose was quite shocked at how her body looked unclothed. She was covered with a light down of dark hair, and her bones and sinews were quite clearly visible, as if she were some sort of three-dimensional anatomical diagram. Apart from the tattoos, another history was etched on her skin: a network of thin scars that criss-crossed her thighs and arms. Rose noticed that while some were older and keloid, others, which must have been made more recently, were still scabbed. And there were what looked like small bruises, too. On her inner thigh, and above her breast. Finger dots.

What a mess, Rose thought. And a small part of the hard thing that seemed to have set into her over the past couple of days melted, when she thought of all that Polly had put herself through. And of course, she needed to show kindness, and so did Gareth. And that, surely, was all he was up to: trying to show Polly some kindness.

'I'm going to leave it a bit. I've got to feed Floss now,' Rose said, unbuckling her from the little car seat.

Polly rubbed sun cream into her papery legs, then stood up and stretched. Despite the skin and the bones and the scars, people looked over at her. Or perhaps it was because of them. But Rose knew that it was also her glamour that drew people's eyes. They wondered if she was some kind of star. And of course, she was—or had been—so they stared even more.

'I'll get the picnic out,' Polly said, rather uncharacteristically. She knelt at the basket in her little bikini and started to unwrap the food that Rose had prepared earlier that morning. Sitting there with her baby at her breast, Rose tried to think back and remember what she had made, but she couldn't. It was as if the morning had been another country. The only thing she could recollect was that this was the first time in years that she had prepared food without filling it with her love.

So there were egg sandwiches. Without cress. And a shop-bought pizza cut into slices. Cheese sandwiches and peanut butter sandwiches. Little sausages without sticks or rolls, bags of crisps and Mars Bars that Rose and Anna had bought from the local shop. And some little purple plastic bottles of something ersatz. Only the big bag of cherries had anything to do with what Rose was coming to see as her former self, and even these were unseasonal, something from which she usually recoiled.

'This looks great,' Polly said, as she popped the cork from one of the champagne bottles. 'Bottoms up!' She poured a large plastic cupful and handed it to Rose.

Balancing Flossie with one arm, Rose drank her champagne. She watched the children splash in the water. They were so far away, she could only make them out because of the pink rubber rings. It looked like they were playing a game that involved using whatever means you had to try to take possession of one of the two rings. The other children in the water seemed to be giving them a wide berth. Rose hoped this was just down to the wild splashing, and nothing to do with anything they were saying. Polly leaned over and refilled her cup.

Rose finished feeding Flossie and laid her down on the blanket, where she stayed still, looking up.

Rose tried to tell herself that she was fixated on the trees above, horse chestnuts in full candle. She lay down next to Flossie, and tried to join her in her reverie.

'Look, Flossie, flowers in the air. How weird is that?'

Polly sang under her breath, one of her own tunes.

There was no response from Floss. Rose looked up at the leaves and blossom as they swayed in the slight breeze, listening to the gentle rustle that mingled with Polly's humming and the chatter of the people in the field. She should take it easy. She hadn't eaten anything all day. She shouldn't drink any more alcohol until after the picnic.

'Here you go!' Once more, uninvited, Polly topped up Rose's cup. Despite the resolution she had made just a couple of minutes before, Rose knocked it back. She had gone beyond the point of worrying how they were all going to get home if she were drunk.

Polly stood up and, putting her fingers to her mouth, whistled loudly. The chatter stopped as every single head in the field turned to see who had produced the piercing sound.

'Fucking hell, Mum!' Nico shouted through the silence, right across the field, and Rose heard the quick intake of breath of offended parents, as they turned to glare at the little dark-skinned delinquent in the swimming trunks.

The three children stomped up the hill towards their picnic. Rose saw Anna forcing herself not to stare at Polly's strange body.

'I don't like any of these sandwiches,' Yannis said, looking at the forlorn little platefuls.

'You've got to eat something,' Rose said.

Polly thrust a bag of crisps and a Mars Bar at him. The others dutifully tucked in.

Rose didn't feel very hungry, but she forced down a sandwich to allow herself to drink another couple of cups of champagne, working her way well into the second bottle. Polly, as usual, ate nothing.

'Can we go back in now?' Anna said, her mouth reddened with cherry juices.

'You've got to let it digest first,' said Rose. She was having to be careful with her words. She could feel a bit of slurring coming on. 'Come and lie next to me.'

Relenting, Anna snuggled next to her. Flossie nuzzled into her other side, and, lying back, Rose allowed herself to drift off, the dappled sunlight warming her face.

She woke sticky with sweat. Anna and Flossie were both fast against her like little press studs. She was so, so hot. Prising them away, she half sat up—bleary, she thought, from the champagne and the heat. Polly and the boys were all fast asleep, lying apart, on their backs, palms up, so that if you looked at them from the air they might appear to be the victims of some catastrophic event. The boys, their faces red-stained with cherry juice, and the blood-red blooms on Polly's dress added a tang of verisimilitude to the scene.

The field was quieter now. There was a muffled quality to the sounds coming from the few children playing in the water, but most of the families were sitting with their lunches, their well-behaved offspring quietly munching on chicken drumsticks and home-made quiche, bare limbs splayed on the

285

grass. A few groups had brought barbecues. Small drifts of smoke rose from their encampments, bringing with them the smell of charred flesh. If you half-closed your eyes, as Rose did, it could have been a battleground after the event.

She was crazy with the heat. Taking care not to wake anyone, she got up, stretched and clenched and unclenched her hands, which had gone to sleep again underneath her girls. Woozy from the champagne, she rummaged in the beach bag and pulled out her swimming costume. Simple and black, with a tummy control panel, it had a plunging neckline that made the most of her cleavage. It was, she thought, just the right side of sensible. She leaned against a tree to pull it on, looping the straps up and under her sundress.

Liberated from her clothing, she pulled on her beach shoes. She hated going into wild water without them. Who knew what she might step on? Holding her arms folded across her middle, she rather self-consciously picked her way across the field towards the river. Then, gasping with the cold of it, she launched herself into the bathing pool and ducked her head under, wetting her hair. She stood up quickly, her heart beating, panting with the shock. Then, again she lowered herself in. The water was shallow here, no more than thigh deep, but despite the sun's best efforts, it still had a chill on it. Later in the summer, after a season's warming, this pool could hold the temperature of a bath. But it was the fast-flowing water beyond that was calling to Rose. She pulled herself onto the weir, then, lying on her stomach, she slid down the algae-green fronded slope into the brown swirl beneath.

If the pool had been cold, this deep water was ice. The shock of it made her head ache and she forgot where her toes and fingertips were. She tried to reach back to the weir, to grab on to one of the jellied strings of weed that clung to it, but it came away in her hand. Gasping, but not yet panicking, she tried to put her feet on the ground, but the river, fed by the recent rain, was too high for that. It carried her away from the bathing-place.

She first tried to swim against the current, in an attempt to get herself back to where she came from, then, when that proved to be impossible, she tried to fight her way towards the far bank, where at least she would have a chance of holding on to something. But the cold, and possibly the champagne, made her movements sluggish. Normally a strong swimmer, she just didn't seem able to make her strokes count for anything. Then she realised she was losing the battle. Her heart started pounding, the adrenaline sent a shock around her body and she seized up as if electrocuted. She breathed in, hugely, involuntarily. With the air, she took in a lungful of brown, dank riverwater. Coughing and waving her useless arms around, she felt herself going under, as if pulled by water babies down to their lair. A thick, bristling thing brushed her leg and she had a second to worry about pike and razor-sharp teeth before she was under and the light faded to a swirling greeny brown that crept into her limbs and over her forehead.

For a second she gave up and felt an enormous sense of relief that she could stop the struggle, but then two strong hands gripped her, one under her arm, the other under her chin, and hauled her backwards, up and out of the water, where, like a baby being born with its passages full of mucus, her reflexes stirred into an attempt at breath. Unable to reach air, she was dimly aware of more hands taking her, dragging her over mud and stone onto grass, where fists pumped her chest and pushed into her shoulder, fingers reached into her mouth and hooked themselves around her paralysed tongue. She retched, coughed and vomited water and cherries, spluttering waste into the earth at her cheek.

'Rose, Rose . . .'

She looked up and into the eyes of her doctor friend, Kate, who was leaning over her in a Speedo suit and swimming cap.

'Where's Flossie?' Rose tried to say, but no sound came out.

'She's back,' she heard Kate say. 'Rose, is Gareth here?'

The last thing Rose remembered before she passed out was Kate punching a number into a mobile phone that someone had thrust into her hand.

Thirty-Three

A low orange light bled into the room from the crack in the curtains. Rose creaked one eye open. She was in her nightdress, in her own bedroom. She tried to run over what had happened, but she couldn't get beyond the point where she fell asleep after the picnic. Her throat felt as if someone had got inside and rasped every surface with sandpaper.

'Floss?' she croaked.

'Ah, you're with us.' Kate bustled across from the armchair, carrying a copy of the *Guardian*.

What is Kate doing in my bedroom? was all Rose could think.

Kate laid a cool hand on Rose's forehead. She held her wrist between her other fingers, taking her pulse.

'Where's Flossie?' Rose said.

'Don't worry, she's downstairs with Gareth. You need to rest. You've had a bit of a time.'

Rose tried to sit up, but the person in her throat seemed to have also left a few hammers lying around in her skull cavity.

'What's going on with me?' she said, trying to hold her head still.

'Apart from anything else,' Kate said, 'you've got a nasty dose of the flu. Which, in itself, would have been enough to knock you out. There's a lot of it about, you know. I've organised jabs for everyone else. But you also nearly drowned through going swimming when reeling drunk.'

'Gosh,' Rose said.

'How much did you actually drink, Rose?' Kate asked.

'I don't know,' Rose said, shame washing over her.

'If Tim and I hadn't decided to go for a swim . . .' Tim was Kate's husband, a six-foot six-inch triathlon athlete orthopaedic surgeon. 'I wouldn't have been able to drag you out on my own.'

'I'm sorry,' Rose said.

'I'm just glad you're all right. I don't know what

got into you, going swimming in that state.'

'It was only a couple of glasses of champagne.'

'It looked like a lot more than that.'

'Oh, I don't really remember. It could have been. Polly's a classic glass topper-upper.'

'It was as if . . .' Kate frowned slightly, then she shook her head.

'What?'

'Well, it was as if you'd taken something else as well.'

'Don't be ridiculous,' Rose said.

'I've made sure it's too late for a urine sample, anyway. We don't want the drugs squad around again, do we?'

'I didn't take anything. I don't do that.'

'It could have just been the fact you were ill, I suppose,' Kate said. 'With the booze on top.'

'What time is it?'

'Six.'

'Jesus. Where did the day go?'

'Rose, no. It's six the following evening. So to speak.'

Rose gasped. 'Flossie!'

'She's fine. She's eating enough solids now, and Gareth has been giving her bottles of follow-on milk.'

'No.' Rose turned her head away.

'You've been awake from time to time, but you've not been exactly coherent. You've had one hell of a fever. I've been keeping an eye on you, though. I thought you'd appreciate not being carted off to hospital.'

'I'm sorry.'

'None of that, now.' Kate moved over and sat on the bed. Her hair was tied back, and her freckled face and clear green eyes made her look so clean that Rose felt like weeping, in her intoxicated, despoiled state.

'Rose, are you all right at the moment?'

'What do you mean?'

'It's just—I've been watching out for you a little bit since Flossie . . . well, since the hospital stay.'

'I've hardly seen you.'

'Ah, but remember, I'm the village GP. Not much escapes me.' Kate took Rose's hand and squeezed it, with so much care that Rose felt a swell in her throat, as if something was about to erupt. And then she couldn't help it: the tears came and she found herself wracked with heavy, cathartic sobbing. She buried her face into Kate's shoulder.

'It's OK,' Kate kept saying, holding her and rubbing her back, absorbing her tears into her clean, lavender-scented T-shirt.

'I'm sorry, Kate,' Rose said over and over. 'I'm so sorry.'

In the end, she fell back onto the pillows, her eyes swollen, her face streaked with snot and tears. Kate handed her a tissue, and she cleaned herself up.

Rose couldn't bring herself to look at her friend and doctor, in case her kindness should set her off again.

'I don't know, Kate. It's just that I need time, I suppose. Floss being like that was such a shock. And . . .'

'And?'

'And, well, I feel alone. So alone. I've never felt so lonely in all my life.' Rose's voice had shrunk to a tiny speck of its normal volume. 'I feel as if there's some sort of buffer, some sort of force-field between me and the real world. I mean, I'm here for the children, but that's about all it feels like at the moment. I feel so useless . . .' Self-pity set her off crying again.

'Have you spoken to Gareth about this?'

'No,' Rose said quickly. 'He's not to know.'

'But he could help, perhaps?'

'He's not to know!' Rose repeated.

'OK, OK.'

There was a knock at the door, and Polly slipped in with a cup of tea for Kate. Rose looked away.

'How is she?' Polly asked, her voice dripping with concern.

'Awake now,' Kate said. 'I think she'd like a cup of tea now as well. Would you, Rose?'

Rose nodded.

'I'll get Gareth to bring one up in a bit,' Polly said. 'I've got to get the children in the bath now.'

'Bring me Flossie,' Rose murmured.

'Sorry?' Polly, not catching what Rose said, leaned over towards her. Rose shot out a hand and grabbed Polly's skinny wrist.

'Bring me Flossie, now,' she said.

'Do you think that's OK, Kate?' Polly asked, pulling her arm away and rubbing her wrist. 'Is she all right to hold the baby?'

'It's what Rose wants. Flossie's had her jab so please bring her,' Kate said, stroking Rose's shoulder.

'Well, if you think so . . .' Polly went out and shut the door.

'I don't want her alone with my baby,' Rose said to Kate.

'Oh, Rose.' Kate folded her hands in her lap, and looked at her for a long while. The silence between them was broken by her bleeper. 'Shit.' She looked down at it. 'I've got to go.' She got up and pulled her bag towards her, taking out her prescription pad.

'I don't want drugs,' Rose said. 'I don't want them in my milk.'

'I think you'd better lay off feeding Floss for the next forty-eight hours, Rose. Just in case.'

'In case?'

'Just to be sure, in case there was anything going on. Besides alcohol.'

Rose turned her face to the pillow and felt the tears come yet again.

'Here's your prescription.' Kate laid the thin green slip of paper on Rose's bedside table and bent over to kiss her. 'Have my cuppa. I don't think Gareth can have heard that you're awake. I'll make sure I tell him on my way out, and I'll make sure that you get Flossie. Take care, and come and see me if you need any help.'

She went out, closing the door quietly behind her.

Rose lay there for a few moments, feeling blasted. Then she lifted a heavy arm over to the bedside table, groping until she found the prescription. She opened it and held it in front of her face until her eyes could focus. There, in Kate's energetic yet ordered script, were six words:

Get her out of your house.

Rose folded the piece of paper and tucked it into her bed-side drawer. As prescriptions went, this was a good one, but she thought she would keep it to herself for the time being.

Thirty-Four

Rose could feel someone in the room, so she forced her eyes open. She had drifted off again; the fatigue had stretched over her like a tight net until she couldn't think or breathe any more.

It was Gareth, hovering by the bed with a mug of tea.

'Hey, you,' he said, putting the tea on the bedside table and kneeling on the floor beside her. He stroked her hair out of her eyes.

'What happened, Gareth?' she asked.

'We're not sure, but we think you were going down with this flu, and then you drank all that champagne—and the cold of the water just set it all off suddenly. You were lucky you didn't drown.'

Rose looked away. Despite his gentle tone, he wasn't going to let her off lightly.

'But Kate says you're on the mend now. You've got to rest, Rose. At least three days in bed, she said.'

'I can't do that. What about the children?'

'We've got it all under control. Polly has very kindly stepped in, and is working wonders in the kitchen. You don't need to worry about a thing. She's really stepping up to the mark. Who'd have thought her so capable!'

Rose felt as if she were shrinking. The duvet and pillows threatened to engulf her.

'Now then, you've got to drink all of this tea. I put three sugars in it.'

Rose made a face. She hated sugar in her tea.

'You've got to. You haven't eaten anything for

294

nearly two days. Go on, now.' He held the mug up to her lips and she forced herself to take a sip.

'That's a girl. We'll bring your supper up shortly,' he said. 'But in the meantime, there's a couple of young ladies who want to see you.' He opened the bedroom door and there was Anna, holding Flossie in her arms.

'Careful with her!' Rose called out.

'Anna's a big girl now, Rose,' Gareth said, and went across to stand behind the girls. 'Go on, honey, don't be afraid.'

Anna edged towards Rose. She looked as if she didn't know where she was.

'I'm fine now,' Rose said. 'Come and sit by me.' She reached out for Flossie, and Anna gladly let her go into her arms. Flossie sat back onto Rose's lap and looked at her, saucer-eyed, as if she were wondering who she was. Then she lifted up her fat little hand and put her thumb in her mouth, silently curling up like a comma in the shelter of her mother's arms.

Anna smiled at this, and, the ice having been broken by her sister, she climbed over to the other side of the bed and tucked herself in next to Rose.

'Are you really better, Mum?' she asked.

'Getting there.' Rose put her arm around her.

She lay there with them for an hour, feeding on the proximity of their warm little bodies. She and Anna chatted about this and that, and Flossie nuzzled herself to sleep. Then Gareth knocked on the door and came in with a tray of food for Rose.

'Supper's ready, Anna. Get yourself downstairs now,' he said.

'Can't I eat upstairs here with Mum?' Anna pleaded.

'No, love. It's soup and it'll spill. You can come straight back up after if you like, though,' he said.

'Can I sleep with her tonight? Can I?'

'Of course you can,' Gareth said kindly.

'What about you?' Rose croaked.

'Don't worry about me. I'm fine to stay down in the studio. I've practically moved in there,' Gareth said. 'Now, let's get you too, madam.' He put the tray down on the bed beside Rose and took Flossie from her.

'I'll be back after my bath,' Anna said, as Gareth ushered her out of the room.

He shut the door and Rose was left alone. She looked at her supper. It was a thin, liquidized vegetable soup, made with no discernible oil, butter or stock, served with a small piece of wholemeal bread. An apple sat unadorned on the tray as a nod towards dessert. To drink, she had a glass of tapwater.

It was no doubt healthy and low fat, but if she were feeling hungry this meal wouldn't go anywhere near to satisfying her. She's slimming us all down, Rose thought. Like the witch in *Hansel and Gretel*, but in reverse.

She ate what she could of the food, then moved the tray to the floor and lay back down on the pillows. The day she had missed had nearly gone now, and the last dregs of the orange sunset stained the white curtains. The bedroom glowed, as if it were witnessing a fire. Rose let herself drift off to the imagined heat and crackle of the flames.

The next thing she knew, the bedroom door burst open and Anna rushed in, clutching a largish wicker-basket to her breast.

'Look, Mum! Look what Polly got me!'

296

She placed the basket on the bed as Rose groggily pulled herself up to sitting. Carefully, Anna lifted a small ball of fluff up to her face, closing her eyes and bending in to feel the softness against her cheeks.

'A kitten,' Rose whispered.

'I'm going to call him Monkey,' Anna said. 'He's a sort of replacement for Manky, but not quite, because, of course, nothing could replace Manky. But he's going to help us all come to terms with our loss.'

'Who told you that?' Rose said.

'Dad and Polly. Polly got him from the pub. Charlie the landlord's cat just had these kittens. Isn't he lovely?' Anna held the little creature out for Rose to take hold of.

'I'm not going to hold him just yet,' Rose said, looking down. 'Sorry.'

'Why not? Isn't he just the cutest?' Anna thrust the kitten forwards again.

'Sweet. We say sweet in this country.'

'Sweet. Isn't he sweet, then?' Anna held the kitten out so its body hung down and its front paws stuck up in the air as if he were reaching out for some invisible bars.

'Yes, he's very sweet. He really is.' Rose looked up at her daughter, whose smile was breaking, tipping over into tears of incomprehension. But she just couldn't find it in herself to do this, to take hold of this animal that Polly had foisted upon them. It all seemed so indecent; just two days after they had buried her old cat. It showed that Polly completely failed to understand her. Either that, or it was a malicious attempt to upset. Rose didn't know what was worse.

Trying not to show her tears, Anna put the kitten down on the bed.

'I thought you'd be pleased,' she sniffed.

'Well, he's a lovely kitten.' This was all Rose could muster in the way of trying to improve Anna's mood. 'And I'm sure you're going to be a great cat-owner for him.'

The kitten looked up at them with eyes that were like oversized sewn-on sequins, all surface glitter with nothing behind them. Rose shuddered.

'Isn't he just great?' Gareth came into the room, with Polly and the boys behind him. Rose saw Polly was carrying Flossie, who was dressed for bed.

'Give her to me,' she said, reaching out. Polly shrugged and, smiling, leaned over and handed Flossie to her. She stood back and wiped her fingers on the front of her apron, which was, of course, Rose's apron. With her hair neatly tied back, her face scrubbed of eye-liner and her simple black smock, Polly was quite clearly playing the part of domestic angel tonight.

'Isn't that great of Polly, Rose?' Gareth had taken hold of the kitten and held it up, smiling and wrinkling his nose at it as if it were a baby. Rose put her arms around her daughters. She felt as if her face were peeling away from her skull.

'Wonderful,' she said.

'Did you like your soup?' Polly sat on the side of the bed and placed her hand on top of Rose's, patting it ever so slightly.

'Great.' Rose made her mouth smile.

'I'm going to give you my full range of healthy, warming meals,' Polly said. 'We'll have you back on your feet in no time.'

Rose could see Nico behind his mother, pulling

a face and sticking his finger down his throat, pretending to be sick. So it seemed he could be on her side. Rose would remember that.

'Can we watch *South Park* now?' Yannis said. He had hung around the edge of the room, leaning against the wall. Rose wondered if she looked scary to him, with her hair loose and matted and her face unwashed. She could still smell the brown river on her skin, and wondered how long it was exactly since she had showered or bathed. She shifted in her bed and a stale biscuity smell wafted up from the bowels of the duvet.

'Go on, bog off, Square Eyes,' Gareth said, ruffling Yannis's hair. He had always loved to play with English idiom. One of his favourites was 'wanker', a word he had never encountered before he arrived at Goldsmiths. The boys charged off with a cheer, but Anna hung back, waiting for her promised night with Rose.

'Go and brush your teeth, Anna, then you can get in with Mum,' Gareth said.

After Anna had gone, Polly leaned towards Rose, her face full of concern, and put her hand on her forehead. 'And how are you now? It seems like a lot of things hit you all at once: the drinking, the drowning and the disease,' she said. 'Poor you.'

'Polly's had a great idea,' Gareth said, sitting on the other side of the bed. He took Rose's hand and squeezed it.

'It would be great for you to have a break, Rose,' Polly said. 'You're overwrought. You're dealing with all the fallout of Flossie's illness, and now you've made yourself sick as well. Our bodies and our minds are so bound up with one another. There is no such thing as an accident, you know.

299

Anyway, we both reckon you need a little holiday, so look!' She spread ten railway tickets onto the bed. 'Five tickets there, and five tickets back. We don't have to pay for Flossie, apparently. It's a total bargain.'

'What?' Rose peered at the tickets.

'I was going to save this for a surprise, but I think the time is right now. We're going to Brighton! You, me, Yann, Nico, Anna and Flossie. I got the tickets the other day when we were in Bath. They're really cheap if you get them in advance.'

'What? When?'

'At the weekend. We're going on Thursday morning, coming back on Monday.'

'But what about school? And Gareth?'

'It'll be fine. Gareth is old enough to look after himself, believe me.'

'Don't worry about me.' Gareth gave her hand another squeeze. 'All we've got to do is make sure you're better for the trip.'

'And as for school,' Polly went on, 'well, for fuck's sake, this will be *educational*. They'll be seeing the spots where their old mums used to hang out.'

Rose looked down at the tickets again, as if by reading the details on them she could make sense of all this.

'But why don't we drive?' she asked.

'I don't want you driving,' Gareth said. 'This is supposed to be a rest for you.'

'Anyway, the train's really cool,' Polly urged. 'It goes cross-country and we get to see the lovely English countryside on the way.'

Rose frowned. 'I'm not sure though if I *want* to

300

go back to Brighton,' she said.

'Course you do. It'll be like we never left.'

'But we *did* leave. Quite consciously on my part.'

'You know what, Rose? You can't keep hiding from your past all your life. You've got to face up to things or they get you in the end. Believe me, I know.'

'Look, if this is some kind of therapy you've dreamed up for me . . .' Rose's argument was hampered by the fact that she didn't want to talk about all of this in front of Gareth. There were things Polly knew that he didn't, and Rose was keen to keep it that way. He seemed oblivious to any undercurrents, though, and just continued to sit on the bed, holding her hand and smiling—a little, she thought, like a zombie, or a man possessed.

'Don't be absurd,' Polly went on. 'We're just going to go back to our home town, meet up with some friends, take the kids to the pier and the Sea Life Centre, show them the scenes of our youthful misdemeanours, visit a few old pubs then come back. What could be simpler? The boys are dying to see Brighton. And they've got Anna all excited too.'

'Where will we stay, though?'

'Lucy's got space, now two of hers have left home.'

'Lucy?'

'You know—Lucy Gee. Tall, skinny, red hair? At school with us? Got pregnant? Went off and got married really young? Well, Mr Lucy went off and left her after the fourth child. Bastard. But that was ages ago, and her kids are all quite old. She's got the house until the last one leaves, so she's got

301

loads of space. We've stayed in quite close contact, me and her.'

Rose was surprised. She wondered, given all that, why Polly hadn't thought of turning to this Lucy after Christos's death, rather than foisting herself onto her and Gareth.

She closed her eyes. Of *course* she remembered Lucy. She could hardly forget her. But she couldn't remember Polly being so intimate with her. And she herself certainly hadn't been close to Lucy. In fact, she couldn't remember having had any friends other than Polly. But, then again, her memory was unreliable: there were chunks of her life she had wiped out of her mind.

The last thing she wanted to do, however, was to go to Brighton. Everything there was too close to the bone for her. But she felt trapped. Stuck between the beaming faces of Gareth and Polly, she couldn't bring herself to refuse. The trip had been so firmly arranged that there was no chance of it not happening.

It was a strange sort of kindness, though, Rose thought, with Polly knowing what she knew.

'Now you lot have got to get out of the way.' Anna had come back in, clutching the kitten. She climbed on the bed. 'I want my mum back for the night.'

Gareth smiled and stroked Rose's hair. 'Goodnight, love; night, Floss, Anna.' He bent over and kissed the three of them. 'Come on, Poll, let's leave the girls to their sleep. And I'll take that little Monkey, Miss Anna.' He scooped up the kitten and moved towards the door, waiting for Polly.

'Good night, Rose.' Polly kissed her on the

302

cheek then got up and followed Gareth out of the bedroom. As she closed the door, Rose heard her laughing at something he had said.

Anna snuggled down next to her, lifting the duvet up over her shoulders.

'Poo, Mum. Stinky old bed.'

Thirty-Five

Rose couldn't sleep. she lay there in a bath of sweat, sandwiched between her hot little daughters, desperate for a pee. She lifted herself up and over Flossie, almost leapfrogging so as not to wake her up. It was only the third time she had stood up in two days, and she had to pause for a few seconds to allow the blood to return to her head. Her bare feet curled under the chill of the wooden floor, as she stood silently in the middle of the room, swaying, waiting for the black dots in front of her eyes to subside.

The house was completely silent. She looked at the clock on Gareth's side of the bed. It was three o'clock. So she must have slept, then. She took a pee, then got her kimono from its peg and, drawing it around herself, feeling a little lighter than she had a few days ago, she cracked open the bedroom door. The landing was pitch black. There was no moonlight to help her down the stairs. She didn't want to switch on the hallway light, so she went back to the bedroom and got the torch from her bedside table. She often used it when Flossie woke up, to avoid disturbing Gareth. It had become something of an irrelevance though, since he hadn't slept in the same bed as her for three nights now.

Swooping the torch across the stairs like a cat burglar, Rose tiptoed down towards the kitchen. The light made this most familiar of places seem strange and new to her, as if it had been rearranged. She flicked the switch on the torch and stood, again in the dark, straining to see if she could discern any movement up at the Annexe. All was silent; all was dark.

She moved across the stone floor that was even colder than the wood under her bare feet, and switched on the lights that ran underneath the wall cupboards. It was all the light she could bear just now. She turned and looked around her. The room *had* been changed. Under her tenure, it had been ordered, with clean surfaces and everything resting in its allotted space. Now it was like it had been when she had returned from the hospital the first time. The story of last night was present everywhere. There was a bowl of vegetable peelings on the counter that filled the air with the sweaty tang of stale onions. The sink was full of unwashed pots. The food processor stood in a queue for its turn to be cleaned, old soup crusted round its edges. The table hadn't even been cleared from what looked like a dessert of oranges. Two empty wine bottles stood at one end, with two drained glasses by their side. The chairs were spread around the kitchen; you could read exactly how each person had pushed themselves away from the table, and in what mood.

A sound like a distant newborn baby's cry made her jump. She looked where it was coming from and saw the kitten, tiny and fluffy, swaddled in a blanket in a shallow cardboard box. Rose had crocheted that blanket. It had been for Anna when she was a baby. Trying not to handle the kitten with the violence she was feeling—she didn't want another dead animal on her hands—Rose picked it up and shut it in the living room. If it shat everywhere, it wasn't going to be her problem. She picked up the blanket, shook it out and, folding it neatly, put it carefully over a chair back.

Rose's stomach turned and she realised she was hungry. She moved to the fridge and opened it. It was empty except for a chunk of cheap cheddar, two cooked sausages and a bowl of noodles: leftovers from meals she didn't know about. In the door stood a pot of natural yoghurt, half a tub of hummus, orange juice and milk and at the back a couple of old jars.

She stood at the fridge and absent-mindedly crammed the sausages into her mouth. She scooped the noodles up with her fingers. Then she took a couple of bites from the cheddar, holding it as if it were a piece of cake. Taking the hummus over to the breadbin, she finished it off with an almost whole loaf of staling bread, dunking it into the pot and scraping it around until there was nothing left. Leaving the empty pot on the crumb-strewn worktop, she went back to the fridge and applied herself to the yoghurt. She worked quickly now, washing the food down with alternating gulps of the milk and orange juice. Kneeling on the floor, she opened a drawer in the freezer and pulled out a tub of Ben & Jerry's Rocky Road ice cream. Squeezing it out of its frozen carapace, she bit into it as if it were a giant ice lolly, barely noticing that her teeth ached with the freeze.

Remembering from long ago how all of this went with her, she pulled out a bag of petits pois and tipped them into her mouth, sucking briefly to thaw them before she swallowed.

She shut the freezer door and stood up, her insides chilled. She needed something to warm herself up now, so she climbed up onto the stepping stool and reached for the biscuit tins. They were still as empty as they had been when she was packing for the picnic. Still on the stool, she found a jar of sultanas and crammed overflowing fistfuls of them into her mouth, then a packet of oatcakes, which she took over to the fridge and helped down with the last of the milk.

Feeling as if she had finally filled the emptiness, she lay on the stone floor and looked up at the ceiling. Her hands strayed to her belly and stroked its now firm, convex shape. For a second she felt nothing but a solipsistic bliss.

But then, as she knew it must, the other feeling crept in. A dull nausea, like the smell of new carpet, began to seep into her toes and move up her body. What on earth was she doing here, on the kitchen floor, with the remains of her disgusting frenzy all around her? It had been almost two decades since she had done this, but it had come back to her like a bad dream that you can never quite force out of your mind. She sat up and crawled to the pantry, where, finding the red plastic bowl she usually did the hand washing in, she stuck her finger down her throat and made herself vomit up every last trace of her session.

Spitting out the last dregs of bile, she felt redeemed, purged, and ready for action.

She stood and reached down her Barbour,

306

slipping her feet into her overshoes. Taking the torch, with sour breath and lumps of vomit still catching in the back of her throat, she tiptoed up the garden steps to the Annexe. She snapped the torch off and stood completely still, holding her breath, straining to hear any sign of Polly being awake. As seemed to be the way with this night, there was no sound. Good. Rose went to open the door at the bottom of the steps that led up to the living area. She didn't know what she wanted to do, nor indeed, fully why she was doing it, but she felt something needed to be proved. Something needed to be made definite.

A sting of shock jolted her. The door was locked. It had never, to Rose's knowledge, been locked before. Even when she, Gareth, Anna and Andy had slept up there, and she had been so paranoid about the silence of the countryside, it had never been locked. What was it with all the door-locking that was going on right now?

'Fuck,' she said to herself. 'Oh fuck.'

She rattled the door a little, thinking perhaps that in doing so she might accidentally wake Polly. If she did, and if Polly came down, Rose would find an explanation for being there at four in the morning, and everything would be all right. The sound of the loose handle on the other side of the door would surely bring her down. It seemed to ricochet around the walls of the darkness of the night. But there was nothing, no response. Except that somewhere, not too far away, a couple of hedgehogs screeched their frenzied, birdlike mating racket.

Rose hurried back up the steps and turned to look into the Annexe window, scanning it for movement. But it just returned her stare blankly, calling Flossie's gaze to her mind.

Her nerves were on the edge of her skin. Was she going to do this all over again? Was she once again going to creep around to the back of her house and spy in on Gareth's studio? Even as she asked herself these questions, she found herself tiptoeing over the black lawn to the hulking shape of the studio. Again, the door was locked, the blinds drawn. She pressed her ear right up against a windowpane. Nothing. It was as if everyone had left in the middle of the night. For a moment that thought had her by the throat—it might be true. Then she remembered seeing the car in the driveway up by the Annexe. They must still be here. Surely?

A chill got her, like an invisible shapeless thing that was swooping at her, behind her head. She had always been afraid of the dark, afraid of the silence of the countryside. Until the Hackney mugging, she had been happy, with a little caution, to walk about city streets at any hour of the night or day. But she had always held a deep fear of the dark of the rural night. This moment, here, right now in front of the studio, was the first time she had remembered this in all the time of their escape to the countryside. Once, long ago, before Anna was born, she and Gareth had stolen away to a small cottage in North Wales. The cottage backed onto a lake that, by day, was glorious, blue and lightly whipped by the mountain breeze. But at night, it took on, for Rose, a malevolent presence. One warm, still night, Gareth had picked up a rug and suggested they walked down to the lake. Rose, keen not to let her weediness be revealed to him at such an early stage in their relationship, had gone along with him. On the way down to the water, he sang 'Blanket on the Ground' in his best Country and Western accent.

But halfway there, even with him by her side, Rose had been seized by an overwhelming urge to run to the cover of a building. She had found her feet taking her away from him, and she was charging back up the path, slipping on the grass, stumbling on stubs of rocks, unable to stop until she was back inside the cottage with all the lights on.

And she was feeling that urge now, outside the studio, in her own back garden. She turned and, not worrying about making a noise, she fled back up towards the house. On the way, she tripped up onto the York stone terrace, barking her shin badly on the hard edge. Undeterred in her flight, she picked herself straight up and hurried towards the kitchen door.

She threw herself inside and slammed the door shut, leaning her back against it, panting, not knowing quite what had propelled her so quickly back up the garden. Looking around at the detritus that covered what had been her kitchen, she had no compulsion to tidy up. Instead she felt a sense of defeat that bordered on relief. Scanning the worktop, she saw Gareth's studio coffee tin. She went over and opened it, smelling its warm interior. It was empty, waiting for a refill.

Something hit her. It was a plan, of sorts, for proving something. Moving quickly now, Rose went to the fridge to get the sealed Tupperware box that Gareth kept his special blend of beans in. Americans are so particular about their coffee, she thought. She moved over to Gareth's beautiful old coffee-grinder and tipped the beans into the funnel contraption at the top, positioning the tin underneath to catch the grindings.

Then she slipped into the pantry and climbed on a stool to reach the secure, high cupboard where the home medications were kept. After Flossie had been born, Rose had suffered from piles so big that they had hit the bed before her backside when she sat down. Not wishing to disrupt her breastfeeding with drugs, Rose sought the help of a herbalist, who had provided her with some dark green tablets that had rocketed through her system so violently that she had only used one. She had left the others tucked away in the medicine cupboard.

Finding the bottle, Rose climbed down and skipped across the kitchen to the grinder. The tablets, she remembered, had a dark chlorophyll taste, but she thought that a smoker like Gareth, who liked his coffee strong and bitter, wouldn't be able to detect it. She tipped the whole bottle into the coffee-grinder funnel and turned the chrome handle, shaking the studio tin to mix the dark green powder of the pills with the brown coffee.

She put the tin up on the dresser shelf, hiding it behind Anna's egg basket. Some part of her needed to think about what she had done in the cold light of day before she unleashed it on her victims. She buried the empty pill bottle at the bottom of the recycling bin, and put the kettle on for a cup of tea. She felt good now. Good enough to have a go at the kitchen. She did her usual, methodical tidy, moving clockwise from the most northern part of the kitchen, clearing, wiping and sweeping; putting some things away and straightening others. She knelt down and wiped the kitchen floor with the dishcloth from the sink. Normally she wouldn't do that in a million years, but the devil had got her. To her it was a subversive act: the best sort, in fact—one that only she would know about.

It was only when she moved backwards to clean the bit she had knelt on that she noticed the blood. For a second she sat back on her haunches and looked at it, wondering where it came from. But then she felt the sting in her shin, and brought her leg forward to inspect it. It was covered in blood that was oozing from a split in the front about three inches long. She must have done that when she tripped on the terrace. She rinsed and wrung out the dishcloth and, deliciously, wiped away the blood from her leg. Squinting and contorting herself to get up close to her injury, she noticed with a sense of detachment that the split went right down to the bone. She must have really bashed herself.

Going back to the medicine cupboard, she reached down her well-stocked first aid box. She poured TCP on a gauze wipe and marvelled at the sting as she cleaned the wound. She found the paper stitches she had bought when Gareth had cut his hand during the build, and pulled the edges of the wound together, binding them tightly to each other. Then she covered the whole thing with a big plaster. She would have to wear trousers from now on. This wound, too, would be her secret. She should probably have stitches, she thought, but she wasn't going to the hospital. There was no way she was going to leave the house now, not when there was so much to watch out for.

She went back to the kitchen and got the mop and bucket. She had made quite a mess, she noticed now. There was blood everywhere, as if someone had taken a newly slaughtered corpse and dragged it around the place, smearing sanguine evidence on every surface.

It took a while to clear up. It was nearly dawn when Rose took herself up to her bed and climbed back in between her daughters. It was extraordinary to her that they had both slept while she had been so busy. She reached across Flossie to open her bedside drawer. Kate's prescription was there, tucked under a tube of hand cream.

She unfolded and studied it. Then she lay back, staring up at the ceiling with its exposed beams that Andy had said probably came from an ancient ship.

Here begins the endgame, she thought. I'll see the end of all of this.

Thirty-Six

For a second when Rose woke, she panicked as she realised she was alone in her bed. Her daughters were gone. She glanced over at her alarm clock and realised that it was gone ten. Of course they were up. Anna would be at school. She lay there in the grey light of the curtained room and tried to recall what had gone on in the night. Her throat was sore, and her shin throbbed. She turned onto her back and felt the creak of her spine and pelvis. It felt as if she had been beaten up.

There was the distant sound of music from the kitchen. Someone was downstairs. It wasn't Gareth, because he always had Radio 4 on when he was in the house. So who was with Flossie? A sudden panic propelled Rose out of bed, wafting her staleness around the room. She grabbed her dressing gown and fled for the stairs.

What she saw from the landing above the kitchen was beyond horrible. Polly was in the armchair, curled up with Flossie, reading a picture book. They both looked utterly contented, as if they had been born to end up just there. Rose gasped and brought her hand to her chest. Hearing the sound, Polly looked up, the smile she had shared with Flossie freezing on her face.

'You shouldn't be up,' she said to Rose.

'I'm fine,' Rose said.

'You don't look fine,' Polly said, not getting up.

Rose went down the stairs and crossed towards Polly, holding out her hands.

'Give me Flossie,' she said.

'I don't think that's necessary. She's fine, look, aren't you, Floss?'

Flossie turned and looked up at Rose, a smile breaking her face open. She looked more present than she had for weeks.

'Besides which, you should rest. You're still ill. And Rose—please don't come down and tidy up in the night. I'm on the case. I can cope, you know. People just do things differently from you some-times, you know?'

Rose stood there, her mouth opening and closing like that of a fish plucked from its bowl.

'Where's Gareth?' she finally brought herself to ask.

'Out.'

'Oh.' Rose moved to the kettle. 'I'll make myself a cup of tea, then I want Flossie back.'

'If you must, then. Sorry, Floss.' Polly stood up and put Flossie down on a play mat that Rose didn't recognise. 'Mummy wants you back.'

Seeing her opportunity, Rose picked her daughter up from the floor and fled back upstairs, her tea forgotten. She grabbed a couple of books from the nursery then went back to her room and climbed into bed. She cuddled Flossie up to her side and started to read to her. She could do this better than Polly.

For a while, the bright colours and bold shapes kept Flossie amused, and Rose started off enthusiastically, pointing out the ducks and going 'Quackity Quack Quack!' in a suitably raucous voice. But soon they both ran out of steam. Thankfully, Flossie started rooting and beating at Rose's breast, and she was only too pleased to let her back onto her nipple. She vaguely remembered Kate saying something about breastfeeding, but she chose not to recall it in detail. Besides, this was what they both needed so much. After a couple of days off, it took them both a while to fall into a rhythm, but it came back quickly enough.

Rose was just feeling the familiar tingle of milk letting down when the door opened sharply, shocking Flossie into a bite, which made Rose yelp, which in turn set Flossie off crying.

'See? I said you couldn't cope.' It was Polly, with a mug of tea. 'I brought this up for you. You seemed to forget to make it for yourself. Now let me have her.'

'Thank you for the tea, but Flossie and I are just

fine,' Rose said.

Polly put the tea on Rose's bedside table, her mouth set into a sharp little pout.

'Drink this then. You need to keep your fluids up.' She turned and left the room sharply, shutting the door behind her with a bang.

'Phew, Floss. I'm not quite sure what we're going to do about her,' Rose said. She sat there silently and sipped her tea. The curtains were still drawn and the warm pool of her bedside light made her feel cocooned there. This was her refuge, for herself and for her baby. When Anna got back from school she would go and scoop her up and bring her back to this safe place.

A feeling of contentment warmed her as she sipped her tea, and she began to relax and feel as if she could sleep a little more. Flossie had settled and her eyelids were heavy in that spinning-away way that babies have. So Rose snuggled down with her and drew the duvet back over them both, burrowing down into a primeval place of shelter.

Much later, she woke to a clean, medical smell. It took a while to register where she was: for the first few moments she thought she was back in the hospital. Then she remembered that she had gone to sleep with Flossie in her arms and now there was no one there. She turned over quickly, and only just managed to stop the scream that sprang to her lips.

Lying in bed next to her was not Flossie, but Anna. One of her eyes was covered with a large pad, strapped around her head with bandages. Rose's movement in the bed had woken her, and her good eye slowly opened.

'What happened, Anna?'

'Monkey scratched me. She was trying to catch my eyelashes. I thought it was funny, but then she got my eye.' Anna spoke in a small voice. 'It was my fault.' Her good eye welled with tears. 'Don't blame Monkey.'

'How bad is it?' Rose said. Why hadn't anyone told her? What time was it?

'They think it'll be OK. It's a bad scratch though, Mummy. It hurts lots.'

'Poor baby,' Rose said, pulling Anna to her.

'They gave me some drops, but it felt like a sharp knife. It's a lot better now, though, without the light.'

'Poor Anna.'

There was a gentle knock on the door, and Gareth came in, holding Flossie.

'Hi honey,' he said, sitting down on the bed next to Anna and reaching over for Rose's hand.

'What's happening, Gareth?' Rose sat up.

'It's not so bad, Rose. They say she'll see again.'

'Again?'

'It's too painful for her to open her eye at the moment, that's all. It's a deep corneal scratch. We've just got to keep it free of infection. They flushed it out at the hospital, and—'

'Hospital?'

'Yeah.'

'When did you go there?'

'This morning. It happened just before school so I dashed off with her to Bath. Didn't you know?'

'No. Polly didn't say.'

'She probably didn't want to worry you. It's not as serious as it looks or sounds.'

'Don't you think I've a right to know if my own

316

daughter has been taken to hospital?' Rose realised she had raised her voice, and was breathing heavily. Anna's one eye was registering some alarm, and she leaned towards Gareth, who had removed his hand from Rose and put it round his daughter instead.

'And you are demonstrating exactly why it was better not to tell you,' Gareth said. 'You're not well yourself. You need to take it easy.'

'I've had enough of this!' Rose said. She jumped out of bed and headed towards the shower. She owed it to her daughters and herself to put herself back in charge. 'I'm getting up. I'm making supper. I'm perfectly well.'

She stopped for a couple of seconds as those black dots swam again. She tried her hardest not to sway or stumble.

'Are you sure you're all right, Rose?' Gareth asked. He had turned himself on the bed so that he was resting his back against the headboard, his big, safe arm around Anna.

'I'm absolutely fine,' Rose said through teeth that were gritted partly through the effort it was taking to remain conscious, and partly to contain the anger she was feeling. If anyone asked her that question again today, she was going to—quite literally, probably—explode.

'Rose?' Gareth asked.

'What?' Don't say it again, she was thinking. She turned and saw him looking at her bloody and bandaged shin.

'Rose? What did you do to your leg?'

'Oh, oh, it's nothing. I—um—fell.'

'When? How?'

Rose rushed to the bathroom and locked the

door behind her, leaning against it until she regained her composure.

Thirty-Seven

Leaving Anna, Gareth and Flossie behind, Rose went downstairs. It was early afternoon, and the kitchen was deserted. Despite all the clutter, she couldn't see any signs of supper preparation. This she saw as an invitation to take on the task herself.

She went over to the hooks by the kitchen door and reached down her blue and pink floral apron. Looping it over her head, she pulled the waist straps really tight and tied them at the front. She reached in the front pocket, found the grip she kept there for cooking, and swept her hair up away from her face.

She leaned against the pantry door, surveying the empty shelves. Where had all the food gone? One lone onion lay in the vegetable basket; a forlorn, half-empty packet of conchiglie rested against it. All that remained of her jams, chutneys and pickles that once covered a whole wall in sturdy jars, was a small group on the shelf that was too high to reach without a ladder.

It was bizarre. Surely they couldn't have eaten the whole lot? Certainly not with the portions Polly had been serving up. It was as if Rose's influence had been expunged from the kitchen. First the form of it—her sense of order—had been dismantled, and now the contents had been cleared away. In a slight panic she rushed to her saucepan cupboard and knife block. With relief, she saw that her Le Creusets and Henckels were all still in order.

She picked up her favourite knife, a twelve-inch deeply curved blade with a riveted black handle. Holding it firmly in her right hand, she ran her left index fingertip along its razor-sharp edge and watched with satisfaction as the tiny cut first gaped slightly, then beaded up with blood.

There were some things that couldn't be removed.

Wiping the knife on the side of her apron, she replaced it in the block and went to the table with a pad and pen, to work out a list for the village shop. She needed to cobble something together for supper. She sat there gazing out of the window at the rain, which had bled beyond its nighttime reign and was now falling steadily in the afternoon, putting paid to predictions of an early, hot summer. Rose had difficulty finding focus enough to get her shopping list down onto paper. As she sat there, doodling, she became aware of a tapping sound coming from the living room. She crept across the kitchen floor and stood like a spy, leaning up against the half-open door so that she could see what was going on.

Polly sat on the sofa. She had kicked off Rose's sheepskin slippers and tucked her feet underneath her legs. Resting on the arm of the sofa was an empty coffee mug, and beside her was the box of Loukoum that Rose had brought back from Karpathos two summers ago and never opened. It was open now, though. And half-empty.

Polly was chewing and looking at something on a laptop perched on her knee. The laptop appeared to be Gareth's 17-inch MacBook Pro, which surprised Rose. He normally didn't allow it out of his studio.

Polly's hair framed her face and shoulders like a curtain of wild seaweed and she was dressed in a beautiful long black floral velvet dress that clung to her. She looked like a dissolute child.

'Hey there, G. How's her ladyship, then?' She spoke, helping herself to another lump of Loukoum, without taking her eyes from the screen.

Rose pushed the door. It slowly opened, creaking slightly, revealing her standing on the other side.

Polly looked up. 'Oh!' she said.

'I'm fine, thanks,' Rose said. 'Look—I'm up. Weren't expecting that, were you?'

'How's Anna?' Polly said, snapping the MacBook shut.

'Careful with that,' Rose said.

'Where's Gareth?'

'He's upstairs with her. She's going to be fine. Bloody cat.'

'It wasn't the cat's fault. She was holding it too close.'

'What are you doing?' Rose went over to the sofa and sat next to Polly, taking the laptop off her and opening it. Polly pulled it back onto her lap and, before the display wokc up, she performed a series of key strokes to close the windows down, so all Rose saw was a snip of flesh and a slice of leather before it dissolved into the plain, non-distracting blue screen wallpaper that Gareth liked to keep.

'I didn't think you knew how to turn a computer on, Polly.'

'I've been having lessons.'

'Ah.'

'I'm researching our Brighton trip. Seeing what's on. We'll probably get a chance to escape the kids on the Saturday. Lucy's got a babysitter.'

Brighton. Rose had completely forgotten.

'You know, I'm not sure about taking the kids out of school.'

'Oh, details, details.' Polly waved her hand in the air. 'We'll phone them in sick. Look,' she said, touching her finger-tip onto the screen, 'Fusion: House, R&B and indie night at the Honey Club. Remember the Honey Club, Rose, eh?'

'But what about Anna's eye?'

'You're not still trying to find excuses? It's only a scratch. It'll probably be better by the time we go. If the worst comes to the worst, there's always doctors and hospitals in Brighton, you know.'

Rose felt hot, as if she had a fever.

'What's that on your cheek?' Polly asked, reaching over and touching her with her thumb. 'Looks like blood.'

Rose rubbed her cheek. It must have been from the knife cut.

'You've got to be more careful, Rose. Anyway, Lucy's dying to see you and the girls. And us, of course. It must be, what—eighteen years?—since we were last back in Brighton.'

'Twenty years, three months and two days,' Rose said.

'Wow.' Polly looked straight at her, frowning slightly. If there was meaning, or empathy in her look, Rose chose to ignore it.

Rose stood up. Up until this point, going back to Brighton had been an abstract notion, but now it was suddenly, horribly, real. The question, though, was how was she going to deal with facing up to the place again, and everything that had—or hadn't—happened in all the time that had passed since she had left her hometown.

The door from the terrace burst open and Nico and Yannis tumbled into the room, a whirlwind of schoolbags, mud and ruddy, snotty faces.

'Scumbag!' Nico cuffed Yannis round the head.

'Fuck off!' Yannis yelled. 'Mum!' he pleaded.

'Shut the fuck up, will you, you two?' Polly said, returning her gaze to the computer screen. 'Some of us have work to do.'

Rose wanted badly to tell the boys to go back out and come in through the kitchen door, where there was a doormat and a place for dirty shoes. Anna would have done that without thinking. But Rose didn't feel able to interfere. Her sphere of influence seemed to be narrowing down to a dot.

'Did you have a good day?' she asked, as Nico sprawled on the other sofa and flicked the TV on with the remote. He still had his dusty shoes on. If her sofa hadn't been a practical slate grey, it would be looking pretty sad by now.

'Whatever,' he said, already distant and focused on the flash of colour and loud sound he had let loose into the living room.

'No school tomorrow,' Yannis said. 'Boiler's bust.'

'Or the next day,' Nico scowled from the sofa.

'Or possibly not till next week, Miss Richardson said,' Yannis reported to Rose.

'There you go,' Polly said, looking up at her. 'It's a sign.'

'How's Anna, Rose?' Yannis quietly took her

322

hand and searched out her eyes.

'She's OK. Bit sleepy. Why don't you run up and see how she is yourself?'

He slipped off. A few minutes later, Nico sighed heavily, dragged himself away from the screen, and got up to follow his brother.

Polly turned back to the laptop. She was busy Googling herself. Rose watched as she clicked on a link. There she was, at twenty, in that iconic photograph where, skeletal, she caressed the mike, practically fellating it. She looked dirty in the picture, in all senses of the word, but strangely beautiful, too.

'Look at me,' Polly giggled to herself.

Rose went over to the door, where the boys had dropped their bags. She picked them up and, leaving Polly, she went to put them on the kitchen coat hooks, fishing out their lunchboxes on the way. Then she returned to the table to resume her shopping list.

She chewed the pencil until her mouth was full of slivers of wood, sharp shards of paint, and charcoal-crunchy pieces of graphite. She was at the point of beginning to write when Gareth came downstairs with Flossie.

'I've let the boys stay up there with Anna for a bit,' he said. 'But she's pretty sleepy. They gave her some wild painkillers.'

'Good,' Rose said, without looking up.

'You've got to take it easy, Rose,' he said, sitting Flossie on her play mat.

'She can't sit up any more, Gareth. You have to prop her up with cushions,' Rose said. 'Or she'll topple over.'

Gareth went through to the living room to fetch

some cushions. He had been gone a few minutes when, as Rose had predicted, Flossie listed to the left then rolled onto her side, cracking her head on the stone floor.

'Gareth!' Rose shouted, rushing over to scoop up Flossie, who was silent, drawing her breath in with shock, the stunned calm before the storm of the wail she was summoning from somewhere deep inside.

Gareth came back into the kitchen, a couple of cushions in his hands.

'I said she'd fall over.' Rose looked at him. He tossed the cushions over to the mat.

'I've got to get back to work,' he said. 'Have you seen my coffee tin? I can't find it anywhere.'

With a small thrill, Rose remembered doctoring the coffee. With the bawling Flossie tucked under one arm, she reached up behind the basket of eggs and gave it to Gareth.

'What's it doing up there?' he asked.

'Just keeping things tidy,' she said, bouncing Flossie up and down to try to calm her.

'OK, then. Bye,' he said, clearly keen to get out of the house, away from the screaming child and the accusing wife.

'Supper at seven,' she said. Putting Flossie on her knee, Rose returned to her list. Gareth hurried out of the back door, clutching his coffee tin. If there was one thing Rose could say about her husband, it was that he was a creature of habit.

A little while later, Polly came through with the laptop.

'I think I'll go up to the Annexe, do a little writing,' she said, stretching herself like a cat in the sun.

'Careful with Gareth's laptop,' Rose said.

'I'll drop it back in the studio,' Polly said. 'I can't use these things for writing. A pen and paper's the technology for me.' She slipped towards the back door.

'Polly,' Rose said after taking a deep breath.

Polly stopped and turned to face her, one hand on the doorknob.

'Have you got any plans yet?' Rose said. 'About what you're going to do and all that?'

'I'm working on it.' Polly's smile vanished. 'Watch this space.' Then she moved quickly out of the door and down the path towards Gareth's studio.

Whatever, Rose thought. She couldn't say she hadn't tried to start the conversation.

She sat and looked around at the kitchen, as if scanning a room full of strangers. She had the odd feeling that it had nothing to do with her. For the first time she could look at the scrubbed wooden worktop without thinking she needed to give it another coat of oil. The wear and tear on it was merely evidence. The copper-bottomed saucepans suspended from the ceiling rack looked like dead things, the shining ladles, spoons and tongs that peopled the wall beside the Aga the instruments of their downfall.

She supposed, then, Polly and Gareth having disappeared to their work, that she was in charge of all the children again. But it didn't feel like it had before, when she had enjoyed her role as the mother of the house. Things had fallen apart. It was as if she had been brought in because of the *absence* of a mother. She had the feeling that there was a vacuum where the woman she had thought

325

she was once stood, and that she was now beside it, looking on.

In that case, she thought, who fills the space I occupy now? And this was a question she really couldn't bring herself to answer.

Thirty-Eight

Unable to leave Anna alone, Rose called the boys to send them up to the village shop with a list and two twenty-pound notes. She also gave Nico her wicker shopping basket. It made her smile to watch him bridling at the feminine nature of the thing. At first, he tried to sling it over his shoulder like an unyielding, awkwardly-shaped duffel bag. In the end, he had to carry it in the only way possible: tucked into the crook of his arm.

'Like Little Red Riding Hood,' Rose said, rubbing it in as he scowled back at her. Yannis giggled behind his hand.

'Shut up, runt,' Nico snarled. But Rose had to give him his due. He strode as manfully as he could up the steps to the lane. From the set of his shoulders, she saw that he was prepared to face any peer ridicule, with fisticuffs if necessary.

The sight melted her heart. What on earth was she doing, taking it out on these two bereft boys? And, to make her actions even more despicable, she couldn't—or rather wouldn't—put her finger on what exactly the 'it' was that she was taking out.

The kitchen had filled with the meaty stink of a full nappy, so Rose tucked Flossie under her arm and took her up to her bedroom, where Anna was dozing. Rose had partly forgotten about the eye, and the sight of her daughter all patched up took her breath away for a second.

At the sound of her, Anna stirred and opened her good eye, looking up at her.

'It hurts, Mum.'

Rose lay the stinking Flossie on the bed and picked up the packet of pills that Gareth had dangerously left on the side. She read that one to two were to be taken every two to three hours depending on the level of pain. She double-checked that these pills had Anna's name on—that they hadn't somehow been replaced by Polly's medication—and then she checked the time. It had been at least two hours since she had gone downstairs to take control, so it was safe to give Anna the pills. But where on earth had the two hours gone? And had she succeeded? Was she back on top?

She swept her hands across the front of her apron, brushing away some invisible crumbs, then sat down and passed the pills to Anna, along with some water that had sat in a glass beside her bed for days. It had developed little bubbles of oxygen that clung to the side of the glass, trying to escape the staleness within.

'Poo, Mum,' Anna said, wrinkling her nose.

Rose had forgotten about the nappy. She got up and lay Flossie on the changing mat on the floor, peeling off her leggings then the sodden, bulging nappy. It was a hell of a weight. Rose had always insisted on using real nappies, but when she was ill she supposed that Gareth and Polly had decided to switch to low-maintenance Pampers.

Gareth and Polly.

'Throw me the wipes,' she said to Anna, pointing to the plastic pack sitting on the floor down by Rose's side of the bed. It was beginning to look like a self-service sick room in her bedroom. There was an aura of unwashedness about it that even the vileness of Flossie's nappy couldn't overwhelm.

Rose carefully cleaned the light brown goo from around Flossie's bottom, breathing through her mouth. The smell of shit—even that of her own daughters—made her gag. She held up her baby's fat little legs, lifting her pelvis off the mat and reaching right round to where the nappy mess had crept up her back. Flossie lay there like a big doll, allowing herself to be moved back and forth. Where was her fight? Rose was sure she could remember epic battles to change Flossie before the hospital stay. She glanced over at Anna, who was lying back like a wraith against the pillows, like Munch's *Sick Child*.

Rose let her head fall to her chest and felt the throb of her shin. The malnourished fatigue of the recently recovered sank through her bones.

How damaged we all are, she thought.

'I think I'm feeling a little better,' Anna piped from her pillow. 'Can I get up now?'

'Let's leave it a bit,' Rose murmured. 'Come down for supper if you feel up to it.'

'I want to watch telly, though,' Anna said. 'With Nico and Yannis. I'm bored up here.'

Rose got up with the stinky nappy in one hand, a freshly powdered and changed Flossie grasped under her arm with the other, as if she were carrying a rolled-up blanket or a bunch of firewood.

328

'Well, if you can't amuse yourself up here, I suppose you'd better come down then,' she said, a little peevishly. 'But I can't help keep you occupied. I've got supper to make.'

'Thanks, Mum,' Anna said, a little taken aback by what, for Rose, amounted to an outburst. She cautiously got out of bed, tucking her feet into her slippers and shrugging her shoulders into her dressing gown. She did all of this with a level of self-consciousness, as if she were trying to convey to her mother what a good girl she was.

Relenting a little, Rose added, 'You can help me out by keeping your sister amused.'

'Of course,' Anna said, relieved to be allowed back into her mother's favour.

Anna had to take it carefully on the stairs. She found that, with one eye bandaged, she had difficulty judging distances. So Rose helped her down, holding her hand all the way.

When they got down to the kitchen, Rose saw the two little boys returning from the shop, marching down the steps to the front door, swinging the basket between them. They were bickering, but the looks on their faces suggested that, for once, there was a good-naturedness to it.

They burst into the kitchen, spilling their boyish energy through the door. Nico put the basket on the table, and fished the crumpled list from his jeans pocket.

'One kilo of organic lamb mince, check. Onions, garlic, rhubarb, spaghetti, tinned tomatoes— Napolina only—FRESH parmesan, semi-skimmed organic milk, pot of double cream, rolled oats and a dozen free-range organic eggs, check. But they didn't have Maldon Sea Salt,' he said, 'so I just got table. I hope that's OK.'

'Thank you, Nico. That's fine,' Rose said. Of course, table salt wasn't the same thing, but it was a practical decision on Nico's part, and she was grateful to him for having shown such initiative. She was sure that, put in the same position, Gareth, for example, would not have bought salt at all.

'Here's the change, Rose,' Yannis said, piling the coins on the table. 'Seven pounds and thirty-one pee.'

Rose looked at these boys and, where she had seen damage in herself and her own daughters, in them she saw only potential for goodness and growth. If there was something she needed to cling on to, it was here, in these two wiry bodies.

'Now, go and amuse yourselves, you lot, while I get supper on.'

As Rose set about making meatballs and tomato sauce, the kitchen began to look a little more familiar to her, as if it were that of the house she had grown up in and to which she had now returned. Of course, it was no longer possible to return to the house she had actually grown up in; it had long since been sold, when her parents turfed her out and left her to fend for herself. And look how well she had done out of that. She wished they were still alive, just so that she could show them all of this—the house, the garden, the life. Just so she could rub their noses in it.

She had reached the simulacrum of a truce with her mother and father in their last few years. It was the birth of Anna that had brought them round. A child that everyone actually wanted on this earth was finally acceptable to them. The sheer hypocrisy of it made her seethe, though. Even now, at such a remove, she felt a clenched fist draw back inside her as if on a spring, like a pinball striker. At any moment the handle might be let go, and all hell break loose.

She wondered if perhaps Brighton was such a bad idea that she would have to refuse to go. But what appeared outwardly to be a threat also contained strengths and opportunities. Yes, it could be a release, in that awful Pollyesque psycho-babble, *to face up to her demons*. But the practical side of her also saw that the trip would give her the ideal circumstances in which to talk to Polly, to begin to move her on and out of their lives. It could provide the starting-point for her own family—and even, if she played her cards right, the boys as well—to resume filling their beautiful house with the perfection that they had originally ordered for it.

She bent down and opened the Aga door to check on the meatballs that sat fatly bubbling in their red sauce. She tore a couple of leaves of basil and dipped them in olive oil, then scattered them on the top, closing the hot, heavy door behind them and lifting it onto its latch. She hadn't completely lost her touch, then. Encouraged, she made a large batch of flapjacks to fill the empty biscuit tins.

She poured herself a glass of good red wine and stood in the middle of the kitchen looking up at the Annexe, enjoying the blackcurranty vanilla scent as it travelled down her throat, filling her belly with warmth. It was a beautiful evening. The sun, which she knew was on its way down behind her, stained the eastern portion of the sky in her

331

sights a violent pink. Little puffs of white cloud were scattered carelessly around. A Tiepolo sky, she thought. She half-expected fat little *putti* to spill down and start careering in from the garden to help her serve the supper.

The more she thought about the Brighton trip in this new light, the more she felt a sense of calm lay an easy hand on the churning that had been creeping around her belly for the past couple of weeks.

The kitchen door opened. Gareth had come up early for supper. His hair was rumpled, his clothes a little stained and dirty. He stood on the threshold looking around him in such a wild way that it spiked Rose's calm.

'Hi, honey, did you have a good day?' she asked in her best Doris Day voice.

'Have we got a spare fuse?' he said.

'In the drawer by the washing machine,' she said, pointing to the pantry, as if he might not know where that would be.

'Fucking new coffee-machine. Pile of crap,' he said.

Shit, she thought.

'I go down there today, gasping for my coffee, and what happens? It farts and—*poof*—nothing. So I'm going to try the fuse first. If it's not that, I'm sending this piece of junk back to Amazon.'

'So you didn't get coffee then today?' she asked. 'How on earth did you manage?'

'Whisky.' He grinned.

'Wow.'

'Oh, for fuck's sake, don't start,' he said, walking straight past her and into the pantry, where she heard him rummaging and cursing into the drawer.

'Supper's nearly ready,' she said.

'I'll take these down after and do it,' he said, putting the fuse and a Phillips screwdriver on the dresser.

'Nico, can you run up and get your mum?' Rose called through into the living room. Instantly the boy, her new little star, jumped up and slipped on his trainers to leap up the steps to Polly's hideout.

She didn't know why he was trying to please her today, but she liked it.

'Anna and Yann, could you be the waiters?'

They came through happily and started to set the table. Rose was as pleased with them as if those little golden cherubs had actually spilled down from the sunset. Perhaps it was the wine, but she was full of hope for the evening.

Gareth sat and poured himself a large glass of red. She looked at the raddled shape of him and wondered how much whisky he had got through during the afternoon.

'How was work though, seriously?' she asked, as she trimmed a lettuce she had picked from her cold frame into the salad spinner.

'I'm getting a little sidetracked now,' he said, looking into his glass. 'It's the drawing. I've realised I haven't been looking enough recently— well, not for the last couple of years, what with the house and everything—so I'm turning to the world around me and I'm drawing and drawing. Giving the brain a rest, you know, and reconnecting the synapses.' He sighed and rubbed his eyes. 'I've gotten a bit rusty, truth be told,' he said.

'You'll soon be back on track.' She leaned over and touched his hand. 'I have every faith in you.'

'Do you?' he said, holding her gaze in his.

333

Something in his eyes chilled her. Her hand prickled.

' 'Scuse me, madam, sir.' Yannis was brandishing a place-mat, shaking it out ready to lay it in front of Gareth. Gareth broke away from Rose and leaned back.

'Why, zank you, seer.' Yannis's waiter had inexplicably become French. 'Can I get you anysing, m'syer?'

'Why, I'm just dandy, thank you,' Gareth said, trying to turn on the jolly.

'No leetle tastee beets?' Anna, who had been putting Flossie in her high chair, joined in with the insistence.

'Do you have any olives?'

'Ah'll just ask Chef. Do we have any oleevs, Chef?'

'Oui,' Rose said, moving to the fridge and finding a rather ancient jar of black olives sitting like biology lab specimens in some cloudy brine.

' 'Eer you are, sir.' Yannis plonked the jar down in front of Gareth.

'My, the presentation in this joint is tip-top,' Gareth said, rubbing his hands together.

'She's not coming.' Nico burst breathlessly into the kitchen. 'She says she's done in.'

'What on earth has she been doing?' Rose asked as she took the spaghetti off the Aga.

'She had to run the house while you were ill, Rose. Perhaps she just wants a night off,' Gareth said, unscrewing the jar of olives and fishing one out with his fork.

Rose hoped that her outraged gasp was hidden by the rush of water as she tipped the spaghetti through a big colander. With tight lips she moved around the kitchen getting the remainder of the meal onto the table, trying her very best not to slam the pots and pans as she did so.

'Can you grate some of this?' she asked, putting a lump of Parmesan, a Microplane and a small board down in front of Gareth.

She doled the meatballs out onto plates that she had piled with spaghetti. Yannis passed them around the table, placing them down in front of their recipients with a neat little bow.

'I mean,' Gareth went on, dusting the final crumbs of Parmesan off the Microplane and onto the board, 'it's not as if Polly's got your constitution.'

'What on earth is that supposed to mean?'

'I mean, look at you, Rose. Just yesterday you were in bed half-drowned with some sort of virus or something, and here you are up, about and back on top of everything. Not everyone's like you, you know.'

'Thank goodness,' Anna giggled.

'What?' Rose turned sharply towards her daughter.

'Joke?' Anna asked, splaying out her hands.

'That's not funny, Anna,' Gareth said.

'Sorry.' She looked down at her plate.

'It's OK, darling.' Rose leaned across and ruffled Anna's hair.

'You're a marvel, Rose, no one can deny it,' Gareth said, tucking into his plateful with knife and fork, avoiding her eyes. 'This is fantastic.'

'Nico, can I ask you to take this up for Polly after the meal?' Rose said, tucking a bowl over the spare portion she had plated up and putting it over by the counter. It wasn't that she was trying to prove the truth of Gareth's words about her domestic brilliance. It was something she wanted done anyway.

'She won't eat it, you know,' Nico said.

'Well, there's no harm in trying,' Rose said.

'I don't know anyone else like you,' Gareth said. 'These meatballs are delicious. More so than usual, even. What did you do?'

'It must be the special salt that Nico got,' Rose said, winking at the boy, her ally. Nico smiled like a cat that had been sitting on a table for hours trying to get someone to stroke him.

'Extraordinary,' Gareth went on, sloshing another glassful from the bottle. 'Shall I open another?' he said.

'Why not?' Rose shrugged, as he got up and went to the wine rack.

After a dessert of rhubarb crème brulée, which Gareth declared to be 'A Total Marvel', the children cleared up while Gareth and Rose sat at the table finishing the second bottle.

'This is nice,' Rose said. 'Bit like the old days.'

'What days were those?' Gareth said.

'Oh, you know,' Rose said vaguely, looking around. 'Can you handwash that?' she asked Nico, who was just about to put her special knife in the dishwasher. 'On second thoughts, I'll do it. It's fiendish sharp.'

When she turned back to Gareth, he was draining his glass and making ready to stand up.

'Best be off,' he said. 'Those drawings won't draw themselves.'

'Oh. OK. All right then. Don't forget that fuse,' Rose added as she got up to wash the knife.

'See you tomorrow, then,' he said, leaning over

336

and giving her a kiss on the cheek.

'What?' she asked.

'Anna'll want to sleep in with you tonight, and what with Floss and all of that, I think I'll somehow get a better night's sleep down in my studio again. I'm planning on working late anyway.'

'OK,' she said. 'OK.'

And, with the fuse and screwdriver in his hand, he turned his back and went out through the door, to spend yet another night in his studio, away from Rose.

Thirty-Nine

Despite Gareth's pronouncements about her constitution, Rose was feeling pretty worn out. The wine hadn't exactly woken her up, either, so as soon as she had the children bathed, read to and put to bed, she drew herself a long, deep bath, tipping in a generous helping of her best Aveda rose-scented bath oil and lighting a couple of candles. As she lay there in her bathroom, the steam drawing great clouds of scent around her piled-up hair, she thought about the look in Gareth's eyes earlier that evening. She had seen it some time before . . .

Then something began to come back to her. If she ever managed to be honest with herself, Rose would have to say she had a difficult relationship with the truth. Like most people, she supposed, there were many secrets she wouldn't tell anyone else about. There were some things some people knew and not others. Then there were a couple that only one or two people knew about and she would quite possibly kill to stop Gareth knowing. That Greek beach with Christos was one of those things. But there was only herself now to know about that. Killing wasn't a necessity for that secret to stay put.

She stirred in the bath, an involuntary movement brought on by the memory of Christos. The scent of roses was renewed, invigorated by her movement, and for a heady moment she was back there with him; that smile of his was tangible once more. But his eyes soon became Gareth's and she remembered when she had last seen that look. During the bad times, the times when Gareth was so low during the build, she had spent an evening with Andy. She had wanted to get out of the house, away from the smell of Gareth's mood, and had suggested a trip to the pub, knowing that Gareth wouldn't come and would therefore have to babysit.

So, after supper, she and Andy had walked slowly down the lane into the blue-black night. It was the beginning of spring and the hedgerow was full of bud. Rose could pick out the light dots of primrose flowers on the dark verge, like a set of gentle lights guiding them along their way. There was a gorgeous lemony scent in the air, of freshness and new beginnings. In her pregnant, height-ened olfactory state, Rose thought she could detect the smell of a newborn's head.

They sat in the pub, and Andy drank three pints of local bitter while she nursed one half of Guinness. Rose was an unapologetic consumer of stout during pregnancy since her first midwife in

London, a venerable lady originally from Jamaica, had told her to view it as medicinal on account of its iron content.

As Andy drank, he talked. He told her, for the first time, about his early romantic yet disastrous marriage to a French woman and how he had never been able to love anyone since. He told her about how, after Françoise and he had separated, he had tried to return to the States to be closer to his parents, but then they died, and Bush got elected, and the War on Terror started. Fed up with it all, he had returned to the foothold he had retained in France, with the dual aim of being closer to his brother and living a simpler life. And as Andy talked, Rose began, once again, to wonder if she hadn't landed the wrong brother.

Lying in her rose-scented bath, she squirmed at the memory. But then, she had to remind herself that, to put it bluntly, Gareth was being an absolute pig at that time. So she could probably absolve herself from anything that went on, that night in the pub and afterwards.

It had seemed to her, as she sat there with her velvety half-pint, that Andy had all the great qualities of Gareth without any of the downsides. Like his brother, he was tall and handsome, to be sure. He was creative and intelligent. He had an enormous sense of play. Yet he lacked what Rose was beginning to see as the dark side, the distaff to all this sun. Gareth must have been handed that particular gift by his birth mother—the one who had killed herself before he had a chance to meet her. It was, no doubt, all her fault.

And then, Andy was reaching across the barley-twist pub table and taking her by her hand.

'You see, I don't think I can bear to see my brother hurting you like this,' he said. He was explaining why he was thinking of leaving. 'I want to kill him when he is like this. The fact it affects you so much makes it even more acute. I'm scared, Rose,' he went on, his voice lowered. 'I'm scared of what I will do to him if he goes on like this.'

Rose drew her hand away and put it to her mouth. But he reached across and clasped it back.

'Come outside with me,' he said, and she found herself getting up and following him across the crowded pub room, waving goodbye to the few people she knew in there, as if to say out loud that there was nothing going on, that she wasn't just about to carry out a secret assignation with this man she was with, while she was carrying the second child of his adoptive brother.

But she was. She knew it. He was offering her closeness, comfort. And, since declaring her pregnancy to Gareth, she had had scant little of that. Carried along by the butterflies in her stomach, she followed Andy across the stile that led up the allotments at the top of the hill on the other side of the village to The Lodge.

And there, on the cool hard ground, in amongst the prosaic late-winter kale, leeks and parsnips, she and Andy fucked like hungry dogs. It ended with her collapsed in a muddy heap on top of him, sobbing partly with relief, partly with the shock of what they had just done. There, in amongst the brassicas, they had built an atom bomb. The fallout potential was stultifying.

'I'd better leave this place,' Andy said, as they crept back to the house.

'Don't.' She turned to him. 'Don't leave. I don't

340

know what I'd do without you.'

'I need to think,' he said.

They went back to the Annexe, tiptoeing in so as not to wake Gareth or Anna. It was one o'clock in the morning, long after they would have returned from the pub if they hadn't taken their little diversion. Rose stripped off in the shower room and washed herself thoroughly, removing all traces of Andy. She bundled up her muddied clothes and put them at the bottom of the laundry basket.

She slipped into bed beside Gareth, who turned over onto his side, facing away from her. She remembered lying there on her back, going over all the possibilities in her mind until she decided on the only viable path, given all of their circumstances. Gareth must never find out. Andy must stay as if nothing had ever happened. They would finish the house, she would have the baby, and everything would be all right again. She had practised this sort of strategy before, and it would work, she knew it.

And was it all all right? Rose thought as she got out of the bath and dried herself off. Was everything all all right again? She reached down for the body cream she had bought with the bath oil and began to rub it into her legs and belly—which, she noticed, hung a little loose after her illness.

In the morning after the allotment episode, she had looked Gareth in the eyes. That was where she had seen that look before, the one he had given her during supper today. After breakfast, she had got Andy on his own and spelled out her plan to him. His decision had been different from hers. He wanted to leave, to go back to his house in Brittany, to give them all some space, as he put it. It took a lot of persuasion, but Rose knew she had a little leverage with him, and in the end he stayed with them as long as he would have, had he and Rose not connected like that. They continued to be confidants for each other, but they never allowed themselves to touch again. It was conceivable, Rose thought, that she found this easier than him. If she were honest with herself—and she had proved to herself that this was sometimes something of a difficulty—sex with Andy had been like lifting the weight off a pressure cooker. She had let go of a lot of steam, and it had, ultimately and not without some inconvenience, made her feel a whole lot better.

After he left, Andy did write to her a couple of times. He knew it was safe, because he knew it was Rose's job to stroll up the garden to get the post out of the US-style mailbox that he had installed with Gareth. But she had simply put the letters unopened in the fire. She wanted done with all that.

Rose pulled on a clean nightdress, a lovely Victorian thing of thick soft cotton. She tiptoed through into her bedroom and crept gently in between her daughters. She lay, looking through the skylight at the pinpoints of stars above her.

All this, she thought. It has been worth holding onto. Hasn't it?

Forty

The gunshot wrenched Rose from a troubling dream of textures first dull and heavy then shiny and bright. The scream that followed, Anna's scream, coming from downstairs, made her realise that she was alone in the bed. Again, someone had come in and taken her daughters from her.

Ice shot through her body. She leaped from the bed and pelted down the stairs. She wasn't yet fully awake when she took in the scene. Polly stood alone in the kitchen, her back to Rose, looking out of the open garden door. She had her arms clasped around her body in the way silly children do when pretending to snog. Because of her posture, her stained peach silk nightdress gaped at the back, revealing her tattoos, her keyboard of rib bones and the semibreves of her spinal column. The morning chill had given her goosebumps, each one pricked out by the pale morning sun that filtered in from the front of the room.

It was a strange, still scene. It stopped Rose in her tracks on the stairs, one foot in the air, not quite landed on the step in front of her, her mouth wide open, as if she were some comic cartoon. Everything was held for a beat, while she took in what else was going on. She followed the trajectory of Polly's gaze and saw Gareth, outside on the back lawn, kneeling over a small, heaped body. By his side lay a gun. *A gun*?

Then she heard Anna's second scream, 'Nooo!!!' as she pelted across the grass towards her father.

Rose gasped and put her fist to her mouth. 'Flossie!'

She launched herself across the room at Polly, swinging her round by pulling her long, dark straggle of hair.

'What has he done?' she demanded, forcing her face up towards that of her friend. Polly had an almost beatific air of calm to her, a hovering sense of victory.

'What has he done? Where's Flossie?' Rose grasped her by the shoulders, feeling the little handfuls of loose skin and muscle. The way Polly's flesh moved along her bones suddenly reminded Rose of the brace of partridges she had plucked and drawn the previous autumn. If Polly were a bird, how easy it would be to remove her feathers, taking them and snapping them out of her gooseflesh, throwing them up in the air, watching them float down like a fistful of fifty-pound notes.

Holding Rose's gaze, Polly gently slipped herself out of her grasp. 'She's sleeping. Behind you,' she said, and lifted her hand to point.

Rose wheeled round and there, flat out on the lambskin, was Flossie, arms thrown to either side. Rose held her breath and watched her daughter's chest. Sure enough, there was a little shift up and down in the front of Flossie's clean, fresh Babygro. As if to confirm her sentience, she gave a little sigh that was almost a gasp, shook her arms a little, then relaxed back down into the depth of her sleep.

Rose turned wildly to the scene on the back lawn. Brushing past Polly, she burst out of the back door. The sharp gravel outside dug into her bare feet, but she scarcely noticed. Gareth now had

344

something in one hand while he hacked at it with the other, with what looked like a knife. Anna was on his back, not playing like she had all those centuries ago back at the castle, but trying to stop him. There was a lot of red, made even more vivid by the sparkling emerald of the lawn.

Rose hurried onto the dewy grass, feeling the damp chill work up the edge of her nightdress, sticking it to her stinging shin. It seemed to take an age—like the dream running that takes a person nowhere—but eventually she closed in on them.

She turned to look back at the house. Polly had resumed her position in the doorway. Rose almost stumbled when she saw the look on her face. It was beyond pleasure. It was a sort of proprietorial ecstasy.

'There!' she heard Gareth cry as he stood up holding the fox's brush aloft in his bloody hand. Anna had slipped off his back and had turned away, holding her head in her hands, sobbing. The look on his face was almost the same as Polly's, and, to Rose's horror, she realised it was directed past her, towards the back door. It was as if she were invisible, had dissolved to nothing. Suddenly the grass began to tilt and melt into the sky and Rose fell, gratefully offering her face to the wet lawn. The last thing she remembered was Anna leaning over her and looking into her eyes with her one good eye.

'Mum?' she asked. Then she dissolved into a haze.

*   *   *

Rose woke up, yet again back in her bed. Anna,

345

Nico and Yannis were sitting cross-legged on the floor, playing a game of cards. Flossie was in her car seat beside Anna, impassively watching the other children, a small dribble of drool on her chin.

'Hi,' Rose said.

'Mum!' Anna crawled over to the bed, surveying her with her one eye. 'Everyone's ill. We don't know what to do.'

'What?'

'Mum and Gareth,' Nico said. 'They've got some kind of stomach thing. They've both gone to bed.'

Rose swallowed. Her mouth felt dry, her throat rasped.

'Dad's in my bed, and Polly's in the Annexe. They've both been really, really sick, and we don't know what to do.' Anna got up and sat on the bed, hoisting Flossie up on to her knee. 'We've been waiting here for ages for you to come round.'

The coffee, Rose thought. There's the proof, then. Then she remembered that look between Polly and Gareth and she shuddered. She supposed she should feel flattered that the children should choose to wait at her bedside for some sort of guidance.

'What was Dad doing out there?' she asked Anna.

'He shot Foxy, Mum.'

'Shot him? Why?'

'Polly saw Foxy trying to catch Monkey. Monkey scrambled up a tree.'

'Where did he get the gun from?'

'Mum bought it,' Nico said. Rose noticed that his voice had got deeper. Was he changing already? Was all this turning him, far too early, into a man? He climbed on to the bed too, on the other side of Rose.

'I thought you knew?' Anna said. 'Weren't you there when she gave it to him?' Her voice had risen to a higher pitch.

'No,' Rose croaked, pulling herself up to sitting.

Anna got her a pillow and propped it up behind her. 'He'd been talking at supper—oh yes, that was when you were poorly—about how he and Andy used to go hunting back in America. He made it all sound so much fun.'

'He said how they'd track a deer for a whole day through the woods, about how to recognise the marks it made as it passed through,' Nico added.

'So Mama said, "Why don't you hunt here?"' Yannis chipped in, clearing up the cards.

'And Dad said that you'd never let him,' Anna added.

'So the next day, Mum walked up to the hunting shop—you know, the one by the garage on the big road?' Nico said. 'And came back with a shotgun.'

'She looked like the girl in *Pirates of the Caribbean*,' Yannis giggled, slipping himself in between Rose and Nico.

'He never said anything about the killing bit, though,' Anna said. 'Why didn't he say anything about the blood?'

Rose closed her eyes.

'I need to talk to your father,' she said, getting once more out of bed.

'He's really sick,' Anna said.

'I don't care,' Rose said. 'I need to talk to him. Now. You lot stay here.'

Ignoring the fact that the children were in the

room, she pulled off her nightdress and put on a tracksuit. She pinned up her hair to make herself feel more in command, then she went out of the room and downstairs to Anna's bedroom, leaving a bed full of concerned children.

She pushed open the door to Anna's room and saw that the curtains were drawn against the morning light. Gareth lay in a huddle in the bed, a bucket at his side. A strong smell of stale fart filled the room. Rose smiled.

'Hello,' she said. He stirred, groaned and rolled over onto his back.

'I don't know what happened,' he said, throwing his arm over his eyes. 'One minute I was standing there, the next I had to run for the bathroom. I feel like I've shat my bowels out.'

You weakling! Rose thought. You pipsqueak! She wondered if Andy would be so sensitive to an overdose of laxatives and emetics, or whether he would just put it all behind him, so to speak, and get up and on with what he had been doing. She suspected the latter, very strongly.

'Then, I don't know, Polly got taken the same way, at almost the same time. I think it's some sort of virus or something, Rose.'

'Or something you ate, the two of you?'

'It's far worse than that,' he groaned. 'I feel like I'm dying.'

'Food poisoning can be fatal,' she said. 'Botulism, for example.'

'Rose?' He took his hand away from his eyes and looked at her. She hadn't moved fully into the room. Instead, she stood there, looking down at him, enjoying the fact that she was so much higher up than him, and that he was so helpless. 'What is

348

it? Is it about the gun?'

'*Is* it about the gun?' she asked.

'I have always wanted a gun, ever since we moved out here. It's what a man does in the countryside.'

Rose snorted.

'I was saving the kitten, Rose. God knows, that damn fox had already killed Manky.'

'That's what you think?'

'Why are you being like this, Rose?'

Once again, Rose felt that lump rise up from her belly and lodge itself in her throat. Perhaps it was that clenched fist, trying to find a new way out. Whatever it was, it made it impossible for her to talk. Instead, she just lifted her hands and dragged them backwards through her hair, pulling her face back like a drumskin, so that for an instant she looked like a girl in a horror movie.

'That's the problem with you, Rose,' Gareth said, making a leap in his mind that she could find no path for, 'You've never seen me as a man. You just see me as a pathway, a means to an end.'

'That's not true,' she said in a low voice.

'It is. And when I finally turn round and say to you that I am a man, you can't take it. You can't take it so much that you just literally black it out, you collapse and fall.'

'So to be a man you have to have a gun, do you?' she asked, the lump working its way up to the air, like a baby forcing its head out between its mother's thighs.

'That's not what I mean, and you know it,' Gareth groaned.

'You have to show your daughter you can kill an innocent animal, do you?'

'It wasn't innocent. It was a murderer.'

'*You're* the murderer,' she thundered. 'You are murdering everything around here.'

'Gah!' Gareth clenched his fists and groaned in frustration. The sinews in his neck stood out like threads. He pulled Anna's princess duvet up over his head and threw his body over to face the wall, sending a flatulent gust of duvet air over towards Rose.

Disgusted, she turned on her heel and stormed downstairs to her kitchen. Automatically, she put her apron on and poured herself a large glass of wine. All this, and before lunch, too. She saw that her hands were shaking.

She needed a cigarette. She went to Gareth's jacket, which was flung over the back of one of the wooden chairs, knowing she would find a packet of Drum and some Rizlas there. As she delved in his pockets, her fingers landed on the large, cool shape of the studio key. She fished it out and looked at it. It was a beautiful thing. She and Gareth had gone to inordinate lengths to source original door fixtures for the house, and although he had made her believe that locks were some sort of bourgeois hang-up on her part, he had been most concerned that the keys were both functional and original. This one was black and curved, as big as the palm of Rose's hand. She imagined that, a couple of centuries before, some hulk of a village blacksmith had hewn this on his anvil, all sparks and smoke and metallic clangs. And here it was now, in her eyes some sort of fetish, the final piece in the jigsaw that would uncover the truth for her.

Pocketing the key in the front of her apron, she took the tobacco out to the side terrace, along with her glass of wine. She took three Rizlas and stuck them together as if she were making a spliff, then rolled herself an enormous cigarette, twisting one end and putting a Rizla packet roach in the other. Using the Zippo that Gareth always rather scummily kept tucked in the tobacco packet, she lit up and leaned back on the stone bench. The sun hadn't yet struck the side of the building, and she felt the cold sting into her back and buttocks.

What with passing out earlier, the previous couple of days spent in bed and her wine breakfast, the tobacco sent her soaring with the kind of rush only occasional smokers know about. For a moment she seemed to leave her body and hover above herself, looking down at the nearly middle-aged housewife that she was presenting to the world, with her hastily pinned-up hair—how long was it, she thought, since she had visited the hairdresser?—lack of make-up and wobbling mounds of cellulite that were scarcely covered by her drab, functional clothes.

She closed her eyes against this vision and tried to think straight. Now she had her proof, she had decided that she was going to perform a guerrilla raid on the studio. But how? She had a window of about twenty-four hours, she reckoned, before Gareth and Polly were back up on their feet. But, with school shut, she couldn't do it while the children were around, so she would probably have to wait until nighttime, which was cutting it a bit fine for the Brighton trip—which, she realised, with a sickening, excited thud, was tomorrow. And then what? What would she find in there? How would she react? That sort of thinking was getting too much like forward planning for her. No, she

351

would wait and see. There was no hurry, beyond the twenty-four-hour stricture. She reckoned she had all the time in the world.

'Mum?'

Rose opened her eyes. Anna had crept right up beside her.

'Why are you smoking, Mum?' Anna had never seen Rose smoke. She had, in fact, extracted a solemn promise from her that she never would. In the light of Gareth's fairly heavy habit, Anna had said she wanted one parent to live until she was grown up, at least.

'Sorry, darling. I'm just not feeling very well. This is sort of like medicine.'

'A cigarette?'

'Yes. Like . . .' and here Rose's brain was racing '. . . like, if you drank a whole bottle of Calpol, you'd have to be made sick.'

'Like Effie did last year?'

'Yes. But if you only have a little bit, if you're ill, then Calpol can be very good for you. It can make you better.'

'And a cigarette is like Calpol?'

'In a way, yes.'

Anna thought this over. 'I hope I never get the illness that needs cigarettes to make it better,' she said finally.

'I hope you don't, either,' Rose said. 'I really hope you don't.'

Rose drained her glass and stood up, grinding the big cigarette under her bare foot onto the stone floor. The mixture of hot and cold was really quite pleasing. Nico and Yannis hung about the back door, looking at what was going on. Nico, bless him, had Flossie balanced on his hip.

352

'How are they?' Yannis asked.

'How are who?' Rose asked, pushing her hair behind her ear.

'Mum and Gareth. Are they going to be all right?' His eyes were round with concern, as he came forward, step by step, afraid of what her answer might be.

'I imagine so,' Rose said.

'They're—they're not going to die, are they?'

'Don't be gay,' Nico snapped.

'Nico!' Rose said. 'Don't say that. I won't have you using the word gay as an insult.'

Nico turned patiently to his brother. 'Don't be a spastic, then. Course they won't die. Will they, Rose?' He looked back to her.

Rose couldn't allow this to go on. She couldn't bear to see those two little faces, part of her gang, looking up at her with so much concern.

'Of *course* not. Of course they're not going to die. It's just a bug—like I had. And look at me— I'm not dead, am I? They'll be fine in a day or two.'

'We can still go to Brighton, can't we?' Nico asked.

'Of course. I'm sure your mum will be fine by tomorrow.'

'Promise?'

Rose knew that the laxative would have worked its way through her body by then. Whether the constitutionally weak and fragile Polly would be able to come with them, she didn't know. But Rose had decided that she'd take the children away come what may. She needed to put some distance between herself and Gareth and the house for a while, to get her head straight.

The children were all standing looking up at her now. Their innocence and worry, the way they looked to her, was too much for her to bear.

'Let's go to the park,' she declared, swaying slightly, breaking the spell.

'Yesss!' Yannis cried. 'Can I bring the football?'

'Bring what you like,' Rose said. 'We'll stay out the whole day if we want to!'

Forty-One

'Hello, stranger.' Simon looked up and smiled as Rose walked over towards the park bench.

She smiled back and sat down next to him.

'Not meaning to be insulting or anything,' he said, 'but you look like death warmed up.'

'No offence taken,' Rose said. 'That's exactly how I feel.'

'I hear you've not been so well. I tried to call by a couple of times, but I kept on seeing *her* in the kitchen and, well, I just couldn't bring myself to go in.' He thrust his hands deep in his jacket pocket and stretched his legs out. 'But I just want you to know the thought was there. I heard about your shenanigans at the weir, too.'

'Bloody village gossip,' Rose said. 'It was all connected, I think, the nearly drowning and the illness. An unhappy collision.'

'There seem to be quite a lot of them around with you lot at the moment,' Simon said.

'I'd like to say that was too cryptic for me to understand but, sadly, I can't.' Rose turned and gave him a wan smile. Simon took his hand out of his pocket and grasped hers.

'Rose, I don't think I can stand by much longer and watch this happen to you.'

'It's none of your business, Simon. Please.'

'I know. But—I hate seeing you like this.'

'Yannis. Get down off there!' Rose yelled at the little boy, who had somehow shimmied himself right to the top of the A frame that supported the swings, and was now turning somersaults around the bar at the top.

Simon joined his two hands together, enclosing hers in his own. He tried to search her eyes out, but she refused to allow him access. Instead she scanned the playground, checking not only on the children in her charge but the other ten or so who were buzzing around the apparatus like wasps round an abandoned wine glass.

'I'm fine, really, Simon. Just a bit of post-viral something or other. Gareth's down with it now. So's Polly.'

'My heart bleeds.'

Rose smiled and, finally, looked right at him. 'You're a good mate, Simon. Thank you.'

He blushed in his usual way, from the sides of his nostrils to the tips of his ears.

'Hey, look!' Nico cried, running over. 'Rose and Simon, sitting in a tree, K.I.S.S.I.N.G!'

'That's enough of that, you,' Simon said. He got up, ran towards Nico and scooped him up. Effie, Liam, Anna and Yannis swept towards them, piling in with whoops and shouts.

Rose stayed where she was, turning the hand Simon had held over and over, inspecting it and wondering how it had deserved such kindness.

'Fancy lunch at the pub?' Simon called from in

355

amongst a tangle of children. 'My treat.'

It was such a long time since Rose had eaten out that she had forgotten that it was a terrible idea to take more children than adults into a pub. Despite the long, fizzy drinks and bags of crisps that Simon had bought them to help pass the time, the children grew bored waiting for their ham, eggs and chips. When the food eventually did arrive, Rose was feeling rather pissed from the two pints of bitter she and Simon had each had, standing as they did on top of the wine. Then there was the usual flurry of activity while salad garnish was deposited from the children's plates onto those of the adults.

In amongst their attempts to keep the noise down and minimise the disruption to the other patrons of the pub, Simon and Rose had little chance to talk any further. For that she was grateful. She felt that the relatively calm exterior she was presenting to the world was only a very thin membrane. Underneath that, there was a scrambled mess of spoiled, rotten matter—like the curdled lump you might find under the harmless-looking skin of a very old tin of gloss paint.

As they ambled back up the lane towards their respective homes, Simon turned to Rose. The beer had mellowed him even further. He had the air of a faithful bloodhound as he looked into her eyes.

'Do you want us to stop by for a bit? I could help you out, sort out anything that needs doing, while you put your feet up.'

'I can't ask you to do that—not to come into the house while *she*'s there. But . . .' a great opportunity had suddenly occurred to her '. . . I *am* a bit done in. Is there any chance you could have

356

the big kids for the afternoon?'

Nico, Yannis and Anna, who had been passing a football between themselves a couple of yards ahead, stopped, turned round and looked at Simon expectantly.

Simon opened and closed his mouth as he looked at them all. This obviously wasn't what he had had in mind. But then he lifted up his hands as if to admit defeat.

'Of course,' he said. 'How could I resist those three little faces? Four little faces,' he corrected himself, turning to look at Rose. 'I'll even take Floss for you if you like. Janka's around, so it's not as if I'll be single-handed.'

'And I'm a great help with Flossie, too,' Anna piped up.

'Of course you are,' Simon said.

'Thank you so much,' Rose said, as they approached the gate to The Lodge. She passed the buggy with Flossie in it to Simon. 'There's nappies and a couple of bottles of milk in the changing bag. I'll be round about seven to pick them up.'

'No rush. There's no school. Come when you're ready. Miranda's up in Town for the weekend, so I'm on my own timetable,' he said, a little ruefully. 'In fact, why don't you come round and watch a film with us later if you're up to it? I've got a great pirate of the new Terry Gilliam. Completely impenetrable plot-wise, but visually amazing enough to keep this lot quiet.'

'I'll see how I feel,' she said.

'No worries if you don't feel up to it,' he said. 'Just wait and see.'

It's as if he doesn't want to leave me, she thought. As if he knows what I'm going to get up

357

to.

'Bye then,' she said finally, then turned and passed through the gate. Instead of going down into the house, she hid behind the hedge until she heard the hustle and bustle of the children disappear down the lane; until she knew she was completely alone.

Although it was only two o'clock, the light had a late-afternoon feel to it, or perhaps it was the beer that made it seem so. Rose crept into the kitchen and fished in her apron pocket to find the key to Gareth's studio.

She tiptoed up the stairs to Anna's bedroom. Gareth was still in there, huddled under the duvet. She held her breath for a few minutes to check he was still breathing. She was soon rewarded with a loud inhaled snore. After he had settled himself again, Rose took herself back down the stairs.

She went out to the Annexe to check on Polly. Tiptoeing up the steps, she knocked on the door.

'Come in,' Polly said in a small voice.

Rose took in the scent of the room. Polly had attempted to mask it with her perfume, but the same dark faecal taint surrounded her as it did Gareth. She lay in the bed, propped up by pillows, one long, thin hand resting on the top of the duvet, the other holding a book of Rimbaud's *Oeuvres Poétiques*, as if she had arranged herself to look like Mimi in *La Bohème*, instead of an Englishwoman with diarrhoea.

The room was a mess.

'How are you?' Rose whispered.

'On the mend,' Polly smiled weakly.

'You still up for Brighton tomorrow?' Rose asked.

358

'Try to stop me,' Polly said, the smile vanishing from her face.

'I'll book a cab to get us to the station; I don't want to disturb Gareth. Do you want a wake-up call?' Rose said. 'We'll have to leave by seven.'

'I'll be fine,' Polly said.

'Good, good. Anything I can get you?'

'Just a glass of water, please.'

Rose went over to the kitchen area and turned on the tap. Standing there at that sink, she was reminded of a different era in her life, one that had been full of hope, when she, Gareth, Anna and Andy lived here and everything was looking up, before the roof went on the house, before she got pregnant, before Polly came to stay. She remembered doing the washing-up in this same spot, after a robust, roast-chicken supper that had felt well-earned after a day of hard graft.

Some part of Rose wished now that she could take a big demolition ball and knock The Lodge and everything it meant and contained down. She would erase it, and then move back into the Annexe to live the uncomplicated life of a hermit, or a nun.

She passed the water to Polly, who took a couple of sips then put it by her bedside.

'I think I'll try and get a little sleep now,' Polly said. 'So that I'm fresh for the morning.'

Fresh, thought Rose. Now, there's a word.

She slipped down the stairs and skirted around the side of the house, just pausing to look up and check that Polly wasn't watching her from the Annexe window. It wasn't that she really cared about being discovered by Polly. It was one thing Gareth trying to stop her—he had the physical

359

strength to do so; but Polly she could cast aside with one sweep of her arm if she so wanted. In fact, she thought as she headed over the back lawn, past the site of the fox murder, it was a wonder that she had managed to restrain herself so far. She could have just reached out and brought Polly down. *Taken her out.* Wasn't that the expression?

Winding her fingers in the curlicues of the key, she slipped it into the studio keyhole. Before opening the door, she paused for a second. Did she really want to do this? If, as she suspected, she were to discover something she didn't want to find, how would that change things? Perhaps it was better to go on not knowing. Perhaps it was better simply to work at ousting Polly so that their lives could, gradually, assume the perfect future they had once envisaged for themselves.

But she didn't have the discipline for that, not at this point. Like a child with a carefully wrapped Christmas present, she wanted to see inside now. She thrust the door open and allowed her eyes to adjust to the gloomy, blind-drawn interior.

She snapped the lights on and the shrouded shapes gave up their secrets. If she were to be discovered down here, she could always say she had come to get the coffee cups for the dishwasher—she could count twelve dotted around the place. And then there were the wine glasses, quite a few of which had a familiar red shade of lipstick around the rim, and the empty bottles, which she could say she was fetching for the recycling.

Really. It wasn't very careful of them.

But there was worse to come. Rose looked around. The place looked like a tip. This was normal. It was the one area of the house where Gareth could let his true nature express itself. Every surface was covered. Rose moved towards a long bench that ran down one side of the room, almost four metres of it. You really couldn't see it through the drift of paper, drawings and pens that smothered it. For a horrible second, Rose thought there were some body parts in amongst it, but when she explored further with her fingers, she realised it was just dried up Sta-Wet palettes full of great nubs of nut-hard acrylic paint in all sorts of flesh tones.

She went over to the old plan-chest that she remembered helping Gareth salvage from the renovation of a couple of the art studios at Goldsmiths. On top was a six-inch pile of A1 sheets of Bristol board. Rose rifled through. Some fell to the ground, and she left them where they lay. The work, all pencil and charcoal, and ink, was of angular curves, of belly skin, stretched between hipbones, of tiny breasts with nipples like thumbs, a rack of ribs for a back.

He had inked some of the drawings. Rose looked hard at those. With their loose black stockings, their curls of pubic and underarm hair, their sad, sex eyes that gazed directly at the viewer, they brought Egon Schiele to mind. But there was something else there. A melancholy air of Christos.

This was extraordinary work for Gareth. Rose could see that. While the influences were plain, he had taken it way beyond. This was work that had Gareth's own stamp on it. His agent, and his gallery, would be very pleased indeed. It was beautiful work—fresh, exploratory, yet commercial

361

and very, very accomplished.

Of course, there was the question of who the model was.

Rose looked at the tumbled, unmade sofa bed that stood over against the far wall. On the floor, just by it, was a pair of black stockings that she recognised from the work. She walked over and picked them up, letting the fine stuff fall through her fingers. Underneath was a little pair of black knickers. Silk. She picked them up and sniffed them, like she did if she found Anna's underwear lying around, to see if it needed washing. This pair certainly needed to go in the machine. But their scent was heavy and musked, a million miles away from Anna's pissy little girl tang. A white residue stained the gusset, as if it had been forced up inside the wearer in a heated moment . . .

Rose knelt on the floor and sniffed the bed, where she found long dark hairs. And my God, she thought, this bed needs stripping and washing. She had to fight every bone in her body to stop herself pulling the sheets away and bundling them up.

She stood up and tried to picture the scene: Polly lying on her back, Gareth doing to her what he had done to Rose only a couple of weeks before. Her bones against his strong chest. Him burying his face down there underneath her concave belly.

The spring that had been drawing back inside Rose was finally released. She grabbed a pillow from the bed and slammed it down again and again, until it burst and its tiny feathers fluttered down, like she had imagined, like the aftermath of a ruck of angels. She ripped the sheets from the bed and emptied tube after tube of expensive paint over them. She dragged the paint-smeared sheets around the room, like naked girls in a 1960s action painting. The feathers joined in with her, swirling and falling, embedding themselves in the paint.

She stopped for a minute, panting, and surveyed her work. Then she went for the drawers where Gareth kept all his equipment. She rummaged around until she found a Stanley knife. She went first to the stinking, stained knickers and shredded them. Then she took herself to the pile of Bristol Boards, to the best work Gareth had ever done, and she slashed each one of the drawings until she was surrounded by a pile of ribbons. Finally, she went to the large, impressive oil and acrylic paintings of Polly that Gareth had propped up around the two empty walls of the studio, the work Rose had failed to notice until now, and gouged each set of staring soulful eyes out, leaving dark holes where there had once been his work, his looking, his taking. It seemed appropriate: payback time exerted by Rose on behalf of his poor birth mother for what he did to her with *BloodLine*.

Then, brushing her hands free of the shards of canvas and paint that covered them, she switched off the light, locked the door and threw the key into the pond. Those ancient keys didn't come with copies. Even if Gareth did get up before they left for Brighton, that should buy her a bit of time to stage her getaway.

363

Forty-Two

Rose had a quick shower, then spent what remained of the afternoon packing for Brighton. She started the task by making a list, on which, amongst the baby wipes, nappies, changes of clothes for herself, Flossie and Anna, she included: *suit of armour, bazooka, landmines (two)*.

By leaving out the ordnance, she managed to boil everything down to one large rucksack and a wheeled suitcase. It wasn't exactly travelling light, but it nevertheless felt liberating to know that she and her daughters had everything they needed for survival in just two bags. She then packed two smaller, wheeled suitcases for the boys. She supposed she would be the only one to think about that, and it wasn't fair on them to be bloody-minded about such things.

She rang Simon to check on the children, and to warn him that they wouldn't be staying to watch a movie, because an early night was called for. In all honesty, this was more for her own benefit than theirs. Her duvet was calling her. She just wanted to hide there until the morning, and then leave.

Instead, though, she had the rest of the afternoon to deal with. She got some chicken stock out of the freezer and heated it up with some thread egg noodles in it to serve to the invalids. To add belt and braces to her plan, she ground another four of the green herbal pills in her pestle and mortar and stirred the powder into Gareth's bowl.

'That should keep him quiet,' she said to the

kitten, who was crying up at her, unfed. 'I'm not going to humour you, you know,' Rose said, ignoring its pitiful mewing. 'You're the devil's work, you are.'

She found a tray and spread one of her lovely Irish linen, lace-edged napkins on it. They were among the few things she had taken from her parents' house when they had kicked her out. She had rarely used them.

She smoothed out the ironed-in creases. *They had kicked her out.* She thought about it. In their view, she had shamed them, so they had actually kicked her, their only child, out of their home. Left her alone, in trouble, with only Polly to rely on, only Polly to sort her out.

How could they do that? And was it any wonder she didn't want to go back to Brighton? But it was too late now. And anyway, she had plans, now.

She poured Gareth's soup into one of her favourite vintage Biot bowls and placed it on top of the napkin. By the side, she positioned a heavy tumbler of water, a small vase with a little bunch of honey-suckle from the garden in it, and a weighty silver soup spoon from the ancestral canteen Pam and John had bequeathed Gareth as a combined apology and family heirloom. If he was feeling well enough, he would be pleased with this arrangement. Pleased enough, hopefully, to drink the whole bowlful no matter how bitter it tasted.

She tiptoed up the stairs and knocked softly on Anna's door.

She heard Gareth mumble something, so she pushed the door open and went inside. He was ashen, but awake, with dark rings under his eyes. What a baby, Rose thought. What a milksop.

'I brought you a little chicken soup.'

'Oy vey.' He tried to smile.

'If you eat something, it'll make you stronger.' She put the tray down in front of him.

'Very pretty,' he said, taking the spoon in his hand.

She hoped he didn't think she was trying to say sorry for her outburst with this tray of food. But it was a risk she had to take in order to keep him quiet. She watched with satisfaction as he took first one then another spoonful of the soup.

'I'll take a bowl up to Polly,' Rose said, turning to go.

'How is she?'

'On the mend. Bit better than you, in fact. She still wants to go to Brighton tomorrow, in any case.'

'Good,' he said. 'You must go. Don't worry about me.'

As if, Rose thought.

Polly was asleep when Rose took another, less well-adorned tray up to the Annexe, so she left it on the floor by the bed. With any luck, she would tip it over when she got up and get cold soup over her nightdress.

Back at The Lodge, Rose was just slipping on her Barbour for the walk over to Simon's house to pick up the children, when she heard Anna's bedroom door swing open and Gareth rush across the landing to the family bathroom. He was in such a hurry, he didn't have a chance to shut the door, and Rose listened with satisfaction to his involuntary exertions. Before she went, she lit a Jo Malone candle on the kitchen table, to mask the stink.

*   *   *

It took a while to get the children to sleep. They were so excited about the impending trip that they begged Rose for details, for snippets of history, for tips as to the best rides on the pier. She put up her hands and refused to say a word.

'You'll find out all about it at the weekend,' she promised. Instead, she read the chapter from *Winnie the Pooh* where he takes a balloon and floats up into a tree.

She put them all to bed, then sat at the kitchen table and drank an entire bottle of Gareth's special champagne. She felt the day called for a celebration. The champagne tasted quite disgusting served warm, but it seemed more fitting that way.

Forty-Three

When Rose went downstairs the following morning, she nearly fell over in shock. Polly was already up, sitting in the kitchen armchair, dressed like a punk Celia Howard in *Brief Encounter*. She balanced a little handbag on her knee; a small suitcase that Rose had never seen before was perched on the floor beside her.

'Good morning!' Polly said, her face bright. 'I fed the cat. He was starving, poor kitty.'

Hungover, still unwashed and in her nightclothes, Rose didn't feel anywhere near as perky. She grunted and put Flossie in her high chair. Then the house erupted, as the herd that was Nico, Yannis and Anna thundered down the stairs.

'Are we going to be late?' they asked.

'Will the taxi be here on time?'

Nico and Yannis directed all their questions at Rose. They seemed to fail to notice that their mother, whose health they had feared for so much the day before, was now alive and well and sitting in the kitchen.

'Hush now, we don't want to wake Gareth,' Rose said. 'It's only just gone six.'

When they were all washed, breakfasted and dressed, they took their suitcases up the steps towards the lane to wait for the people-carrier that the local shopkeeper's husband drove and which served for the village taxi. Rose didn't want him to pull up in the driveway and sound his horn like he normally did. She had left a brief, functional note for Gareth, reminding him to feed the kitten. She had also taken the precaution of not letting him know where they were staying and removing Polly's mobile phone from her handbag while she was in the bathroom. She turned it off, ran it under the tap for good measure, then hid it at the back of the dresser.

It was a misty morning—so misty that you couldn't see your hand in front of you. Rose hoped it was only a local problem—they did live in a slight dip—or they might actually miss the train, and then what would she do?

They stood on a nub of grass at the lane entrance to The Lodge and waited. The older children pulled up long grasses and, holding them like cigarettes, pretended to smoke them, blowing out clouds of breath into the damp air. Flossie was quiet, cocooned in her all-terrain buggy like a sleeping Buddha. Out there in the cold country morning, all done up in her forties gear, Polly looked a little gormless, Rose thought. She was clearly bamboozled by the early hour, the chill, and the fact that she really wasn't wearing enough clothes for someone with no inbuilt insulation.

'Look!' Anna said, pointing at a chandelier of cobwebs, jewelled with diamanté beads of dew. Nico drew back his grass cigarette and swiped at them, bringing the elaborate construction twinkling down with a silent clatter. Anna laughed and clapped her hands. A couple of months ago she would have been distraught. Rose wondered what had shifted to harden her daughter so, and whether it was a good or bad thing.

Thankfully, the taxi turned up on time and Rose's fears about the mist were unfounded. Once they got onto the main road it was plain sailing, and they arrived at the station with five minutes to spare. Even boarding the train was simple, despite all the bags and the children, thanks to an absurdly cheery, red-faced couple of older male station guards who insisted on doing everything 'while you ladies find a nice seat for yourselves and the kiddies'. There was even a trolley service on the train, run by an apple-cheeked young Polish girl. As soon as they sat down on their reserved seats, she wheeled up towards them and offered them tea, coffee and hot chocolate along with fresh sugared doughnuts for the children. Rose paid.

'I'll pay you back. I'm still waiting for the Greek lawyers. They're taking an age—although next week is looking likely,' Polly said.

369

It dawned on Rose that Polly might have come away with no means of paying for anything herself. It was probably something she had never really had to think about before, so the fact she didn't have any money now wasn't going to stop her.

'How are you feeling this morning, then?' Rose asked her.

'Oh, you know, OK,' Polly said.

'At least you didn't end up in hospital for a week.'

Polly looked sharply up at her, but Rose turned to look out of the window.

'Look at that,' she said to the children. A wide waterway carved its way through a fat, springy meadow. 'That water comes from our river,' she said. The river from the bottom of the field by The Lodge. The river that once upon a time Gareth had said he was going to chart with woodcuts.

Mist hung over the top of the water and spilled from its edges into the grass.

'It's almost as if we're in a plane and we're looking down through the clouds,' she said.

Polly leaned her head against the window, preparing to drop off. Rose reached over and tapped her on the knee.

'Shall I take the tickets? In case you're asleep when the guard comes.'

Polly reached in her little handbag and passed a wallet with the tickets in it over to Rose.

They crawled across the West Country, stopping at every station on the way. Polly was soon fast asleep, but Rose was kept busy keeping the children in line. The boys kept attacking each other as usual, but the new development was that Anna was now joining in, holding her own and giving as good as she got. Rose tried to keep them quiet, but it was a long journey, and they were excited. A few of the passengers sitting around them quietly got up and moved further down the train. One or two made their displeasure more evident. An hour into the journey there was an exclusion zone around them.

As they moved into Hampshire, Polly woke up and, borrowing ten pounds from Rose, staggered down the train to find the Polish girl and her trolley. She returned with packets of crisps for the children and a coffee for herself.

'You didn't want anything, did you, Rose?' she asked.

'I'm fine,' Rose said.

'Can we go over there?' Anna asked, pointing to an empty table a few seats away.

'If you're good,' Rose said, and louder, so that everyone on the carriage could be reassured, she went on: 'I'll make you come back here the minute I hear anything I don't like.'

She sat and looked at Polly, this woman who had once been her friend. She wondered if things had always been so difficult between them, underneath the veneer of their shared history and the repeated mantra of referring to each other as best friends. Or was it like a long marriage, dissolved into mute seething where there must surely once have been love? For all her tininess, her little-girl aura, Polly had some nasty hard edges. Rose realised that she had probably always hated her, one way or another. If it wasn't for the downright evil man-snatching that was going on now, it was as an object for jealousy and inadequate self-comparison.

'What are your plans, Poll?' she blurted out when Polly had finished her coffee. The train rattled past a low-tide harbour somewhere near Southampton, with desolate little boats stranded in a space entirely filled with ooze.

'This again,' Polly said, looking out of the window, her reddened lower lip protruding.

'I'd like to know. Gareth and I—'

'Gareth and you what?' Polly shot her a glance.

'Perhaps it might be time to start thinking about finding yourself somewhere proper to live? The house money isn't far off, as you say. You'll probably want to look for somewhere closer to London and if you want to go away and have a look around, see what you can find, I'm happy to have the boys till you're ready for them.'

'Well, that's funny. It was only yesterday that Gareth said, and, now, let me get this right.' She pulled off her red leather gloves. 'Oh yes, he said, "You're welcome to stay as long as you like, Polly. Having you and the boys around, it brings a bit of life to this old place . . .".' She said this in an exaggerated version of Gareth's accent, so it sounded as if it had been spoken back in the dangerous Wild West. She had drawn herself up so she was high in her seat, almost looking down at Rose. Then, without warning, she laughed and laid a hand on Rose's knee.

'Oh, don't look so worried. I'm sure he didn't mean it like that. He might not even have said it like that in so many words.' She wrinkled her nose and tried to catch Rose's eye. 'Poor you,' she said. 'You really do need this little break, don't you?'

'Tickets please, ladies, on this fine and misty morning!' A portly guard bustled down the aisle towards them. What was it with South-West Trains this morning? Rose wondered. It was as if they had only permitted cheerful, wholesome and sunny people to work this route, to act as a foil to her mood. She thought about Gareth and, for the first time since she had done the desecration, she thought about the studio, and she felt sick. Suddenly, her plans—to get to Polly during this trip, to investigate the studio yesterday—revealed themselves to her as the muddled mess they were, and as she bantered with the ticket collector, inside she felt uprooted, lost. After the studio, she probably wouldn't ever be able to talk to Gareth again. What on earth had she done?

'Feet off the seats, sonny boy,' the guard said to Nico as Rose rummaged in her big bag for the tickets. Eventually she found them and held them up, feeling like a child herself.

The rest of the journey was spent in near-silence. The only words uttered by Rose or Polly were directed at the children. It was gone midday when they finally got to Brighton. They walked the length of the iron-arched platform in the cold, bright, sea-tanged air. Each step brought Rose's childhood back to her. She remembered clearly coming back to this station from London shopping trips, hand in hand with her mother, before she became a teenager, before she turned round and disappointed them all. Back when she was a good girl.

They rounded the corner by the Golden Crust Baguette stall to get to the taxi rank. There was no one in the queue, so they made to get into the one cab that was waiting there.

'Oy, oy, stop now,' the taxi driver said, getting

out and slamming the door. 'I ain't taking all of you at once, you know. Not with all them bags and that buggy and all.'

'But that's ridiculous,' Polly said. 'You can carry six, surely?'

'That's not what it says on my licence, mate,' the taxi driver said. 'Unless you know better, that is.'

'Look, I'm fine. Me and Floss can walk,' Rose said. She thought she could do with the fresh air. 'I'd rather. Really.'

'I want to come with you, Mum!' Anna said, hanging on to Rose.

'That's fine, love. You come with me. I'll show you all my old places.' Anna curled into her side and looked up at her with adoring eyes.

'Sort it out, love, then. I haven't got all day,' the taxi driver said, blowing out his cheeks.

'Well then, OK then,' Polly said. 'It's twenty-five St Luke's Rise. Can you remember that?'

'Of course,' Rose said. 'You'll need some money, won't you?'

'Yes,' Polly said, holding her hand out. Rose gave her a ten-pound note. She had resigned herself to the fact that this trip was going to be expensive in so many ways. Finally, Polly, Nico, Yannis and all the luggage got in the taxi, and Rose, Flossie and Anna stood on the pavement, waving as they set off. Rose should have turned left out of the station to get to Lucy's house, which was only about a mile away down and up the hill. But she decided she needed to buy time for herself, so instead she pointed the buggy down Queen's Road, towards the sea, which hung like a great grey blanket between the buildings in front of them.

'Come on, Anna. I'm going to show you some of the best clubs in the universe.'

'What sort of clubs?' Anna asked, hanging tightly onto the buggy handles as they rolled down the hill.

'Clubs for when you are a big girl. Clubs for dancing, and drinking, and having fun.'

'They sound good,' Anna said. 'Except for the drinking thing.'

Rose felt reckless. She felt no responsibility towards Polly, nor towards this Lucy-from-the-past. For once, she thought, she would do what she wanted and not worry about anyone else. They picked their way down to the seafront, past the throngs of people: snow-white girls with pierced noses and soft bellies on display to the sea-chilled air; *Big Issue* sellers with pathetic dogs, the art of avoiding whom had long since escaped Rose; dazed-looking women with buggies like Rose's, held rapt in front of Waterstones as if they could while the whole child-riddled day away just gazing at stacks of the books they used to have time to read.

This Brighton was a different town from the one Rose had grown up in. Instead of a slightly down-at-heel, seedy, kiss-me-quick-hat dive, it now had the air of a slightly down-at-heel cosmopolitan city. Rose wondered if this homogenisation had only recently happened, and how widespread it was. She felt out of touch and impossibly old as she neared the seafront, the anodyne brick and pastels of a redeveloped Churchill Square shopping centre on her right. In her day it had been piss-sodden, bleak and brutalist.

'Look at all the birds!' Anna said.

'Seagulls. They're sort of rats with wings.'

Anna thought about this. 'But they haven't got those horrid tails,' she said.

'True. But they eat absolutely anything. And they attack people. I once read about a man who was killed by a seagull in Rottingdean.'

Anna looked up at her, wide-eyed, and Rose slapped herself on the head. What was she thinking, worrying her sensitive girl like that? She had got too used to the thickened pelts of the boys. 'But he was an old man, and very ill at the time. They've never killed a girl or her mum before.'

'Never?'

'Never.'

They went down the slope to the seafront and Rose was completely taken aback. Where she remembered scrappy clubs amongst decaying fishermen's arches, deep, pocketed pubs and pissy little alcoves, there were now coffee bars on neat terraces that edged onto the shingle. Beautiful glass floortiles pointed the way along the new, curving, granite sett seafront walkway. There were a couple of showers, a kayak rental shop, the odd sculpture. It all looked so unEnglish to Rose's eye. With its brightness, its bustle and its shards of colour picked out against the chalky sky, it was almost an affront to her newly hewn rural sensibilities.

Anna loved it, though. Even Flossie managed to look a little interested in a rack of plastic windmills by a giant, big-girl-sized fibreglass ice-cream cornet.

'Let's have a drink,' Rose said, and they took their seats at a bar terrace on a paved peninsula that reached far out onto the beach, up against a

376

big stone groyne. Rose wondered how the bar fared in the winter, during the storms that flung the stones from the beach up against the promenade. Perhaps they had to rebuild the bar each spring. Or perhaps the winters weren't what they used to be down here in the south.

The afternoon had worn on. The sun was working hard to burn off the grey veil of cloud that touched everything. But, sitting at the bar waiting for their drinks, Anna and Rose felt the sea-chill in the air. Eventually, their order arrived. Rose had a large glass of Shiraz, and Anna a hot chocolate with cream and chocolate flakes, which she declared wasn't as good as the one she had had back at Heathrow when they waited for the boys to arrive with their mum.

They drank up, paid their bill and carried on towards the pier, which looked unchanged, more like the old Brighton. Everything was a little bright, a little gaudy. The people clogging the entrance were tattooed, gold-chained and out for the kind of good time you could only find in Brighton. She took the girls for a walk along to the very far end, past the clash and clatter of the amusements, the hypnotic bass pulse of tinny chart music and the unspeakably delicious smells of fresh, frying doughnuts. Out they went, beyond the phallic helter-skelter, the screaming dodgems and an alarming lever that promised to drop its shrieking occupants several hundred feet into the boiling sea beneath.

'Look, you can see the sea whirling under you,' she said to Anna. They stood on the boardwalk and looked down between the gaps. 'You think you're on solid ground, but you're not. Any minute and the whole lot could collapse and we'd be in the water.'

Rose thought she could see the ghost of herself down there, covered up by some boy or other, his spotty bare back-side going up and down, hammering into her. She shuddered.

'I want to go back,' Anna said.

'Don't be silly. It's been standing like this for a hundred years.'

'But what about that one?' Anna pointed across the choppy expanse of sea to the West Pier that had fallen victim first to storms, then to arson. It was a sorry sight, Rose thought. A skeleton, a once-glorious queen, now a stripped thing, slowly reverting back to nothingness.

'Oh, that's a *very* old pier. Almost as old as the dinosaurs. We've got eras to go before this one falls like that,' she said. In fact, she remembered the West Pier when it was closed, but still more or less whole, its beautiful domed ballrooms rising above the shingle, egging her on as she rolled out of a club at closing time with yet another boy, stumbling down the shingle to have fumbled, transient sex at the very edge, where the sea licked the land. It felt wrong to be standing here with her untainted daughters.

'Come on, Anna banana. Let's go. Do you want to see the house I grew up in?'

They escaped to dry land, then skirted up the hill past the Sea Life Centre. It was Rose's old trip to school in reverse. With every step they took, Rose began to dread seeing her old house.

Looking back, it had been a horrible childhood. Like Flossie, she must have been an accident. But unlike her own lucky little baby, she didn't even

378

have one parent rooting for her. Her overriding memory was of always being in the way, of being an inconvenience in the otherwise smooth running of her parents' guesthouse. If she kept her head down and her mouth shut, they were happy. Anything else, and her father, particularly, would be provoked to acts of violent exasperation.

Having learned this habit of invisibility, when Rose eventually made it to school, she lacked the skills to make friends. Her parents were also parsimonious to the point of disease. Her clothes were all from charity shops, and she was only permitted one bath, of five inches, once a week. There were no toys, no holidays, no new clothes and no birthday parties for Rose.

None of this helped her social life.

Her only comfort was food, which she took to like a lover. So the odd, drab, smelly girl added fat to her list of distinguishing features. It was only when she took to taking lovers like a lover that she began to lose weight and clean up her act.

Small wonder then, that when Polly showed her that bit of kindness on that school morning when she was so sodden from the waves, Rose grasped it with both hands and held it to her chest. It seemed she had been doing just that for all the years since. Perhaps, she thought, as she steered the buggy round a seagull-pecked black rubbish bag that spilled its glutinous contents onto the pavement, perhaps she should give it a rest now, all that gratitude.

'This is it,' she said to Anna, as they stopped in front of the tall, narrow house that she grew up in. It looked a lot smaller than she remembered. Or perhaps she was used now to larger houses, like

The Lodge.

'Posh,' Anna said.

'Someone's done it up,' Rose said, peering over the railings at the front that gave down to a courtyard full of shade-loving plants. Like Brighton itself, the house had acquired a sheen that it had never had in Rose's day. It was a startling white, with glossy black paintwork. The windows, which used to clank in their rotten, peeling frames, had all been replaced with new wooden double-glazed sashes. There would be no draughts now, Rose thought. And instead of slightly mouldy nets, the windows were shielded from the street by smart oak Venetian blinds. All very nice, but also very closed off, like someone with their eyes shut.

'It wasn't like that in my day.'

In her day it was all brown. Rose remembered the guest room in the attic where the Moustache Man stayed on his regular Brighton visits. She remembered lying back on the candlewick comforter and spreading her legs as he fumbled with the zipper on his Terylene trousers. She remembered his 'friend' who sometimes accompanied him, and the way they took it in turns, laughing at her, and slapping her fresh little breasts.

'Don't tell your father, eh, Rose?'

'We'll make it our little secret, eh, girly?'

And Polly, in between times, had egged her on, daring her to push it further, to flirt more outrageously, to flash a bit more flesh underneath her school uniform, for the delight of the paying guests.

'But look how close you were to the sea,' Anna

380

said, looking dreamily at the horizon at the end of Rose's old street. The sun had finally won its battle with the grey, and now the sea reflected the chalky blue that Rose had only ever seen here, on this coast. 'You were so lucky, Mum. I wish I lived by the sea.'

'Who's the father?' her father had screamed, yanking her hair and raising his fist above her that day in the parlour.

Rose really, honestly, didn't have a clue. And she told him as much.

'Slut!' he roared. 'Jezebel!'

It was a good job Polly had stopped him the way she did. Otherwise Rose's father would no doubt have killed his daughter.

'But you're lucky, Anna,' Rose said. 'You've got all the fields and the countryside. Isn't that lovely enough for you?'

'It is lovely, Mum,' Anna said, taken aback by her mother's tone of voice. 'But I like the sea, too.'

'Well, that's funny. I always wanted to live in the countryside when I was here,' Rose said. She had to get away from this place. 'Come on, then. They'll be wondering where we are.'

They walked up the hill to Queen's Park, where Rose stopped to change Flossie and let Anna explore the playground, which had acquired a safe, bouncy pink surface since Rose had played there. She still had a little speck of the black asphalt that used to be here tattooed into her knee from an over-hasty slide descent when she was seven.

Rose ordered a cup of tea and some cupcakes for the girls from the café hut. They were doing a roaring trade with the local mummies and their children. From the crowds of kids clutching blue bookbags, it seemed that school had just got out. A few older, secondary-school children swaggered through the park, smoking. They were an alarming sight. The boys had their shirts hanging out of trousers slung so low that they revealed their underwear. The girls, all well-fed, appeared to burst out of their too tight Aertex blouses. The mothers with young children instinctively shielded them from the sight, tutting to one another. You could see them thinking that their offspring would never end up like this, all dishevelled and sexual, despoiling the haven of the Friday afternoon park. But of course, they were wrong, Rose thought. All lovely things get spoiled with time. The little Rose girl did, that was for sure, all those years ago.

She knew she was procrastinating, but the last thing she felt like doing was going up to Lucy's house and pretending to be friends. It was even worse now she was here in Brighton: walking the streets had woken up pathways in her memory that she had long ago closed down. Lucy was the *other* one who ended up pregnant at school. But Lucy stuck with it. More to the point, her boyfriend did. Her pregnancy hadn't been a mystery, not like Rose's.

But it was time now. She had to face it.

'Anna—come on.' Anna had joined a group of girls on a ground-level, safety-conscious roundabout and was wheeling around, whooping. She was confident, outgoing and, even with an eyepatch, she didn't have any problems making instant friends. This was one of the very few things that Rose could call a victory in her life as it stood today. That thought brought back the studio and what she had done. Had Gareth found out yet?

Her stomach turned and she felt sick. She bent over and retched, turning a few concerned heads her way, causing a few of the mummy hands to be put around small children again, in case this was a crazy lady.

Flossie sat in her buggy, awake now, cramming cake into her mouth and staring at the children playing.

'Anna! We've got to go now.'

'Ohhh,' Anna sang. But she came, obedient as ever, and they pushed on up the steep hill at the north end of the park, avoiding a pile of dogshit that stood sentinel in the middle of the footpath.

At the top of the hill, Rose paused, panting a little. The small of her back felt damp as she reached under her corduroy jacket to rub it. Anna looked up at her with her one good eye, concerned.

'Are we nearly there yet?'

'It's just across the road there.' Rose pointed to the house. Her hand fell as she saw Polly standing in the front bay window, her arms crossed, her face like thunder. She clocked them as they moved along the pavement and she ducked inside. Rose lugged the buggy up the steps that led to the house then knocked on the chipped red front door.

After a few minutes, Polly appeared, with a bright smile on her face.

'Thank God, Rose,' she said in a too-loud voice. 'We were getting so worried.'

Forty-Four

'Is she here then?' a voice came from behind Polly, and a large-hipped, middle-aged woman appeared at her shoulder. There was a tea-towel flung across her shoulder, and her hair was scraped back to reveal a scrubbed, thread-veined face and a dry skin etched with lines. So this was what had happened to Lucy, then.

'Come on in, Rose.' Lucy bustled forward and took the buggy, pulling it down the narrow hallway that was lined with coats hanging from hooks and untidily piled shoes on pine racks. There was a strong smell of dust and Nag Champa incense. 'So, this is Flossie, and where's Anna?'

'Hello,' Anna said, popping her head round from behind Rose.

'Ah, there you are. What *have* you been up to? We were just about to call the police,' Lucy went on, backing into the living room. 'You take them down to the kitchen, Polly, and I'll get this poor baby out of the buggy. My God, she's frozen.'

Polly took Rose by the hand and led her down to the back of the house, to a long kitchen lined with stained pine units and worktops. The cupboards petered out at the far end into a large, heavy wooden table surrounded by mismatched wooden chairs. Every surface was covered with piles of papers, folded washing, half-eaten pies and pots and pans. At the very back was a set of French windows through which Rose could see a pile of mouldering bikes and an uncut jungle beyond.

'Where the hell were you?' Polly hissed, clearing

a chair of a sewing basket and pair of jeans and pushing Rose down onto it.

Rose, who hadn't spoken a word yet, drew Anna towards her. Something was up, and she wasn't quite sure what it was. When she had seen Polly's face in the window, she was worried that Gareth might have found the studio and got in touch. But now she was pretty sure that hadn't happened. In any case, Polly's phone was back at The Lodge, and Rose was certain that Gareth had no idea of Lucy's address or number.

Lucy bustled through to her messy kitchen and stood in the doorway, filling it up with her bulk. Flossie was balanced on her hip, resting her head on her shoulder, her eyes taking in the new space.

'Poor Rose,' Lucy said. 'You've really been going through it, haven't you? Polly's told me all about it.'

Rose frowned slightly. 'I'm fine,' she said.

'Course you are,' Lucy whispered, winking. 'Now, can I get you something to drink, Anna? Would you like a piece of cake? I bet you're all starving.'

'Lucy's a feeder, like you, Rose,' Polly said from over by the kettle.

'We had cake in the park,' Anna said.

'What—the park down there?' Lucy said, pointing in the direction they had just come from. Anna nodded.

Lucy turned to Polly and raised her eyebrows. Polly nodded, as if this were confirmation of something she had been saying to her. Polly moved over to Rose with the cup of tea, and sat down opposite her.

'Look at the state of you all. You all look so

windswept,' she said, smiling.

'I've put the hot water on,' Lucy said, 'so you can have a nice bath and possibly a little sleep before supper. You do look worn out.'

Rose wished she had a mirror, so that she could check the evident horror of her own appearance. She wanted to tell Lucy that she didn't look so hot, either, but she wasn't being given the opportunity for that.

'You're in Molly's room,' Lucy went on, slicing a homemade carrot cake and putting it onto chipped plates. Molly was, Rose remembered, Lucy's oldest child, the one she had had when they were at school. 'Polly's unpacked your stuff for you. You can just take it easy.'

Polly looked at her, smiled and nodded, as if Rose were some sort of idiot.

'Where are the boys?' Rose asked.

'Molly and Frank have taken them to the cinema. Frank's her boyfriend. He's *such* a nice boy. You'll love him,' Lucy said, nodding significantly at Polly. Rose sipped her tea and looked at these two women and wondered what on earth she was doing here.

'Won't Molly mind if I take her room?'

'Not at all! She's happy to have any excuse to spend the night round at Frank's. His parents have one of those big white houses round the park. They're very well off,' Lucy went on.

This all seemed like unnecessary detail to Rose. She looked over at Polly, who continued to smile like a queen bee.

'I could have unpacked my own things,' Rose said. 'I would have preferred to, you know.'

'Oh no. This is your break, Rose. You mustn't

lift a finger,' Polly said.

'Now, why don't you drink up and go upstairs and run yourself a nice hot bath?' Lucy added. 'We'll take care of the girls. You just rest, now. Come on, I'll show you the way,' she said, holding her hand out as if for a child.

Rose looked at the two of them, their faces full of concern, then she turned to Anna who was, she saw with a stab of anger, looking at her with the same expression. Whatever was going on here, she felt suffocated by it. But they were right about one thing, at least. She was exhausted. Her bones ached with all the pushing and ripping and tearing, the late night, the warm champagne, and the sea air. She took the opening that was being offered to her and followed Lucy up the stairs.

'Now, don't you worry about a thing,' Lucy said, handing her a clean, fluffy green towel and a bottle of Body Shop lavender bath oil. 'Molly's room is that one, second on the left. And you're to sleep as long as you need, OK?' Lucy reached forward and stroked Rose's hair. Rose wanted to rip her arm off, but instead she nodded and turned towards the bathroom.

Rose put the plug in, turned the hot tap on full and stood in front of the mirror. Slowly, she took her clothes off. She looked at her body with a sense of detachment. The skin on the pocket of fat that sagged a little below her navel was streaked with a Nile delta of stretchmarks. Her breasts, too, had a flayed appearance: the purple lines, still livid from her most recent pregnancy, looked like veins, or a network of lymph ducts. She took hold of her fleshy hips, a handful at least each side, and jiggled them, watching the loose, uncon-ditioned flesh ripple upwards, sideways and downwards. It wasn't a pretty sight. Perhaps she had only herself to blame if Gareth had strayed. Perhaps she had crossed the Rubicon, done the unthinkable for a woman of her age. Perhaps she had 'let herself go'. Perhaps she was a deserving subject for Lucy's pity.

She turned and poured a slug of bath oil into the tub, swirling it around and inhaling the clean, calming lavender scent. No. Polly was up to something—Rose knew it. She had to stop giving her the benefit of the doubt. She had been far too lenient with her, had felt too sorry for her, had relied too much on their shared history. She climbed into the steaming bath and lowered herself into the too-hot water. As she lay there, her body slowly poaching, she tried to straighten everything out in her head. But she couldn't. She was too far removed now from any sort of context to have a view on anything. Far better, she thought, just to go to the bedroom and get some rest. Things would sort themselves out one way or another.

She dried herself. With the towel wrapped around her, she tiptoed along the corridor. There was a sort of foot-level opening, she saw, on the half-landing that turned and led to the attic floor. She squatted down and peered through the wooden spindles that fenced it off from the room below, which Rose saw was the kitchen. From this spot she could see and hear Polly and Lucy, as they sat at the kitchen table, chatting with Anna. Lucy had Flossie on her knee. Anna was telling Lucy about what had happened to her eye. She and Polly seemed to have turned it into some sort of joke-story—Anna was enacting what the kitten had done, swiping her hand across Polly's face as if it were a clawed paw.

'So, they don't need me, then,' Rose muttered to herself. Polly looked sharply up and clearly clocked her. She didn't alert the others to it. Instead, she just carried on as if nothing had happened. Rose got up and went to the bedroom, where her clothes had been hung on hooks on the back of the door, a travel cot had been put up for Flossie, and Anna's cuddlies had been arranged on a camp bed. Rose picked up her own night-dress, which had been laid out on what was presumably Molly's bed, and pulled it over her head. Then she lifted back the clean duvet and curled up underneath it. Within seconds she was fast asleep, in a deep, dreamless hole.

When she woke, she had no idea what time it was or where she was. Gradually she remembered that she was back in Brighton, in a teenager's bedroom. She could hear the whiffle and snore of her two daughters, who someone had put into the room with her. She got out of bed and tiptoed across to the window. It was raining heavily and the night was pitch black. She could see the outlines of the houses on the other side of the back garden. They were all in darkness, so it must be quite late. Rose realised she felt hungry, and wondered if she had missed supper. Taking care not to wake the girls, she slipped out of bed and padded along the landing. She heard voices coming from the kitchen, so she stopped and squatted by the little galleried opening, putting herself to one side so that she couldn't be seen. At the table were Lucy, Polly and two young people, a heavily pregnant girl and a boy, both about twenty. The boy looked familiar to Rose, but she couldn't put her finger on why.

'I'm sorry, Frank, darling,' Polly was saying. She was leaning across the table, her hand on his forearm. The boy, a pink-cheeked, round-faced, indie-dressed kid with a mop of dark hair, nursed a can of beer. His body was twisted around and his head was inclined in a way that shouted disappointment to Rose.

'She's just not up to it,' Lucy added. 'She's obviously in a real state.'

'I can't believe she did that to her husband's work,' the young woman said.

'She's ill, Molly. She's not herself,' Polly explained.

'I wait for twenty years to meet her, and this is how it ends up,' Frank said, putting his face in his hands.

Rose gasped and put her hand to her mouth.

'You've got plenty of time. She'll get better soon enough, and then you can take it from there,' Lucy said.

'It's just the wrong time, Frank,' Polly said. 'I'm so sorry. I don't know what I was thinking. The signs were all there that the time was right. I just didn't have an idea just how deranged she is. But she is your mum, there's no doubt about that. And you've met your sisters, at least.'

'It's not your fault, Aunty Polly,' Frank said.

Aunty Polly! Rose bit her fingers to stop herself from crying out.

'And thank God you've stayed in touch down the years,' Lucy said. 'It's only because of Polly here that you're even going to get a chance to meet

390

her.'

'It's only because of Polly that we met,' Molly said, taking Frank's hand and looking into his eyes.

Rose's stomach lurched. So this was why Polly had brought her back to Brighton.

'Do you think they're going to take her away?' Frank asked.

'I should imagine so,' Polly said, patting his hand. 'It'll be for her own good. She's probably a danger to herself right now.'

'I feel bad about leaving those children in there with her,' Lucy said to Polly.

'I think it's important to act normal,' Polly said. 'We don't want her to suspect anything.'

Rose looked at the young man, who was sitting so that she could see his face now, turned up to the light. Of course. His features were familiar, because they were her own.

'Do you want to see your baby?' the midwife had said, as Rose lay, weeping and groggy from the Pethidine that Polly had insisted she used.

'She doesn't,' Polly said. 'She was very clear about that.'

The midwife shrugged and carried the bundle of blankets out of the room, into the arms of its new parents. It was all out of Rose's hands. Polly had contacted a Catholic adoption agency which, with her input, had overseen everything.

She must have kept in touch with that agency. Had she kept in touch with Lucy with this reunion in mind? Had she engineered the relationship between the two young people? And *Aunty Polly*? What was all that about?

Rose had been wrong to trust Polly with anything, ever.

All Rose had known about the adoptive parents was that they, too, lived in Brighton. That was one of the reasons she had got out of the town so quickly. It is, as her parents had told her before they left for Scotland, a small town. A place for scandal. A place where you couldn't sneeze without everyone knowing about it.

'Gareth should be here in an hour or so, Frank,' Polly was saying. 'You two had better leave. He's going to be in enough of a state as it is. We'll save all this until he's got over the immediate stuff that Rose has done. Then we'll move on to her past.'

Rose tore her eyes away from the boy, got up and went to the bathroom. Locking the door behind her, she knelt over the toilet, expecting to be sick. But nothing came. She was beyond even that. She closed her eyes and tried to calm her breathing down. Gareth was on his way. They all thought she was ill. Things were not looking good.

Had Polly told Anna about this Frank? About the big secret her mother had kept from everyone? Had she—and here she reached for the toilet bowl again—told Gareth? Gareth who, because of his past, could never, ever know? Rose couldn't begin to think about it. She had an instinctive need to get home, to regroup, to sort herself out. While she was here, in Brighton, she couldn't see straight. And, more to the point, she was in danger. She had to get out, and there was only one place she wanted to go.

A phone. She had to find a phone. She tiptoed towards the front bedroom, the one she imagined must be Lucy's. She could still hear them talking in the kitchen. Their hushed, concerned tones sounded like they were standing vigil over a corpse. Rose was right about the bedroom being Lucy's, and there, by the bed, was a phone. Carefully she picked it up and dialled a taxi number that had been so cleverly designed to be memorable that it came back to her even after a break of two decades.

'Hello. Taxi please, twenty-five St Luke's Rise. To go to near Bath. Yes, the Bath in the West Country. Yes, I know it will cost me. I don't care. And—and please don't call, or sound the horn when you arrive. I'll be watching and when you get here I'll come out. And we need a car seat, for a baby.'

Rose darted back to the bedroom where Flossie and Anna were sleeping. She put on her clothes and threw what she could back into her rucksack and suitcase. Then, very carefully, she woke Anna up.

'Anna, come on, it's a game. We're going to pretend to escape. No one can hear us. You've got to be quiet as a mouse and tiptoe down the stairs.'

Anna was sleepy and confused but, happily, as obedient as Rose had hoped she would be. Rose picked Flossie up, then the three of them quietly waited in the front bedroom until the taxi pulled up in the wet, dark street. It stood there, its orange light reflected in the puddles.

'Quick,' Rose said. 'Down the stairs and straight out into the street. Don't stop!'

Rose led, suitcase and buggy in one hand, Flossie tucked under her free arm, rucksack on her back, and Anna holding on to her skirt as they flew down the stairs and out into the street. By the time Polly, Lucy, Molly and Frank had reached the front door, Rose had thrown everything and

393

everyone into the cab.

Then she stopped, turned, and looked back at the stunned group standing in the doorway. Despite everything that was propelling her forwards into the cab, she found her legs taking her back, up the steps, to the door.

She noticed Lucy taking a small step backwards, to shield her pregnant daughter. But it was Frank that Rose headed for. She took his face between her hands and looked straight into those dark brown eyes as if she were looking in a mirror.

'I'm sorry,' she said. 'One day, I'll make it up to you. I promise.'

As she leaned forward and kissed him, just once, on the cheek, she felt Polly's skinny hand dart forward and grab her arm. But she slapped her away and stumbled down the steps again, hurling herself into the taxi.

She slammed the door shut and saw that Polly had broken out of the doorway and was coming after her.

'Just go,' she said to the driver. 'Get the hell out of here.'

Whatever the taxi driver thought, he didn't want any trouble. He lurched forward, aquaplaning as he turned the corner at the end of the street. Rose looked back for an instant to see Frank standing, stunned, in the street as Polly ran after the cab. He had his arm round Molly, who had her face buried in his shoulder, her round belly pressed into his side.

Then Rose realised, for the first time, that if Molly was pregnant, if Frank was her boyfriend, then that was her grandchild in there. She gasped and clasped her hand to her mouth.

My grandchild!

'Are you all right, love?' the taxi driver asked.

'Um . . .' she said, leaning back and trying to breathe. She focused on the windscreen-wipers as they swished backwards and forwards, giving a second's clarity before the pelting rain obscured her view again. She counted ten swipes.

Then she shook herself. She hadn't strapped Flossie, Anna or herself in. What was she thinking? She got busy with buckles and straps.

'No one's going to come after you, are they?' the driver asked.

'Don't worry,' she said, leaning over Flossie to anchor the baby seat to the car.

'And you know it's going to cost you an arm and a leg?'

'Needs must.'

'Just so long as you know.' The taxi driver, a fatherly, thickset man with a deep Estuary accent, reached forward and switched on Radio 2. Soon the sounds of Easy Listening filled the warm, chemical-coconut-scented cab as it headed west across the sodden country. The rain washed the bollards and crash barriers, the service stations and the mobile phone masts masquerading as trees. It brought the shiny edges into sharp relief so that, even in the yellow sodium glare of the streetlights, everything seemed to be clear; everything looked flushed out, brought up to the surface.

'Look, love, I don't want to interfere or anything, but you're sure you know what you're doing?'

'Oh yes,' Rose said. 'I'm on my way home, actually.'

'That's a relief to hear. Just so long as you know what you're doing. With the kiddies and that.' The man settled back to his driving.

There was very little traffic on the road, and the driver was smooth, fast and confident. Rose wished that the journey could go on forever, because she didn't want to face what awaited her at home. She put her arms round her sleeping daughters, glad that the driver wasn't one of the chatty sorts. She tried to concentrate on her girls, but seeing Frank back there had made it difficult for her to pin her mind down.

Despite all that, the relentless sound of the rain, the rhythmic swiping of the wipers, the gentle music and the warm glow of the car interior began to lull Rose towards an uneasy sleep.

As she finally drifted off, the last thought she had was that it was very likely that, at some point, Gareth would be passing them, coming in the opposite direction. She hoped against hope that when he did, he wouldn't see them. Because then the taxi driver really might have something to worry about.

Forty-Five

It was the deadest part of night when the taxi pulled into the empty parking space at The Lodge. The house stood at the bottom of the steps in complete darkness. There was no wind, and the rain fell arrow-sharp in great, straight torrents, coursing over the edge of gutters, bubbling up at the drain-covers.

'You sure this is it, love?' the taxi driver asked.

'Oh yes,' Rose said.

He got out and gave her a hand down the steps with the suitcase. Rose had her hands full with Flossie, who was still fast asleep, and Anna, who was only just awake enough to be talked down to the house, one step at a time, while Rose held her coat over her head.

'That'll be two hundred and ten pounds, please love,' the taxi driver said. Rose blew out her cheeks and looked in her purse. She had got a wad of cash out for the Brighton trip, so she fished out twelve twenties.

'Keep the change,' she said.

'Thanks, love. And take it easy, eh? And you, Miss,' he knelt and looked into Anna's good eye, 'you look like a brave girl. You make sure you look after Mum and Baby, eh?'

His words brought the hospital stay back to Rose, and how impotent she had felt when the nurses replaced her name with her role. It was ironic, really. What had she known back then about disempowerment?

She watched the taxi driver trudge through the rain back up to his car, then turned to open the front door. It was locked. She rummaged in her bag for her keys then opened the door. Seeing her do this, the taxi driver turned on his engine and, with a roar and a flash of lights, he was gone into the night.

Frank, Rose thought. She had to bite that thought, swallow it down whole.

'I'm frightened, Mummy,' Anna whispered, clinging onto Rose's leg as they went through the door into the dark, empty kitchen.

Frank.

'There's no need, love. Look, we're home.' Rose put her arm around her and pulled Flossie in even closer, so that her head nestled into her shoulder.

'Where's Daddy?'

'He's out, Anna,' Rose said.

Forgetting about the buggy, suitcase and rucksack, which she had left out in the rain, Rose reached for the light switch. The kitchen was a mess. Their breakfast things from the morning before were still out. There were three empty wine bottles and two stacked ashtrays. Drawers had been pulled open, their contents spewed all over the kitchen floor, as if someone had been searching for something. Tea-towels that Rose had washed and pressed into neat piles had been opened up and flung around like dead birds' feathers. A couple of baskets containing what Rose referred to as 'bits and bobs'—a term Gareth had always for some inexplicable reason found offensive—had been upended, their contents of spare batteries, bits of string, rubber bands and drawing pins splattered over the kitchen table.

'Probably it was the key,' Rose muttered.

'What, Mummy?'

'Oh, nothing. I just said I think your daddy was looking for something.'

'He's a messy daddy,' Anna said, sucking her thumb in the way she did when she was a toddler.

'He certainly is,' Rose said. She moved over to the back window and saw that, across the sodden lawn, the studio was lit up. The door looked as if it had been caved in—or, rather, hacked—as it stood in splinters. Gareth had raised the blinds and the room looked empty and silent; the lights were on

398

but there was no one at home. Rose could see, even from that distance, a glimpse of the mess she had made. It looked pretty bad.

Taking the girls with her, she went on a tour of the ground floor of the house, checking that all the doors to the outside were locked, turning on all the lights and looking inside cupboards to make sure there was nothing hiding there. Apart from the detritus in the kitchen, the house appeared to be untouched.

'Come on, let's get you to bed, Mrs One and Mrs Two,' she said to Anna and Flossie, and she took them up the stairs, switching on lights as she went, holding her free hand out in front of them all as if she were carrying some invisible shield. She took them right up to her bedroom, which was exactly as she had left it, the bed pulled over hastily, her kimono draped across the back of a chair. She tucked Anna in, then quickly changed Flossie and put her in the other side of the bed, hemming her in with pillows to stop her rolling out. By the time Flossie was settled with a bottle of follow-on milk that Rose prepared from a Tetra Pak she had stored in the changing bag, Anna was fast asleep again, snoring softly, her good eye closed and her patch staring back at Rose like an accusation.

Rose visited each of the upstairs rooms. She flashed on the lights and checked under the beds and behind the wardrobe doors. She didn't know exactly what she was going to find, but she wasn't taking any chances. It was obvious now; she had always been too trusting. She needed to make sure that Gareth hadn't left any traps behind for them.

But the only real problem he had left was the

kitchen. Which was fair do's, Rose thought, considering what she had done to his studio.

She went back downstairs and took an umbrella from the stand by the coat-rack. Switching on the outside lights, she cautiously stepped up through the puddles to the Annexe. She opened the door, swinging it wide at arm's length, a gesture that felt ridiculous, as if she were in some sort of James Bond movie.

She switched on the hall light and peered up the stairs, listening for any sound or movement. Then, carefully, holding the umbrella a little like a sword, she edged up the stairs until she was in the bed-sitting room. She hadn't been in here properly—without Polly watching her every movement—for a long while.

She flicked the wall switch to turn on the overhead lights. It was certainly Polly's lair, and no one else's. Her clothes were strewn everywhere, covering every surface. There were black cobweb dresses, bras that were, to Rose's view, unnecessary, given her tiny breasts; there were more soiled knickers. Rose knelt and looked under the bed. Reaching so that she nearly gave herself a cold shoulder, she hoiked out a pair of rather too familiar male under-pants. They were tangled with the loden green jumper that Rose knew only too well.

'See. I'm a proper wife now,' she had said as she presented him with it, the result of three months of evenings sitting by the TV, balancing the knitting on the bump that was to be Anna.

There were leather straps on the headboard and, looking through the bedside drawer, Rose found contraceptive pills, two vibrators—one large and one tiny, pink and soft—a tube of strawberry-flavoured lube and a string of Thai beads that had seen, Rose noted, some use.

The bathroom was as she had thought it would be—a jumble of cosmetics for hair, skin, face and body. Polly's distrait, scruff look required a fair bit of behind-the-scenes maintenance. Rose clocked her missing Touche Éclat nestled in between a jar of Eve Lom cleanser and a Nars eyeliner pencil. She thought about reclaiming it, but decided not to—it was probably contaminated by now. The bin was over-flowing with bloodstained tissue, and the toilet required a judicious flush.

She moved to the little bedroom, the room she always thought of as Andy's. It was forlorn and empty. There was no trace of the boys, of course—Rose herself had overseen their removal to the main house. The bunk bed stood there stripped of its bedding. It was as if someone had died.

If only I had gone with Andy, Rose suddenly thought, gripping her chest with her fist. All this wouldn't have happened. It would have been difficult, but not quite as catastrophic as the way things were heading now. So that's what she would do, then. Tomorrow, she'd take the girls and travel to Brittany to live a life with Andy in his cottage on a salt-scabbed escarpment facing west over the wild Atlantic. She would stand on a limpet-crusted rock and inhale the ozone that she imagined was so different from the heavy, domestic air of the Channel she was used to from Brighton.

And there, away from the wedge of Gareth's resentment about his own situation, she would finally be able to set herself free from her secrets and, for the first time ever, begin to live a totally free and open life. She would make it good for Frank. She would make it good for her grandchild. She would atone.

Trying to still her mind by working out the practicalities—would they take a boat, or would they fly; where would she get a car from; and could she smuggle Flossie, who had no passport, in amongst some luggage?—she went to the kitchen area of the bed-sitting room. It was so different from when the space had been her own. Back then there had always been pans draining by the sink, beans soaking in bowls, piles of muddy potatoes newly lifted from her garden, awaiting her attention. Now there was no sign of food preparation or consumption at all. Instead, a guitar stood propped up against the gas stove and the kitchen table was covered with sheaves of yellow legal paper. Each sheet was etched with line after line of Polly's small, crazy hand-writing, peppered with out of place capitals, small flourishes, eccentrically slanted letterforms and a lot of crossings out.

These were Polly's songs.

Rose picked up a sheet near the top, and, holding it up to her torch, she read:

> *You say you can't hurt her*
> *You can: I want you too much*
> *Her clouds close over us*
> *We'll drown in black clouds*
> *You have to bring down the storm.*

So then. This was something beyond the *Widow Cycle* that Polly had gone on about so much. Reading it once more, Rose took the sheet and tore it into tiny pieces, throwing them up and watching them fall. She took another sheet, then another, until the room was covered in drifts of yellow paper, like dog-piss snow. She hoped that Luddite Polly wouldn't have a copy somewhere. She laughed to herself. This was the only weapon she had left to her: the ability to tear it all up, and wasn't she using it well?

What did it matter, anyway? Tomorrow she and her girls would be on their way to France. She kicked the yellow fragments, sending them curling up into the air.

'Hello?'

It was a male voice, coming from the bottom of the stairs. Rose jumped, quite literally. For a second she fell into slow motion, like in a Kung Fu movie. She could hear the whoosh of her movements as she quickly turned and switched out the lights, ready for anything, her hands raised.

'Is anyone there?'

A shadow advanced slowly up the wall, slanting away from the stairs. From his outline, Rose saw the man was holding a stick of some sort. Possibly a hammer.

She backed over to the kitchen cupboard and grabbed a saucepan, swinging it behind her head as if it were a rounders bat, ready to whack.

'Rose?'

Rose took a sharp intake of breath and let the saucepan fall to the floor. It was Simon. Her old friend. Her old mucker.

'Is everything all right?' he said. 'I saw the lights and I knew you were all away, and the car's not here, so I came up to check.'

Rose ran to Simon and threw her arms around

him, sobbing with relief. 'I thought you were—'

'Shhh, shhh . . .'

'I thought . . . It's all coming down, Simon,' she cried.

Simon held her for a long time, stroking her hair as she wept into his chest. He waited until she was quiet, and then he spoke.

'I was coming back from Bath when I nearly crashed into Gareth, driving towards the motorway. He looked like the Horseman of Death.'

'He's going to get me, Simon.'

'Shhh, shhh.' He stroked her hair.

'You were right, of course. They're fucking— him and Polly. She got her claws into him.'

'I'm sorry, Rose.'

'She's not good, you know.'

'I can't disagree with that.'

'Mum!'

Anna's petrified cry pierced the night, shooting straight into Rose's heart. She let go of Simon, and flew down the stairs, stumbling down the stone steps to the house, where Anna was frozen in the doorway. Simon followed behind her, switching off lights and closing doors. Rose could hear Flossie's whining, insistent cry coming from upstairs.

'Mum. Flossie's awake and she wants you. I called for you and you didn't come,' Anna said, folding her arms and looking at her mother, the fear she had felt replaced by petulance.

'Is that all?' Rose said, grabbing Anna by the shoulders. 'Is that all? I thought something awful had happened!' She shook her roughly. Relief that she hadn't been attacked by a monster turned into a rage.

'Ow, you're hurting me!' Anna cried.

'Rose.' Simon stepped in and pulled her away. 'Take it easy, Rose. It's not Anna's fault. Look, she was frightened. Are you OK, sweetie?' He knelt down and stroked her hair.

Anna nodded dumbly, but her eyes showed the shock and pain of her mother's attack.

Rose felt giddy. 'Sorry,' she mumbled, and staggered past them both, through to the kitchen.

'She's got a lot on her plate, Anna,' Simon said as he led her through into the house. 'It's not your fault.'

'No,' Anna said, bewildered.

'Look, I'm sorry, darling.' Shaking, Rose knelt and took her hand. 'Please forgive me.'

Anna looked at her and nodded. Flossie's cries from upstairs had by this time reached a crescendo.

'Come on, young lady,' Simon said. 'Let's go and see to that sister of yours. And it's the middle of the night, so let's get you to bed.' He led Anna back up the stairs. 'I promise you that your mum will be here from now on. She's not going out again, are you, Rose?'

'No,' Rose said, although she was desperate to go down to the studio and see what had happened since she was last there. When Simon and Anna had gone, she curled up deep into the worn, comfortable kitchen armchair. She stayed there for what seemed like an age, holding on tightly to what remained of herself. Then she got up, stretched herself, opened a fresh bottle of Gareth's Laphroaig and set it on the table with two glasses. She poured herself a good two fingers and topped it up with a splash of water. Gareth would have

405

been horrified about that. She switched off the main kitchen lights and lit a couple of candles, which she placed on the work surface.

Eventually, Simon came downstairs.

'That was a mission,' he said, smiling. 'But they're both down now.'

'Good,' Rose said. 'Drink?'

'Like daughter, like mother,' Simon said.

'What?'

'You don't want to be left alone tonight, do you?'

'You got me in one,' Rose poured him a stiff glassful. They knocked the whisky back and she refilled their glasses.

'Thank God for the au pair,' Simon said. 'Miranda's away again, but Janka can deal with the kids if anything comes up.'

'Don't worry, I'm not going to report you to the authorities. So long as you don't tell on me for daughter-shaking.'

They sat down at the table, facing each other in the flickering candlelight.

'I'm worried about you, Rose.'

'I'm a big girl. I'll get by,' she said. She really believed it now. Going to France would solve all her problems.

'Where do you think Gareth is, then?' Simon asked.

'Brighton.'

'Ah.'

'He's gone to get me, so that he and Polly can lock me up.'

Simon looked at her, slightly astonished.

'She's making me out to be mad, you know,' Rose went on. 'I'm trying hard not to believe it myself. She's infected us all, one way or another, hasn't she?'

'Yes.' Simon looked grim. 'She has.' Rose refilled both their glasses.

'Rose,' he said, 'I'm so sorry. I've been a fool. Gareth's an idiot. There's a point, you know, with us men, where there's too much blood in our dicks. It drains our brains.'

'I don't think men have the monopoly on that effect,' Rose sighed. 'Except for the dick bit.'

Simon held his hand out across the table and Rose took it, grateful for his friendship, thankful that he was someone she could talk to.

'We've all been idiots,' she said. 'It's like we're making it up as we go along.'

Simon got up and moved round to her side of the table. He knelt at her feet and looked up at her. He took her face in both his hands and looked into her eyes, his long blond lashes flickering as he spoke.

'I hate to see you like this. I feel it's my fault. If only I had been more forceful right from the start, Rose. If only I had made you get rid of her. But can't you see, too, that Gareth is to blame as much as her? He doesn't know what he's putting at risk. He's got it all. He's made up and he can't even see it. He's got you, Rose, and he can't even see what a precious, precious thing you are. You are so lovely, Rose. If only . . .'

And he pulled her face towards his and kissed her. Perhaps it was the whisky, but she found herself responding to him, letting his tongue into her mouth, pushing hers back into his. Then she broke away and looked at him, her heart pounding.

'We're all fools,' she said, standing up, bringing him with her.

She grabbed at his hair, drawing him back onto the table, so that he was on top of her. He pulled up her skirt and delved his fingers deep into her, pushing her knickers aside. She opened the buttons of his tenting jeans. Then suddenly, violently, he took her by the hips and thrust himself deep inside her.

'What are we doing?' she gasped, but his answer was lost in the drive of his hips. It was almost immediate, the rush and the release. She came instantly, her whole body pulsing, opening and closing like a sea anemone. She threw out her arm and knocked over the whisky bottle. It tumbled over and rolled, spilling its earthy contents on to the two of them before clattering to the kitchen floor and shattering.

Simon, taken by her contractions, pushed into her a couple more times then pulled himself out just in time to come on her belly, which was exposed by her flung-up skirt. He collapsed on top of her, licking the whisky from her cheek.

'Wow,' he said. 'Never in my wildest.'

'I'm sorry,' she said.

'I've wanted to do that for so long,' he whispered in her ear.

'What did you say?' She couldn't believe what she was hearing. Pushing him off her, she sat up.

'It's true. She—Polly—was my way of trying to get you out of my system.'

Rose suddenly felt disgusted, defiled by what they had just done. How low could they sink? Men are dogs, she thought, getting up and pulling down her skirt.

'I have to get some sleep now,' she said. 'I am half dead.'

He reached up and put his hand on her breast.

'You don't understand, Rose. I want to stay.'

She shook her head. 'The children . . .'

'I want to be here when they come back, Rose. They'll come back, you know.'

'This is none of your business, Simon. Don't complicate things even further.'

He looked at her.

'Look, I'll see you soon, OK?' she went on. 'The next bit is for me alone.'

'I don't think—'

'Go. Please.'

'All right then, Rose. I'll go. But call me, any time, if you need help. OK?'

'OK.'

She walked him to the front door, where he held her in a deep, long embrace that felt like it might be the last shot of human kindness she was going to get for a while. Nevertheless, she wanted it to be over, and for him to be gone.

He staggered up the steps like a man who had seen it all, then he disappeared. The night was receding, and the birds were beginning their morning reveille. Rose noticed that the rain had stopped, and it had left behind air that was clearer.

Feeling bruised around the lips and between her legs, Rose took herself upstairs and slipped in between her daughters, where she passed out into a deep and dark sleep that seemed to be threaded with poison. Everything had been done to her, and she deserved none of it.

So fast asleep was she that she didn't hear the phone as it rang on five separate occasions.

Forty-Six

Flossie didn't wake until nine in the morning. Rose, in a hungover fug, rolled over, lifted up her blouse and flipped her breast into her mouth. Flossie latched on almost immediately, and it wasn't long before Rose felt her milk letting down. She was surprised she still had it in her.

The bedroom was at its best in the morning sun, which lit up the far reaches of the eaves, throwing everything into a golden relief. It felt warm and safe in there. Lying with her daughters, Rose felt relieved that things had come to a head. She had the sense that anything was possible during the day to come. Her old optimism had not deserted her, after all. In a strange way, she was excited at the potential for change. She held that picture of Frank, of the kindness she saw in his eyes, in her mind.

As Flossie pawed and sucked at her breast, she focused on the little free-standing calendar she kept on her bedside table. She had put it there when they moved in so that she could keep on top of everyone's comings and goings. The plan had been that she would wake knowing, for example, whether she had to send Anna into school with swimming gear, whether she had to provide tins for harvest festival, or money for a school trip. But it hadn't worked out. She had never kept it up to date, and for the past couple of months it had stood there completely unmarked. Looking at it now, she realised that today was the first of May, a day she had always tried to keep special, as the mark of a new beginning.

'Wake up, Anna.' She nudged the sleeping form beside her. 'Come on, we've got to get out there and wash our faces in the dew.'

Anna was bleary, but she knew the form. It was a ritual she had repeated every year of her life. So, a few minutes later, she and Rose were kneeling in the middle of the back lawn, rubbing dew into their faces, Flossie lying on a rug by their side.

'Bright and happy we shall be, the whole day through!' Anna sang and looked up at her mother, smiling.

'I'm sorry about last night, love. I was just really tired.'

''S'OK. Just don't let it happen again,' Anna said.

Rose put her arms around her and they held each other close, there in the middle of the sodden lawn, while Flossie tried to put a daisy in her mouth.

They went back to the house, where Rose ran a deep, hot bath and tipped in a decadent amount of her Aveda bubblebath. She lay back in the water and scooped up a mouthful of foam, letting it gently pop in her mouth. She saw parts of her body bob up from the clouds of bubbles, little glimpses of crepey imperfection that seemed not to have anything to do with the Rose that was now living in her head.

She gave the girls a breakfast of French toast and maple syrup, and then she brought in the sodden rucksack from outside. She and Anna sorted out the soaked things and arranged them, with the damp buggy, out on the stone steps to dry in the sun. It felt good for the two of them to be working on something together. It gave Rose some hope for a future.

When everything was dry, they would pack it up again and head off.

But underneath this veneer of calm, Rose kept feeling a thrill of dread, a feeling like hunger, that grabbed her guts and twisted them tight. She knew this feeling well. She usually had it when a storm was forecast.

But today, the weather promised to be fair. When they had laid out all the wet clothes and set the upended kitchen to rights, Rose and Anna made sandwiches and took some of the flapjacks Rose had put in the biscuit tins a couple of days earlier. They packed them all in a day-sack and, with Flossie strapped to Rose's front in the baby-carrier, they set off for a long walk, climbing the breast hill and slogging it up to the brow of the ridge that lay beyond. They looked down into the far valley, where there was a field full of sheep, who were moving from one end to another in what looked like a giant 'S'.

'I didn't know sheep could spell,' Anna giggled.

Rose smiled, and even Flossie craned around in her sling to take a look.

They worked their way along the ridge, which curved round into a semi-circle that would, eventually, take them back towards home.

The sun was beating down by one o'clock, and Rose and Anna stripped down to their vests, letting the new season's warmth touch their skins. They made a camp underneath a hawthorn tree in full bloom, and ate their little feast. Rose spread her sweatshirt on the ground and she and Anna lay back, with Flossie sprawled across the two of them.

Rose told Anna the story of Beltane, of fire and new beginnings.

They dozed there in the baking sun, breathing in the sweet, faintly indolic scent of the hawthorn.

'Summer's really here,' Anna said happily.

'I hope so,' Rose said.

Then, one by one, they all dropped off, floating away from the lush landscape into worlds of their own.

*   *   *

When Rose awoke, the sun was well along its path to the west. She felt a little pink and hot. To think that only a couple of weeks ago, she had needed a bulky jumper and her Barbour before she ventured out.

She looked down at her sleeping girls. Flossie had nestled right into Anna's side; Anna had a protective arm around her little sister. Rose felt unimaginably sad for her daughters. They were going to be the long-lasting victims of whatever was to happen today. These girls were the collateral damage. However things turned out, they were going to suffer, one way or another.

Why couldn't things ever stay the same? Why did they have a tendency to fall apart?

In a while, the girls woke up. Rose packed the picnic things, and they set off on their journey round the curving ridge, back to The Lodge. They would have walked a good six miles by the time they got home.

*   *   *

It was nearly four when they returned to the top of the breast hill. From here, they had an excellent view of the house and garden. Rose's heart lurched as she saw the Galaxy sitting in the driveway. Nico and Yannis were playing on the swings at the back.

So this was it, then.

'Daddy's back,' Anna said.

Rose looked down at her and wondered what was going on in her head. Whatever she was thinking, her face gave nothing away.

They stood there, holding hands, looking down on the scene below. The last thing Rose wanted was to take the girls down there, but she had little choice.

They edged their way down. This side of the hill hadn't seen much sun, so the long grass was muddy and slippery, threatening to upend them and send them sliding down towards the house and their doom. Rose preferred a more controlled descent.

As they got closer to the house, Rose saw Gareth's crossed legs in the kitchen window. He was sitting at the table, but not, thankfully, looking up in their direction.

Rose took the buggy, by now completely dry, and put Flossie in it.

'Anna, why don't you take Floss and go and play with the boys?' she said.

'But I want to see Dad,' she whined.

'You'll have plenty of time for that, later,' Rose said. 'But first I really need you to help me out with Flossie.'

Anna rolled her eyes, but knew not to pursue it. She took the buggy and wheeled it round to the back garden. Thinking how mature Anna looked, stepping in there as big sister, Rose didn't like to think how much growing up she would have to do in the next few months.

Taking a deep breath in and out from the tributaries of her lungs, Rose pushed open the front door into the kitchen. Gareth sat, mug of coffee in front of him, waiting. He turned to look at her, his expression as blank as a sheet of baking parchment.

'Rose.'

'Hello.'

There was a long pause. Eventually, he sighed.

'What were you thinking, Rose?' His voice was tired in a way that she had never heard it before, not even at any of his former psychological troughs.

'What do you mean?' she asked. It was a genuine question. She wanted him to take his pick.

'Where do I start? You do a lot of increasingly crazy stuff including trashing my studio and MY WORK,' he barked suddenly, standing up and thumping the table, making the spoon in his coffee rattle so violently that Rose was afraid the mug might break. He took a deep breath, and calmed himself. 'You disappear for hours in Brighton with my daughters, then you set off in the middle of the night to God knows where, abandoning Polly and the boys, and embarrassing everyone.'

'Embarrassing everyone?' Rose said. 'I'm so, so sorry.'

'That's not an apology, is it?'

'I'm not the one that needs to apologise.'

'And what the fuck is that supposed to mean?'

'You know exactly what I'm talking about.'

'You have ruined everything, Rose. It's all down to you, but you're so far gone you can't even see it.

415

We've been watching you.'

Rose felt as if part of her were pouring out of the top of her skull. He stood there looking at her as if she was a crazy woman, as if it were she who was in the wrong, not him and his dog whore. She ran for him, her hands extended in front of her, her claws out. She wanted to push him over, out and away.

But instead, with Gareth being so tall and her being of only average height, he stood firm. His body absorbed the impact of her charge, sending it down through his feet to the stone floor. He grabbed her wrists and held them so tightly that her bones ached, but he was still. He took a deep breath and held her away from him as if she were a dirty thing. He looked her straight in the eyes and Rose realised she was peering into the face of a stranger.

'Rose. Rose. Polly and I are very worried about you,' he said, trying to control his voice. 'You haven't been yourself for a long time. Not since Flossie was ill. And the things you have done recently—well, it's not what you'd expect from someone with young children to look after.'

Rose shook herself free and looked up at him. 'What are you trying to say to me?'

'I'm worried about my children.'

'*Your* children?'

'Listen, Rose, and listen well. We've been talking, Polly and I.'

'I'll bet you have,' she said.

He looked at her pityingly. She stared back at him, willing him to confess.

'Polly called me from Brighton—she had forgotten her mobile—to tell me how worried she was about you and, as you can imagine, I was pretty concerned about you myself, given what you had done to MY WORK.' He pointed through the kitchen to the studio, which stood despoiled and gaping at the end of the garden,

'You do know that you might as well have cut my arm off as do what you did in there? You've never understood my work, Rose, have you? You've just seen it as a way for me to earn money so that you can go SHOPPING AT WAITROSE.'

He paused and ran his fingers through his hair. He took another breath and bit his lips. 'You know what? I don't think you've ever seen me as anything other than a meal-ticket, a sperm bank, a means to an end.'

Not this again, Rose thought.

'Have you ever seen me as a man? As a sexual being?'

Rose snorted. That he should say such a thing!

He glared at her. 'As anything other than second-best to Christos?'

Rose gasped. Any wind left in her sails was ripped away.

Gareth stopped and exhaled. 'And, Rose, you have lied and lied and lied and lied to me. Polly's told me everything.'

He sat down and stared at her: judge, jury and executioner.

'See what you've done, Rose?' Rose wheeled round. For the first time she noticed that Polly was there, sitting part-silhouetted in the corner armchair. Her face was serious, but Rose was sure she could see a trace of victory in her eyes.

'I called Gareth and he told me what you'd done. We decided you needed to see a doctor, but that he should be with you when you did, so he set off to fetch you. Then you pulled your disappearing trick. With the girls, Rose. *With the girls.*' Polly's voice had taken on a deep, understanding tone, and she had shifted her position so that she rested in the chair, one hand under her chin, as if she were auditioning for the part of The Psychiatrist.

'You understand that I had no alternative but to tell Gareth about your history, about the baby?' Polly went on. 'About poor Frank?'

Gareth raised his head. 'Why didn't you tell me, Rose?'

'I didn't want to lose you,' Rose said, in a small voice.

Gareth looked at her with a mixture of pity and disgust. 'Don't you think this is what all this is really about? The visit to Brighton tipped you over, didn't it? Don't you realise that if you lie all your life, it's going to make you ill?'

'I'm not ill,' Rose yelled. *'I'm. Not. Ill!'*

'We've been talking about it, Rose,' Gareth went on. 'I was angry. I wanted to take you to hospital, get you sectioned. But Polly here argued for you. She said that what you need is a rest, away from all your responsibilities, and she said that the girls should be able to see you as well. We have to think of them.'

He walked over and stood right in front of her. 'So this is the deal. We're going to move you up to the Annexe, get you enrolled with a psychotherapist and take it from there.'

'You won't have to do anything. No cooking, no house-work,' Polly said, smiling.

'Polly has very kindly agreed to take all of that

418

on. Which is very good of her, considering she has such a lot on her plate already.'

'I'm going to be recording an album,' Polly said. 'But we can do it in Bath, so I can fit it around the house and the children.'

'You just have to concentrate on getting better, then we'll take it from there,' Gareth said.

They both sat and looked at her, their eyes open wide, as if the plan they were proposing were the most simple and obvious thing in the world. As if they were offering her a kindness. Rose's shoulders dropped, her brow lowered and she found it hard to catch her breath.

'You know though, Rose, that it's over. You know I can't take you back now. Not after all your lies,' Gareth said.

'I know what you're up to,' Rose snarled at Polly. 'Don't talk to me about lies.'

'Poor Mrs Maths,' Polly said, standing up. 'Always putting two and two together.'

Rose couldn't take any more. She launched herself at Polly, dragging her fingers into her hair, tugging at it, snagging her nails in it. Polly was taken by surprise. She fell back against the armchair and Rose found herself laying punch after punch into Polly's head.

Gareth jumped across the room and yanked Rose by her arm, pulling her up and away from Polly, throwing her so that she sprawled down onto the floor.

'Leave her!' he yelled. 'Just leave her alone.'

'Your precious Polly? Your little fuckwhore?'

Polly had got up and was standing by Gareth's side, just behind him, looking down at Rose. She was still smiling.

'Take that back!' he roared. 'Just leave her out of this.'

'It's OK, Gareth. She's not well,' Polly said, touching his arm.

Rose crawled across the floor to the dresser, where she pulled herself up. She had hit her head when she landed and was feeling dizzy, but she had a force propelling her so strongly that nothing could stop her. She reached up with both hands to the shelf on the dresser where Anna's egg-basket lived. She found the two largest eggs, made of onyx and marble and so big that her hands barely fitted around them. She turned to face Gareth and Polly, who seemed suspended across the other side of the kitchen, watching her as if she were an animal in a zoo.

Then, in a heartbeat, she threw herself across the room with an egg in each hand. She flew at Gareth, reaching up and hitting his head with the stones. Taken by surprise, he tried to dodge her, but instead took a crushing blow to the temple, which sent him reeling towards the ground. On his way down, he hit his head on the upraised cover of the Aga. It was so quick that Rose had little idea what actually happened. She jumped back. He was slumped over silently, his face up against the burning hot-plate of the stove, a stream of blood sizzling as it flowed out of his nose.

For a second, both Rose and Polly stood there, frozen with horror. Then Rose rushed towards Gareth and tried to yank him away from the stove. He was a big man and now he was a dead weight. His face ripped as she pulled him off the hotplate, leaving behind a layer of burned skin. Sobbing and retching, she knelt over him and tried to revive him, beating his still chest, trying to get life back into his body.

Nothing happened.

'Gareth!' she cried. 'Gareth!'

'Oh, Rose. See what you've gone and done now?'

Rose looked up to see Polly standing over her, her hands on her hips, that faint smile still on her face. For a second or two, Rose couldn't move. Her mind was blank except for the fact that she needed to act quickly. Then like an animal running for shelter, she scrabbled to her feet and fled across to the pantry, slamming the door behind her and drawing the bolt so that Polly couldn't get in. She stood there, panting, until she could breathe again.

What *had* she done?

It dawned on her that she had run into a trap. If she was going to get out of there, not only was she going to have to face the horror of what had happened to Gareth, she was going to have to deal with Polly, the creator of it all. She was running on instinct now, on the need to preserve the self. Casting around the room, her eyes fell on the gun. Gareth's gun. He had put it up on the top shelf, no doubt in some feeble attempt to hide it. The fool. It was completely visible up there behind the few jars of apple chutney that had escaped Polly's pantry purge.

Clambering onto the work surface, she pulled herself up by her fingertips, levering herself like a mountaineer against the shelves. She could just about reach the gun, although when she pulled it down, it brought one of the chutney jars crashing along with it. The sticky gloop splattered all over

421

the slate tiles. Rose was nearly beyond caring about the mess, although she still added clearing up the chutney to her mental list of tasks. Using some skill she didn't know she possessed, possibly something that had lodged in her from some film or other, she cracked open the gun. It appeared to be loaded. This was a good thing, she thought.

She put her ear against the bolted door. All was quiet in the kitchen. Who knew what she would find when she went back in there? All she hoped was that the children were still outside.

Holding the gun up to her chest, she eased the door open and edged back into the room. Gareth was still on the floor, where she had left him, and he was as still as ever. She would get back to him after she had finished with Polly.

'I was wondering when you were going to come out of there,' Polly said.

Rose wheeled round to see her, back in the armchair. For the first time, she saw that sick little smile waver as Polly clocked the gun.

'What are you doing, Rose?' Polly said, standing up.

'Stay there!' Rose barked, and Polly put her hands up and stood still, rooted to her spot.

Rose edged over to the back door and locked it. Pointing the gun at Polly, she moved around the room, drawing the curtains. Finally, she locked the front door. Now there was no danger of the children coming in. She could do what she wanted now.

'What are you going to do, Rose?' Polly asked again.

Rose circled round to face Polly, pointing the gun straight at her. She lined the sight up so that it was level with Polly's forehead. She had always been a good shot at funfairs with rubber ducks and the like. She was confident her aim was going to be true.

'Rose, I don't know what you think was going on, but really, everything I have ever done has been in your best interest,' Polly said.

'Hah,' Rose snorted.

'It's true. How on earth could it be otherwise?' Polly said quickly. 'We go back so far, Rose . . .'

'I've heard all this before,' Rose said. 'I'm bored of it.'

'Rose. You think this is irretrievable, don't you? You think you're in so deep that you might as well finish me off and have done with it, don't you?'

Rose said nothing. She just reaffirmed her position with the gun and unhooked the safety, curling her finger tight around the trigger.

'I was the only witness to this, Rose. The only witness.' Rose could see Polly's mind working with the desperation of the doomed. She wasn't going to be taken in by it.

'Exactly,' Rose murmured.

'But don't you see? You didn't kill Gareth. He fell. It was an accident. An *accident*, Rose.'

Rose felt the waves of breathlessness coming over her again. She adjusted her stance and did her best to remain steady with the gun.

'It was an accident! A horrible accident. You can walk away from this if you want.' Polly looked relieved at the thoughts that were occurring to her. 'The girls will still have you. But—but if you shoot me now, there's *no way* you'll get away with it. Think what a waste that will be! All those four children with no parent to speak of. If not for me,

423

then for them, Rose. Put the gun down. Look! We can do it!'

And, her hands still up, Polly edged round the room. Rose kept the gun trained on her, as she reached the bloodied onyx eggs. Facing Rose and squatting down, her back straight, Polly picked them up.

'Don't panic,' she said as Rose hitched the gun again. 'I'm just going to take them over to the sink and clean them. Look.'

Holding the eggs up in her scrawny little arms, Polly backed round to the sink and, using a J-Cloth and Ecover, she removed every trace of blood from them. Then she dried them on a tea-towel.

'Put them back in the basket,' Rose said, and Polly did so, climbing on a chair to put the basket back in its place on the dresser.

'There.' She turned and beamed at her friend. 'All back how it was.'

Shaking, Rose let the gun down. She broke it open and emptied it of its cartridges.

Polly came over to her and handed her the tea-towel.

'Best to wipe that of any fingerprints and put it back where you found it,' she said. As Rose took the cloth, Polly's hand took hers. She looked her in the eyes.

'I'm so sorry, Rose. About everything that has happened. About all this. Poor us. Poor him.'

They looked down at Gareth on the floor.

After a moment, Rose broke away and went to put the gun back in the pantry. When she returned to the kitchen, Polly was kneeling at his feet, undoing a shoelace.

'This is why he tripped,' she said. 'He lost it,

didn't he?' she said to Rose. 'I mean, look what he did to his studio. And he phoned me and said it was you. And all the mess everywhere, the whisky. And it's not like he hasn't got a history of, well, difficulty. When he lunged forward to attack you, I didn't know what I was going to do . . .'

Rose backed into the armchair and buried her face in her palms. She felt hands on her knees and looked up to see Polly crouching in front of her.

'Rose. This is what's going to happen. I'm going to take the children round to Simon's,' she said. 'I'm going to tell him there's been an accident. You're going to call Kate and tell her you don't know what to do. Then let her take control. She's good at that. You're upset now. Just go with that. I'll be back in a second and we'll tell our story about how Gareth tripped as he went to attack you.'

Rose nodded dumbly.

'I'm glad, really,' Polly went on. 'It's happened quicker than I had hoped, but everything's back as it should be. We're both in the right place again. Everything else is just water under the bridge, isn't it?'

Polly got up and undid the bolts on the back door, then turned to face Rose again, her eyes burning.

'You know, Christos was never the same after you visited Karpathos, Rose.' Then, with a sudden, violent force, she spat on the floor. *'Never.'*

She opened the door, and went out into the garden.

Trying not to look at Gareth, Rose got up and peered through a chink in the curtains. She watched as Polly went over and gathered up the children. She was smiling and talking to them as if nothing had happened at all. Something she said to them even made them cheer.

She seemed very practised at subterfuge.

Two years later

'MAMAN!'

Flossie toddled across the scrubby grass, her little hands held out to her mother. Anna caught her and tumbled her to the ground. Both girls laughed as they rolled together down the flower-dotted slope that brought them to their mother, who was sunning herself on a rug underneath a cherry tree.

Rose smiled and swept them up, hugging them to herself, breathing deep their scent of salt and sea and sky. They lay back and looked up at the dancing blossom above them. Rose closed her eyes and listened to the distant crash and roar of the waves as they coursed into the sand a few yards from where they lay, discharging energy picked up over the vast swathes of water that lay to the west.

'Maman.' Flossie, who had got to her feet again, was leaning over Rose, brushing her nose with a long stalk of grass. Rose reached up and tickled her tummy and the little girl squirmed in pleasure, her sharp eyes dancing.

Anna looked on, smiling. 'No, we say *Mummy*, Flossie, *Mummy.*'

'No, it's *Maman!*' Flossie insisted.

For the fourth time in so many days, Rose thanked the sky for this brightness that had flown back into her daughters, and into everything around them. It hadn't happened overnight, but here they were at last.

'There you are.' Andy appeared round the orchard fence, wiping his hands on an oily rag. He had been working on the boat for the last couple of weeks, since the weather had turned. He was planning to spend the summer mornings out there again, on the waves, catching fish for the local restaurant. Rose supplied the same place year-round with eggs, preserves and vegetables from the little garden that she had somehow managed to coax out of the wild soil of this small island off the west coast of Brittany.

Despite the money Rose got from the sale of The Lodge, she, Andy and the girls lived a consciously pared-down existence here on the Ile d'Ouessant, and it suited them fine. They were almost self-sufficient and had no TV, no phone, no internet, and very few visitors, except for Frank and Molly, who came over every couple of months with Johnny, Rose's little grandson. Rose was so pleased that she had been able to help them in their very young parenthood by buying them a house in Brighton. It was reparation, of sorts.

She had, at last, found peace.

'Look at you lot, lying around,' Andy smiled.

'Can't a bird take a rest once in a while?' Rose looked up at him. He was so handsome in this light. Happiness suited him.

He scooped up Flossie and, swinging her round onto his knee, he joined Rose on the rug, putting his arm round her and the girls.

'Beautiful day,' he said. 'Fancy a swim later?'

'You're on.' Rose leaned over and kissed him on the nose.

He held her gaze for a moment, then broke away and reached into his pocket.

'Oh yeah. You completely made me forget why I came to find you. This arrived.'

Rose took the letter from him and opened it. She recognised the writing instantly.

Album done. Wiped out. Need a break away from temptations. Boys v. excited about seeing you all. When can we come? Send ferry details etc. Polly xx.

So, then. It had been bound to happen some day. Rose felt a little sick. She folded the letter over and smoothed it in her lap. Shielding her eyes with her hand, she looked out over the orchard fence, at the blurred line of the horizon, where the sea met the sky.

How could she refuse?

A sudden, brisk breeze pushed itself in from the shore. The cherry tree shuddered. A flurry of blossom tumbled down around Rose, Anna, Flossie and Andy, and Rose shivered.